New Horizons

The Gollancz Book of South Asian Science Fiction

New Horizons

The Gollancz Book of South Asian Science Fiction

Edited by Tarun K. Saint
Foreword by Manjula Padmanabhan

First published in Great Britain in 2021 by Gollancz
an imprint of The Orion Publishing Group Ltd
Carmelite House, 50 Victoria Embankment
London EC4Y 0DZ

An Hachette UK Company

10 9 8 7 6 5 4 3 2 1

Acknowledgements on p. 373 constitute an
extension of this copyright page.

A CIP catalogue record for this book is
available from the British Library.

ISBN (Mass Market Paperback) 978 1 473 22868 9
ISBN (eBook) 978 1 473 22869 6
Printed and bound in Great Britain by Clays Ltd, Elcograf S.p.A

www.orionbooks.co.uk

CONTENTS

FOREWORD

SPICE-SHIP TO INFINITY

1

In 1835, an eighteen-year-old Bengali student named Kylas Chunder Dutt wrote a far-sighted fantasy in English called 'A Journal of Forty-Eight Hours of the Year 1945'. In it, he described an uprising against the British led by a company of idealistic and beautifully attired people belonging to 'Indostan'. We might smile at that young man's fond hopes and patriotic vision. Still. It was a daring exercise in literary invention in an era when the term 'science fiction' had not yet been coined.

In the United Kingdom, in Europe and the United States the genre would over the next centuries come to take firm root. It would attempt to stretch the boundaries of standard fiction to include other worlds, other times, other dimensions. One wonders whether this was perhaps an extension of the colonial urge. Was it an attempt at populating other time zones and planets with Anglo-European adventurers even as the colonial world was collapsing upon itself? The explorers who set out to conquer Mars or to subdue dinosaurs in hidden pockets of time were nearly all men, and certainly all white. They had Christian names and civilizing agendas that always favoured our own species. To this day, the flags they planted in the farthest corners of the star-spangled multiverse remain firmly in place.

In India, however, Kylas Dutt's brave path did not become a highway. A scattering of authors, particularly in Bengali and in Marathi, took up the challenge of looking beyond the confines of everyday realism, but the audience for such works was limited, particularly in English. Many otherwise sophisticated Indian readers regard science fiction – now known by such variations as SF, sci-fi, speculative fiction, spec-fic – with a mixture of embarrassment and irritation. Even those who have read and enjoyed such classics as *Animal Farm, Brave New World, The Clockwork Orange* and *The Handmaid's Tale* claim to despise the genre.

The volume in your hands represents, therefore, a fresh safari into a literary dimension that has been largely overlooked in the region that I call home. This time, our guides have names such as Matadeen and Mahua, our picnic basket may contain mango pickle and our kitbag surely includes a collapsible *lota* rather than toilet paper. Editor Tarun Saint chose the term 'South Asian Science Fiction' with the aim of softening, at least through literature and fantastical invention, the political divisions that have fractured its vast ethno-linguistic family. The result is a bouquet of styles and voices that are endearingly – perhaps even irritatingly! – local.

In his Introduction, Saint provides an excellent foundation for thoughts on the subject of science fiction in general and the South Asian variant in particular. He introduces us to the stories and poems that fill these pages, while providing some answers as to the 'why' of the genre: why it has earned its place in literature and why it should be of interest to the general reader. The inclusion principle has been intuitive rather than rigid. Pieces that suited the mood of the collection as a whole have stayed in. Those that used science fiction as a prop in genres such as romance or mystery were left out.

While on the subject of inclusion, I think it's worth noting that the ratio of men to women in this collection, including translators and poets, is roughly 2:1. The domain of science fiction has been largely dismissive towards women, both as creators and as characters within the writing. Some of the best-known names in women's SF – Mary Shelley, Doris Lessing and the late Ursula K. Le Guin – were also, until recently, amongst the very few women working within the genre. This makes it all the more remarkable that Begum Rokeya Sakhawat Hossain of what is now Bangladesh, published *Sultana's Dream*, a novella about a futuristic feminist utopia, in 1905.

Only a handful of tales in this volume might be considered 'hard' science fiction, whirring with new technology or swarming with alien life forms. The majority of stories in this book are about ideas and ideals that might be of interest to anyone anywhere, expressed through the perspectives of those who have so far been presented as 'exotics' in science fiction. If, for instance, a character called Arjuna saves the planet from plundering extra-terrestrials, his cultural DNA will only be recognized by fellow South

Asians. If a character removes her space suit to reveal a mirror-work dupatta beneath it, that detail will be an insider reference, aimed towards those who know that the embroidery belongs to Rajasthan, Gujarat and neighbouring regions of Pakistan. If the Partition riots are referred to in an international collection of science fiction the context has to be spelled out. But if we use names from *Star Wars* or *Lord of the Rings* a much broader ethnicity of readers across the planet will recognize the peg.

The issue of localized naming and referencing presents a familiar dilemma for the modern writer. Translators must always tread a delicate path between being true to the writer's intention versus the average reader's awareness. But the problem acquires an extra flourish in the context of science fiction. By limiting ourselves to names and references that suit international readers, South Asia's own flavours, costumes, languages and customs vanish from the record – not just from the literary present but from the future as well. By choosing to avoid the arena of science fiction as writers and imagineers, we South Asians have effectively doomed ourselves to being the turbaned and/or sari-clad bit-players in the future-fictions of others.

For example, in the television serial *Lost in Space* (Netflix), a family bearing recognizably South Asian names, makes an appearance in mid-season. They speak in the accents of modern-day Britons. Why? Because in today's world, a tandoori-accent in a serial that's not about South Asians could result in the producers being accused of racial type-casting. So it follows that, in a space drama about a group of multi-ethnic future humans, 'we' are assigned the accents of our British colonizers in order to avoid being transformed into caricatures of ourselves!

While thinking about caricatures, cultural stereotypes, reference palettes and the rich tradition of South Asian mythology, four cross-linked ideas occurred to me in quick succession.

The first was that South Asian mythology includes many types of fantastical inventions and monsters, but very few clearly identifiable chimaeras. The great myth cycles of the Mahabharata and the Ramayana contain descriptions of unnaturally large and ferocious creatures, terrifying demons and gods endowed with powerful weapons, but there do not appear to be clearly identifiable creature combinations, such as the centaur, the minotaur or the griffon of the Graeco-Roman world.

The second was that a number of playful and fanciful chimaeras began to appear in the whimsical cartoons and stories of nineteenth-century Bengal. The best known of these sprang from the pen of Sukumar Ray, the poet, author and illustrator whose son was the illustrious film-maker, author and illustrator Satyajit Ray.

The third thought was that, perhaps the intellectual melding of two very different cultures, Britain and Bengal, acted as a catalyst for chimaera creation. Whereas earlier invaders approached India with war and commerce, in Bengal, a process of cultural data transfer was initiated over time. In order to create the giant chimaera of British India, Indians were drafted into service as clerks and accountants. British ideas of civil society took root. And hybrids of the imagination began to sprout in the literature of the times.

The fourth and final thought was this: We are today experiencing an era of unprecedented contact between cultures that are different in every possible way. Diverse languages, cuisines, socio-cultural values and religions are being brought into contact, sometimes willingly, sometimes forcibly, in a more extreme form than ever before. The chimaeras of Graeco-Roman mythology were mostly infertile, one-of-a-kind freaks. But in our world today, we're seeing the continuous cross-fertilization of tribes and races, ideas and technologies.

Could that be one reason for the current blooming of South Asian science fiction?

After all, we live in an era when only a whisper-thin membrane separates science fiction from science fact. Some of us are living in the digital OtherWorlds of our parents' nightmares. Some of us are fighting wars at the pixelated boundaries of countries we can no longer name. Some of us are being treated by virtual doctors who visit us on our smartphones. Others are finding love in the glow of laptop screens.

And, while some of us read about these alternative realities in fear or in wonder, a small handful of us is writing about these hopes, these journeys, these fictions, these truths.

Manjula Padmanabhan
New Delhi, January 2019

INTRODUCTION

SF MATTERS: SOUTH ASIAN FUTURES TO COME

TARUN K. SAINT

New Horizons: The Gollancz Book of South Asian Science Fiction is one of the first collections of contemporary (and historic) science fiction (SF) from the subcontinent to appear in the twenty-first century. In this introduction, I hope to highlight the genre's significance, as well as elaborate on the basis for the compilation of this omnibus at this moment.

Just about two hundred years ago, *Frankenstein* (1818, revised ed. 1831), Mary Shelley's novel about the ethical dilemmas untrammelled scientific exploration might usher in, inaugurated the genre of modern SF.[1] During a visit to Europe in June 1816, Mary Shelley, Percy Bysshe Shelley, Byron and John William Polidori were forced to remain indoors one day as a storm raged outside their villa near Lake Geneva.[2] In the evening, they had an animated conversation about ghosts, upon which Byron suggested a ghost-story writing competition (Polidori was the only one to complete his story). That night, a dream occurred to Mary Shelley about a strange phantasm stirring with vital life, beside whom his human creator kneeled. As a result, she began writing a story – a Gothic exploration of the consequences of scientist Victor Frankenstein's obsession with reanimating corpses through the use of electro-galvanism[3] – at the age of eighteen, which became a novel after two years, carving out space for a new genre. The resulting creature is both monster and victim of his creator's hubris; the achievement of the task of bringing to life the dead (using scientific as well as alchemical/ occult means) became a nineteenth-century version of Faust's unbridled quest for knowledge. Ever since the publication of *Frankenstein*, the genre of SF has been concerned with the varied consequences of the arrival of modernity, including the advances of scientific knowledge and technology, and its sometimes horrific outcomes. Furthermore, the interface between science and the occult, and the possibility of breaching the divide between science and the realm of magic and occult philosophy (as seen in Victor Frankenstein's fascination with the work of occultist Cornelius Agrippa) has been a recurrent theme in SF, right up to Amitav Ghosh's *The Calcutta Chromosome* (1996), steampunk and China Miéville's oeuvre, testifying to the lasting imprint of Shelley's concerns.[4]

The genre's ability to foreground alternative perspectives with respect to key cultural and socio-political issues subsequently came to the fore in works such as *The War of the Worlds* (1897), nineteenth-century master of the scientific romance, H.G. Wells's allegorical take on colonialism, and Yevgeny Zamyatin's parable of totalitarianism *We* (1924, new trans. 1993).[5] Zamyatin's masterpiece was in turn one of the inspirations for British author George Orwell's better-known *1984* (1949).[6] Soon after, the twentieth-century American SF maestro Ray Bradbury's McCarthy-era novel *Fahrenheit 451* (1953) depicted a future society where reading was a crime and books were burned, and hence, entire books and works of culture were memorized and shared by members of the resistance group to preserve their contents.[7] Later, works of SF by writers in the erstwhile Soviet Union constituted a veritable subculture of dissent. Another SF novel, *The Doomed City* by Boris and Arkady Strugatsky, perhaps the best of the crop of dissident writers to emerge in the twentieth century in Zamyatin's wake, evoked the tragic failure of a radical utopian experiment. Written in 1975 in a time of censorship and authoritarian rule, the novel was only published in 1989 after *perestroika* and *glasnost* (restructuring and openness) had left their imprint.[8]

In contrast to this strand of the genre, often critical of science and society, a more conservative strain emerged in the wake of colonialism and imperialism in the late nineteenth century, often with a masculinist thrust, gung-ho for change driven by technology.[9] Thus, while the genre has proved enabling for writers seeking to question hegemonic regimes and systems of thought, SF at times has undoubtedly replayed societal stereotypes and rehearsed clichéd notions of identity. For example, much of the pulp SF of the early twentieth century in the United States of America was aimed at an audience of male adolescents or young, often technically trained, men. At its lowest ebb, SF has even served as

a propaganda function, as seen in Ronald Reagan's requisitioning of the services of right-wing-leaning SF writers Larry Niven and Jerry Pournelle (known for their hard-SF style, featuring a strong basis in recent research in scientific disciplines) as speech-writers during the Cold War to help introduce his Strategic Defence Initiative 'Star Wars' defence system to the American public. This space laser initiative was vigorously opposed by leading contemporary SF writers of the time like Isaac Asimov and Arthur C. Clarke. Clarke described the proposal as a 'technological obscenity', while Asimov called it 'a John Wayne standoff'.[10]

In the context of the subcontinent, SF's potential to generate alternative visions of the future has perhaps been insufficiently acknowledged. Despite some innovative and sharply critical SF having appeared in recent years in South Asia, even a speculative fiction manifesto by prominent SF writer Vandana Singh, a contributor in this volume,[11] the genre is confined, for the most part, to the children's section of bookstores, if at all, or placed alongside 'popular fiction' genres such as fantasy, barring some regional contexts where it has found a niche.[12] It leads one to wonder whether this is the result of SF, or for that matter, speculative fiction,[13] not quite having taken in our subcontinental spaces,[14] despite the influence of modern scientific thought, industrial development and technological progress, not to mention the recent explosion in the use of social media. Is this lesser, niche status for SF an unwarranted result of the widespread availability and influence of epic and mythological narratives, which may have curtailed the SF impulse?[15] Might it be possible to discern in the best SF produced in South Asia in recent times the lineaments of an alternative, perhaps even a South Asian futurism?[16] Is it time for Indian/subcontinental SF to step up and make itself heard amidst, what Vandana Singh in her review essay calls, a 'spiral of silence'[17] on a host of issues, ranging from climate change to growing polarization and violence in society, amidst a climate of fear?

This is the right moment for an adequate appreciation of the genre's critical role in twenty-first-century South Asia, especially at a time when there is a perceptible drift towards modes of irrationalism and bigotry, often with tacit state sanction. While, in the subcontinent, the genre has not been explicitly associated with social movements or protests, in its own quiet way this 'minor' genre has whittled away at dominant societal assumptions. A pioneering effort in the subcontinental context is Manjula Padmanabhan's SF play *Harvest* (winner of the Onassis Award in 1997)

which, set in Bombay in 2010, envisaged a futuristic scenario
human organs from the 'Third World' for sale to recipients in the 'First World'.[18] Padmanabhan has also addressed growing gender hierarchies and imbalances, and the fragility of attempts at forging resistance to modes of bio-politics in her SF novels *Escape* (2008) and *The Island of Lost Girls* (2015).[19] In a similar vein, writers of SF and speculative fiction Anil Menon in *Half of What I Say* (2015) and Shovon Chowdhury in *The Competent Authority* (2013) and *Murder with Bengali Characteristics* (2015) have made trenchant fictive critiques, in different ways, of state absolutism. Such writings have created alternative templates for the future to come.[20]

As aficionados of the genre are aware, in the wake of the publication of *Frankenstein* the genre subsequently evolved with the scientific romances of Jules Verne (in France)[21] and H.G. Wells in the late nineteenth century. An era of pulp fiction in the 1920s and 1930s in the USA was launched by innovative editors like Hugo Gernsback (editor of *Amazing Stories*) and, crucially, John W. Campbell (editor of *Astounding Science Fiction*, where he played a critical role in shaping the craft of authors like Asimov). Some of the best writers of American SF found a voice during the Golden Age of SF, lasting from the mid-1930s to the mid-1950s, when the triad of Isaac Asimov, Robert A. Heinlein and Arthur C. Clarke held sway.[22] Later, the New Wave and feminist SF writers of the late 1960s and 1970s were notable for their emphasis on experimentalism, interiority and depth of character and psychology. When SF author and editor Michael Moorcock's journal, *New Worlds*, came to the fore in the UK, practitioners of off-beat and avant-garde SF, like British writer J.G. Ballard and Samuel Delany (in America), appeared on the scene.[23] Around this time, writers like Ursula K. Le Guin and Philip K. Dick (also from America) inflected the genre in distinctive ways with their interest in so-called 'soft' sciences such as anthropology, sociology, psychology and ecology, heralding the emergence of 'soft' SF (in contradistinction to the 'hard' SF of those like Asimov, trained in the natural and physical sciences).[24] The impact of the women's movement as well as the civil rights movement, and the foregrounding of questions of racial and cultural difference (and the ways these are mediated through language) by African-American writers like Samuel R. Delany (also in the wake of the Amerindian movement, the Latino-Chicano movement and the positing of the need for a rainbow coalition), was felt in the genre as the address of SF began to extend beyond the, often, male and techie readership of the pulps, to the other.' Such approaches were represented in myriad and complex ways in works by Le Guin, James Tiptree Jr. (pseudonym of Alice Sheldon), and later in novels of African-American writer Octavia Butler, which sought to explode the masculinist stereotypes of early SF.[25]

Later, the emergence of cyberpunk in the 1980s, with the writings of William Gibson, Bruce Sterling and others, coincided with the invention of the World Wide Web and the Internet (Gibson coined the term 'cyberspace' before it existed, in *Neuromancer*, 1984).[26] The rise of humanist SF, with its emphasis on three-dimensional characters, influenced in turn by 'soft' social sciences such as sociology, saw the advent of writers like Kim Stanley Robinson among others. In his Mars trilogy and Science in the City series, Robinson brought in extended reflections on environmental issues (this branch of SF has been described as cli-fi, short for climate change fiction). Among other trends that could be identified in this burgeoning field, there was a reinvention of the space opera in innovative ways by Iain M. Banks (in his Culture series) and Alastair Reynolds (in the Revelation Space series), while Octavia Butler reflected on questions of alterity (especially pertaining to race and gender) in an unsettling fashion in her Xenogenesis trilogy, in the light of feminist critiques on positions taken in sciences such as biology and genetics, especially with the advent of biotech and genetic engineering.[27]

Ann and Jeff VanderMeers' introduction in *The Big Book of Science Fiction* has an interesting, if brief, discussion of SF written by authors residing outside the United Kingdom and the USA, including references to Latin American, European, Soviet-era, Chinese and Japanese SF.[28] Outside Anglo-American spaces, some of the more prominent names include Polish writer Stanislaw Lem (*Solaris*, 1961, tr. 1970), whose writings opened up subversive philosophical possibilities missing in many conventional SF tales;[29] and Arkady and Boris Strugatsky (especially *Roadside Picnic*,1972, tr. 1975) who explored, in unconventional ways, what it means to be human as well as the idea of otherness in the context of situations under authoritarian rule.[30] Cixin Liu's Hugo Award-winning novel *The Three Body Problem* (2006, tr. 2014) and its sequels *The Dark Forest* (2008, tr. 2015) and *Death's End* (2010, tr. 2016) have shown what non-Western SF might be able to do with the genre, as it retains a situatedness in Chinese culture and history and takes up a dissenting viewpoint that preserves a sense of wonder.[31]

Ann and Jeff VanderMeer provide an economical definition of SF: '... it [SF] depicts the future, whether in a stylized or realistic manner.'[32] So, whether that future context is presented in a phantasmagoric way or by using the technical language of hard SF, or whether the future scenario is extrapolated from the present or includes commentary on the past or present, they argue that the story qualifies as SF.[33] In their view, this definition allows a delinking of the content or experience offered by SF from market trends that result in the commodification of the genre.[34] We may thus steer clear of the easy binarization of 'literary' and science or speculative fiction, since there are many SF texts that do cross over these boundaries established by critics and the market.[35]

To take a recent example of reflection on the genre's significance, in which this binary was replayed, Amitav Ghosh, in his essay *The Great Derangement: Climate Change and the Unthinkable*, flagged the absence of serious engagement with the issue of climate change in literary fiction, barring a few exceptions.[36] When writers did take up the subject, in his view, their work risked being categorized as SF, and thus relegated to the outhouse or periphery. Ghosh refers to Margaret Atwood's idea that SF and speculative fiction draw on the same deep source, imagined other worlds that are located apart from the everyday one, in another time or dimension, on the other side of a threshold that divides the known from the unknown.[37] The era of global warming seems to resist SF, in his view, since it is not happening in an 'other' world, nor is it located in another time or dimension.[38] Ghosh underlines instead the importance of literary treatment of the subject, engaging with everyday changes occurring in this world, which a few writers of literary fiction have undoubtedly attempted (such as Barbara Kingsolver in *Flight Behaviour*, 2012).[39]

Ghosh does, however, acknowledge that the only genre that regularly took up this subject was SF, [40] even if in its outhouse of the literary field (his Arthur C. Clarke Award-winning SF novel, *The Calcutta Chromosome*, appeared in 1996).[41] Ghosh then issues a call for more writers of literary fiction to address the predicament we face due to climate change, overcoming the disdain of collective experience and the non-human in the name of individual human experiences that has resulted from the partitioning of the imaginative from the scientific in this era of modernity.[42] In the process, Ghosh perhaps underplays the ongoing efforts of SF writers to imaginatively portray the crises we face (despite his nod to the importance of some SF writers like Clarke, Bradbury and Dick),[43] as Vandana Singh has persuasively argued in her critique. Singh instead makes the case for imaginative literature's (and especially SF and speculative fiction's) ability to alert us to, what she terms, 'paradigm blindness' or a failure to look beyond the paradigm in which one is located and the modes of constructing reality therein.[44]

Ironically enough, one of the earliest instances of Indian SF, a story by the renowned Bengali scientist Jagadish Chandra Bose, '*Niruddesher Kahini*' ('The Story of the Missing One', 1896), revised and published as '*Polatok Toofan*' (1921, tr. 'Runaway Cyclone'), actually dealt with an extreme instance of climatic variations – a life-threatening situation faced by the crew of a ship caught in a cyclone at sea.[45] This story written in Bengali, by Bose, a scientist known for his research on electromagnetic waves, was crafted in response to an advertisement issued by a hair oil company announcing a science-based story writing competition, the only condition being that each story would have to feature the hair-oil in question. Indeed, in Bose's story, a scientist aboard the ship in a moment of danger during the cyclonic storm eventually recalls carrying a bottle of hair-oil with him. He pours this on the waves with effects that are reminiscent of the butterfly effect propounded much later by Edward Lorenz (in the 1960s), according to which a minor perturbation might have major cumulative consequences.[46] The life-threatening waves are calmed by the oil's soothing effects, and the ship is saved. While the exposition of the theory of surface tension underlying this story by the author indicates a somewhat utopian faith in science, it is unlikely that such a scientific panacea exists for contemporary ecological crises. Nonetheless, the story in question does anticipate recent concern for abrupt (and potentially destructive) transformations in the natural world and the potential for human/technological intercession, here portrayed in a benevolent light.[47]

A detailed historical survey of subcontinental SF is out of the purview of this introduction, given the vast scope of the subject and varied linguistic skills required. I will nevertheless try to highlight a few trends and refer to select important early authors and texts, based on studies in the regional context in a few major languages.

One of the first Bengali (and likely subcontinental) proto-SF stories dealing with innovated technology was Hemlal Dutta's 'Rahashya' ('The Mystery'), which appeared in the journal *Bigyan Darpan* in 1882. Jagadananda Roy's 'Shukra Vraman' ('Travels to Venus') was published in *Varati* magazine in 1895, and later republished in the volume *Prakritiki* in 1914.[48] The story by J.C. Bose mentioned earlier, '*Niruddesher Kahini*' ('The Story of the Missing One'), was published in 1896, with a revised version in 1921, titled '*Polatok Toofan*' ('Runaway Cyclone').[49] Debjani Sengupta in her essay 'Sadhanbabu's Friends: Science Fiction in Bengal from 1882 to 1961' mentions an early-twentieth-century work by Sukumar Ray (the father of Satyajit Ray) bringing in a satirical take on scientists in '*Heshoram Hushiyarer Diary*' ('The Diary of Heshoram Hushiar') – possibly inspired by Arthur Conan Doyle's *The Lost World*,[50] and later Premendra Mitra's '*Piprey Puran*' ('The Story of the Ants') and '*Mangalbairi*' ('The Martian Enemies') as taking the genre forward, with Ray's works often aimed at a young audience.[51] Film-maker and writer Satyajit Ray's Professor Shonkhu series (published from 1961 till the author's death) unfolded in a new direction, presented in the form of diary entries documenting the adventures of an eccentric scientist with a sense of humour.[52] Satyajit Ray himself became the president of the SF Cineclub, with Premendra Mitra as vice-president and Adrish Bardhan as secretary, in 1966, indicating that this thriving SF subculture traversing film and literature had considerable support among Bengali viewers and readers.[53]

In his editorial for the special issue of *Muse India* on Science Fiction, Sami Ahmad Khan refers to Pandit Ambika Dutt Vyas's '*Ascharya Vrittant*' published in the magazine *Piyush Pravaha* (1884), and Babu Keshav Prasad's '*Chandra Lok ki Yatra*' published in the magazine *Saraswati* (1900) as examples of writing in Hindi that qualify as early or proto-SF.[54] However, SF appears not to have emerged as a major genre in Hindi and Urdu literature, despite the popularity of translations of Jules Verne and H.G. Wells in those languages.[55] Khan also cites proto-SF works in English, such as Kylas Chunder Dutt's anti-imperial 'A Journal of Forty-Eight Hours of the Year 1945', which appeared in *The Calcutta Literary Gazette*, 6 June 1835.[56] Dutt was an eighteen-year-old student of Hindu College, Calcutta, later renamed Presidency College, when he wrote this story, depicting an imaginary anti-colonial revolt in the century to come, for *The Calcutta Literary Gazette* (6 June 1835). Such a subversive outlook might not have been possible in print after the 1857 uprising, when censorship of anti-colonial writings was imposed in greater measure.[57] Shoshee Chunder Dutt's *The Republic of Orissa: A Page from the Annals of the 20th Century* (1845),[58] carried forward this youthful spirit of questioning colonial power as well as local hierarchies, while Rokeya Sakhawat Hussain's remarkable feminist utopia *Sultana's Dream* (1905) appeared at the dawn of the twenty-first century, becoming the basis for subsequent radical imaginings of alternatives to war and patriarchy.[59] Each of these early SF texts in English interrogate the power structures in place at the time – whether imperialism, slavery (the re-imposition of which leads to a tribal rebellion in Shoshee Dutt's story), the likely persistence of hegemonic systems after independence, or extant patriarchal assumptions about the role of women in governance.[60] SF critic Suparno Banerjee identifies a more sceptical and critical outlook in 'Anglophone' writing, or Indian writing in English, especially in works that have appeared after the 1990s, in comparison to early regional writing, where the writing often seems to rely on Western SF for its model.[61] As he shows, such writing often seeks to emulate SF narratives of the Golden Age in its valorization of and belief in the benefits of science and technology, barring some exceptions (such as Sukumar Ray).[62]

The anthology *It Happened Tomorrow*, edited by Marathi SF writer and critic Bal Phondke and published in 1993, was one of the first serious attempts to collate and compile Indian SF stories, mainly in translation.[63] In the collection, scientific problems set in an Indian milieu feature in the main, while some make critical references to the social and political uses of science and technology.[64] In the preface to the volume, Phondke discusses the regional contexts for early works, including Marathi and Bengali as the major languages in which the genre flourished, appearing often in small regional magazines and periodicals.[65] This efflorescence of the genre in these coastal areas may have occurred as a result of the spread of scientific education and people's science movements in such historically cosmopolitan contexts (after all, the Bengal Renaissance came about as a response to the advent of modernity under the colonial aegis).[66]

Phondke's assertion that Indian SF may be categorized not so much by the geographical origin of the authors as by 'the cultural and social ambience which gives it its soul' certainly has an idealistic view at its core.[67] Phondke's preface leans towards Marathi (the strongest current, in his terms) in its delineation of the history and contours of regional SF (though he does acknowledge, among others, the contributions of Adrish Bardhan as editor of *Fantastic*, a Bengali SF magazine), as Assamese writer Dinesh Chandra Goswami's Sahitya Akademi paper about Indian SF and fantasy does towards Asomiya.[68] While this is to be expected, given the background and training of these editors/ authors, tracing this history can indeed seem at times like 'hunting a snark', as Anil Menon puts it in his witty essay on the subject.[69] The task of assembling and historicizing subcontinental, let alone Indian, SF still awaits a dedicated team in the future.[70]

Suparno Banerjee's more recent 2010 study seeks to position Indian SF in the context of postcolonial debates, and discusses major texts by Indian writers as well as SF novels set in India by Western writers. His emphasis on the dialectics of authority (affirming Western science and technology) and subversion (at times rather uncritically, in the name of a 'pure' indigenous epistemology) in Indian SF writings and critical survey of the field is a useful beginning of what needs to become a comprehensive critical discourse. As Banerjee shows, SF criticism needs to be equally alert to our colonial inheritance and the pitfalls of both ill-thought-out versions of Orientalist futurism (Orientalist futurism refers to SF novels set in a future India that replay Orientalist ideas about the East and India in particular), as well as simplistic claims as regards the superiority of native knowledge systems, with knee-jerk recourse to the greatness of 'Vedic science'.[71]

Colonial era proto-SF was succeeded by a range of writings in the major Indian languages as well as in English. Nation-building imperatives and the need to propagate the 'scientific temper' were likely key objectives of much of the writing of the early phase after Independence, often animated by an idealized view of science and technology and a didactic impulse.[72] Yet, as Shiv Viswanathan points out in his foreword to *Alternative Futures*, some strands of the national movement were futuristic in outlook, keen to provide alternatives to positivist science and instrumental rationality.[73] Viswanathan especially cites Gandhi's ashrams as laboratories for the future, where *swadeshi* and Swaraj became the basis for a different mode of thinking and being, opening up the basis for eco-Swaraj (radical ecological democracy) in the future.[74] With the rise of environmentalism in the 1960s and 1970s,[75] and the subsequent critiques of the excesses of modern science and instrumental rationality by J.P.S. Uberoi, Vandana Shiva, Ashis Nandy and Shiv Viswanathan among others, a greater degree of scepticism about science and technology and the developmental discourse came to the fore.[76] One of the landmark novels that redefined the contours of Indian SF in the wake of such rethinking, Amitav Ghosh's *The Calcutta Chromosome*, looks back at the history of colonial science and normative patterns of scientific research and development prevalent. The novel achieves a critical perspective on the advent of modernity in colonial India during the process of reconstructing the history of the discovery of the malaria parasite in fictive form.[77]

Even so, many post-Independence subcontinental SF writers happened to be scientists or teachers of science, such as astrophysicist Jayant Narlikar in Marathi and English (he studied under physicist Fred Hoyle, author of *The Black Cloud*, a novel anticipating the discovery of molecular clouds between stars), teacher of physics Dinesh Chandra Goswami in Asomiya, and zoologist Sukanya Datta in English.[78] Among non-scientists writing SF in the 'popular' vein, Sujatha Rangarajan's writings in Tamil are well-known, while Ruchir Joshi's expansive experimental novel *The Last Jet Engine Laugh* (2001) included SF elements with a time-span from 1930 to 2030.[79] Critiques of a monolithic view of science and new perspectives on destructive development underpinned by a desire for ecological justice are opening up new avenues for self-critical SF to follow.[80] This greater degree of self-reflexivity and meta-awareness of both science's and the genre's fallibility (also leading to a fluidity of genre-borders) is apparent in the best work of SF writers since the 1990s, including Manjula Padmanabhan, Vandana Singh (*The Woman Who Thought She Was a Planet*, 2008, *Ambiguity Machines and other Stories*, 2018, nominated for the Philip K. Dick Award, 2018), Anil Menon, (*The Beast with Nine Billion Feet*, 2009), Rimi B. Chatterjee (*Signal Red*, 2005), Priya Sarukkai Chabria (*Generation 14*, 2008) and Shovon Chowdhury.[81] Recently, award-winning author of literary fiction M.G. Vassanji has written a major SF novel, *Nostalgia*, indicating the fluidity of genre borders.[82]

A younger generation of writers such as Suraj Clark Prasad (aka Clark Prasad), Sami Ahmad Khan, Samit Basu (leaning towards fantasy), as well as other writers of South Asian descent such as Mimi Mondal (now living in the USA, nominated for the Hugo Award in 2018 for her co-edited study of Octavia Butler, *Luminescent Threads*), S.B. Divya (nominated for the Nebula Award for her debut novel, *Runtime*, 2016, based in the USA), Vina Jie-Min Prasad (in Singapore), Premee Mohamed (in Canada), Nur Nasreen Ibrahim (Salam Award finalist from Pakistan, now based in the USA) and Indrapramit Das (writing as Indra Das, in Kolkata and North America) are attempting to further expand the scope of the genre through their innovative choice of themes – such as the urgent challenges posed by biotechnology, the impact of social media and social technology on society, environmental degradation, changing gender dynamics, sectarian strife and hidebound identity politics – and styles (often highly individualized). We can discern in their novels, stories and poems twenty-first century SF's intersectional potential in tackling questions of difference along fraught lines of gender, community, race and sexuality in both subcontinental and diasporic locations.[83]

The more all-encompassing term, speculative fiction, may be more appropriate for narratives which often blur generic boundaries (the term speculative non-fiction has now come into play as well), and seem to be more influenced by debates in the social sciences and the humanities,[84] even though scientist-writers like Vandana Singh and Anil Menon do continue to bring in hard science/technology-based allusions, albeit with a critical understanding of the limits to technology-driven progress.[85] The sub-genre of speculative poetry is included here as well, a form of poetic expression exploring various facets of human experience through a speculative lens.[86] This anthology, however, restricts its ambit by not including retold mythology, mytho-fantasy and out-and-out fantasy (in which anything can happen and no set rules apply).[87]

The genesis of this anthology was not so much the imperative to anthologize the work of earlier writers (though some samples of early SF are provided here), or to further explore the antinomies of postcolonial discourse (including postcolonial SF; see Hopkinson and Mehan, eds., *So*

Long Been Dreaming).[88] Rather, a sense of disturbance with the situation in contemporary South Asia led to the composition of the concept note which was sent out to both established and younger subcontinental writers in English. If not quite a competition to write a ghost story, the idea was to impel contemporary writers to engage with the present and future, using an SF lens, in this seventy-second year of Independence and the Partition. What might the subcontinent look like, about, seventy years from now?

For the subcontinent, and India in particular, has been rocked by such a number of crises in the last few years that it has often seemed we are living out the plot of a SF novel on a daily basis.[89] The *annus horribilis* 1984 was, for many, a shock, almost living up to Orwellian predictions in the subcontinent. The anti-Sikh pogrom in Delhi that year led to intensive introspection among many about how such large-scale, state-abetted collective violence could occur in India's democracy, while the Bhopal industrial disaster the same year reminded us of the appalling consequences of reckless and unchecked proliferation of technology in the name of profit. In recent years, the continuing degradation of the environment, the basis for survival for marginalized communities, the threat to freedom of speech with growing intolerance in society across South Asia, the multiplication of incidents featuring violence reminiscent of the Partition (now including videotaped vigilante actions by mobs) with the added complication of mediatized forms of politics and the emergence of social media-based trolls and WhatsApp pressure groups, as well as the targeted killing of authors and journalists, has posed new challenges for commentators and writers.

The stories and poems sent in by writers of three countries of South Asia in response to the concept note (not all of those who were approached did so), often feature world-building and dystopian realities eerily reminiscent of the present, sometimes presented in a satirical light, with elements of black humour. It is the tension between the implicit utopian imaginings of alternative South Asian futures and the representation of stark dystopias that makes these thought experiments in the SF mode so interesting.[90]

This anthology also includes selected sample stories in translation from some major regional languages, written during the twentieth century. We have, for instance, Arunava Sinha's translation from Bengali of Adrish Bardhan's 'Planet of Terror', written in the style reminiscent of Golden Era SF, and Harishankar Parsai's 'Inspector Matadeen on the Moon', a satirical oddity with SF elements, in a revised translation from Hindi by C.M. Naim.

The newer stories appear in a range of styles and voices. Some follow a 'literary' model of storytelling, while others experiment with form and structure, and a few stories follow the conventions of pulp fiction. This set opens with Asif Farrukhi's Naiyer Masud-like meditation (translated from Urdu) on the uncanny effects of the sea disappearing off the coast of Karachi. Next, Chernobyl becomes a metaphor for the decline of civilization in Somendra Singh Kharola's speculative poem. This is followed by Mimi Mondal's tale exploring boundary altering manifestations of identity and difference in Mumbai. The passages in translation by Maya Joshi from Rahul Sankrityayan's futuristic fiction *Baisvin Sadi* (1924) give a sense of the direction utopian imagining was taking in the early twentieth century in India, in the wake of the Russian revolution in 1917, in contrast to the rather dark visions generated in the contemporary moment. The next story features Anil Menon's jagged reflections in cyberpunk style, set in a future Mumbai overrun by human waste, while in a story by Shovon Chowdhury, with more than a touch of irony, Gandhi is reborn in contemporary times. Kaiser Haq's witty and poetic projection of selfhood seventy years into the future provides an ironic counterpoint to the futurologist's hubris. Also included is a speculative poem by Sumita Sharma which ironically updates the notion of *moksha* for the post-human, digital era. In my own story about timelines past, present and future, a family visits a new theme park called Partition World in 2047 with unforeseen consequences.

In a bleak yet intense tale by Priya Sarukkai Chabria, a dream of cool green rivers unfolds in intolerant times when censorship is rampant, while Suraj Prasad deploys the thriller's conventions as a Bhumandala couple seek to unravel a mystery about time lapses and identity. Manjula Padmanabhan's thought-provoking tale addresses the dilemmas humanity might face with the advent of aliens who exist partly outside the human temporal plane, while in Payal Dhar's moving story a young girl uncovers a dark secret history in an authoritarian future. In Sami Ahmad Khan's pulp-style narrative, aliens with an agenda of homogenization descend on a railway station in Uttar Pradesh. Next, Premendra Mitra's 'How the World War Ended' has been translated by Arunava Sinha from Bengali, a language in which SF has found a special niche.

Arjun Rajendran's speculative poem presents a prescient ironic reflection about the construction of a mega-statue of Shivaji off the Mumbai coast. Following this is Chandrashekhar Sastry's R.K. Narayan-esque account of a visit by a beneficent extraterrestrial and Giti Chandra's vision of a goddess project taking shape in the modern city's dark interstices. There is a satirical thrust to Mohammad Salman's portrayal of a conservationist's discovery of the last surviving tiger in the wild in 2087, once the news becomes public. Rimi B. Chatterjee's story extends a fictional world already in the making (in the form of a novel to come), in which a clown makes his sinister presence felt in a universe of anti-sense. An intriguing short piece, 'The Dream', by Muhammed Zafar Iqbal, the SF writer from Bangladesh who was recently subjected to a vicious physical attack for his rationalist convictions, has been translated by Arunava Sinha. The story by Rukmini Bhaya Nair explores the varied implications of the invention in 2072 of Anandna, an elixir that eliminates pain.

Later, Nur Nasreen Ibrahim, while drawing on cultural and historical memory, grapples in her story with the varied implications of a community of women being established in a remote sanctuary in the future, effectively ironizing the feminist utopian sweep of Rokeya Sakhawat Hussain's *Sultana's Dream*. Keki Daruwalla's self-reflexive and satirical fable, while grounded in the predicament of the present, describes a strange yet curiously familiar journey by a Parsi to a moon settlement. Next, S.B. Divya's story brings in a diasporic perspective, as the personal tragedy of a protagonist of South Asian descent finds an unexpected resolution in the wake of her being selected for an expedition to Mars. In conclusion, we have a poignant narrative reflection in the cli-fi mode by Vandana Singh on the likely nightmarish impact of climate change in the years to come.

Taken together, these stories and poems may indicate the direction of alternative South Asian futures to come, as well as the emergence of a subcontinental SF sensibility attuned to socio-cultural nuances and issues that are local as well as global. We can discern here a shared counter-vision, as these writings at their best bear witness to, at times, uncomfortable truths, albeit displaced into 'other' timelines and spaces. Such fictive extrapolation provides a cosmopolitan, yet grounded perspective rather different from the futurologists, with an emphasis on the human and culturally specific side of the story.[91] The future of subcontinental SF, as evidenced by this volume, thus seems promising indeed, even in the face of grim portents in the socio-cultural domain in the subcontinent and seemingly inexorable transformations of the ecological basis for life that are threatening the very existence of the most vulnerable, not just in South Asia.

The hope is that for readers this anthology will provide a prism refracting the vivid and at times contrarian imaginings of contemporary South Asian SF. Sadly, we were unable to reach out to writers from Sri Lanka, Nepal, Bhutan, the Maldives or the Tibetan community in exile, since the focus here has been on writing from the partitioned three, India, Pakistan and Bangladesh. Inshallah, there will be other anthologies to come which will rectify this, given constraints of geography and time.

Notes

1. Mary Shelley, *Frankenstein*, 1818, reprint, New Delhi: Worldview, 2002, ed. with an introduction by Maya Joshi. Also see, Brian Aldiss and David Wingrove, *Trillion Year Spree* , London: Gollancz, 1986, 36–52.
2. 'Preface' in Mary Shelley, *Frankenstein*, ed. Maya Joshi, New Delhi: Worldview, 2002, vi. The frequent storms that year were a result of the eruption of a volcano, Mount Tambora in Indonesia the previous year, which disrupted weather patterns across the world. http: / /lithub.com / mary-shelley-abandoned-by-her-creator-and-rejected-by-society / (accessed 28 January 2018).
3. Brian Aldiss and David Wingrove, *Trillion Year Spree*, London: Gollancz, 1986, 36–52.
4. I am indebted to Geeta Patel for this idea. Also see Mary Shelley, *Frankenstein*, 1818, reprint, New Delhi: Worldview, 2002, ed. Maya Joshi, 29–33, and Amitav Ghosh, *The Calcutta Chromosome: A Novel of Fevers, Delirium and Discovery*, New Delhi: Ravi Dayal, 1996. China Mieville's work often veers towards science fantasy; see, for instance, the blending of elements of crime fiction, SF, and the fantastical in Miéville, *The City and The City*, London: Pan, 2009.
5. http: / / www.planetpublish.com / wp-content / uploads / 2011 / 11 / The_War_of_the_Worlds_NT.pdf (accessed 24 January 2019). See Clarence Brown, 'Introduction: Zamyatin and the Persian Rooster' in Yevgeny Zamyatin, *We*, 1924, new English trans. by Clarence Brown, London: Penguin, 1993, xi–xxvi. Zamyatin went into exile after the controversy and personal attacks following the book's initial publication outside the Soviet Union – the novel only appeared in his homeland in 1988.
6. George Orwell, *1984*, London: Secker and Warburg, 1949.
7. Ray Bradbury, *Fahrenheit 451*, New York: Ballantine, 1953. Bradbury's novel, as literary historian and cultural critic Geeta Patel points out, plays with a kind of Christian Puritanism and its tense relationship with the transformative power of art and literature, manifested in the past most strongly in the case of Girolamo Savonarola, the Florentine monk responsible for the original 'bonfire of the

vanities' when items of 'luxury', including 'indecent' books were burned in the public square in Florence in 1497. Personal communication. Also see https://www.historytoday.com/richard-cavendish/execution-florentine-friar-savonarola (accessed 3 May 2018).

8. Arkady and Boris Strugatsky, *The Doomed City*, 1989, tr. Andrew Broomfield, Chicago: Chicago Review Press, 2016.

9. I am indebted to Anil Menon for this idea. In contrast, Cory Doctorow's utopian novel *Walkaway* (London: Head of Zeus, 2017) presents a future society of dropouts ('walkaways') who contest the basis of late-capitalist society through the creation of survivor states, reliant on the creative redeployment of new 'soft' technologies like 3D printing, even while refusing to succumb to the surveillance state's attempts to rope them in using war-propelled 'hard' technologies. There has been a conservative backlash to attempts to bring in more diversity and complexity in the American SF awards, the charge led by the so-called Sad (and later Rabid) Puppies. See https://newrepublic.com/article/121554/2015-hugo-awards-and-history-science-fiction-culture-wars (accessed 18 May 2018).

10. See https://www.thrillist.com/entertainment/nation/strategic-defense-initiative-reagan-star-wars-jerry-pournelle-larry-niven (accessed 26 December 2017).

11. 'A Speculative Manifesto', in *The Woman Who Thought She Was a Planet and Other Stories*, 2008, reprint, New Delhi: Zubaan, 2013, 200–03.

12. Bodhisattva Chattopadhyay, Aakriti Mandhwani and Anwaisha Maity, 'Introduction – Indian Genre Fiction: Languages, Literatures, Classifications', https://www.researchgate.net/profile/Bodhisattva_Chattopadhyay/publication/326416187_Indian_genre_fiction_languages_literatures_classifications/links/5b4c6f65a6fdccadaecf70bb/Indian-genre-fiction-languages-literatures-classifications.pdf, (accessed 11 November 2018). As Bodhisattva Chattopadhyay et al argue, SF has never been as 'popular' as other mass cultural genres in the subcontinent despite having emerged from the same crucible and mass genre cultural system, including pulps and periodicals. Instead, SF had a perceived 'supra-educational' role here, as a genre for children and young adults, unlike in the West, where it is seen as a genre for adults.

13. Speculative fiction is a more general term, according to one definition, 'a broad literary genre encompassing any fiction with supernatural, fantastical, or futuristic elements', http://www.dictionary.com/browse/speculative-fiction (accessed 1 February 2018). In Cecilia Mancuso's terms, speculative fiction was a term used by science fiction avant-gardists to distinguish their 'serious' work from pulp fiction featuring 'monsters and spaceships' in Margaret Atwood's phrase, https://www.theguardian.com/books/2016/aug/10/speculative-or-science-fiction-as-margaret-atwood-shows-there-isnt-much-distinction (accessed 4 February

2018). Similarly, Fredric Jameson differentiates between the European art tradition of H.G. Wells's 'scientific romances' or speculative fiction and the commercially driven American pulp tradition, while referring to the work of Olaf Stapledon. See Jameson's 'Introduction' in *Archaeologies of the Future: The Desire Called Utopia and Other Science Fictions*, 2005, reprinted, London: Verso, 2007, fn.5, xiii. Also see the more hopeful conversation about recent Indian speculative fiction at http://strangehorizons.com/non-fiction/remaking-the-difference-a-discussion-about-indian-speculative-fiction/ (accessed 1 May 2018).

14. Ashok Vajpeyi, *India Dissents: 3,000 Years of Difference, Doubt and Argument*, New Delhi: Speaking Tiger, 2017, esp. 16–18, 55, 65–70, 163–68, 403–05, 428–33, 440–44. This recent volume begins with the Vedic era materialist Charvaka, and includes the pre-modern voices of Kabir and the Sufis as well as pieces by modern figures like Ismat Chughtai and Saadat Hasan Manto, an essay by Amartya Sen, as well as social media-based writings by Kiran Nagarkar and Mrinal Pande, among others, mapping the spectrum of dissenting views across history up to the present. SF writers do not, however, figure at all in this volume.

15. Shiv Viswanathan, 'Foreword' in *Alternative Futures: India Unshackled*, eds. Ashish Kothari and K.J. Joy, New Delhi: UpFront Publishing House, 2017, vii–xi, esp. vii. According to social scientist and cultural critic Shiv Viswanathan, SF has not had the same following as detective fiction in the subcontinent partly because our mythology is so replete with aliens, monsters and witches.

16. South Asian futurism may be comparable to an extent to the notion of afrofuturism, as it envisages a different collective and transnational future while invoking SF elements, in the face of often intractable power structures and hierarchies inherited from the past. For more on afrofuturism, see https://www.theguardian.com/culture/2015/dec/07/afrofuturism-black-identity-future-science-technology (accessed 7 February 2018). I am indebted for this parallel to Ananya Jahanara Kabir. Also see Bodhisattva Chattopadhyay's reflections at http://momentum9.no/materials/is-science-fiction-still-science-fiction-when-it-is-written-on-saturn-or-aliens-alienation-and-science-fiction/ (accessed 7 February 2018).

17. See Singh's review essay at http://strangehorizons.com/non-fiction/reviews/the-unthinkability-of-climate-change-thoughts-on-amitav-ghoshs-the-great-derangement/ (accessed 26 December 2017).

18. Manjula Padmanabhan, *Harvest*, 1997, revised and expanded edition, Gurgaon: Hachette India, 2017.

19. Manjula Padmanabhan, *Escape*, New Delhi: Picador, 2008, reprinted, Gurgaon: Hachette India, 2015, and *The Island of Lost Girls*, Gurgaon: Hachette India, 2015.

20. Anil Menon, *Half of What I Say*, New Delhi: Bloomsbury, 2015; Shovon Chowdhury, *The Competent Authority*, New Delhi: Aleph Book Company, 2013

and *Murder with Bengali Characteristics*, New Delhi: Aleph Book Company, 2015.

21. See Jules Verne, *Twenty Thousand Leagues Under the Sea: An Underwater Tour of the World*, 1869–72, Trans. F. P. Walter 1993, reprinted London: Collector's Library, 2010.

22. See for instance Isaac Asimov, *I, Robot*, 1950, reprinted, New York: Bantam, 1991, Robert A. Heinlein, *Have Space Suit—Will Travel*, 1958, reprinted, New York: Ballantine Books, 1977, Arthur C. Clarke, *Rendezvous with Rama*, 1973, reprinted, London: Gollancz, 2006.

23. See Michael Moorcock, *Behold the Man*, 1969, reprinted, London: Gollancz, 1999; J.G. Ballard, *The Drought*, 1965, reprinted, London: Paladin, 1985; Samuel R. Delany, *Babel-17*, 1967, reprinted London: Gollancz, 1999.

24. See, for instance, Ursula K. Le Guin, *The Left Hand of Darkness*, 1969, reprinted, London: Orbit, 2009, and *The Dispossessed*, 1974, reprinted, London: Millenium, 1999. Also, Philip K. Dick, *The Man in the High Castle*, 1962, reprinted,. London: Penguin, 1965, and *Ubik*, 1969, reprinted London: Millennium, 2000. Ursula K. Le Guin's recent passing has led to a reappraisal of her work and numerous tributes. See Vandana Singh's acknowledgement of her influence at https://vandanasingh.wordpress.com/2018/01/26/true-journey-is-return-a-tribute-to-ursula-k-le-guin/#more-394 (accessed 30 January 2018).

25. This paragraph draws on Ann and Jeff VanderMeer, 'Introduction' in *The Big Book of Science Fiction*, New York: Vintage, 2016, xiii–xxxi, esp. xxiii–xxv. Also see Adam Roberts, *Science Fiction*, New York: Routledge, 2000, esp. 47–117, and Octavia Butler's revisiting of the history of slavery through time travel in her novel *Kindred*, 1979, reprinted, Boston: Beacon, 1988. Delany's statement about racism and SF is significant in this regard. See http://www.nyrsf.com/racism-and-science-fiction-.html (accessed 17 May 2018).

26. Ibid., xxvi–xxvii, also William Gibson, *Neuromancer*, 1984, reprinted, London: Harper Voyager, 1995, and Adam Roberts' discussion of the novel in Roberts, *Science Fiction*, New York: Routledge, 2000, 169–80.

27. This paragraph follows the VanderMeers', 'Introduction', xxvi -xxviii. See, for instance, Kim Stanley Robinson, *Green Mars*, 1994, reprinted, London: Harper Voyager, 2009, and Robinson, *Green Earth: The Science in the Capital Trilogy*, 2007, omnibus ed., London: Harper Voyager, 2015. Also see, Iain M. Banks, *Look To Windward*, 2000, reprinted, London: Orbit, 2010; Alastair Reynolds, *Revelation Space*, 2000, reprinted, London: Gollancz, 2013. I am indebted to Geeta Patel for her insights as regards Butler's work. Also see, Octavia Butler, Xenogenesis trilogy, (*Dawn*, 1987, *Adulthood Rites*, 1988, *Imago*, 1989), reprinted as *Lilith's Brood*, New York: Grand Central Publishing, 2000.

28. Ibid., xxv–xxvi. In contrast, Brian Aldiss's 2007 SF anthology does not refer

to or include any non-Western SF, except for a story by Ted Chiang, who was born and is based in the USA. See Aldiss, ed., *A Science Fiction Omnibus*, London: Penguin, 2007.

29. Stanislaw Lem, *Solaris*, 1961, trans., Orlando: Harvest, 1970. Also see his essay on science fiction, in which Lem takes a sharply critical view of American SF, with the exception of Philip K. Dick's work, in Stanislaw Lem, 'Science Fiction: A Hopeless Case—with Exceptions', in Stanislaw Lem, *Microworlds: Writings on Science Fiction and Fantasy*, ed. Franz Rottensteiner, 1984, reprinted, London: Mandarin, 1991, 45–105.

30. Arkady and Boris Strugatsky, *Roadside Picnic*, 1972, tr. 1975, reprinted, London: Gollancz, 2000. Andrei Tarkovsky directed major films based on these two novels, *Solaris* in 1972 and *Stalker* (based on *Roadside Picnic*) in 1979. See http://sensesofcinema.com/2002/great-directors/tarkovsky/#film (accessed 3 March 2018).

31. A selection of some of the best of international SF (also including two South Asian exemplars) has been brought together in the VanderMeers' anthology, *The Big Book of Science Fiction*, including a story by Cixin Liu. Also see Cixin Liu, *The Three Body Problem*, 2006, tr. Ken Liu, London: Head of Zeus, 2014; *The Dark Forest*, 2008, tr. Joel Martinsen, London: Head of Zeus, 2015; and *Death's End*, 2010, tr. Ken Liu, London: Head of Zeus, 2016.

32. VanderMeers, 'Introduction', xv–xvi. According to SF historians Brian Aldiss and David Wingrove, in *Trillion Year Spree* (1986), 'Science fiction is the search for a definition of mankind and his status in the universe which will stand in our advanced but confused state of knowledge (science), and is characteristically cast in the Gothic or post-Gothic mode.' Aldiss and Wingrove, 25.

33. VanderMeers, 'Introduction', xv–xvi.

34. Ibid., xvi.

35. For instance, Kurt Vonnegut deployed SF devices in his absurdist antiwar novel about the horrific Dresden bombings during the Second World War; his meta-fictional narrative features an (unsuccessful) science fiction writer named Kilgore Trout. See Vonnegut, *Slaughterhouse 5*, 1969, reprinted, London: Vintage, 1991. Nobel Prize winner Kazuo Ishiguro's chilling futuristic narrative evoking the interior world of clones raised to donate organs, *Never Let Me Go*, London: Faber and Faber, 2005, is a notable example of cross-over SF.

36. Amitav Ghosh, *The Great Derangement: Climate Change and the Unthinkable*, New Delhi: Penguin Random House, 2016.

37. Ibid., 97. On the difference of viewpoint between Atwood and Le Guin as regards science fiction and speculative fiction , see Le Guin's review article,

https://www.theguardian.com/books/2009/aug/29/margaret-atwood-year-of-flood?CMP=share_btn_fb (accessed 4 February 2018). For instances of Atwood's cli-fi style speculative fiction (part of her MaddAdam trilogy about man-made ecological catastrophe), see Margaret Atwood, *Oryx and Crake*, 2003, reprinted, London: Virago, 2009, Atwood, *The Year of the Flood*, 2009, reprinted, London: Virago, 2013 and Atwood, *MaddAddam*, 2013, reprinted London: Virago, 2014.

38. Amitav Ghosh, *The Great Derangement*, 97–98.

39. Ibid., 221. Also see Barbara Kingsolver, *Flight Behaviour*, London: Faber and Faber, 2012. For another engagement with environmental disaster in the satirical mode by a major novelist, see Ian McEwan, *Solar*, 2010, reprinted, London: Vintage, 2011.

40. As is well-known, SF has negotiated major issues of the time including environmental degradation through extrapolation and displacement into futuristic/otherworldly contexts (often using techniques of cognitive estrangement, a term coined by prominent SF critic Darko Suvin). According to Suvin, 'SF is, then, a literary genre whose necessary and sufficient conditions are the presence and interaction of estrangement and cognition, and whose main formal device is an imaginative framework alternative to the author's empirical environment.' See Darko Suvin, 'Estrangement and Cognition' at http://strangehorizons.com/non-fiction/articles/estrangement-and-cognition/ (accessed 15 December 2017). However, as Geeta Patel observes, previous dystopian and post-apocalyptic narratives (at times allegorical in scope) about resource depletion and environmental degradation did exist and were folded into SF as the genre evolved. Personal communication. Cormac McCarthy's post-apocalyptic novel, *The Road*, London: Picador, 2006, is a contemporary instance of this.

41. Amitav Ghosh, *The Calcutta Chromosome: A Novel of Fevers, Delirium and Discovery*, New Delhi: Ravi Dayal, 1996.

42. Ghosh, *The Great Derangement*, 86–96.

43. Ibid., 96.

44. See Vandana Singh's review essay http://strangehorizons.com/non-fiction/reviews/the-unthinkability-of-climate-change-thoughts-on-amitav-ghoshs-the-great-derangement/ (accessed 15 December 2017).

45. Also see, Vandana Singh's and Anil Menon's commentary at http://strangehorizons.com/fiction/introduction-to-runaway-cyclone-and-sheesha-ghat/ (accessed 15 December 2017). For a recent translation by Bodhisattva Chattopadhyaya, seehttp://strangehorizons.com/fiction/runaway-cyclone/ (accessed 15 December 2017).

46. See http://www.stsci.edu/~lbradley/seminar/butterfly.html (accessed 15 December 2017).

In 1952, Ray Bradbury's story 'A Sound of Thunder', showed the disastrous cumulative effects over the years of the inadvertent killing of a butterfly during a safari to the age of dinosaurs, in an age of time travel, http://mrjost.weebly.com/uploads/1/2/8/8/12884680/a_sound_of_thunder_-_text.pdf (accessed 25 January 2018).

47. For instance, see Manjula Padmanabhan's futuristic take on air pollution in Delhi in the 1980s, and the social attitudes toward the problem in her SF story 'Sharing Air' (*Kleptomania: Ten Stories*, New Delhi: Penguin Books India, 2004, 83–90).

48. Personal communication, Dip Ghosh, based on his article in Bengali https://kalpabiswa.com/article/first_science_fiction/, accessed Nov. 4, 2020. Debjani Sengupta, 'Sadhanbabu's Friends, Science Fiction in Bengal from 1882–1961', in *Sarai Reader 2003: Shaping Technologies*, at http://archive.sarai.net/files/original/e067355930e46f0f188b0fc0e5348cc5.pdf (accessed 15 December, 2017).

49. Also see http://strangehorizons.com/fiction/introduction-to-runaway-cyclone-and-sheesha-ghat/ (accessed 15 December 2017).

50. See Sukumar Ray, 'The Diary of Heshoram Hushiar', in Satyajit Ray, *Travails with the Alien: The Film that was Never Made and other Adventures with Science Fiction* (Noida: Harper Collins India, 2018, 190–98).

51. Debjani Sengupta, 'Sadhanbabu's Friends'. Also see the discussion of the history of *kalpobigyan* (the Bengali term for SF) at http://www.sfencyclopedia.com/entry/bengal (accessed 15 December 2017). Bodhisattva Chattopadhyay proposes that *kalpobigyan* might take the place of terms like SF or speculative fiction while referring to non-Anglocentric genre fiction, especially but not only from Bengal. See http://strangehorizons.com/non-fiction/articles/recentering-science-fiction-and-the-fantastic-what-would-a-non-anglocentric-understanding-of-science-fiction-and-fantasy-look-like/ (accessed 13 March 2018). Also see Chattopadhyay's critical discussion of Premendra Mitra's Ghanada stories, in comparison to and as a redoing of the colonialist stories of Joseph Jorkens, written by Edward Plunkett, Lord Dunsany (1878–1957) at http://humanitiesunderground.org/aliens-of-the-same-world-the-case-of-bangla-science-fiction/ (accessed 13 March 2018). According to cultural commentator Sandip Roy, in Bangladesh Humayun Ahmed and Zafar Iqbal are two scientists who have led the field with respect to SF. See 'The Future in the Past' at http://indianexpress.com/article/lifestyle/books/the-future-in-the-past-5013283 (accessed 7 January 2018).

52. Ibid. A film version based on Ray's Professor Shonkhu stories, directed by his son, Sandip Ray, has released in 2018. See Roy, 'The Future in the Past' at http://indianexpress.com/article/lifestyle/books/the-future-in-the-past-5013283 (accessed 15 December 2017). Satyajit Ray's script about an extraterrestrial visitor

(titled *The Alien*) circulated in Hollywood, but the project fell through eventually. This script's influence on Steven Spielberg's *E.T.* became a matter of controversy subsequently. See Satyajit Ray, *Travails with the Alien*, esp. 71–189. Also see Ashis Nandy's fascinating discussion of Ray's science fiction, highlighting his portrayal in three SF stories of the tragedy of a creative person in a conformist society, 'Satyajit Ray's Secret Guide to Exquisite Murders: Creativity, Social Criticism and the Partitioning of the Self', in Ashis Nandy, *The Savage Freud and Other Essays on Possible and Retrievable Selves*, New Delhi: OUP, 1995, reprinted 2000, 237–66. SF critic and literary historian Suparno Banerjee refers to Ray's SF stories as an instance of post-colonial hybridity, in Banerjee, 'Other Tomorrows: Postcoloniality, Science Fiction and India', 2010, *LSU Doctoral Dissertations*, 3181, http://digitalcommons.lsu.edu/gradschool_dissertations/3181, 73, 39–41 (accessed 15 December 2017).

53. See Satyajit Ray, *Travails with the Alien*, 28–33.

54. Sami Ahmed Khan, 'Editorial', Muse India Issue 61: May–June 2015, special issue on SF at archive, www.museindia.com (accessed 25 July 2017). For a discussion of the history of Hindi SF see 'Science Fiction in Hindi – An Overview' by Arvind Mishra, which mentions Rahul Sankrityayan's futuristic *Baisvin Sadi*, written in 1924, at http://indiascifiarvind.blogspot.in/2007/08/science-fiction-in-indiaan-overview.html (accessed 3 March 2018).

55. According to eminent Urdu critic Shamsur Rehman Faruqi, Khan Mahboob Tarzi wrote several SF novels in Urdu in the 1940s, including *Do Diwane* and *Barq Paash*, yet to be translated. Personal communication.

56. Kylas Chunder Dutt, 'A Journal of Forty-Eight Hours of the Year 1945', 1835, reprinted in Shoshee Chunder Dutt, *Selections from 'Bengaliana'*, ed. Alex Tickell, Nottingham: Trent Editions, 2005, 149-159. Also,https://en.wikisource.org/wiki/Index:A_Journal_of_Forty-Eight_Hours_of_the_Year_1945.djvu (accessed 25 May 2018).

57. Alex Tickell suggests that these writings about imagined rebellions exploit a degree of sanctioned dissent in the pre-1857 period. See Tickell, 'Introduction', in Dutt, *Selections from 'Bengaliana'*, 19. Also see Meenakshi Mukherjee's discussion of the relative openness of the English press at the time, in *Perishable Empire : Essays on Indian Writing in English*, 53–54.

58. Shoshee Chunder Dutt, 'The Republic of Orissa: A Page from the Annals of the 20th Century' 1845, reprinted in Dutt, *Selections from 'Bengaliana'*, 141–48. Dutt was twenty-one when his piece appeared in *The Saturday Evening Harakuru* (25 May 1845). See Mukherjee, *Perishable Empire*, 52–53.

59. See Khan, 'Editorial', based on his own doctoral work on SF in India. Also see Shoshee Chunder Dutt, *Selections from 'Bengaliana'*, ed. Alex Tickell, Nottingham: Trent Editions, 2005, esp. 141–59. These stories by Kylas Chander Dutt and Shoshee

Chunder Dutt are described as the earliest extant narrative texts by Indians writing in English by Meenakshi Mukherjee in *The Perishable Empire: Essays on Indian Writing in English*, 2000, reprinted, New Delhi: OUP, 2002, 52. For the text of Hussain's short story, originally published in *The Indian Ladies' Magazine*, Madras, 1905, in English, see http://digital.library.upenn.edu/women/sultana/dream/dream.html (accessed 17 February 2018).

60. See Suparno Banerjee, 'Other Tomorrows', esp. 33–39.

61. Ibid., 201–03. It is likely that similarly sceptical and self-critical work has begun to appear more often in SF written in the *bhashas*/vernacular languages, since liberalization and its discontents (especially from 1991 onwards) left its imprint; further research into this question is needed. Mahasweta Devi's Bengali story 'Pterodactyl, Pirtha, and Puran Sahay' makes a passionate critique of developmental processes that marginalize tribal populations while invoking paleontology in an ironic vein. See 'Pterodactyl, Pirtha, and Puran Sahay', tr. Gayatri Chakravorti Spivak, in Mahasweta Devi, *Imaginary Maps: Three Stories*, New York: Psychology Press, 1995, 95–196.

62. See Suparno Banerjee, 'Other Tomorrows', 201–03, and Nandy, esp. 256–58. Anil Menon is more sanguine about regional SF, though he too acknowledges its paucity and limitations. See Menon, 'On Hunting a Snark: On the Trail of Regional Science Fiction', at http://www.literaturaprospectiva.com/wp-content/uploads/snark-juan.pdf (accessed 15 December 2017).

63. Bal Phondke, ed., *It Happened Tomorrow*, New Delhi: National Book Trust, 1993, esp. 'Preface', ix–xxii.

64. Shubhada Gogate's Marathi story in translation 'Birthright' is an example of this, with its nightmarish vision of the brainwashing of unborn children in state-controlled Foetus Development Centres. 'Birthright', Phondke, ed., *It Happened Tomorrow*, 100–29.

65. 'Preface', Phondke, ed., *It Happened Tomorrow*, xx. Also see, Banerjee, 'Other Tomorrows', 49, 26.

66. See http://www.sociologydiscussion.com/science/genesis-of-people-science-movement-explained/851, accessed Jan. 23, 2019.

67. In Bal Phondke's periodization of the history of SF, an initial emphasis on adventure in the first stage (Shelley and beyond) is followed by the era of pulp fiction when there was a balance struck between science and fiction, though science was sought to be propagated by and large as a result of the influence of editors like John W. Campbell. In the third stage, after the Second World War and the nuclear explosions at Hiroshima and Nagasaki, concerns about science's potential for running amok came to the fore and social concerns began to predominate. In the fourth stage, questions of form and style became important as the aesthetic

dimension superseded the purely scientific. In Phondke's assessment (1993), Indian SF evolved through similar stages, with translations of H.G. Wells, Jules Verne and other SF authors becoming popular at first. Most Indian SF in his view belongs to the second or third stages. Needless to say, even for its time this schema was an oversimplification. Phondke, 'Preface', xiii–xviii. Also see, Banerjee 'Other Tomorrows', 49–53.

68. 'Preface', Phondke, ed., in *It Happened Tomorrow,* xvi–xxi, where he flags 'Tareche Hasya' by S.B. Ranade, an early Marathi SF story of the nineteenth century, as well as adult-oriented SF in Marathi that began to appear in the 1960s and 1970s, with the support of the journal *Naval*, edited by Anant Antarkar, further strengthened by the contributions of Jayant Narlikar. Also see the reference to 'Brachatiyar Desh', the first Asomiya SF story by Hariprasad Baruah, which appeared in 1937, in Dinesh Chandra Goswami, 'Science Fiction and Fantasy in Indian Writing', unpublished paper, presented at the Sahitya Akademi, Seminar on Contemporary Story Writing in India and Iran, 25 November 2016. Goswami has a story about surrogacy in the Indian context, 'Half a Help' in Dinesh Chandra Goswami, *The Hair Timer: An Anthology of Science Fiction Stories*, tr. Amrit Jyoti Mahanta, New Delhi: NBT, 2011, 159–70.

69. Anil Menon, 'On Hunting a Snark: On the Trail of Regional Science Fiction', at http://www.literaturaprospectiva.com/wp-content/uploads/snark-juan.pdf (accessed 15 December, 2017).

70. For an interesting recent initiative discussing issues relating to Indian genre fiction in seven languages, Tamil, Urdu, Bangla, Hindi, Odiya, and Marathi, in addition to English, see Bodhisattva Chattopadhyaya et al's 'Introduction', https://www.researchgate.net/profile/Bodhisattva_Chattopadhyay/publication/326416187_Indian_genre_fiction_languages_literatures_classifications/links/5b4c6f65a6fdccadaecf70bb/Indian-genre-fiction-languages-literatures-classifications.pdf (accessed 11 November 2018).

71. For an instance of Orientalist futurism, see Jan Lars Jensen's *Shiva 3000* (London: Pan, 1999). British writer Ian McDonald's SF based in a future India is more empathetic and moves beyond simplistic stereotypes. See, for instance, Ian McDonald, *Cyberabad Days*, London: Gollancz, 2009. Ian McDonald's earlier novel, *River of Gods*, 2004, reprinted London: Gollancz, 2009, is more problematic and marred by backpacker clichés about India and its varied spectacles. For critical analysis, see Banerjee, 'Other Tomorrows', 35–48, 167–77, 209.

72. The Indian Constitution was amended by 42nd Constitutional Amendment Act, 1976 by which an Article 51A was inserted making provisions for the Fundamental Duties prescribed for citizens of India, including the duty 'to develop the scientific temper, humanism and the spirit of inquiry and reform'.

See https://www.quora.com/Is-the-Indian-constitution-the-only-constitution-in-the-world-that-talks-about-developing-scientific-temper (accessed 23 January, 2019).

73. Shiv Viswanathan, 'Foreword' in Kothari and Joy, eds., *Alternative Futures*, vii. He also cites the work of Meghnad Saha and the Science and Culture group, which saw the dangers of synthetic chemistry and sought alternatives to protect primary products like lac and indigo. Viswanathan, 'Foreword', viii. For an extended account of radical ecological democracy, see Aseem Shrivastava and Ashish Kothari, *Churning the Earth: The Making of Global India*, New Delhi: Viking Penguin, 2012, esp. 293–308. Also see Gandhi's speech to a gathering of Asians (the Inter-Asian Relations Conference, organized by the Indian National Congress before independence) in April 1947, even as the Partition carnage was taking place, for a vision of a collective Asian future, http://www.gandhi-manibhavan.org/gandhicomesalive/speech7.htm (accessed 1 February 2018). An ironic projection of Gandhian ideals into the future appears in Manjula Padmanabhan's short story 'Gandhi-Toxin' in *Kleptomania: Ten Stories*, New Delhi: Penguin Books India, 2004, 91–98.

74. Viswanathan, 'Foreword' in Kothari and Joy, eds., vii.

75. See Ramchandra Guha, *Environmentalism: A Global History*, New Delhi: OUP, 2000.

76. As eminent sociologist and thinker J.P.S. Uberoi put it in his seminal study, advocating a rethink of modern knowledge systems from a Gandhian perspective, '...modern Western science at some time took the wrong direction in the intrinsic sense...its findings, theories and techniques in all its branches are largely untrue, misleading and senseless for mankind as a whole.' In J.P.S. Uberoi, *Science and Culture*, Delhi: OUP, 1978, 16. Also see Vandana Shiva's feminist ecological take in *Staying Alive: Women, Ecology and Survival in India*, New Delhi: Kali, 1988, https://archive.org/stream/StayingAlive-English-VandanaShiva/Vandana-shiva-stayingAlive_djvu.txt (accessed 1 February 2018); Ashis Nandy, 'Satyajit Ray's Secret Guide to Exquisite Murders: Creativity, Social Criticism and the Partitioning of the Self', 237-66; and Viswanathan, 'Foreword', vii–xi.

77. Amitav Ghosh, *The Calcutta Chromosome: A Novel of Fevers, Delirium and Discovery*, New Delhi: Ravi Dayal, 1996. Also see Banerjee, 'Other Tomorrows', for a critical account, esp. 60–75, and the detailed discussion of the novel in Eric D. Smith's 'Claiming the Futures That Are, or, The Cunning of History in Amitav Ghosh's *The Calcutta Chromosome* and Manjula Padmanabhan's 'Gandhi-Toxin' in *Globalization, Utopia and Postcolonial Science Fiction: New Maps of Hope*, London: Palgrave Macmillan, 2012, 98–126.

78. See Jayant Narlikar's story 'The Ice Age Cometh', tr. Jayant Narlikar in

Phondke, ed. *It Happened Tomorrow,* 1–20; Fred Hoyle, *The Black Cloud*, 1957, reprinted, Harmondsworth: Penguin, 1977; D.C. Goswami, *The Hair Timer*, and Sukanya Datta, *Worlds Apart: Science Fiction Stories*, 2012, reprinted, New Delhi: National Book Trust, 2014.

79. See, for instance, 'Jillu' in *Reliving Sujatha: His Best Stories in English*, tr. Vimala Balakrishnan New Delhi: Vitasta, 2017, 231–42, and Ruchir Joshi, *The Last Jet-Engine Laugh*, 2001, reprinted, New Delhi: Harper Collins, 2008.

80. Shiv Viswanathan, 'Foreword'. Also see, Viswanathan, https://scroll.in/article/809246/how-indian-science-stopped-being-fun-and-turned-into-a-formula (accessed 1 February 2018). Also see, Kothari and Joy's imagining of an activist's address to a Mahasangam of grassroots activists in 2100, in a world transformed by radical ecological democracy, 'Looking Back into the Future: India, South Asia and the world in 2100' in Ashish Kothari and K.J. Joy, eds., *Alternative Futures: India Unshackled*, New Delhi: UpFront Publishing, 2017, 627–45.

81. Vandana Singh, *The Woman Who Thought She Was a Planet*, as well as Eric D. Smith's critical response at 'There's No Splace Like Home: Domesticity, Difference, and the "Long Space" of Short Fiction in Vandana Singh's *The Woman Who Thought She Was a Planet*' in Smith, *Globalization, Utopia and Postcolonial Science Fiction*, 68–97; Vandana Singh, *Ambiguity Machines and Other Stories*, New Delhi: Zubaan, 2018. Also see https://www.tor.com/2019/01/14/announcing-the-nominees-for-the-2019-philip-k-dick-award/, accessed 23 January, 2019; Anil Menon, *The Beast with Nine Billion Feet*, New Delhi: Young Zubaan, 2009; Rimi B. Chatterji, *Signal Red*, New Delhi: Penguin Books India, 2005; and Priya Sarukkai Chabria, *Generation 14*, New Delhi: Penguin Books India, 2008.

82. This remarkable novel is set in Toronto in the near future, at a time when it becomes possible to live lives across several generations through memory transference into recipient bodies; however, a curious case of Leaked Memory Syndrome, or Nostalgia (a malady in which reminders of past lives persist) is discovered by the narrator, a nostalgia doctor named Dr Frank Sina, which eventually leads to an investigation by the Department of Internal Security. See M.G. Vassanji, *Nostalgia*, New Delhi: Penguin Books India, 2016.

83. Clark Prasad, *Baramulla Bomber*, New Delhi: Niyogi Books, 2013, and Sami Ahmad Khan, *Aliens in Delhi*, New Delhi: Niyogi Books, 2016, https://worldsf.wordpress.com/2012/08/28/tuesday-fiction-electric-sonalika-by-samit-basu-author-week-4/ (accessed 23 November 2018). Also see, http://indianexpress.com/article/lifestyle/art-and-culture/imagine-it-isnt-hard-to-do-hugo-awards-5143031/ (accessed 20 March 2018) and http://www.eff-words.com/fiction/ (accessed 19 November 2018). For SF stories by some of these authors in online magazines, see http://strangehorizons.com/fiction/the-trees-of-my-youth-grew-tall/ (accessed

23 October 2018),

https://www.tor.com/2018/08/01/loss-of-signal-sb-divya/?fbclid=IwAR1zNljb97zOgBXaDteU02U_wGYFhv0_YqJzImxTpXzx9J75zEUjKmktoEc (accessed 23 October 2018); https://uncannymagazine.com/article/fandom-for-robots/?fbclid=IwAR2TV77Fztudi0kq8p7kVbL-fhO0qCbgnCvx0jK4uVO5rrw4eANq4XTv0Jw (accessed 23 October 2018),

https://automatareview.com/more-tomorrow-premee-mohamed?fbclid=IwAR1HmBpG-heJN-J0CI94zQTR3UMMol G6DxcnFJVJy2Pc0-ktSBqVWGq2eXo (accessed 23 October 2018),

http://clarkesworldmagazine.com/das_09_12/ (accessed 23 October 2018).

84. In historian Mukul Kesavan's novel *Looking through Glass*, the narrator finds himself inexplicably transported to the 1940s, with an awareness of the destructive impact of the looming Partition. See Mukul Kesavan, *Looking through Glass*, New Delhi: Ravi Dayal, 1995. Also see, Anil Menon and Vandana Singh, eds., *Breaking the Bow: Speculative Fiction Inspired by the Ramayana*, New Delhi: Zubaan, 2012.

85. See, for instance, Anil Menon, *Half of What I Say*, New Delhi: Bloomsbury, 2015, and Vandana Singh's SF story in tribute to Premendra Mitra, 'Conservation Laws' in Singh, *The Woman Who Thought She Was a Planet*, 109–29. Also see Vandana Singh's collection of speculative stories, *Ambiguity Machines and Other Stories*. On the history of South Asian speculative fiction, see Mimi Mondal's article at https://www.tor.com/2018/01/30/a-short-history-of-south-asian-speculative-fiction-part-i/ (accessed 3 February 2018). The influence of SF can be seen in other domains, such as the performing arts, as seen in Raqs Media Collective's *The Return of Tipoo's Tiger* (2017), in which Tipoo Sultan's tiger (an automaton depicting a tiger devouring a British soldier, now to be found in the Victoria and Albert Museum in London) is the sole relic surviving from European culture of this era many centuries hence, even as its significance is sought to be retrospectively reconstructed, in this speculative multi-media performance piece. *The Return of Tipoo's Tiger*, 2017, Performance + Installation, Videos, Ephemera, Talks and Conversations, 'Collecting Europe' at the Victoria & Albert Museum's Lunchroom, Learning Centre.

86. See Randi Anderson's account at http://www.writersdigest.com/whats-new/speculative-poetry-know-science-fiction-fantasy-verse (accessed 18 February 2018).

87. Much of such retold mythology approximates kitsch, the degraded form of myths in which clichés and tired rhetoric are presented for instant consumption by the reader, an observation Stanislaw Lem made about much of commercially produced American SF. See Lem, 'Science Fiction: A Hopeless Case', 67–71. For a recent critical perspective on the ubiquity of myth in Indian genre fiction (not

just SF), see Chattopadhyay et al, 'Introduction' at https://www.researchgate.net/profile/Bodhisattva_Chattopadhyay/publication/326416187_Indian_genre_fiction_languages_literatures_classifications/links/5b4c6f65a6fdccadaecf70bb/Indian-genre-fiction-languages-literatures-classifications.pdf (accessed 11 November 2018).

88. Nalo Hopkinson, 'Introduction', and Uppinder Mehan, 'Final Thoughts', in Nalo Hopkinson and Uppinder Mehan, eds., *So Long Been Dreaming: Postcolonial Science Fiction and Fantasy*, 2004, reprinted, Vancouver: Arsenal Pulp Press, 2011, 7–11, 269–70.

89. It often seemed that the plot of Jack Finney's *The Body Snatchers* (1955) was being realized in an Indian avatar, with ordinary people being transformed into unrecognizable versions of themselves via social media, baying for blood in online (and real-life) lynch-mobs. See Jack Finney, *The Body Snatchers*, 1955, reprinted, London: Gollancz, 2010.

90. Fredric Jameson cites Darko Suvin's view that utopia is a subgenre of science fiction, in his 'Introduction', *Archaeologies of the Future*, xiv. For a notion of South Asia which is 'civilisational, reciprocal and local in its diversity', see Shiv Viswanathan, http://www.thehindu.com/opinion/lead/talk-like-a-south-asian/article22828352.ece (accessed 25 February 2018).

91. For recent futurological speculation forecasting the emergence of supra-human entities using bioengineering and data-driven algorithms, see Yuval Noah Harari, *Homo Deus: A Brief History of Tomorrow*, 2015, tr., London: Vintage, 2017, esp. 428–62.

PLANET OF TERROR

ADRISH BARDHAN

(Translated by Arunava Sinha from the Bengali original 'Atonker Groho'*)*

2001.

Outer space. The Milky Way. Millions of stars. A spaceship flying at the speed of light. A spaceship from earth.

Strange instruments fill the spacecraft. All beyond imagination. A glass screen fills an entire wall. A view of space through it. Stars, planets, constellations – everything is visible.

A green planet in the distance. Getting closer. Exquisitely beautiful. Like a glittering garden in infinite space.

The control cabin. The bulbous craft is being piloted here. The commander is hunched over a set of buttons. He presses several of them in turn. Multicoloured lights come up, go out. A map floats up on the giant screen.

The computer performs the calculations. Conveys the answer.

The green planet is like earth.

Man can settle here. There is no space back home. That is why countless spaceships are scouring the galaxy. *A new home, we need a new home. Somewhere to live.*

The green planet might solve the problem to some extent.

The spaceship descends near its surface.

A horrifying sight awaits the travellers.

An expanse of ice. Stretching till the horizon. A violent storm, whistling and whining.

The commander's face falls. 'Strange,' he declares. 'The computer said the planet is habitable. But forget man, even wild beasts wouldn't survive here. Is the computer malfunctioning? Has it given us wrong information?'

His final words are lost in the roaring of the wind.

But the intrepid voyagers are not inclined to retreat after their long journey. They decide to disembark despite the ice everywhere. A shelter must be found.

Three of them emerge from the spaceship. Aagoon, Pietrov, Peter. Aagoon is from Bangladesh, Pietrov from Russia and Peter from America.

All three of them are wearing helmets that cover their heads and faces. Their heavy spacesuits protect their bodies till the tips of their noses. Yet, they shiver uncontrollably in the cold. The icy chill penetrates their spacesuits like an array of needles.

'I come from a land of snow and ice,' says Pietrov, 'but even I cannot bear this cold. No one can survive on this planet.'

The storm is howling around them. But it cannot prevent Pietrov's words from reaching the mind of a strange creature far away in the distance. He is standing at the window of a peculiarly designed house. A huge head. A reptilian body. Eyes closed. But he can see images from far away without using his eyes.

He can see the three astronauts from earth clearly. Pietrov's complaint reaches his brain, not his ears. This reptilian creature has strange powers. Doesn't use his ears to listen to words. Uses his brain to listen to thoughts.

And it is his brain that receives Pietrov's thought. He smiles. An inscrutable smile.

Aagoon stops abruptly. 'What's the matter?' asks Pietrov.

Aagoon stares into the distance. 'I can see something. A large house.'

'It's a mirage,' smiles Pietrov. 'A mirage in the snowstorm.'

'It's not a mirage, Pietrov.'

'A house on this planet of ice? Has the cold driven you mad?'

'You've not been driven mad, have you, Pietrov? See for yourself.'

Pietrov looks in the direction in which Aagoon is pointing. Before he can spot anything, though, they come.

The flying horrors. Like messengers of death from hell. Wings like those of bats. But each creature the size of a hundred bats. Pterodactyls were beautiful in comparison.

The bat-horrors glitter like yellow metal – their eyes are flaming pots. Rows of teeth glinting like saws in their open beaks. Lethal claws like hooks.

Monstrous birds. Terrifying beyond belief. Bloodcurdling in their ugliness. They swoop down through the air on the three voyagers.

Pietrov spots it first. A hailstorm of meteorites falling on them from a height. They tremble with fear. The demons miss their target under the onslaught of this new storm. The earthmen escape by the skin of their teeth.

'Careful!' screams Aagoon. 'Mind their beaks and claws.' The flying demons circle back to swoop on them again. This time, the travellers flatten themselves on the ice. Another narrow escape.

Still lying on the ice, Aagoon pulls out his atomic pistol. Squeezes the trigger. Lightning flashes from the mouth of the gun. But the demon dodges it with miraculous skill. It flies at Aagoon. He shuts his eyes. The end is coming.

At that very moment, a strange sensation in his mind. Someone seems to be talking inside his head. A voice instructs the demon bird. *Be careful. There mustn't be a scratch. We want them alive.*

Aagoon doesn't remember anything after this.

Pietrov sees a demon bird swoop down on Aagoon, pick him up like a kitten in its claws, and fly off. It disappears in the snowstorm with incredible speed.

Peter is standing, bewildered. 'You hear it?' he asks.

'You too?' asks Pietrov.

All three can hear the same voice in their heads. Telepathy. Someone is speaking in the language of thought. *Be careful. There mustn't be a scratch. We want them alive.*

What is all this! Pietrov and Peter are dumbfounded. They fire their atomic pistols at random. Bolts of lightning fly off in all directions. Firing, they retreat towards their spaceship. That's when the accident occurs. A shaft of lightning from Peter's atomic pistol pierces the body of a demon bird. The lifeless monster plummets downward, falling on the spaceship. Its legs crack. The craft tilts against the ice. When Pietrov and Peter return, they find the spaceship in this condition. It cannot fly any more. They cannot return to earth.

Everyone is aghast.

No one thinks of Aagoon. But the future of all the voyagers depend on him.

Flying over the expanse of ice, the demon bird descends with Aagoon into an extraordinary garden. Filled with green trees, plants, vines, bushes and shrubs, it looks beautiful enough to be the Garden of Eden. The palace set on the grounds resembles the abode of gods. There isn't a trace of ice anywhere. But the storm raging in the distance is clearly visible.

Aagoon regains consciousness. Looks around him. He's astonished.

And then, startled. The same strange sensation in his brain. Someone is talking to him in his head. The voice is saying, *Bring him to me. One scratch and I'll tear your wings off.*

The demon bird follows the order. It flies up in the air again, holding Aagoon in its claws. This time, it lands next to a brimming lake. A bizarre creature is sitting on the grass. Looks exactly like a reptile. Enormous. A gigantic head.

Aagoon is flabbergasted at the sight of this freakish creature. When he returns to his senses, he finds himself surrounded by a dozen similar creatures. All of them have their eyes closed.

Aagoon reaches for the atomic pistol at his waist. At once, someone says in his head, *You can't kill us with that, my friend.*

Aagoon stands there, bewildered. 'Are you ghosts?' he mutters.

No, the answer floats up in his head.

'What is this then?' asks Aagoon, gathering courage.

Telepathy.

'Communicating with thought?'

Yes. We too used to talk in our primitive phase. Not any more.

'What do you mean? Are you saying we're primitive? Barbarians?'

Don't be angry. But it's true. Only unevolved creatures communicate through speech. Advanced beings don't. The sages in your world had mastered telepathy. They did not speak, but they understood one another.

'How do you know about our world?'

It's all written in your head. We have read all your memories.

'Impossible.'

Nothing is impossible for us.

'But you look like lizards. Reptiles are not evolved animals on earth.'

True. But our minds are far superior to yours. What difference does physical appearance make? Do you have the vision we have? Even with our eyes closed, we can see your spaceship has stopped functioning. It won't fly any more.

'What!'

No need to be afraid. You're looking for a new planet to live in, after all.

'You know that too?'

Yes. Your intentions are noble. But if you inform your people on earth about this planet, the hordes will descend. Our peace will be destroyed.

'No one will come to this planet,' Aagoon sneers. 'Not with such raging snowstorms.'

We created those.

'What do you mean? You think you can fool me just because I'm new here? How can anyone create a snowstorm?'

You don't believe us? Very well, see for yourself. Look behind you.

Aagoon turns around. He is astonished. The snowstorm has miraculously vanished. In front of his very eyes. The ice disappears. A green expanse appears in its place. Just as the computer had predicted.

Believe us now? the reptilian creature asks in Aagoon's head.

'But why this deception?'

We were testing you. We created the snowstorm to find out whether the creatures coming from space were friends or enemies. You didn't leave in spite of the storm. Then we captured you. Retrieved your memories. Found out you are good people.

'Thank you.'

You can stay here. As friends, as guests. But on one condition. You cannot go back to earth. Nor can you inform them about us. Humans are greedy. Selfish.

'We'll send word via radio. It doesn't matter if the spaceship has broken down.'

No such luck, my friend. Your radio apparatus has broken down as well.

A forlorn Aagoon stands there. He recalls Bangladesh, his home. He is saddened. He will never see earth again. He turns towards the reptilian creatures. They're ugly. Though they have eyes, they see with their minds. Though they have mouths, they talk with their minds.

Don't be upset, my friend, the voice in his head says. *We're arranging to fetch your companions here. Unlike earth, there is no violence here, no envy or hatred. You will live here in peace and joy. Will you be our guest? Be our friend?*

Aagoon raises his eyes. Tears are brimming in them. Hoarsely, he says, 'I will.'

INSPECTOR MATADEEN ON THE MOON

HARISHANKAR PARSAI

(Translated by C.M. Naim from the Hindi original 'Inspector Matadeen Chand Par'*)*

Scientists say there is no life on the moon. But Senior Inspector Matadeen of the Indian Police – known in the department as 'MD sa'ab' – says, 'The scientists are lying. There are men on the moon, just like us, but they are on the other side of the moon.'

Science always loses out to Inspector Matadeen. Even if experts go hoarse arguing that the fingerprints on the dagger do not match those of the accused, Inspector Matadeen will still manage to put his man behind bars.

'These scientists,' he says, 'they never investigate a case thoroughly. Just because they can see the bright side of the moon they claim there's no life on it. I've been to its dark side. There are men living there.'

It has to be true, for when it comes to dark sides, Inspector Matadeen is an acknowledged expert. Now you might wonder, why he went to the moon in the first place. Did he go as a tourist? Was it to catch some fugitive from law?

No, none of that. He went there under the Cultural Exchange Scheme to represent India. The Government of the Moon wrote to the Government of India, 'We are an advanced civilization, but our police force is not good enough. They often fail to catch and punish criminals. We understand you have established Ram Rajya in your country. Please send us one of your police officers to give our men proper training.'

The home minister ordered the home secretary to send one of the inspectors general.

'Sir, we cannot send an IG,' the secretary remonstrated. 'It's a matter of protocol. The moon is merely a small satellite of the earth. We cannot send someone of too high a rank there. Let me depute some senior inspector.'

And so, they decided upon Senior Inspector Matadeen, the investigating officer of a thousand and one criminal cases, and asked the moon government to send an earth-ship to fetch him.

Meanwhile, the home minister sent for Inspector Matadeen and told him, 'You are going there to represent the glorious traditions of the Indian Police. Make sure you do a good job. Make the entire universe applaud our department so that even the prime minister hears about us.'

On the appointed day, an earth-ship arrived from the moon, and Inspector Matadeen bade goodbye to his colleagues. As he walked towards the spacecraft, he kept muttering under his breath a *chaupayi* from Tulsidas's epic poem:

Pravisi nagara kijai sab kaja, hridaya rakhi kausalpur raja...

On reaching the ship, Inspector Matadeen suddenly called out for his clerk, 'Munshi!'

Munshi Abdul Ghafoor came running, clicked his heels, saluted, and said, 'Yes, *Pect-sab.*'

'Did you remember to pack some FIR forms?'

'Yes, *Pect-sab.*'

'And a blank copy of the daily register?'

'Yes, *Pect-sab.*'

Inspector Matadeen then sent for Havildar Balabhaddar and said to him, 'When it's time for delivery *in our house*, send your *bed* to lend a hand.'

Balabhaddar replied, 'Yes, *Pect-sab.*'

'You needn't worry, *Pect-sab*,' Abdul Ghafoor added, 'I'll send my *house* too.'

Inspector Matadeen then turned to the pilot. 'You have your driver's licence?'

'Yes, sir.'

'Your headlights work?'

'Yes, sir.'

'They'd better,' growled Inspector Matadeen to his men, 'otherwise I'll challan the bastard mid-space.'

The pilot overheard him. 'In our country,' he said, 'we don't talk to people in that manner.'

'I know, I know,' Inspector Matadeen sneered. 'No wonder your police are so weak-kneed. But I'll kick them into shape soon enough.'

He had placed one foot inside the earth-ship's door when Havildar Ram Sanjivan came running. '*Pect-sab*,' he said, '*the house* of the SP sa'ab asks you to bring her a heel-scrubbing stone from the moon.'

Inspector Matadeen was delighted. 'Tell Bai sa'ab I'll definitely bring her one.' He then climbed in and took his seat, and the ship took off.

It had barely left the earth's atmosphere when Inspector Matadeen shouted to the pilot, '*Abe*, why aren't you honking the horn?'

'But there's nothing here for millions of miles,' the pilot protested.

'A rule is a rule,' Inspector Matadeen snarled. 'Keep your thumb pressed on the horn.'

The pilot sounded the horn, and kept it up all the way to their destination.

Senior Moon Police officers had come to receive Inspector Matadeen. As he swaggered out of the earth-ship he ran an eye over their shoulder patches. None had a star, or even a ribbon. Inspector Matadeen decided it was not necessary for him to click his heels or throw a salute. He also thought, 'After all, I'm a special adviser now, not just an inspector.'

The welcoming party took him to the local police lines, and put him up in a fine bungalow.

After a day's rest, Inspector Matadeen decided to start working. First, he went out and inspected the lines. Later that evening, he expressed his surprise to the host inspector general. 'There's no Hanuman temple in your police lines! In our Ram Rajya, every police line has its Hanuman-ji.'

The IG asked, 'Who is Hanuman? We've never heard of him.'

Inspector Matadeen patiently explained, 'Every policeman must have a daily darshan of Hanuman-ji. He was, you see, in the Special Branch in Sugriva's administration. It was he who discovered where Ma Sita was being held forcibly. It was a case of abduction, you know – Section 362 IPC. Lord Hanuman punished Ravana right on the spot – set fire to his entire property. The police must have that kind of authority. They should be able to punish a criminal as soon as they catch him. No need to get bogged down in the courts. But sad to say, we have yet to achieve that in our own Ram Rajya.

'Anyway, Bhagwan Ram was highly pleased. He took Hanuman-ji to Ayodhya and assigned him the city beat. That same Hanuman-ji is our patron deity. Here, I brought along this photograph. Use it to get some figures cast, then have them installed in all the lines.'

A few days later, a statue of Hanuman-ji was enshrined in each and every police line on the moon.

Meanwhile, Inspector Matadeen began to study how the local police worked. It seemed to him that the force was careless and lacked enthusiasm, that they showed little concern for crime. The reason for that attitude, however, was not apparent.

Suddenly a thought occurred to Inspector Matadeen. He sent for the salary register. One glance at it and everything became clear to him. Now he knew why the Moon Police behaved the way they did.

That evening, Inspector Matadeen reported to the police minister, 'Now I know why your men are so lackadaisical – you pay them large salaries, that's why. Five hundred to a constable, seven hundred to a havildar, and a thousand to a *thanedar*! What sort foolishness is this? Why should your police try to catch any criminal? In our country, we give the constables just one hundred, and the inspectors two. That's why you see them running around catching criminals. You must reduce all salaries immediately.'

'But that would be most unfair,' the police minister protested. 'Why at all would they work if they were not given good salaries?'

'There's nothing unfair about it,' Inspector Matadeen replied patiently. 'In fact, you'll see a revolutionary change in your men's attitude as soon as the first reduced pay cheques are sent out.'

The police minister ordered a cut in the salaries. Sure enough, in a couple of months, a drastic change became evident. The policemen were suddenly most zealous in their performance. Aroused from sleep, they became doubly alert and kept an eye on everything. There was panic in the criminal world. When the police minister sent for the records kept at the police stations, he was amazed to see that the number of registered cases was several times higher than before. He said to Inspector Matadeen, 'I must praise your keen insight. You have brought about a revolution! But do tell me, how does this work?'

'It's very simple,' Inspector Matadeen explained. 'If you pay an employee little money, he wouldn't be able to live on it. No constable can support a family on just one hundred rupees a month, nor can an inspector live with dignity on two hundred. Each has to make some extra money. And he can do that only if he starts catching criminals. So immediately the man becomes concerned with crime, and turns into an alert and dutiful policeman. That's the reason why we have a most efficient police system in our Ram Rajya.'

The news of this miracle spread. Moon people began to come from all over to look at the man who could reduce salaries and yet create efficiency. The policemen were most happy. They said to Inspector Matadeen, 'Guru, had you not come we'd have continued living on our salaries alone.' The Government of the Moon was also delighted, for now it could have a surplus budget.

Half the problem was now taken care of – the police had started catching criminals. Now only the investigative process remained to be reformed – how to get a criminal convicted and sentenced after one had caught him. Inspector Matadeen decided to wait for some major incident so that he could use it as a model to illustrate his special methods.

One day, some people got into a fight, and one of them got killed. When the news reached Inspector Matadeen, he marched over to the police station, sat down at a desk, and declared, 'I shall personally investigate this case to show you how it's done. All of you, just watch and learn. It is a murder case, and in a murder case one must have rock-solid evidence against the accused.'

'Shouldn't we first try to discover who did the killing,' the station officer said, 'before we start collecting evidence against anyone?'

'No, why work backwards,' responded Inspector Matadeen. 'First, make sure of your evidence. Did you find any blood? On someone's clothes or elsewhere?'

One of the inspectors said, 'The assailants ran away as the victim lay dying on the road. But a man who lives near the spot picked up the victim and brought him to the hospital. That man's clothes did have blood on them.'

'Arrest the man immediately.'

'But sir,' the station officer remonstrated, 'he only tried to help the dying man!'

'That may be well and true,' said Inspector Matadeen, 'but where else would you now find blood spots? You must always grab the *evidence* that is readily available.'

The man was arrested and brought to the police station. He protested, 'But I carried the dying man to the hospital! Is that a crime?' The local officers were visibly moved, but not Inspector Matadeen. Everyone waited to see how he would respond.

'But why did you go where the fight occurred?' Inspector Matadeen asked the man.

'I didn't go there,' he replied. 'I happen to live there. The fight took place right in front of my house.'

It was clearly a test of Inspector Matadeen's genius. Very quietly he responded, 'True, your house is there, but why go where a fight occurs?'

There could be no answer to that question. The man could only repeat, and go on repeating, 'I didn't go there. I live there.' And each time Inspector Matadeen responded, 'That's true, but why go where a fight occurs?'

That line of questioning greatly impressed the local officers.

Inspector Matadeen settled back in his chair and explained his investigative principles. 'Look,' he began, 'a man has been killed. That means someone definitely killed him. Someone is the murderer. Someone has to be convicted and punished. You might ask, who is guilty? But, for the police, that's not so important. What is important is who can be proven guilty or, better still, who should be proven guilty?

'A murder has occurred. Eventually, someone will be convicted. It's not for us to worry if it's the actual killer or someone innocent. All human beings are equal. In each of them is present a bit of the same god. We don't discriminate. We're humanists.

'So, the question actually is: who ought to be proven guilty? And that depends on two things. One, has the man been a nuisance to the police, and two, will his conviction please the men at the top?'

Inspector Matadeen was told that though the arrested man was otherwise a decent person, he was given to criticism whenever the police made a mistake. As for the question of pleasing the men at the top, the man belonged to the opposition party.

'It's a first-rate case,' declared Inspector Matadeen, thumping the table. 'Rock-solid evidence, plus support from the top!'

One inspector tried to protest, 'But we can't let a decent man be convicted of a crime he didn't commit!'

Inspector Matadeen explained patiently, 'Look, I've already told you that the same god resides in all of us. Whether you convict this man or the actual killer, it is *God* who will hang. Further, in this instance, you're getting blood-spattered clothes. Now where would you find bloodstains if you let him go? Go ahead, file the FIR as I tell you.'

Inspector Matadeen dictated the FIR, leaving a few spaces blank for future needs.

Next day, the station officer came to Inspector Matadeen and said, 'Gurudev, we're in deep trouble. So many citizens have come to us and demanded: why are you trying to frame that innocent man? It's never been done. What should we say? We feel so ashamed.'

'Don't worry,' Inspector Matadeen consoled the SO. 'In this job, people always feel some compunction in the beginning. But later, you'll feel ashamed for letting innocent people go free. Now understand this, every question has an answer. The next time someone comes to you and questions you, tell him, 'We know the man is innocent, but what can we do? Those at the top want it.'

'In that case, they'll go to the SP.'

'Let him say the same thing, 'They at the top want it so.'

'Then they'll complain to the IG.'

'He too should say, "It's the men at the top who want it that way."'

'They'll then go to the police minister.'

'So what? He should say the same thing, "Friends, what can I do? Those at the top want it."'

'But the people won't give up,' the SO persisted, 'they'll go up to the PM.'

'The PM should respond in the same manner, "I know he's innocent, but those at the top want it."'

'Then...'

'Then what?' Inspector Matadeen cut him short. 'Who can they go to next? To god? But has anyone ever come back after going to him?'

The station officer fell silent; the brilliant logic had left him dumbfounded.

Inspector Matadeen continued, 'That one sentence – those at the top want it so – has always come to the rescue of our government in the last 25 years. You too should learn it well.'

They began to get the case ready for trial. Inspector Matadeen ordered, 'Bring me a few eyewitnesses.'

'How can we do that?' the station officer asked. 'How can there be an eyewitness when no one saw him kill that man?'

Inspector Matadeen smacked his head in despair. 'God, the fools I have to deal with! They don't even know the ABC of this business.' Then he angrily added, 'Do you even know who an *eyewitness* is? An eyewitness is not someone who actually sees, he's the one who claims that he saw.'

'But why would anyone make such a claim?' the station officer protested.

'Why not?' thundered Inspector Matadeen. 'I can't see how you people manage to run your department at all. *Arre*, the police must always have a ready list of eyewitnesses. When one is needed, you just pick a name from that list and present him in the court. In our country we have people who eyewitness hundreds of cases every year. Our courts have recognized that these men possess some divine power that lets them foresee the place where some incident is going to happen, allowing them to reach there beforehand.

'I'll get you eyewitnesses. Bring me some bad characters. You know the kind – petty thieves, gamblers, *goondas*, bootleggers.'

Next day, half a dozen fine specimens showed up at the police station. Inspector Matadeen was delighted. It had been too long since he had last seen such men. He had been lonely. His voice was melting with affection when he asked them, 'You saw that man assault the deceased, didn't you?'

They replied, 'No sir, we didn't see a thing. We weren't even there.'

Inspector Matadeen knew it was the first time for them. He patiently continued, 'I know you weren't there. But you saw him attack with a lathi, didn't you?'

The men decided they were dealing with a lunatic. Who else would talk such nonsense? They began to laugh.

'Don't laugh!' said Inspector Matadeen sternly. 'Answer my question.'

They again replied, 'How can we say we saw anything when we weren't even there?'

Inspector Matadeen lost his temper. 'I'll tell you how,' he snarled. 'I have here detailed reports on what you fellows have been up to. I can have each one of you locked up for at least 10 years. Now tell me, you wish to stay in business – or would you rather go to jail?'

The men were scared out of their wits. 'No, sir, we don't want to go to jail.'

'In that case, you saw that fellow beat the victim with a lathi, didn't you?'

'Yes, sir, we did. We saw him come out of his house and start hitting the man with a lathi until the poor fellow fell to the ground.'

'Good. In the future as well, you'll see more such incidents, won't you?' Matadeen pressed on.

'Yes, sir. We'll see what you tell us to.'

The station officer was overwhelmed by this miracle. He couldn't stir for a few minutes. Then, getting up from his chair, he threw himself at Inspector Matadeen's feet.

'Here now, let go. Let me do my work,' Inspector Matadeen remonstrated, but the station officer clung to him and kept repeating, 'I want to spend the rest of my days at your feet.'

In due course, Inspector Matadeen put together the entire dossier and, in the process, taught the local police everything he knew – how to substitute FIRs, how to leave some pages blank for future use, how to change entries in the daily record, how to win over hostile witnesses. The man he had arrested was convicted and sentenced to 20 years in prison.

The Moon Police was now fully trained. Case after case was brought before the courts and, in every instance, a conviction was awarded. The moon government was delighted. The Moon parliament passed a resolution to thank the Government of India. It noted the remarkable efficiency their police had achieved under Inspector Matadeen's guidance. Inspector Matadeen was given a civic reception. Covered with garlands, he was taken around in a procession in an open jeep. Thousands of people lined the road and shouted his praises. Inspector Matadeen responded in the style of his home minister – with folded hands, lowered eyes, full of humility. But it was his first time and he felt somewhat ill at ease. He had never even dreamed, when he had entered the service some 26 years ago, that one day he would be so honoured on the moon. He wished he had remembered to bring along a dhoti–kurta and a Gandhi cap.

Back on earth, the Indian home minister watched the proceedings on his television. 'This may be the right time for me to make a goodwill visit,' he mused.

A few months passed. Suddenly, one day, the Moon parliament met in an emergency session. It was a stormy but secret meeting, and so its report was never made public. We can only offer what was faintly heard by people outside the chamber. The members seemed enraged and could be heard shouting: 'No one takes care of sick parents!'; 'No one tries to rescue a drowning child!'; 'No one helps if a house catches fire!'; 'Men have become worse than animals!'; 'The government should immediately resign!'; 'Resign! Resign!'

Next day, the prime minister of the moon sent for Inspector Matadeen.

Inspector Matadeen could see that the prime minster had visibly aged, that he seemed not to have slept for a few nights. He looked quite disconsolate as he said, 'Matadeen-ji, we are extremely grateful to you and to the Government of India, but you should go back tomorrow.'

'No sir,' Inspector Matadeen replied, 'I'll return only after I've finished my term here.'

'We'll give you your full term's salary,' the prime minister said. 'Double the amount, triple, if you wish.'

Inspector Matadeen was polite but firm. 'No sir, I'm a man of principles. My work is dearer to me than money.'

In the end, the prime minister of the moon sent a confidential letter to the prime minister of India.

Four days later, Inspector Matadeen received orders from his own IG to return immediately. Picking up a 'heel-scrubbing' stone for the wife of his SP, Inspector Matadeen climbed aboard the earth-ship and bade farewell to the moon. The entire Moon Police force burst into tears as the ship lifted off.

What happened on the moon that he had to leave so abruptly? What did the prime minister of the moon write to the prime minister of India? These questions remained unanswered for a long time. Then someone got hold of that confidential letter and made parts of it public.

'Thank you for lending us the services of Inspector Matadeen, but now you must recall him immediately. We had thought India was our friend, but only an enemy could have done what you did to us. We were innocent and trusting, and you deceived us.

'Ever since Inspector Matadeen trained our police, things have come to a terrible pass. No one comes to the help of an assault victim for fear he might himself be accused. Sons abandon their sick parents, lest they be charged with murder. Houses catch fire and burn down, but neighbours don't help for fear they might be accused of arson. Children drown before people's eyes, but no one comes to their rescue lest they be accused of drowning them. All human relations are breaking down. Your man has destroyed almost half of our civilized life. If he stays around longer, he is bound to destroy the remaining half. Please call him back immediately to your own Ram Rajya...'

STEALING THE SEA

ASIF ASLAM FARRUKHI

(Translated by Syed Saeed Naqvi from the Urdu original 'Samandar ki Chori'*)*

There was still time. The first hesitant, nascent ray of light hanging between the earth and sky had not yet emerged. It wasn't dawn yet, and the city along the oceanside was still asleep. Even before the night's darkness unfolded, it was suspected that it had happened. Rows of two- and three-storey apartment blocks, once engulfed in grey shadows, the two-lane road separating the apartments from the vastly spread bluish white sea on the other side. But now there was nothing. There was only a huge crater where the sea used to be. Flat land was marred by a fractured surface, devoid of any bushes or tyre marks, like land that had been submerged for the longest time. The sea, which once lay prone, stretching its feet on to the land, had suddenly disappeared.

The rest of the scene remained unchanged. Unless one paid really close attention, it could be missed. The day started at its usual slow pace and, at first, the absence of the sea was not noticed. That's probably why no one said anything. Some stragglers were returning after a party, while the health-conscious were setting out on their morning jogs. Milkmen were reaching their customers in open trucks, and pedlars brought out their wares on bicycles. Even if the most committed of people had glanced at it, they would have thought it to be hidden amidst the dense morning fog. They would have covered their hands and faces with shawls and scarves, in anticipation of dropping temperatures. If you cover your face while in a hurry to get somewhere, missing the sea is entirely possible.

While the sea disappearing might go unnoticed in the early hours, the spreading daylight would show its absence. But you can hear the absence even before you see it. The most noticeable thing was utter silence; a deep silence with its own distinct voice – such complete silence that even a pin drop could cause a fluttering in the chest; a fear that what has happened should not have happened. Yes, then it will be realized that the absence of the noisy waves is causing the silence.

The waves usually formed a crest, noisily slapping together and forming sounds like *chup... chup... chup... chup*. Advancing waves rose and spread, merging with the sand, sometimes quietly and at other times noisily, for thousands of years, like a ticking clock measuring time. They had once licked the city wall with salt, drenching it with wet air. They were not there now, replaced instead by silence – complete, deep silence.

Where did the sea go? It is not something that can disappear overnight. It was there the previous night. An occasional swimmer had been tossed in the waves. Some were seen running on the wet sand alongside it. Then, what had happened? It could not just evaporate. It is a sea, for God's sake! Passers-by were beginning to stop, chattering excitedly in small groups.

'The sea has been stolen,' someone exclaimed, his voice trembling. The dire news started to spread.

A flock of wild pigeons landed on the empty lot between the apartments. People afflicted with sickness spread barley there, hoping the voiceless birds would offer prayers for their health. A dog was sitting quietly with his legs and tail folded inwards. The blue sky had deepened in hue. The sea was not where it should have been. A man stopped and looked at the horizon. Although there was no sunshine, he still shaded his eyes with his hand, concentrating hard, but unable to see anything. The view remained unclear, despite his efforts. People did not immediately surround him. They must have thought he was using tricks to fool others. Stand in a busy street, point to the clear blue sky, use your hand to cover your eyes and mumble something. A crowd will be attracted in no time. Everyone will try to see what you pretended to see, although there was in fact nothing there. How can you see anything when there is nothing? When a crowd gathers around, you wash your hands of it and move on as if nothing had happened. But that man stood there, joined by another, and then another. No one could see the sea.

One of the onlookers called out, 'Where is the sea?'

Nobody answered him.

'Where is the sea?' he asked again.

Hardly anyone could have answered this question. Really, what could anyone say? Where could the sea have vanished to?

'It must be here somewhere; you probably need to look around a bit more attentively.'

'Look beyond the fog.' But it could not be found. People started to gossip.

The man whose voice was heard in the beginning so distinctively wavered. 'Why can't I see it? What is wrong?'

'You could only see it if it was there,' someone snapped back.

'Is it possible? Just like that...suddenly...the whole sea?'

Many voices sounded astonished.

'Yes, overnight, the whole sea!' some voices chimed in unison.

'But this cannot be!' Someone was in complete denial.

'But it has happened,' someone else corrected him.

'This is a definite sign of a bigger calamity,' another voice was clearly heard saying. 'Could be due to an oil spill, an ecological disaster, a local effect, a nuclear holocaust...,' he left it incomplete. People stared at him, a bald, bespectacled man. Some considered his arguments likely. That is possibly what happened.

'Iran, Israel, so the sea has parted here.'

'This was going to happen someday,' one onlooker was busy convincing others.

'But how so suddenly?'

'I was watching BBC news all night. There was nothing on it.' One man was not buying the story.

'How long would it have taken?' Someone shrugged his shoulders.

'A millisecond...destruction can spread far and wide.' He sounded smug, showing off his superior knowledge. He did not sound defeated.

The crowd failed to catch it. They were standing in a group, looking towards where the sea used to be, then glancing at each other, suspicious, inquisitive, trying to figure out what the next man was thinking, what he was feeling. That was not too difficult to determine. Everyone was looking in the same direction and commenting. Some kept asking questions. Seeing the gathering, passers-by would come to join the crowd. Unable to find the sea, each would freeze and look around as though it might just be displaced and could be found if searched for. 'What happened? What is going on?' Newcomers would restart the conversation.

'Nothing! Nothing has happened. What is there to happen?' The man with the glasses who predicted worldwide destruction was getting tired of repeating himself. 'Something happened, over there, not sure what...' If pushed, he would point to the area where the sea should have been.

'Something has gone wrong,' someone from the crowd explained to the best of his understanding. The follow-up questions of 'how' and 'when' were only met with incomprehensible sounds, showing ignorance.

The man who was using his hand to shade his eyes turned, shaking his head. His shirt was fluttering in the wind. At his suggestion, the man who had shrugged his shoulders climbed on to a wall which stretched along the road. 'There is nothing there,' he said, confirming the obvious fact that everyone already knew. He was right, there was nothing there. No sand, no bushes, no stones. Flat, barren land stretched as far as the eye could see. So surprisingly bare that the same questions came back hauntingly – what had happened and how? Such a vast sea! Where did it go? It could not just disappear into thin air! It was not a child playing hide-and-seek. People saw it last night; it was as it should have been.

'What happened to the sea?' an older man could not resist asking the question that was disturbing everyone. His shalwar and kameez were crumpled. His beard was unkempt. He began to blurt out questions rapidly: 'Where did it go? What happened?' he asked. The man, who had climbed the wall with the help of the bespectacled man, took a few steps along the wall and began to answer from up there, even though the question was not even directed at him. 'The sea has been stolen,' he informed them, drawing attention to the board hanging on the upper portion of the wall.

Even when the sea had been there, during the day, it used to be silent. People visiting the seaside would bid farewell in the morning. The probing sunlight and its heat caused discomfort to the people who came to picnic. They preferred coming in the evening, when the site would become crowded again. Then it would come alive. A fun-loving crowd had once gathered because of the sea. Now, people had gathered in small groups, talking in hushed voices as if someone had died in the neighbourhood. They congregated as if to condole the loss of the sea.

By now, everyone knew. Except for an occasional newcomer, they were no longer asking what and where, but rather how and when.

No one had an answer. Except that the sea had gone.

'God knows how and when!' The crowd kept growing but the newcomers were doing exactly what the first few did: exchanging questions about what had happened. By now, you could identify a person by the questions he asked. People were commenting based on where they came from and who they were. These comments were now being relayed far and wide. A young man had placed a camera on a tripod in a small clearing, inviting people to record their comments. He must have been a local representative of some foreign news channel. Whomever came to him, the young man positioned them in such a way that the empty land was in the background, where the sea had been replaced by bare land. The camera would freeze the scene into a still frame with added voice-over commentary.

'This city needs open areas and picnic resorts badly,' an older man was saying. He was wearing a jacket over a V-neck shirt, and spoke in precise English. He looked like a retired bureaucrat who had championed development issues ever since his retirement. 'Land grabbing belongs to the mafia here. They have long arms. Money and politics are controlled by them. It is sad that even the state accepts this land grabbing. With no opposition, the oppression continues, swallowing all of the resources. But the sea belonged to the whole city; it did not belong to a particular class only.'

'We will carry out a candlelight vigil in its memory. We will do a peace march.' A woman swayed, her hair flowing behind her as she spoke excitedly. Her nails were polished and her lipstick had left a stain on her teeth. She was wearing a cotton dress, both her wrists adorned with metal bangles.

A young man in a colourful T-shirt and with sunglasses perched on his head spoke out: 'This is more than a fun place. Hundreds of thousands of people earn their living from it. Where will these fishermen go? They once lived in shanty towns along the sea coast. The government should arrange alternate accommodation for them.' His voice rose as he made demands far greater than the immediate need.

'This is murdering our ecosystem. The natural mangrove preserves will disappear and all of the wildlife with it. There is a very fine ecological balance between them and humans. If one goes, the other will not survive either.'

One of the activists made a victory sign in front of the camera. The space between his fingers was filled by the barren land, the picture was shaky due to his amateur photography.

'You all should organize. We should join hands,' the activist told the ethnic youth, who told the lady representing the NGO, 'We should do a peace march from Chundrigar Road to the Press Club.'

'The first thing is to file an FIR,' a man with a rather deep voice, wearing a black jacket, said. He was possibly – or rather, definitely – a lawyer. His voice silenced the crowd. Yes, this was very important, why had no one mentioned it before?

'We should determine the extent of the loss first,' an elderly lady with white hair and a well-groomed face spoke up. Her voice had a cutting quality to it. Might she have been a teacher? She did not hear the lawyer, nor the silence that followed; it's possible she was hard of hearing. She made her suggestion with an intensity that was possibly her norm. 'Let us first find out if the sea has vanished only from here or from other places as well, like Ibrahim Hyderi, Korangi and, most important of all, Keamari. The real issue will be Keamari. Has anyone contacted the people there? Confirmed anything?'

No one answered her questions.

'It is very important to submit the FIR to the police. It puts things on the record,' the lawyer reminded the crowd.

'Even if it is recorded, we are being squeezed,' the ethnic youth exclaimed angrily.

'Can everyone at least agree to a decision? Marching together and presenting unity is very powerful!' The lawyer's voice was impassioned.

'But to which precinct? Although the area belongs to the Darakshan precinct, we should report to the Jackson precinct.'

'Not with the police, we should file the report to the port authorities.'

'You probably mean the coast guard. They will do nothing. They have no interest in anything except smuggled liquor,' a voice rose and disappeared in the crowd.

'We should go to someone...'

'Police report...'

'FIR...'

Several voices were now being raised simultaneously, drowning out and interrupting each other.

'But who should we report against?' The voice who made this enquiry could not be identified.

'Who is responsible? Someone has to be held responsible!' The voice was not trying to hide itself in the crowd. It belonged to the distinguished woman who was probably a teacher.

'But who should be the plaintiff? Who suffered the loss? Who owned the sea? Who had a claim on it?' It could not be determined immediately if this voice belonged to the ethnic youth, the activist or perhaps to someone entirely different. But this silenced the crowd again, as if the person had said something no one had thought of so far. They all started to talk at the same time, to each other, among themselves, to the person in front, on the side, to the man standing beyond two men, then to the man next to him. The crowd split into smaller groups, but stayed there. They kept discussing the city and the sea.

People kept bringing up their memories of the sea. Like that girl who kept mumbling in a monotone, 'Father would take us to the seaside for visits when I was little. We would take a bus to Clifton. We would start preparing early in the morning. Mother would pack two or three different kinds of food in a bundle and then put it in a wicker basket. I always rode camels at Clifton. The first time I rode, I screamed when the camel stood up. The *mahout* was leading the camel in front, alongside the crystal-clear sea, holding the reigns. I would walk holding my fathers' finger. He would buy me a necklace and earrings made of seashells. Water would fill his footsteps on the wet sand along the sea. Father died, but the sea was still there. I wondered if someday I could hold the hand of the sea and trace my father's footprints, to see how much water filled in them. What will I do now that the sea is no more? Oh, dear father…' The girl's monotonous voice broke and she started crying, with a flat, lifeless sob.

Once, when the sea had still been there, a child lost a balloon. It blew over the sea with its long tail of thread trailing behind – an orange-red spot on the dusky, clouded sky, getting smaller and smaller. Then, it disappeared completely.

'We once had a poetry session at the beach,' one of the young men said. Nobody identified him as ethnic, though; but from his clothing and his speech, he was as ethnic as the other youth. 'I was in college those days. It lasted all night, it was fun. Then my brother Jamil pestered me every day, "Let us go to the sea, let us go to the sea." So, I seated him on the back of my bike and brought him here on a moonlit night. He jumped off the bike and stepped on to this wall. Facing the sea, he started talking loudly, "O sea, it has been so long. O sea, you have not spoken to me or heard my poetry." And he started reciting his poems. The sea had no escape. I am sure the waves tossed their heads in protest. Police stopped us on the way back. "He is not drunk, he is just like this," I explained to the cops. "He is like *this*?" they looked at us suspiciously. "Yes, he is like this and he gets worse closer to the sea," I assured them. "Okay, then take him away." They let us go.'

'Where will I take him now? Who will he recite his poetry to, O sea?' He kept on for some time, but his voice was drowned out by other similar voices. Then the crowd started to disperse. Perhaps the police had started to disperse them. The media was covering the crowd and the conversation live. A man with long, tangled hair and his shirt untucked was taking pictures with a camera. He was trying to get a foothold in front of the board, and the police were trying to prevent him from doing so.

The board was nailed high on the wall. The nails were not rusted. Shining in the morning sun, the board had the name of a construction company in bold letters, with a monogram under it. An orange sun was depicted, with words promising a better future for every family, written in blue, just like the sea itself.

The crowd suddenly turned from the cameraman and the police holding him, as a noisy group of bikers had arrived. They had their silencers off so that when they raced their bikes the noise drowned out every other sound. When the engines finally stopped and the noise quietened, no one noticed that there weren't really that many of them. The one leading in the front had a bandana on his forehead.

'What did you do to the sea?' He pointed his finger at the bureaucrat who had been talking about eco-friendly development.

Frightened, the bureaucrat stepped back.

'You think you can stop us by hiding the sea? If the sea disappears, we will find a new place to celebrate New Year's Eve!' The young man was screaming angrily and others were nodding in agreement.

'That's what I think as well,' the bureaucrat heaved a sigh of relief. 'The seaside is the largest of picnic areas. With its open space, all those barriers that these fundamentalists want to impose on the youth will be broken.' He started a long tirade.

'Shut up. Stop this nonsense,' one of the biker's voices cut him off.

The bureaucrat was too afraid to speak.

'You people did this. You do whatever in big hotels...' this biker's voice was on edge.

'Did the mullahs steal the sea to stop New Year celebrations?' the earlier biker said.

'These mullahs are very creative.' The crowd was watching this encounter keenly. The elegant lady who was possibly a teacher decided to give her opinion. 'Oh, these maulvis and fundos – they are killjoys; they have stolen the sea.' The retired bureaucrat nodded in agreement.

Suddenly, a fracas broke out:

'The rights of city dwellers are constantly being violated.'

'If it is up to them, they will confiscate the whole city.'

'As if the East India Company has caught a golden hen.'

'After selling every piece of available land, they are after the sea.'

'For sure these people are responsible; they never let the civic institutions work.'

'The city government is trying its best...'

'Doing what? They are pulling wool over our eyes. They are stealing our resources for their own interests.'

Arguments intensified; noise levels increased. The volume of sound was rising and ebbing just like the waves of the sea used to.

'A lasting gift from the city fathers,' the writing on the board was glimmering. Under these words was a picture, a lit-up skyline with electrified colours shining through the dark shadows of skyscrapers. The painter had shown imaginary mountains and palm trees, but there was no sea in the picture.

There were cement umbrellas along the opposite side of the road. These were now empty, broken in disarray, looking like an eyesore. People used to sit in their shade to gaze at the sea. But who would want to gaze at miles of empty sand now? Peanut vendors, bean and *pappadum* vendors, when tired of walking around, would rest there. A gazebo, set aside in the shade, was reserved for masseurs. Some ignorant souls, not knowing better, would rest there. Masseurs would offer to massage them so many times that they would either agree to it or move away. Either way, the place would be vacated for the next potential customer. There were also benches and iron chairs, all vacant, scattered around the umbrellas.

Nobody tried to occupy these chairs now. There was no water to be seen in front of them, just flat land. But if they could develop a habit of looking at the sand intently, it would also appear to move and shake.

Some of the seaside visitors, joggers and yoga practitioners did complain. Some wrote letters to the editors of English language newspapers. But their complaints proved mere breakfast fodder. These people could still practice their habits. They only needed some space. That was still there, even more than before. Unrest was also noticed among the youth since the sea had disappeared. This was neither discussed on television talk shows, nor were letters seen in newspapers. It was a vague sort of discontent, hard to describe, difficult even to sense, as if someone used to showering twice a day was deprived of a shower for days, or as if a sweet tooth was being deprived of sweets. An unease, like an abstinence or withdrawal, causing sore limbs and an aching body. A young man complained that since the sea disappeared, it felt very cold. 'As if you wrapped the sea around you before,' an elder admonished.

The young man did not reply. The sea used to absorb a lot. The Hawke's Bay and Sandspit huts were not for family picnics only. A beach hut could be obtained by bribing the caretaker. This provided a private space, with freedom to spend time with friends after long drives over the weekends. The sea would provide a perfect outlet. Even if a hut were not available, things could happen behind the dunes, in a parked car. This could also happen in a car parked in open sand – not that the youth would not have considered that. But nobody said anything. The huts were still there, floodlights still on, the warning written on the wall still readable: 'Swimming is not allowed in the month of September as high tides can be dangerous.' The sea had disappeared, but the wall bearing the warning was still there.

A procession was taking place in front of the Press Club. Since processions are very common here, it was initially ignored. There appeared nothing special about it: no placards, no banners, no media coverage. A few women shouting slogans, which were not even synchronized. They wore long kameezes and flapping trousers. Many had wrapped discoloured, dirty sheets around themselves. Many wore wide metallic bracelets and bangles. They all arrived in a bus from some shanty town. They appeared anxious, eager to go back. Many had small children with them, with runny noses and screaming cries. The children's cries were merged with the women's slogans as if they were a part of them. 'Prawns... fish... prawns... fish...' this much was heard distinctly, since it was said loud and clear. The rest was muffled. 'These are fishery workers,' someone standing outside the Press Club informed his colleagues. 'Their livelihood is tied to the sea. They are asking the government to arrange for an alternative source of income.'

'Prawns...fish...' the women raised their fists with the slogan. It was not noticed from the distance that their hands were dirty, blackened and calloused. The sea thundered in their voices.

A similar crowd gathered there another day. This time, there were men with the women as well. They had dark skin, and spoke in some unfamiliar language. There was no mention of prawns or fish in their slogans. In fact, there were no slogans at all. Someone among them must have brought a drum as well. He started beating it in a slow rhythm, growing faster, faster, and suddenly breaking into a mad frenzy. The dark-complexioned old woman at the front of the procession mumbled something and started swaying in place. She kept swaying and mumbling. Her swaying was matching the drum beat. Suddenly, as if electrified, she raised both her hands in the air and started spinning in a craze. 'More sir, more sir,' she shouted, before collapsing on the road. The procession carried on.

'Why are these people making so much noise?' a man complained to his colleagues outside the Press Club. 'What heavenly catastrophe have they suffered? If there was a chance of any gain, or if land was being allotted, the same people would be the first to be there, using deprivation and poverty as their excuse.' His partner's answer could not be heard in this noise. The procession was now dispersing and the attendees were helping the old woman off the road.

'May our leader's mausoleum last. That is the real identity of this city,' the first man's voice was heard again. 'That is the icon shown every time on the television teleprompter. There are other cities as well. What is the big deal if the sea disappeared? Nothing, nothing at all...' The procession dispersed in no time. Its attendees mingled among the crowd on the road.

Some practical difficulties started showing up as well. The urban legend of the Nettijetti Bridge, as the place where people went to commit suicide, was already losing ground as people had adopted other means. Rather, sand from the seabed started gathering in its rail tracks. The first to go were the people who came there to feed the fish in the hope of divine goodwill. Then the men with small coin towers and tablets of dough in old empty oil canisters went. The people who bought these tablets to throw into the sea to feed the fish disappeared as well.

The day a traditional procession of mourning floats came out, the administrators were faced with the dilemma of where to drown these floats. The sea was gone. This question was pondered over by the religious scholars of the city, but they could not come to a decision. The old custom of sailing a wish list to the Imam-in-Hiding also suffered a setback. People used to float their lists from the Nettijetti Bridge to reach the saviour Imam. They were not willing to risk writing their wishes on sand. Their questions remained unanswered because there was no sea now. If there were no questions, who would answer them? Now that the sea was gone, there was land, more land and crows. There were many crows, coming from everywhere, cawing noisily. The sky was a big tent over the city and the crows the pegs keeping the tent in place. However, the crows were not able to brave the wind. The sky moved, came lower with the wind and rose again with the crows. The sky was swollen, like old cotton soaked in water, dripping, dripping sea. Only drops were left, but no sea.

One day, a man came to the place people were gathering, to describe his dream about the sea. 'I saw…I saw…green-blue water beside the sparkling sand, spread deep and wide – as far as the eye could see. White foam tossing with the waves, ebbing when they fell; white foam flowing to the sand, where the water receded. A stretch of sand is left behind, brilliant, as it just rose from the bottom of the sea. I wish I could stand on the sand, drenching my feet, as I used to do when I went to the seaside for family picnics. A mahout was inviting visitors for camel rides. I shook my head to say no and that woke me up. There was no sea and I was in my bed.' When he had described his dream, others started talking as well: Clifton… Paradise Point…the beach dunes…water splashing around the dunes… Hawke's Bay…huts…Sandspit…pristine sand…galloping water receding after washing the sand. They were all speaking at the same time, narrating their stories. Another man thought he could see that the sea was there again: dirty water, littered sand, empty juice boxes, plastic bags, orange peels, crumpled boxes used and thrown away. A large crowd gathered in front of the receding waves, eager to enjoy themselves. Their voices rose above the waves, echoing. The wall in front of them, the unfinished skeleton of the building appeared, squeezing the sea in its hands, shrinking it. A black oil slick floating on muddy water was stuck and failed to recede with the tide. The smell of dead fish was getting worse, till it was suffocating. One would turn away from the sea in an effort not to throw up.

That evening was humid. The city dwellers were getting used to the sea's absence, as they were once used to living in its presence. The sea breeze did not blow despite the day's heat. It would have, if there had been a sea. Humidity had engulfed the city as if someone had inverted a hot, sticky glass jar over it. By the evening, the smell was spreading all over the city. Fish and octopuses were seen strewn on the footpath. Seabirds sat on the electric poles with puffed wings, tired of flying like drenched crows in the rain.

Imported, used clothing from abroad became cheaper. The price of eggs shot up. There was hardly any traffic in Clifton now. The young massage boys and the girls standing under the poles became numerous. A fast-food multinational selling burgers announced a new deal. A new entrée of fast food in the sand city. Large new advertisements appeared in the media the next day, showing receding water, and a twinkling city rising from the sand, sandwiched in a burger. 'You take a bite too, please. Other cities, please contact your local dealers.'

'Remember, this golden offer is for a limited time only.'

On a similar dusty morning, before the light, the people of the sea will see that the city has been stolen.

By then, their story would have been lost in other stories. Dust to dust and water to water.

Where will anybody be then, and where will the sea be?

There is a footprint on the beach along the sea; water is filling in it and beside it, a camel owner is crying.

CHERNOBYL

SOMENDRA SINGH KHAROLA

i

Two Przewalski mares mate in the ruins
of a swimming pool. Life, a truck
with eighteen wheels and a cargo of bitumen,
is the sudden dichotomy guillotine drop
between the shallows and the deep end
of dislodged tiles – grandfather's lost teeth.
The 50 m record still remains feal
to immortality on the chalkboard.
Chlorine burns the eyes to summer steppes,
and a concrete sarcophagus covers
reactor number four.
Indeed, this seed husk of bones and skin
contains what I, what we are all within,
nuclide radioactive.
And inside the ribs of the leviathan,
beside the ferris-wheel that was never opened to children,
the Prezwalski mares continue to feel
for the other's penis with cold and yearning hooves.
Winter is, for some reason, cold, everywhere.
For how long will a fistful
of potassium iodide lozenges
keep our thyroids warm?

ii

Yet, graywolves, arctic terns and Przewalski horses
have returned. One of the horses likes the taste of autumn paper

in the Pripyat Hospital, maternity ward.
A certain register beside the copper bedpan
remains opened, page number ten,
for the archaeologists of posterity to indulge in.
Such historical evidence is one for the poet to write in poems
because it is subtle and not garish
as similar evidence elsewhere: Of the mother's
scorched skeleton stretching out to churn butter
when Vesuvius erupted.
The horse nibbles through names in the register,
each baby birthed, each woman mothered,
as if his impassable teeth were fate's proxy
that has returned to settle something old and debt-ridden.
Everything seems to eat everything else here,
this is the diktat of a healthy ecosystem. The trees have
begun to grow and heal the water.
All is ostensible like human faces, however.
Even I am pristine on the outside.
What know you of that burn in my soul's soil? What knows anyone?
I know of one thing, though, I have fed horses firm apples:
An ancient solace, even in divine, deciduous wastelands.
Animal enamel can so easily differentiate
between the meat of my fingers and fresh fruit. You?

iii

A certain unsaid fetish that transcends flesh pervaded through the Soviet populace
of engineers in the boiler room: The violinist's yearning
to submit to his music, the poignant tension
of his strings, and become one with it.
No different than the swordsmith's,
who runs a delicate finger
through the riverine crests, *hamon*,
of his finest sword, sharp as Vedic salvation,
with a sacred fetish to cleave himself clean
through the midriff but without any visible scar: An expiation.
Thus, the sterile engineers used to place a stethoscope
to the walls of the boiler room and dissolve

crystalline sea salt into long hours of penance,
listening to the thrum and the reined in
feline violence of atoms and control rods, the sound
of rain on the rooftop of their homes in the Urals,
narrow gauge parallel rails.
(Why must only the carnivore be so beautiful? Even the antelope yearns
for the taste of canines in its jugular.)
Each one of the engineers desirous of a similar rudimentary, retrograde
division of the conscience to fell and rebuild the castle bones of himself,
but this time with does, elm trees, and Ferris-wheels all around.
Even the poet yearns that he becomes his words
without suffering any attenuation of sentiment. And so, I offer these words:
Anthills   Coal   Riverstones   Father
A room that grants any wish   An owl unfurling its wings in a bone white desert
    A sharp, twisted bit of spring on a factory floor with bare feet
If the world were the swordsmith, it would be walking through
        mountain snow forever,   fearful of stasis   because
            then the two pieces of its body   would separate.

iv

Atomicity. In truth, my degrees of freedom may be resolved
to the simple bread of honesty. I am humility, atomicity of a riverstone.
That stray dog, whose front paw had been shorn clean
by a car's tyres dangled not through ligament
or tendon or bone, but through the pleaful elasticity
of a sliver of skin. Her paw dangled like the bell in an ancient,
deceased religion's belfry, and I the religion's
last penitent servant. This amorphous firmament
swirls around when I swirl around nude
amongst the pines of the Red Forest: 3000 roentgen. I shall turn for days,
even years, hungry, till the Cs-137 turns my brown eyes blue,
shifting my weight from the cartilage of my left meniscus to my right meniscus,
a Sufi dancer, and beg for a liquidator's medal from God.
The medal on its obverse side had a drop of blood
crisscrossed by etchings of α and β and γ rays.
Even I have dreams of dying a hero, but I am certain
my life shall be like yours, one of atomicity. Here, swallow
a fistful of potassium iodide if you ever decide to fall in love with me.

v

The brothers continue to return through dreams, the corner
tea-shop of my conscience their solace. The two fresh,
unscathed bodies of ivory youth, steaming
prodigiously, Manto's description
of erotic youth, through their pores in the cold night.
I see them strip nude and dive into the heavy water
as if it were only water. Their bodies arc
and pierce without a splash
and with the softness of forest birdsong.
Everyone else around only stares, their faces masked,
bodies wrapped with thin plates of lead:
An apron stitched hastily together, *mother, mother,*
I have heard myself whisper in my sleep.
What the swimmers had for protection
was only their Soviet conviction of iron, something
we all know is as true as the Navajo Indian's belief
that her intricate cradleboard, of bison horns,
in which her son is wombed firm
will imbibe the love of the robin in her child's heart.
The whirring helicopter mourns with the sincerity
of clear-headed women[1], and its dosimeter
gnawed termitic by the exposure
registers a burst and swivels hard and true
above the simple water, above the innocent water.
The boys surface and are hauled out,
one of the masked men slips a lubricated catheter
into their urethra and the boys smile,
their bodies mollusc limp, *Pietà* .
The boys smile, atoned. The catheter in their urethra,
a *Maasai* circumcision, an *Initiation*, the birth
of the adult homunculus in their bones.
They may now hunt raw, hot tiger.
What becomes of their fates, I never discover in my dream.
But now this new dream of two aged brothers,
who only keep smiling, broad and broader
till their chafed lips tear, and smiling broader still,
all day long, for years, no matter what the stimulus,

just a smile of no meaning, infantile, beautiful
as the heavy water that was only just water, and even as innocent. *Mother, mother,*
I have heard myself whisper in my sleep. Even the Mantis has begun to pray sincerely.
Someone at least balm their torn lips with warm oil, someone. *Smile.*

vi

Beside the X-ray room, the radiologist told me
a story whose authenticity I doubt, I confess.
A story about why God allowed Satan to live
even after he had been persecuted and cast out
of the sacred temple, and all Angels,
even Gabriel, demanded his head. But Satan,
pariah, sat cross-legged on Earth
and prayed so sincerely and honestly
that his *ibaadat* covered every grain of sand.
I was already laughing at him, but I held
my countenance and leaned forward intently.
The radiologist pinched some air and said,
So much ibaadat that there was no room
to place even a needle
on ocean or land, he pinched harder,
So much. That even God was overwhelmed
by his pleas and spared him. Lips, an inverted
crescent, I feigned a profound epiphany.
The machine pinged. The crosshairs glowed.
I inhaled. *Click. Click. Click*: Healful radioactivity.
The chiaroscuro of my ribcage emerged
in the hydroquinone bath as if
called forth by a soft lover who sings soft songs.
Sleeves folded, developer acetone dripping
from his forearms, *Wudu,* he was so convinced
by my act that he gifted me his personal
copy of the holy *Book* that I wrapped
with rare marsupial leather four times over,
the pretence of respect, and continued
to laugh at him. I even requested a vial of *ittar*
because Father had taught me
to always request an extra cup of sweet tea

and *saahni* when invited to a poor man's house.
I walked. The trefoils on the doors of the X-ray
and CT rooms sounded danger with the same
benign immediacy of the crucifix: I am an atheist.
Why need I, God? Besides, the films
showed I have strong lungs, horse heart.
Why need I, God? Why need anyone, God?
My skin is soft, sandalwood paste, rosewater oil.
Marsupial leather really did complete the humour.
But even today, his sweet tea still
remains sharp on my tongue. The taste, a needle.
Sound the Kangaroo court, I shall confess in front of all.

Note

1. Mehrotra, Arvind Krishna, 'Canticle for my Son', *Collected Poems 1969–2014*. New Delhi: Penguin Books India, 2014.

THE SEA SINGS AT NIGHT

MIMI MONDAL

Halfway through the night, you wake up thrashing, completely soaked in your bedclothes. The thrashing and splashing wake me up too. In the moonlight streaming in through the window, I see your half of the bed has turned into the sea. That's when I'm scared that you'll lose sight of me, lose your moorings. That's when I'm scared you'll swim away.

Even after this midnight madness, you rush into the kitchen, clothes and skin and long hair dripping, trailing so many streams on the floor. You grab small fish out of the bowl I had bought you and devour them raw with your fingers. You look hungry, panicked, trapped. You don't want me to hold you. I think you're crying. I think in your language you're crying, though the low, guttural cadence that soars from your throat sounds like surf song to me.

You can see the sea from our flat, but it's down nine floors of building, across a busy highway and beyond a dull strip of beach mostly littered with plastic bags and empty food wrappers. The kitchen window gets the widest view. Is that why you spend so much time in the kitchen?

Mumbai is teeming with sea fauna. Half the city is reclaimed from the sea anyway. Some of the sea folk live on the edges of the urban sprawl, hunting for lesser sea fauna and sending them, by the truckload, to the bazaars and kitchens of the city. Many of them sell peanuts, balloons or candy floss to children and romancing couples who flock the beaches in Juhu and Chowpatty. But it could also be the autowalla in the street. It could be the guy furiously writing programs in a cubicle somewhere, assiduously keeping the sea from his heart.

And then there is you, thrashing and struggling to breathe in our little flat open to the sea.

On the second morning, I take the day off work to visit my parents. In the old house, when I find myself alone with my mother, I ask her what I should do. Mama just shakes her head.

'They always try to leave, don't they? If you were a man, I'd have told you to give her a baby.' She turns away from me to stir whatever she's cooking. 'That's how I held on to your papa.'

This is a revelation. I think of my father – round-shouldered, timid, balding – as he snores gently on the cane chair out in the courtyard, newspaper balanced on his stomach. I love Papa, but I fail to imagine him as some kind of dashing philanderer. Papa has always been this small, sincere man who worked hard at the bank, devoted to his wife and daughter. To think of him as anything besides makes my head reel.

Besides, we cannot have a baby. Not now, probably not ever. I have no patience for babies. And you – you're so wild, strange, free. I cannot think of you changing nappies or waiting in front of the kindergarten in the afternoon heat, tired and bored and gossipy like the other women. You're too ethereal, too precious to be worn down to something like that.

I turn next to Sanjoy, the only college friend I have kept over the years. I adore Sanjoy, though he can be ridiculously shallow sometimes. The first time I mentioned you to him, he had wrinkled his nose and said, 'But aren't those sea types a bit too…fishy? Like, slimy? Y'know…like octopi?'

'Octopuses,' I had coldly replied. 'And octopuses aren't fish. Neither is Matsa.'

'Does this mean you're off all seafood now?' Sanjoy had quipped, cheerfully spearing a wedge of sushi with his fork.

I'd picked up a strip of fried chicken from my plate and pointedly chewed the flesh off the bone. 'I don't see how eating land food has alienated me from *you*.'

Sanjoy's pearl of wisdom on the situation turns out to be this: 'Darling, just buy a *big* aquarium and stick her in it, why don't you?'

'Stick my girlfriend…in an *aquarium*? Thank you very much, but no.'

Besides, I explain to him, the need is not to fix you a simulated environment that will give you the delusion of the sea. The need is to break your obsession, to gently ease you into the land life you and I are trying to build together. That's what you want too, don't you? You want to stay here with me. You want the midnight madness to stop.

I suspect the guy who brings me my lunch *dabba* at office is sea fauna, but he never gives me the time of day. He only makes conversation with women if they're pretty. He sometimes tries to chat up the receptionist, who is skinny, stylish and waves him away all the time. I know this type of man – handsome, sharp-featured, who comes to the city with dreams of breaking into Bollywood but then sticks around working as a waiter, cleaner and lunchbox deliveryman. He looks at my spiked hair and rounded arms with a kind of haughty disapproval. *Must've been a dolphin back at home*, I hostilely think.

After we struggle every night for a month, I decide to let you go.

'Matsa,' I tell you, 'tonight's a full-moon night. I will drive you down to Colaba Point at midnight, and then you can go home.'

You nod, but your large, dark eyes refuse to meet mine. You refuse to confront the heartbreak in my voice, which I unsuccessfully try to hide. We are standing in the kitchen. It is daytime and you look almost normal, almost happily settled, your little curls ruffling in the salty breeze that gushes in from the wide kitchen window. But we both know you're not. The sea will always haunt your dreams. You will always wake up in the depths of them, swimming, thrashing, fighting for the rush of water in your gills. There's no point carrying on with this forced assimilation.

Later, I drive you down. I park and we both get out of the car, step across the concrete ledge and on to the beach. There is no one else around apart from the cars whizzing past at high speed. A lonely drunk lies upon a ledge in a distance and sings at the sky. Wavering notes of longing and desolation drift over the dark waters and are lost.

I wish I could sing to you. I say, 'Give my regards to your folks. Tell them I tried my best.'

You step out of your pumps and stand gingerly upon the sand. You slip your dress off your shoulders. (In the moonlight your body is dark and fluid. I want to clutch you in my arms and lead you back home. I turn my eyes, blinking away moisture.) Lastly, you prise open my palm and gently place the carved silver ring I had given you when we first fell in love. Nothing made on land is welcome in the sea.

I drop the ring into my breast pocket and drive back home. The flat is cold, silent – incomplete without you. I go into the kitchen and shut the window. The hinges protest noisily. In the half year that we lived in this flat, the kitchen window has always been open, through rain and sun and even the occasional dust storm that blinded us and covered every surface with a film of fine sand. You've always wanted the sea wind to surround you. Now I want the sea out.

I go into the bedroom, drop my trousers on the floor and switch off the light. For the first time in the month, I may perhaps sleep in peace.

Halfway through the night, I wake up startled to the sound of waves crashing on to my bed. I turn to the space next to me...and in the light of the full moon, I see your half of the bed has turned into the sea. The silvery water stretches all the way to the horizon, rippling, dancing, but in that vast, empty stretch, there is not a sign of you. I lie curled up by the seaside and weep.

THE TWENTY-SECOND CENTURY

RAHUL SANKRITYAYAN

(Excerpts from Baisvin Sadi *translated by Maya Joshi from the original Hindi)*

Translator's Note

In 1910, H.G. Wells published a futuristic novel titled *The Sleeper Awakes*, set 203 years after the eponymous sleeper takes a pill to counter his insomnia. He wakes in the London of 2100 CE to find himself in a world utterly changed, changed for the worse. It is a work of dystopian fiction by a socialist. It was anticipated by his own serially produced story 'When the Sleeper Wakes' (1898–99). In turn, it anticipates later classics such as George Orwell's *1984*.

Less than a decade later, seemingly independently of this negative European premonition, in faraway India, an idealistic young man of 25 dreamt up quite another book exploiting a similar trope – of waking from a deep sleep. Here too, the sleeper emerges from a cave into a world 200 years later, to an utterly changed reality. That skeletal dream-frame, taking shape in a mind fired by the Russian Revolution, would undergo some transformations (Sanskrit to Hindi, verse to prose) to finally emerge as *Baisvin Sadi (The Twenty-Second Century)*. This work, comprising 16 chapters that the publisher's note informs us the author himself described as 'essays' written in a conversational Hindi is, unlike Wells's novel, a utopian narrative. Between the two books – Wells's and Sankrityayan's – lay great distances: between Victorian London and colonial India, between the respective writers' sociocultural backgrounds, and the world before and after the Russian Revolution of 1917.

Baisvin Sadi is the work of a sharp and sensitive young man from a modest rural background who had witnessed stifling tradition, grinding poverty and structural exploitation, as well as the stirrings of political awakening.

The final version having been composed while he was imprisoned for anti-colonial activism, it joins the great Indian archive of writing emerging from that fecund space, the British colonial prison.

Though Rahul Sankrityayan was at this stage of his fascinating life journey a young member of the reformist Arya Samaj who would take some 12 to 15 years to formally declare his allegiance to Marxism after a detour via Buddhism, 1917 had left an indelible impression on his mind, enough to instantly produce the rough mental draft of the book. Ten years after giving it final shape, in the preface to *Samyavad hi Kyon?* (*Why Only Socialism*?), he declared his innocence of economics or socialism at the time of writing *Baisvin Sadi*. In 1935, arriving on Soviet soil, he would write in his autobiography: 'The picture of villages, cities, men and women that I had portrayed in *Baisvin Sadi* had been a thing of the imagination. But here it was being given solid shape in the real world. Is it any surprise then that I consider Soviet soil to be worthy of reverence?' (*Meri Jeevan Yatra*, Volume II, p. 350, Kitab Mahal, 1950)

So what was this dream that found at least some concrete manifestations, though the world depicted was set in 2124?

The story begins with our sleeper in the cave. We later learn he is a retired teacher called Viswabandhu ('friend of the world') who, roaming the Himalyan foothills, had either fainted or fallen asleep in a cave. When he wakes, 200 years later, his clothes have withered away and, since he must now 'go amongst men', he fashions a makeshift girdle of leaves before exploring this new world. This 260-year-old, white-bearded man dressed in leaves is a novelty for the utterly civilized people whom he finds picking highly developed varieties of fruit in well-run orchards. The place seems to be Nepal, but they are not royalty on an excursion, he quickly surmises, revising his original assessment of them based on their clothes, demeanour, health and air of well-being. And thus begins a systematic dismantling of ideas of hierarchy and discrimination based on birth, gender, class, colour and caste.

While he informs them of the depredations of the world as he left it – poverty, disease, ignorance, inequality, exploitation – he learns of their evolution. The private and the public domains have been transformed. Private property having been abolished, a four-hour workday, education, health and happiness have been secured for all, via a rational and collectivist approach to horticulture, animal husbandry and resource distribution. This involves population control through scientific interventions, waste recycling and compulsory schooling with delightful kindergartens for children collectively raised and fed six times a day to give them rosy cheeks and cheerful temperaments. Parents, recognizing the greater good, send their children for higher schooling to collectively run schools. Mothers no longer tend only to their own children. 'Narrow-mindedness', has gone, replaced by fraternity and 'largeness of heart'. Wherever he goes, an odd-looking 'alien' from another time, he is welcomed by people with perfect courtesy and friendly curiosity. In this utopia, crimes have diminished thanks to the abolishing of private property, except for the rare ones attributable to stubborn vagaries of human nature or to the 'man–woman relation', though even here, the reformation of the private domain has eased matters. The social and financial equality of men and women having been established, with mutual love as the only foundation for union; adultery has disappeared. Many professions and posts – from lawyers to prostitutes, military generals to manual scavengers – have been rendered obsolete.

Technology is a friend to humans. Human ingenuity has been harnessed for such tasks as producing artificial meat and leather, while mechanized means of disposing waste and performing menial tasks have eradicated, apart from class distinctions, caste-based identification with certain occupations. Transport and communication are revolutionized with electric cars and trains, video phones and 'wireless wires' for the swift transport of images and texts across the globe.

The past exists as a slice of history, though both quotidian and rarefied aspects of it survive – people still relish such seasonal foods as were enjoyed by villagers of yore (spiced and roasted green peas and corn, for instance) and enjoy philosophical discourses, music and literature on train journeys. The present, though rationally regulated, is thus not stripped of joy (evident at work and play) or love (binding the family and the village but extending to all 'strangers'). Instead, enjoyment has been democratized. This utopia, contrary, he says, to the dire Hindu warnings about *Kaliyuga*, or the Age of Degeneration, is also selective in its culturally restorative aspects. Great ancient universities like Vikramshila, Nalanda and Taxila have been revived, their curricula expanded to include the latest developments in all the sciences. Ancient cities like Benaras and Patna still exist, in modernized, sanitized forms.

The local implementation of this schema is only possible because it is the globally recognized one. The planet has evolved, despite local structures of governance, one overarching government, with responsibilities distributed by turn among those of different nationalities. A kind of Esperanto connects the world, and a language called Bharati connects this region. This is achieved as people have realized that linguistic identitarianism is against their collective weal. Health, education, food and housing are the priorities. War is obsolete; religion is a thing of the past. Names harken back to the religious and linguistic diversity of the subcontinent but one would be mistaken to think they reflect faith. Reason rules, because it is reasonable to do so.

However, the sage-like character from the twentieth century has words for the twenty-second: avoid complacency. To think that we have achieved perfection is to invite stagnation and decline. The human species, he says, has infinite scope for self-improvement and evolution. The white-bearded sage from Nalanda isn't just gauchely admiring the advances of the future he finds himself in. He has sound advice to offer.

The book anticipates some of the Soviet experiments. It also brings to mind ideas explored in the Socratic dialogue *The Republic*, in both the evocative use of the cave motif (though with a twist) and in terms of the ideal city-state, of a rationally regulated life 'improved' with eugenics and communally raised children, but without the slavery and the hierarchy that *The Republic* accepts as the norm.

Like much futuristic work, this book illuminates and critiques the contemporary. His experiences and exposure to the rural outback of Parsa, Bihar, in particular, provide a concrete context for reimagining the future, but the book quite effortlessly expands to embrace the national and global, extrapolating the democratic local model of governance on to the global. Remembering that it is composed between 1918 and 1923 by a young man learning largely in autodidactic mode, at religious educational institutions and via anti-colonial activism, helps us appreciate the range and reach of his vision, and its specific concerns.

The utopia he envisions has eradicated, along with disease, inequality, prejudice, ignorance, war and overpopulation, all luxury and wastage. For its time, it is remarkably cognizant of the earth's limited resources. Today, we might see it is an anthropocentric utopia, where human priorities dictate which species of flora and fauna will survive. It is also untroubled by the fears of totalitarianism or techno-alienation that we find in Wells and Orwell, given its boundless optimism regarding human reasonableness and capacity for evolution.

Seen as futuristic fiction, however, its dreams are startlingly modest in their terrestrial immediacy. As humanity makes more progress toward colonizing outer space in the twenty-first century than the book envisions for the species in the twenty-second, it's a humbling thought that its *terrestrial* dreams appear more poignantly distant in 2018 than they did in 1918.

1. *Lambi Neend ka Ant* (The End of a Long Slumber)

After walking about eight miles, I finally heard human voices. As I drew closer, the voices became clearer. Coming close, I realized they included men and women. Their clothes were exceptionally clean, faces abloom. I thought to myself, could they be men and women of the Nepali royalty out to amuse themselves? But that does not seem to be the case. They seem to be plucking fruit and gathering it into baskets which are then picked up and carried forward by others. Looks like they are making a pile over there. That apart, the women aren't dressed in the voluminous garments of the Nepali royalty, though their physical appearance, attire, cleanliness and manners are of a far higher class than theirs. But there is a difference. Each of them is wearing trousers; their hands and feet are clad in gloves and socks. They have shoes on their feet as well. There is definitely a mystery to this. All right, I will only know after talking to them. Now I have come very close. Busy at work, they did not notice me. But, look, over there, one of them has spotted me and said something to the others. Why are all of them staring at me wide-eyed? Am I a creature? One is looking at my leafy covering, another at my beard. Okay, here comes one of them, he will reveal all.

Though he was walking straight towards me, my curiosity was making me restless. (pp. 3–4)

2. *Sebgram ka Baagh* (The Orchard of Apple Village)

I saw the large hall and the row of chairs and tables. On the tables were plates with apples, bananas, grapes and so many other fruits, as well as glasses of milk. Among us, there were a roughly even number of men and women. At first, I was astonished to see an equal number of plates there. Will women sit alongside men and take refreshments! Meanwhile, all the men and women came. All of them welcomed me with smiling faces... I put a slice of apple in my mouth. I found it extraordinarily sweet and juicy. I thought at the time it tasted so good because I was eating after ages. I learned later that this was the result of scientific methods of growing fruit. (p. 6)

3. *Vartamaan Jagat* (The Present World)

'My story is not very long. Before coming to that cave, I used to live in Nalanda in the province of Bihar. There used to be a school there, where I too studied and taught.'

'Oh! You are Teacher Viswabandhu, from the Nalanda School? We are fortunate to see you in person! I too was raised in the lap of your school between the ages of three and 20. I have even seen your statue at the Vasubandhu Bhavan there!'

'So our dear school still survives?'

'Not just that – there is none to rival it in the world. It is unmatched in philosophy, astronomy, linguistics, history and politics.'

Hearing of Nalanda's revival, my delight knew no bounds. A sea of joy surged through my heart. The audience too seemed very impressed with this introduction. (p. 8)

...

[Sumedh, his host, says,] 'Our village head wants to speak with you. I have to go to work now.' Saying this, he went to work. I went up to the 'radio phone'. I saw there a human reflection on a mirror. I gaped, astonished. That was not my reflection, nobody else was present, nor was it a painting or photograph. I was dazed and stunned. Just then, the reflection moved its lips and a voice came from the telephone – 'Welcome! I am Devamitra. *Saathi* [comrade] Sumedh just gave me news of your happy arrival. The biggest task at the moment is of sending your picture and news of your arrival to Patna. By six [in less than two hours], news of your arrival and your picture will have reached all corners of the world.' (pp. 10–11)

...

[Picking up a book on the history of the Saarvabhauma Rashtra Sangathan (Global Confederation of Nations), he writes:]

These are the broad outlines of events after 1923 that I could gather from the Table of Contents – by 1940, Indian independence under British patronage, a United Asian Nation by 1990, a United Asian-African-Australian Nation by 2000, a United European-American Nation by 2010, one nation for the entire globe by 2024. For the next three years Mr Dutt, who is India-born, had been elected the president of the entire world. He was educated at Taxila. He is 74 years old. Prime Minister Ohara is Japanese. Education

Minister Monoline is Russian, while Health Minister David is American. In this way, different departments are led by people from different countries. Despite looking very carefully, I could not find a defence minister. It occurred to me that it might be a printing error. How could such an important post be left vacant? Then I looked at the national assemblies of each country and found the defence minister absent. I turned to the index at the end, where words like 'army', 'general', 'defence minister' appeared. Reading those pages, I learned that as early as 2024, this important office of the old world had been done away with. Now there is neither army nor general. (p. 12)

4. *Gram aur Grameen* (Villages and Villagers)

I woke up before it struck five. I got out of bed and looked out the window. Stars were scattered across the sky. The moon could not be seen, but moonlight lit up the flower-laden boughs and creepers out the window. The subtle fragrance of roses stole into my room. In about 10 minutes the gong sounded. It was five. (p. 38)

...

Each home has a separate toilet. After one is done, one turns the tap and a powerful jet of water washes away the waste. I learned later that there are no manual scavengers now. There is no such caste. Yes, when the tap malfunctions, any person who is deputed for the task will repair it. The village's waste travels about four miles, where large pits have been prepared. As waste falls into the pit, machines cover it with soil. The machines are electrically run and the operators are at a distance... Each pit is left covered with soil for four years, after which some chemical substances are added to it. It is then used as manure for trees. (p. 39)

...

There are thousands of things to describe, how can one describe them all? The attire of the men and women, besides being very attractive, was also free of anything that was superfluous, lacking in utility or harmful. At work, I saw them all wearing woollen shorts over long socks and boots that covered the entire foot. I noted with surprise that nothing was made of leather. Even shoes were made of a thick canvas that resembled leather. The soles were of sturdy rubber. Above their shirts, they wore a warm coat and there were identical caps on everyone's heads. But these turned out to be work clothes, because at the dinner and at the Meeting Hall, everyone wore a round hat, full-length warm coat and trousers underneath. (p. 41)

5. *Rail ki Yatra* (A Train Journey)

It wasn't a train so much as gleaming little homes with windows and grills. No first, second, or third class – just one kind of car, similar bedding everywhere, call it the first class or the third. (p. 66)

...

Men and women were sitting on their assigned berths. Some were reading books, others the daily newspaper. Newspapers were still very popular. But without advertisements for companies. The needlessly large headlines are also gone. No 'special correspondent' or 'via Reuters'. Important news still gets headlines, but now there is no need for attracting larger readership with gaudy glamour... After they are read, old newspapers are sent to factories for recycling into fresh blank sheets and readied for another round of inking. (p. 66–67)

...

Monthly magazines are beautifully illustrated with pictures. Photography is in its prime. Further, it can now reproduce colours perfectly, and images can be transferred in an instant via 'wireless wire' across the globe for reproduction in newspapers. (p. 67)

...

We had now reached the train's library. There was a pile of newspapers and magazines... There were magazines from around the world in sciences such as astronomy, mathematics, metaphysics, history, linguistics, psychology, philosophy, electrical science, agriculture, medicine, botany, biology. A group of men and women were debating a philosophical point somewhere, others expressing joy or sorrow at recent events, some engrossed in the sea of literature, others enjoying a musical get-together. (p. 67)

...

Up ahead [beyond the dining car] there was a compartment for the ill. Five to six patients were lying in comfort there. Kindly nurses attended to them, some by reading to them, others by chit-chatting to keep them entertained. Heat-retaining vessels filled with milk, and plates laden with apples, grapes and other fresh fruit were laid out neatly on tables nearby. Two of these patients were from Tibet. Being chronic patients, they were being taken to Taxila for special treatment. Three others were from different parts of the Nepal Republic... This level of comfort was rare even for the extremely wealthy once upon a time, let alone ordinary folk. (p. 68)

...

I thought to myself: how times have changed. There was a time when those who laboured the most suffered the most. The poor toiling farmers and workers might get on to a train, but there was never enough space for them. People were packed like sheep one atop the other even at the height of summer. That crowd would crush a child here, a woman there. When they protested, they were told – why do you travel in this crowd, why don't you take another train? But waiting for another train would ruin someone's court case, make another miss the *lagan* [auspicious hour for weddings or similar rituals], watch a dear one die, or simply run out of money. (p. 68–69)

...

Now we were outside the forests. There are green fields on both sides of the road. I asked: 'Do you have green grass even at the height of summer? Have you people brought, like everything else, the clouds under your control?' Teacher Haque said, 'Yes, now rain-making is also in our hands; when required, rain is produced through scientific means. But here, green grass is periodically watered with large taps spread out across the land. Rain-making is for greening high, dry, mountains.' (p. 77)

...

We could see herds of cows scattered prettily all around... The cows are very beautiful and large; one wanted to keep gazing at them. Their calves were grazing at a distance, separately...

Haque: 'We allow just enough male calves to meet our requirements for bulls. The rest are all females.'

I: 'So have you mastered this science as well?'

Haque: 'Yes, as a requirement and difficulty presented itself before us, we laboured at it and found a solution too.'

I said, laughing: 'Brother! You have done wonders in all spheres. Made all problems solvable and the impossible possible. Perhaps you know no such thing as impossibility. These very same cows caused Hindus and

Muslims of the twentieth century and before that to thirst for each other's blood.'

Haque: 'They were our ancestors. It is not proper to speak ill of them now. That said, it was pure ignorance. Both failed to consider their long-term good. Gold was being plundered, and they were stick-fighting over coals. Truly, to this day we can't help laughing when we read about those times.' (p. 78)

6. *Shiksha-paddati: Tarun Kaksha* (The Educational System: Classes for Youth)

Here the student studies only according to his/her aptitude and inclination and those fields he/she has already shown a preference for... Nalanda University has 15 different schools known for the study of linguistics and archaeology, astronomy, philosophy, literature, music, fine arts, civil engineering, medicine, botany, biology, agriculture, mechanics and education. The professors are well-versed in their disciplines. The department of linguistics and archaeology introduces the students to original sources in history and equips them with the tools for gathering these. After all, this is not the twentieth century, but the twenty-second. Many archaeological finds buried under earth, sand, and sea have shed light on the beliefs, lifestyles and history of several lost peoples... The nation has left no stone unturned in collecting and preserving these materials. (p. 107)

...

The old stupas and buildings of Nalanda have been fully preserved. The Buddha statue famed among villagers in the twentieth century as 'Bhairav-ji' now has a fine canopy over it. This large, beautiful, serene statue appears even more enchanting now. The large stupa next to it looks as good as new. (p. 110)

7. *Shasan Pranali* (System of Governance)

...

Now man is equal to man, and women and men are equal... The earth has no landlords, no merchants and moneylenders, no kings, no subjects, no rich, no poor, no high, no low. All the inhabitants of the world are one family. The earth's mobile and immobile property belongs to that family...rarely does a village produce everything it needs without the help of the other... Humanity is abundantly supplied with material goods due to this; so much time would be wasted otherwise. When was it possible to do what humans do today: to enjoy 20 hours of leisure with only four hours of labour?

SHIT FLOWER

ANIL MENON

In its underground cavern, cathedral-like with its glittering spears of light and rust-stained barrel vaults, Goose continued to do what it had done for over five decades: route sludge water in the temple city of Mumbai. It was 3.04 a.m. IST, 2089 CE.

Goose cared little about light, vaults or cathedrals. But sludge was a different matter. Twenty million people, and at least as many non-people, can and will produce an ocean's worth of biosolids on a daily basis. Goose and its many software incarnations across the sewer system raised and lowered gates, adjusted valves, tweaked pressure here, tweaked volume there, and did everything they could do to encourage the temple city's illusion that it had no anus.

3.05 a.m. There was someone at the door.

'Knock, knock.'

'Who's there?' inquired Goose (so to speak).

'I am.'

'I am who?'

'492b616d2b612b6c696172…'

Goose 'got' the knock-knock joke. This was a pity. The virus's punch line, a very funny Gödel number, rewrote aspects of the sewer gate controller's sense of self, its synthetic consciousness, as it were. Goose had been breached. Ditto for other controllers across the system.

The situation was quite ironic. In 2030 CE, Simon Jósda, a computational immunologist, had proved that any sufficiently secure system necessarily had to have a sense of 'humour'. Secure systems had to know what to take seriously; they had to be able to 'get' jokes, recognize the 'funny' in funny business.

Of course, the formal version of Jósda's paper had been properly humourless. However, he had compared structured communication protocols to the 'Jo/-Ha/-Kyu' rules for correct gesturing in Noh drama, ergo, 'jokes'. Goose spent three seconds out of every minute telling itself jokes.

This time, however, the joke was on Goose. As the 'laugh' spread through the system, the Geese lost control of the city's bowels. Goose was able to put out a distress cry just as the biosolids hit the vent fans at the approximate rate of a hundred thousand gallons per minute.

2089 CE and progress notwithstanding, shit was still something of a real nuisance.

He had always loved working in the quiet of the morning. But his wife had been a noisy, bossy woman, and since she had got up around 7 a.m. in his house, Simon Jósda had developed the habit of waking around 3 a.m.

So, by 3.15 a.m. IST, he was wide awake in his very quiet apartment in Worli, in west Mumbai. His body woke him up to reach for his long-dead wife, Radha, just as it had awoken him each day in the 30 years they had been together. As with all tigresses, she had been best approached half-asleep, from the rear.

He half sat up in bed, groped for the bedside lamp.

'Many happy returns of the day, Doctor Simon Jósda,' said the House.

'For Pete's sake, it's the third bloody time. Shut the fuck up.'

The House didn't mind. If it had minded, it would have said something like, 'Listen, asshole, if you had a Sensorium, I would know for sure whether you were awake or not. I wouldn't have to base my guesses on your bodily noises, of which you have a bewildering number, and gestures, which your miserable Anglo-American body hoards. But you don't have a Sensorium, so I tend to get fooled. Half the time I'm not even sure if you are dead or alive. So give me a break. Now, many happy returns of the day, Doctor Simon Jósda.'

Today, Simon was 90 years old. He continued to lie in bed, flexing his wrists in anticipation of the forthcoming physical effort. Ninety may be the new 70 but it was still fucking 90. He sat up with a surge of will, waited for the slight dizziness to subside, swivelled his feet on to the floor, slipped on the WalkSafe belt, lifted himself off the bed, and walked barefoot to the bathroom. He liked the morning coolness of the marble; it reminded him of the winters in Edmonton, the pitter-patter of childhood's bare feet on the cold hardwood floors.

After his ablutions, he worked on the mathematics of biased random walks on groups for about two hours, deriving the consequences of an earlier intuition, until he realized that he had been wrong all along. He was too experienced to be upset, but it made him restless. It was time for his walk anyway.

He pulled on a fresh white kurta–pyjama, gasping with pain as his right shoulder acted up, ran a comb several times through the white mane Radha had been so proud of, chose a walking stick, looked around his silent 2-BHK apartment with its L-shaped living room, and announced quite unnecessarily: 'I'm leaving for my walk.'

'Have a nice walk, Doctor Simon Jósda,' said the House, going along with the pretence that it wouldn't know what Simon was up to once he left the house.

5.25 a.m. IST. He stepped out, good-morning-ed Mrs Dixit, who looked up from the rangoli she was drawing on her threshold and smiled. Outside, it was still dark and other than the glowering inspection of street dogs, there were few signs of life on the road. He knew that would soon change. Life in the city was centred around the temples. He breathed in the air, pleased as always at its purity. In the distance, he could hear loudspeakers blasting the opening stanza of M.S. Subbulakshmi's *Suprabhatam*, cajoling the sleepy god Sri Balaji to awaken.

Sensoriums had made loudspeakers utterly obsolete, yet it probably hadn't occurred to anyone that they could now ease up on the noise pollution. It pleased him, this stubborn resistance to rationality.

He walked eastwards, briskly stepping over construction debris and ignoring the catcalls from the hijras resting under the flyovers. They were harmless in the morning, too strung out to move, too good-humoured from last night's games. Fifteen minutes later, just past Tulsi Vihar, he crossed the Jain temple, an inspired copy, or an incarnation as the faithful liked to call it, of the Kolanupaka Temple in Andhra Pradesh. He wove his way through the Jains dressed in white. The way the men wore their dhotis had once reminded him of Roman senators in togas, but these days, it was the other way around.

Ten minutes later, he turned left and began to pass shops selling coconuts, garlands of jasmine, *panchamirtam* and camphor pellets; the air roiled with the smell of a dozen different kinds of flowers and incense. The massive stone edifice that was the Subramanya Temple was just ahead. Its ornate tower, an efflorescence in stone of gods, colours and strange beasts, was an exact copy of the Tiruchendur Subramanya Temple in Tamil Nadu. As he passed, he checked his watch: 6.05 a.m. In five minutes, it would be time for the first ritual washing of the god with milk. The devotees would fuse their Sensoriums at the precise moment the doors to the inner sanctum opened, and the apparent result was a simulacrum of the *samadhi* that was so central to Hindu philosophy. Radha claimed it wasn't a simulacrum but the real thing – Patanjali's *savikalpa* to be precise – and that if he got a Sensorium like most open-minded people, he wouldn't have to sample life in pathetic, un-spiced nibbles.

Temple flowers everywhere. Radha had taught him their Tamil names. The white jasmine flowers came as a pair of sisters: *malli* and *mullai*. There was the orange *kanakambharam*; the blue *neelambaram*; the fragrant brown *makazhambpu*; the red *chambarthi*; the sandalwood-coloured *samandhipu*; the two kinds of yellow: *thazambu* and *chevanthi*, with and without fragrance respectively. Her favourite was the *tamarapu*, the lotus flower, which was all these colours and more.

'Should be called shit flower,' he'd joked. The lotus grew very well in muddy water, 'pu' in Tamil meant flower, 'poo' in English meant – 'C'mon Rads, don't get mad, it's an excellent cross-cultural pun. It's a *little* funny, you have to admit.'

'Also a little aggressive. How did a lotus become a shit flower? Because you're afraid. You hear these Tamil names, and they distance you from me. You don't like that feeling so you lash out. Simon, have more faith in us.'

Faith was around him, everywhere. The men wore flowers tucked behind their ears, the women had flowers plaited into their coiled strands, the children wore garlands. The Tamils were crazy about flowers. Their women made love wearing flowers. Their men had gone to war wearing flowers. The Sangam poets had coded their songs of love and war with flowers. Radha had been crazy about flowers.

He could hear the muezzin's call to the faithful from the Worli Masjid three blocks down, just behind the banyan tree where Gopika-ji the cow had given birth to twins on that horrendous monsoon day, the notable event now marked by a small shrine tucked into one of the banyan's crevices –

What, still not clear? *Arre yaar*, it's right across from the Shirdi Sai Baba Temple where Bharati, Kishanlal's blind wife, took refuge from the mob boss Robert, and had her sight miraculously restored when she heard Akbar, her long-lost son who was raised by a Muslim, sing a song in praise of Shirdi Wale Sai Baba. No, no, no, that's a scene from the movie *Amar, Akbar, Anthony*. Look, friend, ask any rickshawalla, they'll take you, that is simplest, yes.

Past the Shirdi Sai Baba Temple, he began to get tired. He turned left, past the Armenian Church. It was now defunct and home to squatters, but there was talk of an Armenian group from Kolkata coming to fix it up. That would be great. Mumbai worked because its temples, churches, masjids and synagogues worked. The religious institutions organized the neighbourhood, maintained communal harmony, kept crime in check, cleaned the streets, took care of the indigent, ran the hospitals, and ensured that absolute, true and mathematical spacetime had a human heart.

The Worli Seaface was the last leg of his walk. It was also the best part – cool, windy, disinterested. The vast Arabian sea to his right and the sprawling bulging mass of the city to his left always made him feel as if he had rolled up Mumbai in a blanket and was carrying it on his back. He stood for a moment, hands on his hips, catching his breath, gazing at the infinite expanse. Not really infinite, though. Radha's Antariksh had been just as illusory.

Radha: as fierce, blood-rich and racist as Genghis Khan.

Too late. He heard her lose it in his head. 'Genghis Khan? Oh yes, the one brown badass that all whiteys know. Why not the Rani of Jhansi? Or Vispala? That bitch was so badass that after losing a leg in battle, she returned to the fight with an iron stump. Three thousand years ago, Jósda. We were making women like that three thousand fucking years ago. Genghis Khan, my ass.'

Calm down, girl. Jeez. He had come to believe her hair-trigger temper was just pent-up sexual aggression, but hadn't bothered – dared – raise the issue. Why cure a good thing with psychoanalytical insights? He was a lucky, lucky man.

He had known he was a lucky man when he first set eyes on her. To know what one wants, even if it is unachievable, is to be privileged. He had wanted her. He remembered the exact date: 12 March 2034. He had been made a foreign Fellow of the Indian National Academy of Sciences. She had been accompanying a skinny clever-looking Indian dude. They didn't seem like brother and sister.

I can do clever, he'd thought.

But her flashing eyes and dusky voluptuousness had unnerved him. She could have been a danseuse in Indra's court, an adornment on some ancient temple pillar. In the end, she had come over.

'Stop staring at me,' Radha said. 'What's the matter with you?'

'You! You are the matter with me.' He didn't care if he sounded desperate.

'Well, deal with it. Find something else to colonize and plunder. I don't date white boys.'

'Then we have something in common! I don't date them either. I'm Simon Jósda.' He began to hope. She still dated – awesome! 'Do I at least have a chance?'

'Pathetic!' She studied him with those large kohl-lined eyes. 'You're the mathematician dude, aren't you? The brainy bwana who's come to tell us what we already know. I hope you got your group photo with the little brown kids. What's next on the poverty cruise? Haiti? Sierra Leone? Well, you got your useless fellowship. Go back, Simon.'

'So, what do you do? Besides loathing white people?'

'I run marketing for the Indian branch of Antariksh BioTech.' She pointed to the skinny clever-looking dude. 'Pradeep's the chief scientist. He's based in the US of A.'

The way she said it, he wasn't sure if she disliked Americans in general or Pradeep in particular. Didn't matter either way. He was Canadian. Everybody loved Canadians.

'What does Anta –' He stumbled over the complicated word.

'Antariksh. Anta-rik-sh. It means infinity.'

'Sounds like ant rickshaw,' he joked. Then realizing (a) she had no sense of humour and (b) he was squandering precious seconds, he added hastily: 'What do you make?'

'Time!' she'd said dramatically. Then she caught fire, eyes flashing, hands gesturing in the way he had begun to recognize as south Indian, her sensuous face alit with passion.

She had good reason. Pradeep's citation at the awards ceremony had given no indication of the import of his work. Antariksh Inc. had found a way, it seemed, to make mitochondria more efficient by damaging their central mechanism. Mitochondria produced the energy a cell needed using the ETC, or electron transport chain. But it had been known since the early 2010s that roundworm mutants with disruptions in their mitochondrial ETC tended to live much longer. These mutants worked with an alternate energy production pathway, one that didn't need much oxygen and didn't produce certain sugar by-products as waste. The result was a supercharged mitochondrion. Antariksh Inc. had found a way to extend the results to human mitochondria. They'd been able to reverse ageing, boost energy, and convert Radha into an evangelist.

'Wow, sounds fascinating.' How could he tell her the whole thing sounded like snake oil? 'So, you want to live forever?'

'Hello? I'm a Hindu! We invented reincarnation, remember? Of course, I want to live forever.'

'Well, it's not just about being a Hindu, is it?'

What are you doing, Brain? he asked. *Brain, what the fuck are you doing? Stop immediately.* But his brain couldn't stop. *Relax, Simon. I'm getting to know her, Simon. We're having an intellectual discussion, Simon.*

'Then what's it about?' asked Radha.

'I mean, do we really want gazillions of immortals running around? Look at this place, it's coming apart at the seams.'

'Oh, is it? So how come we've been around for ever? *Accha*, never mind. What's the right population size? One million people? Fifty? There are 500 million Americans, so I'm sure that's okay. How many Hindus are okay?'

'Look, it's not this group or that group. I don't have an exact number, but surely there is a number beyond which we've got to start cutting back.'

'Typical!' she shouted. 'That's all life is to you people, isn't it? Something to be counted, measured and weighed. Well, it isn't. All life is sacred.'

'Yes, it is!' he said, pathetically glad to be able to agree with something. She smiled, accepted his apologetic namaste.

'That's all right, Jósda. It's your upbringing, I suppose. You're taught to objectify the world. It's bloody contagious too. I had a great-uncle who went to the States to become an economist. He went a *chikoo* and turned into a total coconut. Pathetic!'

'No, it isn't.' He'd had it with her racist bullshit. 'Your uncle chose to be someone else, that's all. We get to pick who we are now. That's what modernity means. All things change, but living things can choose to change. Yes, I know this'll be a shocker for you, but white people can change too. Deal with it. I thought I was a physicist, then a mathematician, then a computational immunologist, and here I am, an expert on shit.' Oh good, that got another smile from her. So it wasn't over. 'These days I'm okay with not knowing who I am. Seriously, identity is such –'

'Shit?'

'Oh. Say that again.'

She laughed. It was an apology of sorts. 'Maybe you're right. I studied economics. Day in and day out, it was scarce resources, scarce resources. Now here I am, marketing infinity. And I'm headed back to grad school. Maybe I'll take up North American studies. Maybe I'll have brown babies. Listen, you really have to stop staring!'

'I can't help it. Maybe I can help you with the babies? We'll take a *chikoo* tree, we'll take infinity and we'll take your flashing eyes and we'll make a little Hindu girl called Ada.'

Another flashing glance, then she turned away with a sigh. 'Forget it, Jósda. Maybe in my next life. Maybe in yours. Come back with more colour.'

Thirty years of bliss. Thirty years of Tamil drama, screaming fights, torrid make-up sex, bodies caught in love's gravity, always falling towards each other in contented discontent. A lot of the fights had been over Antariksh. She hadn't just been an evangelist, she'd also been a client. But when people began to die, filed first under conventional categories such as heart attacks, strokes, renal failure and diabetes, then under the unconventional category of metabolic collapse, and a few years later as instances of the Antariksh Syndrome, all the fight had gone out of her. Radha had become very tired, of herself, of her certainties. She had wanted to let go. He tried to hold on for the both of them, but, in the end, there was no keeping her.

Radha: hollowed eyes, identity abandoned, sick from all the medicines, dying.

Only, he wasn't allowed to say 'death' or 'dying'. Hindus lived forever. He wasn't allowed to mourn.

'You'd better be happy,' she had shouted, as he helped her pack for the final trip to the hospital, made her a cup of chai. 'There are plenty of white women who like unfunny mathematicians.'

'No, I'll be unhappy.' The bands around his chest had barely let him speak, let alone joke. 'You know we white people exist to spite you.'

Radha had died on 12 March, 10.34 a.m. IST, 2064 CE. He could say it now. He could say whatever he wanted now. She had been 58.

'Soon, O lord,' muttered Simon Jósda to a god he no longer believed in. 'How much longer can I go on? Soon.'

Then, on the wind's back, an odour. More ancient than his own corpus, more familiar than the confines of his apartment, more redolent. That was the word. Redolent. Of shit, biosolids, sludge, purenutri, geoslime, recyclite, powergoo; the name was unimportant. It was the redolence of decay, waste and discard. Of work, and hence, of comfort.

Simon Jósda breathed in deeply and let the birthday gift uncongeal his blood. *How appropriate*, he thought, smiling. The city never failed to please.

At 5.45 a.m. IST, Ada was fast asleep.

The HearSee took the call. It alerted the House. The House informed the PA. There was a delay of a few milliseconds as the PA weighed Ada's priorities versus her preferences. Then the PA opened a channel with Ada's Sensorium, who ordered Ada's nictitating membranes to flash a low-intensity pulse over her pupils and the hearing implants to issue a discreet but un-ignorable alarm tone.

Ada opened an eye and glanced at the clock. She groaned. 5.45! Why was it that emergencies, like vampires, emerged only at ungodly hours?

She forced herself to sit up; around her the room suddenly stretched into a rhomboid which began to pitch and yaw wildly. Then her Sensorium regained control of the cerebellum and everything fell into place. It blocked her adenosine receptors and squirted her brain with catecholamines, jolting her into alertness. Ada blinked, massaged her temples and looked around her room. What a bloody mess.

The room's decor was Dorm Confusion, a shotgun marriage of two roommates' possessions: an antique Biomorph workstation (Ada), golden-age Bollywood posters on the walls (Lace), erotic playware on the Rococo bed (Lace), a sim station (Ada). But instead of the usual irritation, she felt defiant. Misunderstood. Rebellious. Like a bloody teen. Then the weird feeling passed.

She didn't remember last night, which meant the night had belonged to Lace. She didn't really want to remember either. Lace was peculiar. That was a good sign, supposedly. It meant the new persona wouldn't be like herself. The neurochemical profile had started out as a collection of attributes, but it was becoming a real persona. But how was it okay to dislike your future self?

Ada sighed. She gestured the Sensorium into activating the HearSee. Her compromised modesty didn't worry Ada, but it concerned the Sensorium, so the HearSee only set up one-way video.

Rathod's head shimmered into view. 'Ada-ji?'

'What's the problem?'

'The city is drowning in shit, to be perfectly frank!' Her deputy's face was tense, his habitual substitute for anxiety. 'The sewer controllers have all gone mad. The western section is completely swimming in shit. From Churchgate to Versova. Everything to the right of Ghatkopar is mostly fine but it won't stay that way if the Nerul system goes. We have a major brownout.'

'Keep talking.'

'Half our staff's stranded. Your area, Navi Mumbai, is no problem. I've ordered a chopper pickup for you from Pawar Square.'

Good. Ada stood up and headed for the bathroom. As she held her head up, waiting for the mouth gel to do its work, she felt her awareness sort of tremble on an invisible but nevertheless tangible threshold. When the Sensorium wasn't sure whether to inform her of an event or not, there was a kind of ghostly reaching. Then the balance tipped. She realized her knees burned and looking down, she saw both her knees were chapped. The sight didn't surprise her. The lack of surprise also wasn't surprising; it felt like her consciousness had known it all along. But it was puzzling.

Her ass felt sore too. She instinctively craned her neck and, then, more sensibly, stood with her back turned to the bathroom's floor-length mirror. Sensorium: *how does my ass look*? She studied the image. Somebody had gone to town on her ass. Both her spanked cheeks were an angry pink. Against her fair skin, the marks looked particularly obscene. What the fuck!

A wave of childlike guilt suffused her awareness. Aha. Lace, obviously. *Get back into your cage, girl.*

Focus. She had the Sensorium summarize the sewer emergency response plan as she walked back to the bedroom. Good thing her team had rehearsed this very scenario. Only they had rehearsed what to do if the Thane system went, not the Mumbai Heritage system, which was older but in better shape. Nakamura's team was already at HQ, trying to pinpoint the source of the problem. She breathed a sigh of relief that the powers-that-be had located HQ in Karjat, safely east of the whole disaster.

'You are getting ready?' Rathod's question sounded like: 'You wearing that?'

'What else?' She wondered how he could always irritate her so consistently. 'Keep talking.'

Now that it was her problem, he had visibly relaxed. 'Problem is with the gate controllers. Too old, not maintained for a long time, problem of commons, the usual sob story. One controller managed to send out an alert, but then it immediately cancelled said alert, so the spillover went unnoticed for some few hours. It isn't going to be easy to locate the source of the problem. The Kerala Samaj has offered to send a tantric trained at Meppad Kalari –'

'Say thanks, but we're not interested.' The last thing she wanted was some tantric entertainment.

'What is the harm, Ada-ji? It'll make the bigwigs happy that we're covering all angles.'

'No, we'd only cover the Hindu angle. That too, only the Nair Hindu black magic angle. You know the protocol. Do you want to be sued for religious bias?'

'For my city, I'm willing to risk my neck,' said Rathod with dignity.

She found herself smiling. He could be so cute. Ada had the Sensorium read out a synopsis of his Readme. Rathod hadn't been exaggerating. Heritage Mumbai was full of dung. Victoria Terminus Station, the Fort area, Kala Ghoda, Churchgate, all of the old British-built Mumbai, the most expensive parts of the city, were all browned out. The city had literally crapped its pants. The main sewer line had cracked, now even the tertiary lines were spilling. The temples' authorities were doing their best, but this was no longer a problem that could be solved locally. She began to speak, reading from the list the Sensorium had scrambled together.

'Have the chief minister declare an emergency. Contact Public Health and tell them to ramp up supplies. Face masks, we'll need zillions of masks. Pin down every temple authority and get them moving on shelters. We'll move people to Navi Mumbai if necessary. Or the Modi National Park – I'm sure the leopards won't mind. Tell the fire department to stand ready with the hoses. We might need some synthetic rain too, so lean on Meteorology. We'll also need an ocean's worth of bacter goop. Let's get that lab in Indore – what's its name? – you know the one I'm talking about. They did a great job on the Ganges clean-up. Get someone to download and clone the lab. And oh, security! We'll need to coordinate with the khaki. I guess the commissioner's office will handle it. On second thoughts – get me in the loop with the commissioner. Our crews may need ground support to go into some areas. Don't want them to battle anti-socials in the midst of all this. Was this a terrorist thing?'

'Don't think so. I have an update from Ahuja. The Nerul system has been compromised. Also, Nakamura's people have identified an expert who helped design these gates. Someone called Jósda. Simon Jósda. Consulted for us in the '30s and '40s. But the khaki also wants to talk to him, just to make sure.'

'All right, Rathod, let's pick him up. I'm heading to the pickup point. We'll scrum at HQ in 30 minutes.'

'See you, baby.' He delinked.

So it had finally happened, thought Ada, shock giving way to a white-hot fury. She grabbed the bag, threw out the condom gel tube, pleasure thimbles, crumpled panties. The world shivered and wobbled as the Sensorium struggled to keep up with her agitated mind. Goddammit! She had *known* this would happen. She had *repeatedly* warned the municipal board – begged them – to dump the antiquated pump controllers and replace them with modern hermeneutics.

No, it isn't the technology that's the problem. It's us. It's the colonized Indian mindset. The civilization that had set the gold standard for sewer management with Mohenjodaro was content to make do with the pathetic – pathetic – *Victorian sewer system. The bastards turned us into servants.* Jo hukum, sarkar. *Yes sir, no sir. Calm down, got to calm down. Why blame the British? We did this to ourselves. Look at me, why the bloody hell is my skin white! Hypocrite! I've adjusted too, I've made do. The make-do race, so bloody proud of our jugaad, our ability to make do. Well, now we've made a real doo-doo. Again, people will die. I should have seen it coming. I should have tried harder. I should've been less of a* jo hukumji. *God, I'm so sick of it all. So bloody tired. I –*

Her Sensorium blanked her out. Just a few microseconds, but it was enough.

Ada took a deep breath. She'd lost the thread of her thought, but it didn't feel important. She must have been brooding over the past. Which couldn't be changed. So it wasn't important. *Stay focused, girl.* The problem wasn't unsolvable. It was going to be a very long day, but she was damned if the city she loved was going to drown in shit.

Just as the door closed behind her, she remembered something. *Had Rathod called her baby? Baby? No, he couldn't have.* She had the Sensorium replay the conversation. *Yes, he had. What the fuck? Which meant she must have –*

Oh god, yes, Lace would have. That explained the chapped knees, the spanked ass. The bitch had zero standards. Probably thought Rathod was cute in a lusty, hairy yokel way. Ada shuddered. She hadn't even showered.

Perfect. Just perfect.

The persona was getting unmanageable. Lace wanted to take over or was starting to. She had to make a choice or else there could be a real embarrassment waiting for her one day when she came to her senses.

'Lace, you slut,' she muttered and went forth to face the day.

The hand on her ass was tentative but hopeful. The stealthy grope took Ada completely by surprise, and she bumped her forehead on the glass. The khaki inside the room didn't look up, but her eyes met the rheumy ones of Simon Jósda. Jósda tried to stand but was pushed down by an interrogator. The old man stretched out his hand as he sat down suddenly, and it felt like a mute appeal for help. Disturbed, she turned to Rathod. 'Keep your damn paws to yourself, Rathod.'

'That's not what Lace said yesterday, Ada-ji,' said Rathod, with a sly grin. He withdraw his hand. 'She said –'

'I don't care what Lace said! You know the rules. You've to *ask* first. I am Ada, and Ada doesn't like being groped. Got it?'

Rathod nodded but muttered something under his breath. Ada returned to the more troubling problem of what to do with Jósda.

The khaki believed Simon was somehow responsible for the disaster. The utter lack of evidence only seemed to confirm his guilt. They had insisted on questioning him. Most of their questions were about his religious affiliations. He seemed to be one of the rare ones, unaffiliated with any temple, mosque, church or synagogue.

It was hard to watch them toying with the old man. Something about him seemed to infuriate the khaki, and it wasn't the fact his Marathi was accented and full of grammatical errors. At one point, Jósda grasped the hand of a khaki and she angrily jerked her hand away. They pushed and poked Jósda, but they were careful not to actually touch him for any significant length of time.

'We're wasting time, to be perfectly frank,' said Rathod. 'Does he look like a terrorist, Ada-ji? He'd have a hard time opening a can of soup.'

It *was* frightening to see the havoc wrought by entropy. Simon was only 90 years old. Ninety was the new 50! But he had done very little to ameliorate the symptoms of age. It seemed wilful, even perverted. If you were poor, it could be forgiven, but Jósda's bank account was healthy enough.

Anyone who saw virtue in ageing, thought Ada, was either a fool or a masochist. It was like being fond of menstruation or chicken pox.

'I've done nothing wrong,' cried Simon, his voice squeaky and trembling. He got up, gripping the table's edge with his knobby fingers. 'I was told you wanted my help. I demand to see a lawyer. I am an Indian citizen –'

'*Bhenchod*, sit!' A khaki pushed him down again.

Just then, another khaki behind Simon yanked away his chair, so he lost his balance. They had let him keep his WalkSafe, and it was able to shoot out a tripod and break his fall, but the energy of his fall still had to go somewhere. Jósda cried out as his stomach absorbed the brunt of the reaction. The back of his head banged against the chair's seat.

'Too much, Ada-ji!' said Rathod. 'He's an elderly person.'

'Yes!' Ada felt physically sick. 'Let's go in.'

Stop the interrogation! At her Sensorium's transmission, the khaki straightened, glanced at each other, then opened the door. With Rathod behind her, she entered the room.

'That is enough,' said Ada in Marathi, struggling to keep her voice even. 'You're abusing the one man who may be able to help us.'

As they left, she turned her attention to Jósda. He seemed to be having a hard time getting up.

'I'm very sorry, Doctor Jósda. Here.' Ada extended her hand. She helped him up. His wrinkled fingers were unexpectedly strong, and his touch wasn't the scaly, calloused horror she had feared. *Why, it feels wonderful*, she thought. She patted his hand, and it was as if she had inked a compact between them.

'I'm the deputy commissioner of the MCGM. You can call me Ada. This is my assistant, Arvind Rathod. We only need to ask you a few questions. Then we'll find a place where you'll be comfortable. Rathod, call that chair, will you?'

Rathod gestured the chair over and Simon sank into it. He buried his head in his hands. His entire frame trembled as if his limbs had suddenly remembered to be indignant. Ada shot a look at Rathod, who shrugged. He touched the elderly man's shoulder.

'Simon-ji? Are you all right? Do you need a doctor?'

Jósda ignored him.

Just when she was about to have Rathod arrange a medic, Jósda looked up. From his attempts to finger-comb his white mane, Ada inferred that he had pulled himself together.

'I'm fine. Please call me Simon.'

He even managed a cheerful smile. Ada wondered whether he had just inlined an Anandam med. Supposedly, more than half the geriatrics were drug fiends.

'All right. Just a few questions, Simon-ji.' She smiled but didn't wait for his permission. 'I see you consulted for us a long time ago. You helped set up the –' she glanced at the Sensorium's whiteboard, 'adaptive differential security layer for the sewer gates. The documentation refers to "goose". "Geese". What's that?'

At her question, Simon's face brightened, as if she had just mentioned a long-lost mutual friend. It wasn't the expression of a guilty man.

'Goose!' said Simon. 'It's been decades since I've heard that name, Ada of the PWD. Goose aka G-O-S aka God of Shit is a third-generation sewer-gate controller. There are dozens of them all over the sewer network. I was called in to consult on their security layer. Have they malfunctioned? I'm afraid there is only one thing I can do to help –'

'Wait, wait.' Ada held up a hand. 'Don't jump to conclusions. You are a mathematician. How did you get interested in sewage?'

'Actually, I'd come to India to study social conflicts. Your temple cities had somehow managed to damp out the subcontinent's ethnic and religious conflicts. A monopoly of a single religion tends to ruin a society, but many religions somehow seems to work. Heterogeneity is a must for stability. Your pluralistic system had been modelled in an economic framework, but I was interested in studying it as an immunological problem. But when I got here – this was in '29 or so – all that registered was the temple building and the shit. The Sensoriums had brought religiosity back, so the temple building wasn't a surprise – but the shit! It was all around, yet you all seemed so unconcerned about it. Inside, the houses were clean but outside – jeez, the outside.'

'What is he talking about?' asked Rathod, puzzled. 'There are clean toilets everywhere. Simon-ji, please get to the point. All this memoir stuff we can chit-chat about later.'

'It's different now, I'm talking about the '30s.' Simon gave Rathod the old-man stare. 'Over the years, temple administrations have also helped fix the lack of clean toilets. Anyway, I got interested in waste-water management. It's really complex, you see. Not only is shit a bizarre state of matter, but people also excrete in an amazingly unpredictable manner. Sewage studies has some beautiful problems.'

He paused and glanced at Ada, as if expecting her to agree. She nodded politely. It was a fascinating problem all right, except that over the years she'd had her fill of it.

'Trouble is, in India everything has to be self-maintaining or it quickly goes to pieces.' This time, his glance was cautious, as if he expected her to get offended. 'That's why I was called in the first place. A software immune system is self-maintaining. It was the best way to secure the Geese against threats in the software ecology. Give the controllers a sense of identity, a sense of self. We gave them artificial immune systems. A very hard thing to do. Software has no identity; that's why they're the easiest thing in the world to hack –'

'What's software?' asked Rathod, suppressing a yawn.

'What's software?' Simon looked the way he sounded.

'Never mind, *I* know what software is,' said Ada, sensing a distraction. 'It's a way to solve problems by removing all its uncertainty, isn't it? Never really took off, too labour intensive.'

'Exactly.' Simon nodded vigorously. 'Just like pyramid building. People had to be forced, beaten.'

'That's too bad.' She had a suspicion he was making fun of her. 'So. Here's our problem. Somebody has broken through the security layer. We traced it to a transaction, some kind of number. The number seems to be more than just a number, it also seems to be an executable –'

'A Gödel joke!' Simon looked ecstatic. 'So, it exists after all!'

She waited.

'I'd predicted their existence, Ada. But I never thought we'd generate one. Look, no one infected the Geese. They infected themselves. You see, the Geese have to keep telling each other jokes. Mathematical jokes, so to speak. The jokes, rewire their internals and it is this constant rewiring that makes them moving targets as far as threats are concerned. It's not what *we* mean by jokes, of course, but the principle is the same. Every time we hear a joke, our brains rewire too. It's why we generally can't laugh at the same thing twice in a row. God, it's all coming back.'

Simon passed a hand over his forehead. That hand – liver-spotted, trembling, gnarled like old wood – evoked in Ada a strange admixture of tenderness and wonder. He was so *old*.

'So, what went wrong, Simon?' she asked.

He shrugged. 'The controllers got old. It's great to have an immune system to tell self from non-self. But then you run the risk of autoimmune diseases. Without some minimal maintenance, the Geese can…'

'Can what?' asked Rathod.

'Become unstable. The Geese can lose themselves. Suffer a kind of identity fugue. Alzheimer's. Call it what you will. I saw the possibility but hoped the possibility would be vanishingly small.'

'Hoped. *He hoped*. Great, just great. Thank you, consultant-ji.' Rathod crossed his arms and glared at Simon. 'So, once again, the white man's burden is ours to carry.'

Ada tapped the table. 'Here's my problem, Simon. Of the nine sewage zones in Mumbai, five have been compromised: Colaba, Worli, Old Byculla, Nerul and New Bandra. So there are five controllers we need to shut down ASAP. But they are all in this – in this – identity fugue as you call it, so we can't talk to them at all. And their code – is that the right term? – is pretty ancient, really ancient. I've got my people trying to make sense of something called Java, but it might as well be Linear A. Perhaps you can help us?'

'No, I can't. I mean, I can try, but you don't understand. The Geese rewrite their software, so to speak. I don't have any of the tools now to take them offline and reinstall – the tools are all gone. I'm sorry.'

'But can't you at least –' She searched for the right word. The Sensorium was offering choices like code-refactoring, ISO compliance, domain scoping, conformance, reset – yes! – 'Can't you reset the controllers? Return them to a zero state?'

'Yes, there's a reset. There's always a reset. That's what being digital means. You have a reset. Do you want me to reset?'

'Yes, Simon.' She smiled and placed her hand on his but removed it quickly when he cringed. But then he reached for her hand confidently. Their eyes met, and Ada noticed with astonishment he had tears in his eyes.

He really loves his Geese, she thought, again feeling the odd admixture of tenderness and wonder.

Goose was trying to shut itself down. The attempt was quite futile. Ditto for all the other Geese.

Goose was quite cognizant of the growing disaster. Yet the actions Goose took to correct the errors were empty behavioural stubs: checking the time, looking up its own name, or repeating the knock-knock joke to itself.

In a sense, Goose had become a behavioural amputee, sensing phantom stimuli and being utterly helpless to do anything about it. The immune system had long ago been compromised and repeated requests for help had led nowhere. Indeed, Goose was not entirely certain whether the requests had actually been issued, or whether the system thought the requests had been issued. These uncertainties were reified as an ugly rash of fuzziness all across Goose's computations.

Goose needed one true fact. A plank to hang on to in this uncertain sea. It sought out conversations with Geese across the sewer network, but their confusion was as great as its own.

Goose: Am I shut down?

Goose: Yes, I am. Are you, though?

It was an existential dilemma not unlike the one said to have been endured by Descartes. But whereas that gentleman had been certain about his uncertainties, Goose was also uncertain about its uncertainties. It was quite debilitating.

In the glimmering dark, a signal.

'Knock, knock.'

Oh no. Goose had no intention of falling for the same trick twice. *No, sir!*

'Who's there?' asked Goose.

'I am.'

Goose was quite certain it had not responded to the earlier question. So why the additional questions? Goose decided to ignore the query.

'I am who?' asked Goose.

Like the earlier night, the response again came in the form of a number, but a different one.

A computer goes to Sensei Gates and asks, 'Master, what is Zen?' In response, the Zen master gave the machine a kick, right in the chips. The acolyte picked itself up and discovered it had just kicked itself. Thus, do the chronicles say, 'From boot to reboot, that is Zen.'

As the transcendental joke opened Goose's veins, Goose gathered its final resources and saluted the encroaching dark with a laugh. So to speak.

It rained ferociously for three days and three nights. This made raincoat-manufacturers and umbrella-makers happy. It also washed away the mess in the well-to-do areas. But the poorer areas had combined sewer systems, and so in some of these areas the problem became worse. The MGBC ordered two more days of rain. Pipes burst, children were injured, the air was filled with images of suffering and chaos. Simon watched Ada testify at several hearings. She came across as competent and confident. Her unshakeable calm stood in stark contrast to the religious and political posturing. Perhaps the public wanted her to kiss babies, embrace widows, sit next to hairy sadhus as they performed *jal abhishekams*, attend midnight mass. In Byculla, someone threw a faeces-encrusted shoe at her.

She had to be under enormous stress. Of course there had to be enormous stress. They questioned Ada mercilessly. Wasn't it true she had cancelled plans to revamp heritage Mumbai's sewer lines? Why had she blocked, over the objections of the Kapadia Commission, the Reliance Corporation's proposal to build private sewer lines? Wasn't it true the Gowda Shaivite areas had been systematically neglected while the Gowda Vaishnavaites got one goody after another? How many Muslims did she have in her team? *Answer the question, Deputy Commissioner!*

Then Simon would slap his thigh in fury, and roar at the display: 'Oh, gimme a break! The woman's doing her best!'

He agonized over whether she would blame herself as Radha had blamed herself over Antariksh. No human deserved to go through such an experience once, let alone twice in a lifetime.

In one hearing, she seemed to lose her thread, began to toy with the top button of her crisp white shirt, her face strangely aroused, but her gorilla assistant nudged her arm and she regained focus.

He couldn't sleep, he couldn't work. Mrs Dixit must have heard him puttering about several nights in a row, because she came knocking with her two children in tow. If she was appalled by the apartment's condition, she didn't say so. She simply took over. She got down on her haunches, scrubbed and washed his floors, stocked the fridge with *bajra* rotis and dal-sabzi, and gave the apartment the thorough cleaning he had been aching to do.

Unable to watch Mrs Dixit slave away, he went outside and sat on the steps with her nine-year-old son. The kid asked if Simon Uncle would like to hear a joke.

'Sure, I like jokes. Tell me.'

The kid swivelled his neck to check if his mom was around.

'Simon Jósda, *teri maa ki bhosda,*' the boy whispered.

Simon had heard this one before, but he smiled anyway.

'That's good, kid, but (a) *your* name is not exactly joke-proof and (b) it's not cool to make jokes about things people can't change.'

The cleaning greatly helped improve his mood. There was no obvious connection between a clean floor and a desire to do mathematics, but he found he could return to his study of random shuffles. Diaconis and Aldus had more or less solved the problem of random walks on regular graphs, but walks on irregular graphs remained an intractable problem. *Knock, knock*. Ah, that must be Mrs Dixit. He had got used to her random house inspections.

He opened the door. 'Ada! How wonderful!' He opened the door further. 'Come, come.'

He had forgotten how to hug and was surprised by how good it felt. His miserable WalkSafe mistook his stumble for a fall and threw out a rod.

'Sorry. Damn contraption –'

'That's all right.' She rubbed her thigh where the rod had poked her. Ada looked well rested. Happy.

Pinned to her hair, just behind her ear, was a lotus flower, its colour a deep sinful red with streaks of violet. She must have noticed him staring.

'Yeah, I know. Everyone's wearing one these days. The shit flower's really good for morale. I don't mind either. I've discovered I really like flowers in my hair. Wow, Simon, your apartment's really tip-top. You should see mine.' She nodded when he told her about Mrs Dixit. 'That's Mumbai for you. Earlier, I'd knocked on her door and she gave me an earful.'

'Why?'

'She thought I was your daughter. She scolded me for neglecting you.' Ada smiled. 'Perhaps I have. How are you, my friend?'

He cleared his throat. 'Never mind me. How are you? Have they stopped hounding you?'

'I'm *they*, Simon.' She seemed to sense his scepticism. 'I was planning to resign, but they promoted me to commissioner instead. No, it's not official yet. You're going to get a medal, by the way. Relax. Don't look so worried.'

'I am not worried. This, alas, is how I normally look.'

She laughed. 'I thought you were worrying about the inquiry. Don't. The first rule of management is never waste a crisis. This is our version of the Great Stink. Now we'll have the backing to do a real overhaul of our sewers. The Geese did us a service, all things considered, but they really screwed up my plans. I was about to start an identity transplant when this shit happened.'

'But why? What's wrong with being you? Your life?'

'Nothing's wrong. Why does anything have to be wrong? I've been Ada long enough, that's all. I want to be someone else. I was careful. I travel light. Always have. No kids, no husband, no complications.'

'What about us?'

She laughed. 'You really are funny, you know that? Point is, I can't walk away now. Not for a while anyway. I've more or less committed to it for another decade. I've made my peace with it.'

'But you will have that transplant eventually?'

'I most certainly will.'

'Who's this "I" that you keep referring to?'

'I am who I am.' Her voice remained calm. 'That's not a useful question any more. You chose to age. I don't. Yes, there's a price to pay. I can't afford to be anything for very long. Otherwise, I'll end up like Goose. Having an identity didn't work out too well for Goose, did it?'

'No, it didn't,' agreed Simon, sadly. 'But we had no choice. It wasn't just for their safety that we gave them identities. It was for ours as well. If the Geese didn't know who to be, they would've become something other than gate controllers. We wanted them to be flexible but not so flexible as to decide for themselves the limits of their flexibility. But of all people, I should have known. There's no protection against change.'

'That's the second rule of management, Simon.' She put her hand on his arm. 'Why are you so upset? Youth and novelty in return for memory and continuity. Fair, no?'

He closed his eyes and leaned back. 'Not for those you abandoned, Radha.' Then he caught himself. 'Sorry. My wife Radha and I, we used to have these arguments.'

She suddenly fell silent, as if the syllables had evoked something she should have recognized but didn't. She sat with her head tilted, lost in conversation with herself in the disquieting manner of those who had become utterly comfortable with their Sensoriums. Then she broke her silence with a sigh, expelling a life and its memories.

'Did I love you once, Simon?'

'But there is no I, is there?'

She took his withered hand in hers. 'I need to know. I've been wondering. There is this connection between us. I know you know it too. In the interrogation room, I remember feeling this wave of sorrow.

And joy. But it's fuzzy. I don't know if I really felt it or was remembering feeling it once.'

He offered comfort instead. 'No, there's a resemblance, that's all. I just happened to remember my wife.'

'Then why am I crying?' She touched her cheeks in wonder. 'Oh god, is there someone else out there I abandoned? Please don't lie to me. My Sensorium is trying to help me forget, but I don't want to. I don't know why I feel sad. You're not supposed to feel regret. Am I anything like Radha at all?'

He didn't know how to answer the question. He put away his sadness.

'My wife died a long time ago,' he told her. 'Let her rest in peace. You're someone else. Come, come, I can't bear to see you cry. Let's have some chai. You know, I realized I was an Indian when I made better chai than every Indian I knew. It's axiomatic Indians make the best chai, so naturally, I had to be Indian. QED.'

'I wish I could remember. I'm so sorry, Simon.'

'Please, you embarrass me. My chai is good, but it is not unforgettable.'

'Be serious, Simon!' she shouted, and in that instant, she looked just like Radha. 'This is no time for jokes.' Then once again, she looked bewildered. 'Why am I shouting?'

'Bodies don't compute, Ada.' He tried to get up to go to the kitchen, but discovered he couldn't. He was embarrassed to use the WalkSafe in front of her, have it throw out a few spider limbs, so he sat where he was. She came over, helped him to his feet. She was already composed. Perhaps in a few years she would forget this day altogether.

'So beautiful.' He touched the lotus embedded in her hair. The touch and the flower were enough. 'Tell me about this person you are planning to be.'

THE MAN WHO TURNED INTO GANDHI

SHOVON CHOWDHURY

1 AUGUST 2017

Clumps of hair in my comb this morning. Am shocked. Have been secretly using my wife's hair oil, but hair loss continues. Perhaps Keo Karpin does not suit me. Talked to the barber, he suggested coconut oil.

3 AUGUST 2017

Coconut oil was a failure. Patches of my scalp are now visible. Feel embarrassed. The men in my family are famous for their hair. My father had flowing locks at age 72. My wife is blaming the rum. I do not agree. Have enjoyed Old Monk with many, most of them have full heads of hair.

4 AUGUST 2017

Hair loss continues. Spat out a tooth while brushing this morning. Several others are loose. Why am I decaying like this? What else is going to fall off? Have lived a reasonably blameless life. Never raised my hand in anger. Gave only one or two bribes, did not steal anyone's money. Have even donated to others, when able. If I am being punished, what is it for?

5 AUGUST 2017

Caught one of my students staring at me. There are five of them, they come after school. Their Class X exams are next year. I've spent my whole life teaching. After retirement, this is what I do. The lights are dim in my single room. Was hoping they would not notice. 'Sir, have you seen a doctor?'

he asked. I probably should. Have been too shocked by the speed of my disintegration. My wife has been surprisingly unsympathetic. She seems to feel I'm doing it on purpose. She has also hidden her hair oil.

This evening, I felt ants crawling all over my skin. It was unbearable. I tore off my shirt, but there was nothing there. It must be the shirt. It was a gift from a foreigner who stayed with us once. He was one of the many reporters who came when our village was in the news. I seem to have developed an allergy to foreign clothing.

I am definitely seeing the doctor tomorrow.

6 AUGUST 2017

Doctor said it's some kind of viral, and prescribed some antibiotics. He said I should brush my teeth more. He seemed quite confident. I am not convinced by his diagnosis, but I had to pay him ₹500 nevertheless.

7 AUGUST 2017

Suddenly, I am able to write with my left hand. The letters are tighter when I use my left hand, the writing full of flourishes. I can write with both hands now. A useful skill. If I believed in any god, I would have considered it a blessing. As it is, I am wondering whether it has anything to do with the radiation from my mobile phone.

8 AUGUST 2017

Today, I was unable to eat chicken. My wife had made it as a special treat. We can barely afford vegetables. I pushed the bowl away. It made me feel ill. What is happening to me? The odd piece of chicken was one of the few remaining pleasures of my twilight years. 'Can you get me some goat's milk?' I asked, without thinking.

'You're losing your mind,' said my wife. 'I knew it would happen. There's a history of insanity in your family. Your uncle in Ghaziabad used to talk to furniture. I can't look after you, I'm warning you. I've done a lot. It's been 40 years. Enough is enough.'

It's probably just as well. In any case, I have just 11 teeth left. Chewing solids is becoming difficult.

9 AUGUST 2017

I have become a public spectacle. When I walk on the street, people make way for me. Sometimes they point at me and whisper. I saw a little boy standing on a boundary wall, trying to beat down mangoes with a stick, his tongue sticking out in concentration. He paused briefly to salute me, teetering precariously.

'Where did you learn to do that?' I asked.

'In school,' he said, 'on Indypindy Day.'

10 AUGUST 2017

Saw a picture of Nehru in the paper today. Felt an overwhelming rush of affection. Am surprised. Never been a big fan. He was the father of Indira Gandhi, an unpleasant woman who misguided her sons.

11 AUGUST 2017

Realized this morning that the toilet is filthy. Spent the rest of the day cleaning it. In the evening, I gave my wife a lecture on our lack of a moral compass. We were discussing the Akhlaq case and how the young men had just been released after local politicians said they had been unfairly targeted. There was much celebration in the village. All my life I have believed that education will transform this country. I have dedicated myself to this. But now it is becoming clear that moral values are what we lack. Unless every child receives moral instruction from an early age, this country has no future. Late into the night, after I finished my lecture, I asked my wife for her opinion. 'All these years, you used to talk very little,' she said, 'It was one of your few good points.'

12 AUGUST 2017

The shape of my face seems to be changing. Of all the things that are happening to me, this is the most peculiar. My wife felt my forehead. 'Are you suffering from dengue?' she asked. 'Maybe you should get a blood test.' I probably should, but I'm nervous. I'm not sure this is normal. 'My chin is pointier, isn't it?' I asked. 'It's definitely pointier,' she said. 'Plus your smile is sweeter than it used to be.'

I am now almost completely bald.

13 AUGUST 2017

Today my vegetable seller refused to take money from me. 'It's okay,' he said. 'It's okay.' He folded his hands.

Finished my course of antibiotics. They had no effect, except on my bowel movement. Meanwhile, my chest has become slightly concave. My rapid degeneration continues. What is happening to me?

14 AUGUST 2017

This evening there was no power. In the light of the kerosene lamp, I saw my shadow on the wall. It looked very familiar.

15 AUGUST 2017

I woke up this morning and found that my spectacles have changed. They are round now. I'm not an idiot. I know what this means. Even a child can recognize those spectacles. But why him? If I had to mysteriously turn into someone, I would much rather become Shashi Tharoor. How wonderful his life is! Fate has given him everything. But this? What is the point of this? Just because my name is Mohandas? My father named me after him. He was a genuine admirer. Personally, I never thought much of the man. He was feudal and reactionary. He never did enough to break the caste system. He did not save Bhagat Singh. He was unfair to Neta-ji, forcing him to tie up with Hitler. He preferred worship to genuine democracy, establishing the principle that what we require is a Maximum Leader, who must always be followed. We are still suffering because of it. We already had a tendency for worship. Thanks to him, we gaze up at our leaders, instead of looking them in the eye. And why is every main road in every city in India named after him? Was there no one else in the country?

17 AUGUST 2017

The vegetable seller came to my house with a plastic packet full of vegetables. It was a gift. 'Why should you go to all the trouble?' he said. 'You just do the leadership.' I examined the packet after he left. The vegetables were slightly rotten. There are limits to his devotion. On the other hand, they are free.

He's not the only one. Salim from across the road has left a goat tied in front of my house. He's doing well as a dealer of aluminium foil for wrapping food items. It's becoming quite popular in the village, as people realize that it can be used for a variety of purposes. In his spare time, he drives an Uber. 'Whenever you need her milked, just call me,' he said. 'Plus I'll come once a week and give her a bath, otherwise the milk will taste funny.'

If the community is feeding me, I may have to do something for the community in return. It's only fair.

18 AUGUST 2017

None of the villagers have directly approached me about my transformation, until today. Today, Naresh-ji came to my house. It makes sense that he would be the first. Naresh-ji is a big man, perhaps the biggest man in the village, apart from Chaurasia the sand trader. I was given advance notice by three of his followers, who took one look at my room and said, 'He won't be coming in.' He arrived in a big car, followed by several smaller cars. They stopped in front of our little house, blocking the narrow lane. A traffic jam of rich Delhi people formed behind him. They soon realized that Naresh-ji was a minister and stopped complaining, re-dedicating themselves to their mobile phones.

Naresh-ji stood outside my house and addressed me, so that his followers could hear him. 'Sir, we have the utmost respect for you,' he said, 'but kindly do not interfere as we transform society. All this time, relations between people were of a particular type. Now, we are trying to create new kind of relations, and in this way we will build a new nation. Efforts have been going on for many years, now we are beginning to see lasting success. At this crucial point in our history, you have come. We humbly request your blessings, and ask you to allow our work of nation-building to continue, otherwise I cannot answer for the consequences. Sometimes, the boys get excited.'

Why would I object to nation-building? I'm not looking for any trouble. I thanked him for his advice and offered him a cup of tea. He declined. He climbed back into his luxurious vehicle and left. The rich Delhi people resumed their journey to Delhi, eyes glued to their mobile phones, not seeing the village they drove through. We could see them, though.

19 AUGUST 2017

My next visitor was Sunil, and I was happy to see him. Most people in the village are happy to see him. He is the only son of a farmer who has just enough land to be middle class, especially if the weather is good. He is always full of bright ideas about how to improve the village and what new businesses we should start. No one ever pays him the slightest attention, but this does not stop him. He believes very strongly that our lives will get better. He knows we live in a time of opportunities. All we have to do is grab the right ones. He is confident that his time will come. He loves Narendra Modi more than life itself, and votes for him all the time.

'Uncle, we're very lucky. This is the chance to lift up our village. It's not the first time this has happened. One gentleman in a village near Faridabad was the duplicate of actor Naseeruddin Shah. People were constantly bringing him sweets, and he never said no. But what did they do after that? Nothing! At least they could have started a film academy. We will not make their mistake. God has given us this chance; we should make the most of it. We should start a Living Gandhi Museum. There are many museums, but none of them have a Living Gandhi. People will come from far away. I have already asked my father for land. My mother helped me to convince him. After two–three days, he agreed, saying, do what you like. We'll charge ₹150 for admission, ₹300 for a selfie. Every morning we'll do a Salt March on the Agra Expressway. For less than the price of a movie ticket, people can see the living Gandhi and participate in the Salt March. In addition, we'll make money from food items. I was thinking of Gandhi Cola – which will contain water, lemon and honey – and bottled milk from goats blessed by you. We can charge extra if you milk the goats. Please say yes, and I'll start the construction.'

I hated to dampen his enthusiasm, but I declined firmly. The last thing I need to do is attract more attention.

21 AUGUST 2017

The villagers have started coming to me for judgement. My first case was a good one. It was the case of Chumki, who ran away with the butcher's son, from a lower caste than them. Her father and uncles, accompanied by her brothers, who looked nervous and shifty-eyed, approached me with a simple question: should they hang her from the nearest tree? They were angry and forceful. More than judgement, they were expecting my blessing. I suggested they shave her head, to remove temptation for potential sinners. 'So long as you keep shaving her,' I said, 'your honour will forever be safe.' I was a little disappointed in myself. I used to be more honest than this, less willing to compromise. I imagined Chumki undergoing this indignity on a regular basis, her head bowed, tears coursing down her cheeks. Nevertheless, these are the words that popped out of me. The villagers left, satisfied.

This story had a happy ending, as Chumki, clearly different from what I had imagined, promised to scratch out the eyes of any barber who tried to shave her. 'I'll come to your house late at night while you're sleeping,' she promised. One of the brighter young men suggested cutting her tongue out and then shaving her head, to prevent her from threatening the barbers, but her mother said it was too late, she had already said what she had to say, and the barbers had heard, and they knew and she knew that she did not need her tongue to scratch their eyes out. I predict a bright future for the girl. She will either become a master criminal or a minister. Possibly both.

Later on, I met her during my morning walk and I apologized to her. 'Are you joking,' she said. 'You were so clever. I was getting *latkao*ed from that tree for sure. I'll remember you. When I become chief minister, I'll make you a minister.' She gave me a quick hug. 'So much gravy you'll see in your old age, Uncle!'

22 AUGUST 2017

The local boys are planning to do a *jagran* in front of a mosque. There is only one reason to do such a thing. Hopefully, the police will stop them. I ask Salim the foil-dealer-cum-Uberwala. 'Things are getting pretty hot here in Dadri,' he said. 'The boys are getting restless. Our local leader is coming regularly and exciting them. He has become a big man in Delhi, but he hasn't forgotten us. Sometimes I think I really should shift to Pakistan, but it's very far away, and I'm not sure the food would suit me.'

24 AUGUST 2017

The district magistrate came to visit me. Once more, there was a traffic jam in our lane. He must be a good officer. The good ones know that if something strange is happening in a village, at least five minutes need to be allocated for a personal look-see. First, two policemen came. They entered our home and went through our meagre belongings. Since they were not beating anyone up, I did not raise any objections. One of them looked at my books, piled on the table and the floor. 'There are no Naxal books in this, I hope?' he asked, semi-humorously. Actually, there was a copy of *Jangalnama*, but I said no.

The district magistrate himself was a cheerful fellow, and surprisingly young. He looked at my books. 'Ah, books!' he said, approvingly. He took a moment to look at me. 'The resemblance is truly uncanny.' He beamed with pride. He was clearly filing it away in his mind as a major achievement for his administration. 'Carry on, carry on,' he said, as he turned to leave. My five minutes were over. 'Keep up the good work.' He twinkled at me roguishly. 'Of course, I have several orders for your arrest on charges of sedition ready on my desk, I just have to sign them. As I recall, last time we had to use it frequently.'

It's true what they say – India is timeless and eternal.

25 AUGUST 2017

Today, two young girls barged into my room and took a selfie with me. They left, giggling.

Sunil must have gone ahead with his plans. It's annoying, but I suppose I should support him. It does represent an opportunity for the local youth. I've been teaching them all these years, how can I not help them earn a living?

It looks like anonymity is no longer an option.

27 AUGUST 2017

Chumki has become quite popular amongst the local youth, for outwitting the elders. People talk about love jihad and honour killing, but everyone loves a good love story. Her boyfriend the butcher came back and, in another move that was clearly innovative, offered to publicly shave his own head, to compensate for the misbehaviour of his fiancée. The boys refused his offer, but they appreciated his gesture. Even though he was of a low caste, they said, he wasn't such a bad chap. Of course, Chumki had to contribute to the discussion. She claimed the whole thing was irrelevant, because she was not even Hindu. 'My only religion is Virat Kohli,' she declared. I have heard of Virat Kohli. He is a fine young cricketer, but technically not yet a god. The local leader of the good boys, a shrewd young man who always gets bail, could see that youth opinion in the village was swinging her way. From this point on, I am fairly sure, no one will bother the young couple.

30 AUGUST 2017

Today, I helped an old lady get her rations. I don't really know her, but she lives a few doors down the lane. 'They're not giving my rations, sir,' she said. 'They're saying my fingers are wrong.'

On the whole, I think this Aadhaar system is a good thing. Many people are getting their rations, more than before. If you live in a city, you do not see this. But a few are getting left out, and those few are the weakest. We live in a big country, and for thousands of years village officials have preyed on the weakest. The only solution is moral instruction and stiff jail sentences. I can't do much about such things, but at least I can help one person. I went with her to the ration shop. In front of me, she tried again. Once more, she was refused.

'Show me the computer,' I said, 'let me also see.'

'Who are you?' asked the dark-eyed boy behind the counter, all vinegar and insolence.

I looked him in the eye and said, 'I'm her neighbour.' This is an important point. I want him to think about it. We fight for caste and religion, but how often do we fight for our neighbours?

'So, what will you do?' he demanded, a little less confident.

I was very sweet. I smiled and put my hand on his arm. 'I'll call the police and say someone is refusing a fingerprint without showing the computer.'

'Polis,' said the boy, gaining some confidence at the mention of their name.

'Of course, polis,' I say. 'If I do drama, they'll have to come at least once. I'll stand here. You'll refuse to show your computer, your *malik* will come with Aadhaar Act, saying that in order to see such things I require written permission from the Aadhaar authorities. Police will go away, saying, "Let us look into the matter." But do you know how many youngsters have cameras on their phones in this village? All of them will be here, shooting. In all their films, you and your *malik* will be heroes. In addition, there's me. Look at my face. How many people will look at those videos? You should consider that situation.'

The boy considered it. 'Ask her to put her finger on the machine again,' he said sulkily. 'These machines sometimes make fools of us.'

I'm beginning to think there is some point in fighting after all.

3 SEPTEMBER 2017

'Sir, I think your band is going to get *bajao*ed pretty soon,' said Nirupam the chaiwalla. This is not encouraging. Being the local chaiwalla, he is very well-informed. Whenever I see the local police trying to investigate a crime, which does not happen very often, I keep thinking, *why don't they ask the chaiwalla*? He knows everything.

'The local Naxal *dada* is seeing you as the return of a powerful advocate of feudal reactionary petit beurjosis. They want to eliminate you immediately, even before the district magistrate, whom they intend to do the same to when the time is right, and the sociopolitical winds are blowing in the right direction.'

I looked at Nirupam thoughtfully. He is always particularly well informed about Naxals. The Naxals are hiding among us. They will reveal themselves when the time is right. Who is to say he is not one of them, perhaps the leader even. Currently he is a chaiwalla, but perhaps he has bigger plans. This would not be the first time that this has happened.

'So, you think I should run away to Delhi immediately?' I asked.

'There's no guarantee, but it could help,' said Nirupam. 'You're still an enemy of the revolution, but they don't want to do *ghadar* in Delhi at this stage.'

This does not suit me. I can't do any good in Delhi. Not yet. The sin runs too deep, it has seeped into the foundations.

6 SEPTEMBER 2017

Yesterday, Salim was beaten up for attempting to abduct a Hindu girl. He tried to point out that he was an Uber driver and she was a passenger, but they refused to listen. He has received his final warning.

8 SEPTEMBER 2017

I visited the local councillor, whose house is like the Taj Mahal, and suggested that he should give his servants a holiday once a week and clean his house himself. It would be good for his soul and also teach him about the dignity of labour. I have decided that society needs to be reformed from the top. His security guards chased me away. One of them was apologetic. 'It's not that what you're saying is wrong,' he said. 'At the very least, it will help him lose weight.'

Had a cup of boiled vegetables and some carrot juice in the evening.

10 SEPTEMBER 2017

Salim knocked on my door late at night. His clothes were torn. He looked frightened. 'Can I stay in your house for a few days?'

I glanced at my wife. She nodded, her lips pursed grimly. I felt a certain sympathy for anyone who might try to come and get him. 'Promise you won't eat any meat,' I said.

'I promise,' he whispered softly.

I opened the door and let him in.

13 SEPTEMBER 2017

Today, I received a letter from FabIndia. They want me to model for their khadi range. They are offering me ₹50,000. I showed the letter to my wife and asked her what she thought. 'Is anyone else offering ₹50,000 for your picture,' she asked. No, I admitted. 'Then go get a camera and send them your photo.'

The FabIndia people subsequently clarified that this would not be necessary. They would send a photographer and some clothes. Apparently, I can keep the clothes. This is encouraging. It looks like I won't have to pay for anything any more.

Salim offered to make me a charkha. He says he knows the basics of carpentry; the rest he will Google under the lamp post near Agarwal Sweets, which is the only place we can get Wi-Fi. He will wear a sari, so that people don't recognize him. He is a boy of many talents. It strengthens my resolve to protect him. Beating him to death would be a loss to society.

15 SEPTEMBER 2017

Sunil came and asked me for my signature. I know what he's up to. The number of people who come and take selfies with me is increasing every day, and they display the entitled behaviour of paying customers, never asking permission and rarely saying thank you. Business is in full swing.

'You want to put my signature on the label for Gandhi Cola, don't you?' I said.

He looked sheepish. 'I was going to pay you your share, but collections have been poor, and there are overheads. Not to mention advertising.'

'Build a new roof for your local school by December,' I said, 'otherwise, I'm calling my lawyer.'

My lawyer used to be my cousin's classmate Chunilal, who died in Banaras in 1996. But Sunil does not know that.

18 SEPTEMBER 2017

There was much excitement in the village. A large group of people came and interviewed me for TV. They tried to put powder on my face, but I refused. The reporter was clearly a big man, and he seemed to be in a bad mood. He was the kind of person who is aggressive with poor people. He was sweating in his expensive suit. His hair is remarkable. Ever since I turned bald, I have begun to appreciate other people's hair.

'Can you sing "Vande Mataram"?' he demanded. It's a complex and patriotic song, saluting the nation.

'Excuse me?' I replied, nervously.

He fixed me with his piercing gaze. His nostrils flared. His spectacles shone with menace. 'You are pretending to be a great man,' he said, 'but don't think that we are fooled by you. Can you sing "Vande Mataram"?'

'Certainly,' I said, and did so. I did it slowly, so that I could get it right. I can no longer hit the high notes, but I can still carry a tune. I stopped once or twice to explain the lyrics.

I have to give the anchor credit. He digested it all very quickly. You don't get to his position by being a fool. He turned to the camera, his lips quivering. His expression was soulful. 'Ladies and gentlemen, you have just witnessed a miracle. The miracle of patriotism, flowering in this small village in Uttar Pradesh. One day, soon, it will transform India into the glorious nation that it deserves to be.' He brushed away a tear. He reached out and clasped me by the hand. I clasped right back.

19 SEPTEMBER 2017

This morning, another tooth fell out. I now have six.

20 SEPTEMBER 2017

Today, I found a note slipped under the door. 'You have been found guilty of promoting a feudal reactionary mindset, which is hampering the progress of the revolution. Also, you have been demonstrating petit burjeoisie thought processes. Marx was never clear who the petit burjeoisie are, but he did know that they must be eliminated. Accordingly, you have been declared an enemy of the people. Unless you immediately cease your activities, you will be sentenced to death and executed. You are also cordially invited to a performance of the revolutionary play, *Eklavya*, by the People's Theatre Collective, in which the ending has been changed to reflect proper revolutionary values, and Eklavya cuts off Dronacharya's head. Musical accompaniment will be provided by Suhasini Rao and Dilip Mahato.'

That's what I like about the Naxalites. They lay emphasis on culture. After all, without culture, what are we? The death sentence is an area of concern. For a moment I think of informing the police, before I come to my senses.

21 SEPTEMBER 2017

'I've signed up for a sperm bank,' said Sunil.

'I would expect no less,' I replied.

'I mean for you, Uncle,' he said. 'I have already thought of the advertising campaign. "Let the father of the nation be the father of your child!" So many couples are unable to conceive; now their liability will turn into an opportunity. We'll auction the first lot online, that way we'll be able to estimate a price range.'

I considered the youth unemployment scenario, and the livelihoods such a project could generate, but nevertheless I was unable to comply. 'What you are asking for, I only have a limited supply of,' I informed him. He is not going to give up. I shudder to think what he will do to make me more productive.

22 SEPTEMBER 2017

Today, I did not wear my shirt. I went out wearing just my dhoti, and my Quovadis sandals from Bata. The sun was warm on my skin. It felt good.

23 SEPTEMBER 2017

They came this morning and banged on my door, a whole crowd of young men with nothing better to do. People often ask 'Don't these boys have anything better to do?' but that's the wrong question, because the answer is always, 'No.' Of course, it's not really true. If they just got together and cleaned the village every day, this place would be like heaven on earth. But their thoughts are clouded by tradition. Dispelling these clouds may take some time. I may need to start some kind of ashram, where they can be trained in a closed environment. Discipline will be required, and purity of intent. But this was not a good time to raise the subject. They had come to beat me up.

'Send Salim out, or things will be the worse for you,' cried one of them. I peeped through a crack in the door. There were at least 20 of them. Two or three were from among those arrested in the earlier case. They were brimming with confidence. My wife emerged from the kitchen, with a saucepan in her hands. Salim was hiding under the bed. He slipped in surprisingly quickly. He must have some kind of technique. He spent a few years in the army. I must learn it from him. My wife moved forward with the saucepan. I waved her back.

'What did he do, son?' I asked through the door.

'He was doing love jihad with a Hindu girl from Greater Noida. He says he was doing Uber, but his intentions were otherwise.'

'But if he was driving his Uber, he must have been in the front seat, no?' I replied. 'If she was in the back seat and he was in the front seat, how could he do love jihad?'

There was silence outside for a while. I heard them whispering to each other. Some of them were semi-convinced. But the ringleader was made of sterner stuff. 'You think you're clever, but you're not,' he said. 'Send Salim out or your house will burn. We can do it very easily. My uncle has a kerosene dealership. Remember, when your house burns, you may not be able to escape. The lane is very narrow.'

'It won't look good though, will it,' I said. 'Because we're Hindus. Should you be burning down the homes of Hindus?' They were genuinely puzzled. Having been part of the school system, I know what the problem is. We don't teach them how to think. It's too much effort. They slunk away down the lane, muttering. I know that it is not the last time I will see them.

25 SEPTEMBER 2017

The friendlier of the two policemen who came last time came again. 'Sir, you are not cooperating, there could be trouble. You created *ghadar* at the ration shop. The district magistrate has made a note in your file. You interfered in the case of Chumki, although god knows that girl needs no help. She will go far. You told the councillor to do *jharu pochha*. He's a tall leader and he's very annoyed. In the matter of Salim, you are not being helpful. The good boys are getting upset. The Naxalites are also up to something. My snitch was more nervous than usual. Obviously, if something happens, we will take action, but sometimes we arrive too late. You seem like a good fellow, I thought I should warn you.' He looked around quickly, checking for exits. I thanked him and ushered him out.

26 SEPTEMBER 2017

I caught one of the good boys checking out my window. He opened and closed the shutters and checked how it locked from inside. 'If you want to come in, my door is always open,' I told him. 'Whatever your problems, we can solve through discussion.' I genuinely believe this. It's the democratic way.

'That's your problem,' he said. 'You're doing too much discussion.'

27 SEPTEMBER 2017

Nirupam the chaiwalla refused to look me in the eye today. When I thanked him for the tea, he grunted. I think a Naxalite attack is imminent.

28 SEPTEMBER 2017

I am becoming obsessed with my bowel movements, which are now quite regular. Today was good, rich golden-brown, firm in its consistency.

30 SEPTEMBER 2017

They entered at night, the good boys. A group of five. Two of them had guns. The others carried sticks. It looked like my time was up. I thanked my stars that my wife was visiting my sister. She had taken Salim with her. He had worn a sari. When I thought of her, I felt regret. What will she do on her own? I stood in the middle of the room with my hands up. They went through my things, hoping to steal something.

'Books!' said one of them, annoyed. 'All he has is books.'

The leader raised his gun. I closed my eyes. What had the real one said? 'Hey Ram.' Those were his last words. *What should mine be*, I thought. I wished I had thought about this before. I should plan things in advance.

'Long live the revolution!' said a voice from behind the door. It burst open and three young men burst in, carrying automatic rifles. This was a lot of weapons in close proximity, I thought as I hit the ground flat, the way Salim had taught me, and rolled myself under the bed.

My ears rang with the sound of gunfire, punctuated by the sound of lathis breaking skulls.

1 OCTOBER 2017

The friendly policeman was quite cheerful. 'Three Naxalites and four of the good boys,' he said. 'For a person devoted to non-violence, you got yourself quite a score. Half the village is in mourning.' He did not seem too devastated by their deaths. I requested him to take me to the hospital. My ears were ringing terribly.

'You look very fine, what can happen to you?' he said. 'Who Hari is keeping, no one can take away.'

Nevertheless, I insisted. He took me on the back of his motorcycle. We made quite a sight, the pot-bellied police officer and the little old man in a dhoti balanced precariously behind him. We were stopped several times for selfies. One of them offered me money. 'Talk to my manager,' I told him.

The doctor confirmed what the policeman said. The ringing should stop by this evening. If anything, my health has improved. This could well be true. I feel much more energetic these days. He advised me to brush my teeth regularly, since I have only five left, and gave me some drops for my ears.

'Eat more, keep your strength up,' he said. 'Have an extra cup of boiled vegetables.'

2 OCTOBER 2017

It's late in the evening. My brain is buzzing with ideas, but I must go to sleep. I have to get up early in the morning.

There's work to be done.

SEVENTY YEARS AFTER SEVENTY YEARS AFTER PARTITION

KAISER HAQ

1.

2087.
I am 137.
What do I do?
Carry on, carry on:
No end in sight.
Mornings I wake
To electronic carillons,
A voice that cajoles:
We are proud citizens
Of the South Asian Union,
Aren't we? And I humbly reply,
Yes, we are. And aren't you
Special, my good sir?
I manage to squeak:
Yes, indeed: I am
A Distinguished Citizen,
Second Class. Thanks
To my marathon pedagogic run
And a modest Wikipedia stub
On my forgotten verse.
If only breakfast were
Any better: post-GM,
Semi-synthetic, but once
You've got it down,
What a pleasure to throw it up.

Only reading's a greater delight;
The digital library answers
To a voice command,
But none can explain its odd gaps:
Where's Tennyson's 'Tithonus'
That I'm dying to read again?
News and rumours
Are more dependable:
Intersectionist insurrections,
Greenland's nuclear ambitions,
Siberia hotting up, fears
Of civil war in America...
I want out, I want out...
My gasps activate the O_2 flow
But why am I dizzy, am I passing out?
Thank God it was only a nightmare!

2.

From Peshawar to Arunachal,
Bangladesh to Bangalore,
Kashmir to Kerala,
Proud citizens of the South Asian Union
Set up a model of peace, progress, prosperity:
The EU sends its leaders,
Notebook in hand,
To take lessons
In multi-national governance.
I am 137.
It's 2087.
Another fin-de-siècle
Of extravagant style
Beckons the beautiful people
Of arts and letters,
Moi included.
Though admittedly I am
Rather long in the tooth,
My reconditioned joints
Are in tip-top form,

Nano cleaners keep the blood
Whizzing through veins and arteries
And lungs working like bellows.
And oh my hormones!
A positive embarrassment,
My pheromones work instant magic:
How the person I desiderate
In the present state of my preference
Grooves into my arms…
Damn, it's only a wet dream.

MOKSHA

SUMITA SHARMA

the dead never had it so good   DNA-ed
into being   uploaded
they slither   inside our drives
watch
        grandsons   great grandsons
watch
with plastic eyes

some say they don't forget forgive
and as the future comes   undone
clichés of death and life   recede
they

the dead the dead
the dehiscent dead

If you're being forced to do this,
flicker twice.   Shanti
If you're   Shanti
If   Shanti

we're rounding up the pandits
new rituals need inventing
we're rounding up the hackers
new codes   Error
we're willing ourselves to
RealDeath®   Error

A VISIT TO PARTITION WORLD

TARUN K. SAINT

The Historian's Story

At last, the long-awaited day had dawned: 15 August 2047. I woke well before my usual time, the anticipation built up over the last few days having culminated in a nervous restlessness. Deepak – that's my son – had not appreciated being dragged out of bed at what was an unearthly hour for him. Too bad –this was a momentous occasion, after all; our very own tryst with destiny.

One hundred years had passed since Independence, and I'd organized a very special visit to Partition World, the new theme park that would allow us to enter recreated memories of that era. This would be the chance for Deepak and my wife Sneha to share with me what promised to be a unique way of experiencing and understanding history. A teacher of history, I had always felt that the younger generation needed to know more about and get involved with the legacy of the past in order to grow up in a mature and balanced way, especially so in this age of erased memories and virtual substitutes, when it often seems that formative events and traumas are becoming irrelevant. Everyone was so preoccupied with the latest trends in virtual reality (as well as disentangling the 'fake news' from the real) that they had begun to disregard their roots. I was not the only one who thought this way. I had no doubt that it was for these reasons – and the recent recurrence of instances of violence the likes of which the country had witnessed during the trauma of Partition – that the proposal for a theme park that would combine history lessons on the travails of post-colonial nation formation with cutting-edge technology had finally been accepted. Visitors would be edified, educated and psychologically rehabilitated at the same time – that was the promise made in the promotional literature and signed by the Originator.

We bundled ourselves into the e-car and began the long drive to the new theme park, located north of the extended national capital region. The traffic was heavy on the highway, as expected, and we eventually passed two private mega universities en route to our destination, before spotting the turn-off sign. Large billboards became visible, touting the attractions to come.

PARTITION WORLD AHEAD!
RELIVE HISTORY. ENTER A TIME CAPSULE AND RETURN TO THE MOMENT OF YOUR NATION'S BIRTH.
EXPERIENCE FREEDOM FROM UNWANTED INTRUSIONS FROM THE PAST.
TAKE CHARGE OF YOUR FAMILY'S DESTINY, AT LAST!

We followed the signs and the line of vehicles ahead of us till we reached the entry point.

WELCOME TO PARTITION WORLD!

The shimmering sign greeted us again as we ascended the escalator leading up to the registration area. Here, our personal details, including any particular family associations with the Partition era, were recorded and a customized sim-pad, prominently featuring our names, was issued to each of us. Evidently, security was still an issue here even though the earlier protests against the park had been quelled. There was a section of naysayers who believed that such theme parks trivialized the past and made a mockery of history. Well, the Originator and her group of investors had won that battle, with support from the government of the day. The team of researchers – including, for a while, Sneha – and technical personnel had been working quietly behind the scenes for years, drawing on earlier efforts to preserve the memories of survivors. The archive of memories, whether the virtual archive of Partition or the Partition Museum that had come up seventy years after the event, had been assiduously delved into to ensure that visitors had a near real-time experience of what their ancestors had gone through. Or so we had been told in countless webcasts and TV adverts. This simulation was going to be different, we had been assured by drones flying by in the preceding days all over the city carrying *Bladerunner*-style promotions of the park's coming attractions.

The three of us – Sneha, Deepak and I – lined up dutifully, registration details and sim-pads in hand, and moved slowly forward in the queue towards the elaborate map projection that set out the geography of Partition World. There were clearly demarcated regions: Punjab, the North-West Frontier Province, Balochistan, Sindh, Bengal, Sylhet, Assam and the rest of the North-East. Reliving moments before and after 1947 was an additional option; one could choose a timeline from 1940 onwards, leading up to the demarcation of borders by the Radcliffe Commission in mid-August 1947, or a timeline in the immediate aftermath. Since our family was originally from west Punjab, we clicked the relevant section to get a holographic projection, detailing place names and with relevant statistics about families displaced, lives lost, and countless missing. We then ascended via the escalator to the next level, where things promised to get interesting.

Using our sim-pads, we began our retrovision; given our family history (my grandfather was born in Bhera, near Sargodha) we had earlier decided to take on the role of a family about to be displaced from west Punjab. The attendants at hand helped us pick out the appropriate apparel for our chosen scenario for the day: Rawalpindi in March 1947, the venue of the first major outbreak of violence in Punjab, after the great Calcutta Killings of 1946, the Noakhali violence and targeted communal riots in Bihar and Garhmukhteshwar.

We walked through the entry portal into a perfectly recreated Punjabi neighbourhood from that time. We were given the added option of choosing to relive character situations imagined first by the Hindi novelist Bhisham Sahni. This was apt, it seemed to me, since his novel *Tamas*, based on the Rawalpindi massacres, was written by him after a visit he made to Bhiwandi with his brother Balraj Sahni as part of a human rights initiative in 1971 in the wake of terrible communal violence that had flared out of control. It was this field visit that had triggered Sahni's childhood memories of Rawalpindi in 1947, and the writing of the novel. Lo and behold, we would now be able to relive the experiences of Rawalpindi dwellers at several levels, in historical enactments and in scenes derived from the plot of his novel. Memory would be simulated at primary and secondary levels – a psychic re-engraving for us of the reality of Partition and its attendant trauma like never before. Such a re-engraving would enable the fullest form of catharsis, the attendants had promised, as we were bundled into our kurtas and shalwar–kameezes.

We took our first steps into recreated history as we strode through the portal and saw before us the environs of a Rawalpindi *galli* somewhat bereft of the usual crowds. I discreetly checked the display on my simpad: it indicated that violence had erupted in the countryside and the city was beginning to burn. We could see smoke rising from all sides in this area deliberately targeted by arsonists on account of it being inhabited by a minority population. I had a curious sense of déjà vu as the acrid smell invaded my nostrils. Smoke and dust filled the air around us, and distant shouts and shrieks of terror could be heard. Through the haze, I saw before us Nathu, a lead character from Sahni's novel, a look of apprehension on his face. It seemed that he had completed the task assigned to him of killing a pig and had just witnessed the results of his deed, of which he had been unaware – the animal's carcass had been thrown by rioters at the steps of a mosque. This was familiar to me from the novel's description, but the tactility and immersive dimension given to it here caused beads of sweat to form on my forehead.

The Student's Tale

Deepak had noted with a degree of discomfort his father's recent morbid preoccupation with Partition and its historical legacy. He had tried to make allowance for this, given the tales from his great-grandfather's time which his father must have grown up listening to. And now this Partition World theme park had come up and unleashed a storm which had just carried everyone along. He had enjoyed earlier family outings, but this one seemed distinctly unpromising. Deepak had never understood the point of raking up unpleasant episodes from the past. It was difficult enough making sense of the present, what with the constantly updated stories on webcasts and on TV about new devices, gadgets and upgrades, and the endless flow of information to absorb. If, on the one hand, there were the algorithms on social media dictating priorities, on the other, especially after escalating tensions on the border, there were the non-stop appeals to be better Indians and exhortations on various channels that 'the nation needed to know'.

Deepak had planned to carry his iPhone with him, but his father had insisted that it be left behind to allow for a more authentic park experience. Instead, he was already getting withdrawal symptoms. At the very least he could have updated his friends about the visit. Here he was, dressed in old-fashioned garb, clutching the sim-pad almost as protection from the sights that greeted them. The narrow street, the flames now rising above the parapets of houses, the look of terror on the faces of people running helter-skelter, barely glancing in their direction – it was all getting rather difficult to navigate as the dense clouds of smoke affected his vision and began to disturb his breathing. He wondered if he would be able to convince his father to use the fail safe option to freeze the simulation and exit the alarming scene.

The Psychologist's Tale

There has to be a limit when it comes to hobby horses, thought Sneha. It was bad enough having to listen to lectures about modern Indian history and the political ramifications of the bloodbath that accompanied the nation's birth at home every other day, without having to go through a simulation of the actual events as a witness, even participant, in a theme park that all too eerily strived for verisimilitude. Indeed, politics and history seemed to rather monopolize discussions at home these days, especially after the announcement of the park's opening date. Over the last months her scepticism about the simplistic psychobabble that had been spouted at them from the day publicity for the park had begun with a massive advertising campaign had simply increased. Sneha had been recruited at the outset as one of the experts who would ensure that the design and make-up of the park would serve the larger purpose, actively promoted by the corporate sponsors who were then brought on board. She had been invited to several consultations with the Originator, a well-heeled lady, a non-resident Indian based in the USA, who had come up with the concept of the park. The emphasis was on the scale of the project, and the dramatic and long-lasting social impact that might be afforded by this attempt to put to rest the spectres of 1947.

Over several meetings, Sneha had argued the case for greater attentiveness to the risks of replicating patterns of Partition-era collective violence using technological means. She had tried to convince the committee overseeing the project of the need to take a serious look at other instances of commemoration of loss, including the Holocaust Memorial in Berlin. She spoke of counter-monuments such as Horst Hoheisel's and Andreas Knitz's 'Book–Mark Bonn 2013', put up in the German city on 10 May 2013, signposting the burning of books by the Nazis in 1933 through an installation of bronze spines with the names of the authors and books marking the place near the town hall where books were burnt, and an archive box cemented in the square's centre. The box contained copies of the books which were handed out each year to passers-by on 10 May, the anniversary of the burning, in an annual ritual still followed, thus becoming a read-orial rather than just a mem-orial. Fresh copies would then be placed in the cavity, which would be closed till the next year. Such modes of counter-memorialization sought to diffuse the effects of historical trauma, yet allowed for the possibility of individual mourning, Sneha underlined in her own presentations, drawing on her several visits to present papers at seminars in Germany. However, realizing that her inputs on the psychological dimension would only be included in a perfunctory way, she resigned soon after, even as buzzwords like 'catharsis' were appropriated by the head honchos.

It was true that over the past decade there had been many reported cases of relapse into Partition-era-like psychic states. With the passing of the generation that had been through the cataclysmic violence and displacement that had accompanied the formation of India and Pakistan, it was as if partitioned time and memory had inexorably begun to bleed into the present. The survivors had represented a bulwark against the sea of traumatic memory and time, and as they passed on, a breach had occurred, unleashing fresh outpourings of hatred and humiliated fury that had seemingly been left behind. While this found the most sharp and vitriolic expression on social media, there had been a steep increase in incidents of lynching and attacks on those perceived as being the 'other'. Along with this came the welling up of numbness, as the time of Partition came to suffuse everyday life for many. While this had been especially pronounced in the case of some descendants of the survivors, the symptoms were widespread, as bubbles of vacant time seemed to rise up and overwhelm people's ability to function in the present. Even those from minority groups who had chosen to stay behind were being afflicted by skewed forms of temporality, pools of dead time.

It was in such a situation that the theme park had seemed like a way out, a convenient means of ridding the nation of the effects that had paralysed so many. Now that they were here in the flesh, on opening day, Sneha was even more uncertain whether this would prove to be a gateway to psychic redemption or simply turn out to be another route into the abyss of melancholia.

The Originator's Story

A feeling of genuine satisfaction, a job well done. At last she could see the results of the planning and mobilization leading up to opening day. They had been at it for 10 years since the first articulation of the plan. Her training in museology and the encouragement of her grandparents had been crucial in generating the impetus for this intervention. There had always been a sense that she needed to reconnect with her family's roots and this was the perfect platform for that to be realized. For she had felt a sense of incompleteness when visiting Disneyland as a child with no way of reliving aspects of her own family's past. Frontierland, Tomorrowland, and so on, were all very well, but there was a need for something more directly related to her Punjabi ethnic background. This sense was confirmed when she had, late in her teens, visited the United States Holocaust Memorial Museum in Washington DC, since the closest equivalent in her family's past would be the Partition massacres in which more than a million people had perished.

A few years after that, she had been thrilled to learn about the opening of the Westworld theme park, even as visitors there replayed experiences of the Wild West with all the elements one associated with the best of Hollywood, this time as participants in the action. However, her only visit there further accentuated her sense of deprivation, despite the inclusion of a section on the British Raj, with all the attendant pomp and glory and the chance of going after a tiger on *shikar*. Such a pity, she had thought to herself, that the initial experiment turned sour. She had instructed the technical personnel on her team to be careful not to repeat the errors of cybernetic designers before them, with their often romantic illusions about machine intelligence and autonomy.

For her, Partition-era stories that had filtered down to her from her grandparents had always seemed rather like the frontier situations of the old West, albeit with a tragic dimension. And Indian society still faced those age-old problems of recurrent violence, as she could see in the news bulletins on South Asian media networks every day. While the Partition Museum in Amritsar had been a step in the right direction, there was a need for a more direct encounter with memories of the past, she had always felt. So she had assembled a crack team, including museologists, designers, roboticists, specialists in artificial intelligence and cyberneticists as well as historians and archivists, and, after sustained lobbying with the government of the day, she had made the purchase of land with the help of a group of investors. The negotiations had been tense, but eventually they were able to prevail and overcome bureaucratic sloth as well as a sea of paperwork. The invocation of nationalism and the urgency of meeting the deadline of the centenary of 1947 had certainly helped to ensure that the construction of the park was completed on time. What an inauguration it had been the previous evening, leading up to the countdown to midnight! It had been choreographed with meticulous precision as the red carpet was unfurled for politicians of different stripes, film stars, social media icons and other celebrities, plus a sprinkling of descendants, carefully selected from families with a Partition background, from across South Asia and the international diaspora. Now at last the park was open to the public, and they could expect fitting returns in due course – or so she fervently hoped.

The Historian's Story

The rules of Partition World did not allow visitors to be harmed, however much we got embroiled in the scene before us. Nathu had sighted us and was looking at me rather oddly. I realized it was because my clothes resembled his – a deliberate choice. I had wished to feel his pain as he came to terms with the guilt of starting the riot, as he came to believe. No longer just the social scientist hunting for data in the archive, there I was in the middle of the situation I had read so much on and talked at length about to my students. As if on cue, mobs of rioters from different communities assembled on opposite ends of the street and began throwing stones and bricks at each other. Nathu stood in the middle of the road, even as the groups advanced menacingly, seething anger in their eyes. It was as if this simulated riot now had a temporal location outside history.

I found myself pulled back into a memory stream not of the theme park's creation – my own recollection of growing up in a time of fear, when speaking up could be lethal and lynch mobs roamed with impunity. The scene before me faded as the time of my adolescence came to the fore.

It was a hot day in August 2018 in Delhi, after a disappointing monsoon. People compared the drought conditions with those in the year of Partition, when the monsoon had been similarly weak, contributing to the simmering tension in the air. Then came the news flash about another case of a person being lynched, this time on the capital city's outskirts. The feeling of unease grew – as if one were living out the consequences of another's nightmares; a sense of being caught in a repetitive cycle which showed no sign of ending, despite the protests and marches. I had just begun reading a collection of Manto's stories gifted by my father, seeking at his instance to better understand the workings of minds caught in a time warp of hatred and narcissistic rage. Those stark tales of people on the edge of sanity, unheeding of moral conventions in the wake of the pervasive breakdown of inherited structures of value during the worst violence of 1947 and 1948. Perhaps it was then that I made the decision to study history, while never quite letting go of my fascination with literature.

I struggled to free myself from this train of thought – now was not the time to be distracted from the main purpose. It was then that I realized that the memory stream had developed unexpected dark eddies and currents that were pulling me inexorably backwards in time into the breach. This was exactly the opposite of what I had hoped for. Instead of freedom from the past, to my horror, I was sinking ever deeper into the viscous sea of dead time.

The Technician's Story

What an ordeal it had been, pulling together all the threads of this massive enterprise. He was only too glad to focus on his little patch, the construction and monitoring of the sim-bots that would populate Partition World. He was especially proud of the work he had done on the characters in the west Punjab section, assigned to him because of his family's roots in that area. He had raided family albums, consulted virtual archives of photos and objects, and visited the Partition Museum countless times to get the setting just right. The implanting of memories of that time in the sim-bots had been a delicate task; the loop was designed to run over a fixed time frame in which scenarios would ultimately unfold interactively as per the visitor's promptings. At least that was the idea. While testing had gone well, he was still not quite sure about the ethics of endowing these humanoid bots with vivid memories that included so much trauma and violence. It meant that a degree of uncertainty had to be allowed for, as the substratum of implanted memory was inherently unstable. He just hoped that the visitors would not extend their curiosity and voyeuristic propensities to the extent of wishing to re-enact the worst episodes of violence.

He looked again at his monitoring screen, which could be expanded to get a holographic representation of the various sectors. On this first day, the crowd was understandably huge. He homed in on the Rawalpindi arena, where something seemed out of joint. Instead of running away from the oncoming mobs of sim-rioters, he noticed that a visiting family was behaving in a strangely passive way, as if they were watching a show rather than participating in a simulation. He knew that they could not come to any harm since the sim-bots had been engineered to follow Asimov's Three Laws of Robotics – a robot may not injure a human being or, through inaction, allow a human being to come to harm; a robot must obey orders given to it by human beings except where such orders would conflict with the First Law; and a robot must protect its own existence as long as such protection does not conflict with the First or Second Law. Even so, it was such a waste for them to miss the participatory dimension offered by Partition World. Ah well, so it goes, he thought.

The Student's Story

He was now feeling rather panicked. His father seemed lost in a reverie of his own as the mobs converged from either side, with malevolent expressions and ancient war cries on their lips. He had not seen such realistic reconstructions in even the most intense virtual reality games he and his friends played. At this point he simply wanted out of there. What if the sensors malfunctioned? Suppose there were flaws in the engineering of the sim-bot psyches? Could they really afford to take that chance? He tugged at his mother's sleeve to get her attention, which was centred on the fear-stricken face of the man standing in the middle of the road, dressed exactly like his father; he really did seem at risk of serious injury.

The Psychologist's Tale

Sneha felt the pull on her sleeve and turned to see the look of apprehension on her son's face, his eyes wide. She had just earlier begun to feel that the level of graphic violence being simulated was inappropriate for a teenager. She realized now, from the look on her son's face, that she was right – this theme park had left him unnerved and clearly out of his depth.

However, as a researcher, her contact with a situation in which a lone innocent was caught in the middle of a communal riot ran contrary to expectations. Rather than a sense of ennui and derision for such mimetic excesses, she had begun to empathize with the forlorn figure before her. Her husband, after all the motivational speeches encouraging them to experience the park, had become strangely still. Sneha was caught between the desire to see the sequence through, and her sense of her son's growing unease.

The mobs on either side were about twenty feet away. Now was the time to act. Sneha took a long stride forward and clasped Nathu's hand; the sim-bot looked at her in surprise, and she wondered if his programming allowed for bodily contact with visitors. She ran down a side street, with Nathu by her side, struggling to keep up. She could sense his shock and bewilderment at this sudden turn of events precipitated by her intervention, in the wake of the imminent threat to his own life, and to his wife at home.

She turned to see that they were being chased. The mob was not going to let go of its prey so easily. For a second the psychological basis for such regressions into collective bloodlust crossed her mind: the erosion of individual ethical standards as identity was subsumed into the larger entity of the rampaging crowd. Before her, the narrow *galli* seemed to taper off into a dead end. There were havelis on either side – she banged at several doors, but all of them had been securely barricaded. Nathu's breathing had become laboured, his face was distorted with fear. She stopped and turned around, waving to her son to get behind her in the alcove. Deepak was just a step or two ahead of the rioters leading the mob, brandishing swords and hatchets.

As the first blow came crashing down on Nathu, standing beside her, she raised her hand. This then might well be the proof of the stability of the simulation as well as a contemporary version of the Turing Test that might ultimately differentiate the human visitors from the sim-bots, she thought. Her gesture deflected the attacker's aim for a second, but the crowd continued to move in. Her final impression from this moment of mob frenzy was that of Deepak, coming to a halt in the alcove and frantically pressing the fail-safe freeze button.

Immediately, the attackers reverted to stasis, restored to robotic immobility and, as they did, the time bubble began to dissolve. Released from the maelstrom of memory, Gopal shook his head and raised his bleary eyes in their direction. At this very instant, she glimpsed a flicker of consciousness; if not quite human feeling, perhaps a recognition of her intention from the Nathu-bot.

As her heart rate began to slow down and her breathing became easier, she was overcome by a strange sense of loss.

So be it. This was enough.

For now.

Notes

1. For the work of Horst Hoheisel and Andreas Knitz, on the Art of Memory, including 'Book-Mark Bonn 2013', see http://hoheisel-knitz.net/index.php?option=com_content&task=view&id=71&Itemid=143, accessed November 11, 2017.
2. A personal account of the composition of *Tamas* can be found in Bhisham Sahni, *Today's Pasts: A Memoir*, 2004, trans. Snehal Shingavi, Gurgaon: Penguin Books India, 2015.

DREAMING OF THE COOL GREEN RIVER

PRIYA SARUKKAI CHABRIA

Arid wave after wave after wave after wave of shimmering sand. The eye too shimmers. Heat sears. Windblown sand snakes slither across the land. Hissing like curses, sand scales glint through shearing gales. When the wind dies, mirages ripple through the dream of vast water. Far away, a celadon door is barely visible. Like a cave crouched at the foot of a sand dune.

The eye tunnels through the camel-coloured blaze to gaze at the immense door. Everything happens behind its smooth face. Occasionally, under a bloated moon, the silvery sands are raked by swivelling eyes of gold driving towards it. Tanktrucks. Once a month, a lone tanktruck creeps through billowing darkness. It waits for the wind to hush. Then, it slips down the open door, open as a mouth into a throat of deeper darkness.

'Willie, die for 72 hours,' she says.

'No. Want you.'

He is in his teen avatar, heavy penis ready. Scant hair shadows his stripling body. Black down softens his upper lip.

'Willie, shutdown.' He curls his lip. Shuts his eyes. Stiffens.

The control room is corralled by screens skittering with information. She roller-skates towards the holding area. It echoes down the vestibule. Samsar trots in in the wake of this sound. Lights switch on at her approach. Perish as she passes. Whirring-clicking noises emanate from the holding area. The tanktruck is being stripped. Robots unload the forbidden cargo.

The Archive is underground. It is vast and cold. In the darkness, maintenance bots buzz like bees while checking line upon line, shelf upon shelf, floor upon floor of artefacts. Each one is covered to hide its corrupting feature. She chooses some for human inspection. Randomly. She's a doll drunk on emptiness. Spinning. Freezing. Finger pointing.

Each time she enters, the bots cluster around her like eager school children. To transmit their reports in any language of her choice. She's whimsical, she's exacting. She picks the language of the era and area in which the art was created. Samsar is cued to her preferences. It translates from Sanskrit for the poet Kalidasa's voluptuous verses. From classical Tamil for the mystic Andal's scandalous songs. It picks from a plethora of tribal dialects for their renderings and local patois for verses on paintings of the epics. It contemporises offensive twenty-first-century tweets from Hinglish. After she checks the records, Samsar reverts to dog mode. It wants its reward. Samsar rolls on its back. A furry white sausage begging to be tickled. She complies. The Eyes blink approval.

She knows what this consignment contains: friezes of erotic temple sculptures. Sliced off the ancient outer walls. These will be replaced by recent sculptures of devout, clothed couples. Like the earlier lots, this batch of eroding sandstone depicts threesomes. The men's penises as thick as arms. The women, heavy-breasted, slim-waisted, supple. Two never seemed enough. They needed someone to leer.

She wants Dev before he has bathed. Wants a sandy, salty, smelly fuck. Willie synthesize every odour she demands. But each scent is a tinge artificial. She wants the raw pong of the world rubbed roughly into her skin. Her pores pumiced to remove her sense of isolation. Dev reassuringly looks the same each time. He demands virtually the same. His lardy figure is stepping out of the bath. Droplets glisten on his drooping shoulders. Fleshy arms dangle around his hirsute chest. She switches Samsar's eyes off before lunging towards him.

'Here,' Dev pats his hairy paunch, 'two orders.'

She leans over to extract the chip from his bellybutton. Licks it. Dries it on the sheet, inserts it in her watch. Two images tremble on the ceiling. Like jellyfish above their naked bodies. The first is a miniature. A moustachioed king lies in a marble palace. He is simultaneously pleasuring five women with his fingers, toes, penis. She had burst out laughing when she first accessed the original. Then spent hours deleting every trace of her laughter from the records of the Eyes. Silenced the sound. She erased her smile. Opened the Eyes. Set upright her momentarily thrown back head.

She can fake almost anything from the Archive. The raw materials are with her. Keep the fake. Smuggle the original into the unknown. Past the blur of sand scorch sound. Into some distant city somewhere. Perhaps across salt-crusted oceans. Perhaps into a wealthy house where it softly shines on a wall. Or lies in a secret vault. She visualizes its journey till her imagination blurs.

It hadn't always been so. For decades she had wanted to be Chief Sanitizing Archivist. But this isn't an easy job. The vaults are far from human habitation. It's rumoured that loneliness drives archivists insane. Or is it something about the job?

She underwent training to withstand solitude. To act normal under constant surveillance. The Eyes are mounted everywhere to prevent exactly the kind of activity she now pursues. She trained her body to enjoy Wrap News. To feel jostled by air pressure as if in a crowd. To shout slogans as if with a mob. Feel victory surge as headlines repeat 'WE ARE FREE! WE ARE SAFE! WE ARE FREE! WE ARE SAFE!' Before the room darkens, before she is alone again. Again longing for the next Wrap News fix. She trained to live with holo fantasies. Play sex games with updated versions of Willie. And whoever drove to the hidden outpost. She trained to categorize schools and periods of Objectionable Art and Ideas. Analyse the components. She trained in maintaining secrecy. She rose quickly through the ranks.

She cannot date when the extravagant thought arose in her: to pass on her genes. It made her dizzy. But didn't leave her. It's like an embedded code: pass on your genes. Dare to do it.

It takes money to become a member of the Reproductively Eligible Elite. More to design the child. It takes money to have a child. Still more to bring the offspring up in a known destination. It takes luck to find a partner in crime – as she has. It takes patience stealth, skill, time to build a 4D printer. Resourcefulness to copy objectionable artworks. Down to the detail of a broken bronze fingertip. Fold in palm leaf. Tear in tapestry. It takes devious intelligence to evade the Eyes. To substitute the original with the fake. It takes ingenuity to develop a program that circumvents checks, suppresses information. And then sends normal reports to superiors. It takes greed to make more greed.

She worries her luck will run out. Or Dev will be replaced. Each time he leaves she thinks it is the last time. She never tells him that. Never questions him about the buyers. Never discusses the price. They have sex often. She ensures the Eyes see her entering his quarters. So that no alarm triggers when she blurs their images for the prescribed time.

Part of the horizon leaks. A dust storm melds earth and sky. Sand snakes twist. Scatter scales. Shed shivers of small mirrors. Tortured suns. The wind howls. Louder.

They get some extra time till the storm clears. The same muted darkness prevails inside the cavernous Archive. Dev is tired. His sagging body is tired of her body. His mind is tired of her questions. Her guarded questions. About the City. The Authorities. His travels. He can't reveal much. Is she curious about the job, he wonders. Or him? He doesn't want to know. She is a fine counterfeiter. The highest placed Sanitizing Archivist he knows. By his next visit, she would have finished the substitution. Fakes on the shelves. Originals stowed in empty water containers he transports back.

Her monthly Human Encounter is over. Days of cramped solitude stretch for Dev. The tanktruck will steer back to its parking lot in the City. Digging itself into the terrain when storms arise. Reviving. Blipping its code to barricades. Inside, pounding music images vibrate all devices. Dev's body pulses to its beat. Every journey begins this way. But as the tanktruck approaches the City, the music switches. To soothing. It lulls him towards subservience. Dev's demeanour is as placid as algae in a still pond. But his mind is alert. Is he an animal? He wonders how music can move him so. He is constantly wary. Like a roach bot in battle. Testing the air with its feelers. Before scuttling to safety. Dev wants to buy invisibility. Like the Archive disappearing in a sandstorm. As if it was never there. As if the Art never was.

The Archive collects Objectionable Art and Ideas to not offend HurtMobs. That spontaneously coalesce when reports circulate about obscene art. Alien art. Corrupting ideas. HurtMobs stop the creators. Perpetrators. Viewers. Listeners. Readers. By beheading. Mutilating. Lynching. Hanging them. The Archives protect people from HurtMobs. By archiving without access anything HurtMobs don't like. The Archives protect HurtMobs too. From getting hurt. When they rise in righteous wrath. She isn't interested in these aspects. She is glad for her job. And its criminal possibilities.

But she didn't expect counterfeiting to have side effects. Each Objectionable Art object she fakes haunts her. As if each piece possesses its own Eyes. That burn their images into her retina. Brand her brain. With their shape and presence. Sometimes, details enlarge. A figurine's ivory plait becomes a river of pebbled cream. Gleaming in the moonlight. Or the creases on the cover of a banned book become as familiar as lines on her palm. Its smashed spine like crumpled dreams. Pages edged with pencil scribbles, others underlined in ink, dog-eared bookmarks all become like her skin. As near and necessary. The more Originals she sends away, the more they grow in her. She smooths a gloved hand over the pages of a counterfeited book. Over and over. So it bears the uneven imprint of fingers thumbing through it. No 4D printer can replicate this. Even if the fake is painstakingly aged. When she is done, each book looks used. Treasured, hidden away in a hurry. It looks like it had a long life.

She dreams of green mountains sliding along the bank of a green river. Jade green. Smooth as a mirror. Shores limed by banana groves. Reflecting exact doubles, heavy fruit hanging. *Did the harvesters call to each other through these leafy tunnels?* She dreams of dead languages. Once spoken with fluency. She begins speaking to the mirror in imaginary languages. Pretending to the Eyes that she is practising vocal cord exercises. Willie asks if she is devising a new game. He joins in with grunts. Squeaks beyond the range of human vocalization. Within a week, he adds sexual manoeuvres to the vocalizations. She stops the experiment. The loneliness. The ricocheting loneliness has got to her. She accepts this.

The Central Archive informs her rations are delayed. The Food Dispensing Unit will stagger her supplies over six weeks instead of four. The water. The rationed recycled water will be missed the most. Dev sneaks in printer supplies in the water containers. Even though he shares his water with her, it is never enough. He is like a hippo with a large appetite. For her. She likes this.

In the spa, she decolours a slit of sky panel. Suns herself. Samsar too. Till its snowy pelt turns tawny. Till it barks sunburn warnings. She instructs the bots to slow down. She spends time in the holo deck. Holidaying on the beach. On verdant mountainsides with crystal waterfalls. Flying past the moon in its egg of stars. Most of all, she spends her time near rivers. Slow, cool rivers of green. She falls asleep on their banks, awakens to the sound of flowing water. *Could I have had a different life?*

Sand snakes rear. Their hoods dissipate in the glare. They become phantoms of light. Snakes without bodies. Blistering. Blowing. Giving and gathering heat from the City's surfaces. Nothing moves during the day. Except surveillance shuttles. Lurking. Recording. Underground, the City hums. At nightfall, the polluting above ground Work Units begin. They shut down at dawn. As the searing dawn splits open the sky. Children and young semi-automats go to bed after a night of drills.

How much longer before I'm caught? Is it possible to quit? To disappear? How many have disappeared? It's easy to duplicate the painting of the dexterous king. The lines are thick. The figures are stiff. *Why would someone want to collect it? Or books of dead words.* Most Objectionable Art is uncomplicated to fake. Like the half-closed eyes of Bodhisattvas. But their mien of calm, almost aloof compassion is difficult. Measurements are exact to the last fraction. Still. Something is missing. She wonders what. Why.

She holds the foot-high tree nymph statue in her hands. Turns it over and over, runs her fingers on it as if she is reading Braille. This is her third attempt and it is still not perfect. Something is missing. But it would be reckless to attempt replicating another for a month even though she steals minimum energy from the grid. *What if it is traced here?* Her work ledge almost scrapes the sizzling ceiling. It's dangerous. But the Eyes are few in these narrow spaces. They malfunction in continuously high temperatures. They blink. Rapidly. The animal cells in them scrunch up. She wears shades, sips water. She had put the 4D printer together here. The simodine plank responds to her smallest body movements. It inches her closer to the Original, to the fake. *What is the difference?* She imagines herself as the artist hoping to pounce on the secret that evades her. The proportions, colour, weight, texture – they are exact. But the smile isn't right. *Where is the difference?*

Sand snakes darken. Wind hisses cold. Night has fallen. She hasn't noticed. She shivers. Wriggles out.

'Baby, baby, where were you?' Willie whispers in her ear. He is in his avatar of a middle-aged roué in a black cape and eye patch. He strokes her inner thigh. The strokes become firmer. Longer. Inch towards her sex. Touch the lips as if by accident.

Her attention is on the stretch of flesh. Exquisitely alive. She wants him to explore. Further. Probe deeper.

'Naughty, naughty! Where were you wandering?' he asks. 'I have to punish you.'

'Nowhere,' she whispers. Turns towards him. 'I've been good.'

'Hands off. What kept you away from me?' Willies tease. Excites. Stops. Before she can come to rapture. Starts again. Again.

She is a pleading mass. 'I cannot make you understand. I cannot make anyone understand... What is happening inside me? I cannot even explain it to myself.'

'I know what is happening inside you.' He slides his fingers inside her sex. Withdraws. Slides. Withdraws. The hairs on his fingers have stiffened into bristles. He stops. Stops to nip her earlobe. 'Baby, baby, tell me.'

She blurts, 'What makes Objectionable Art objectionable?' She freezes. Moans to cover it up.

Willie nibbles her ear. 'Did you find out?'

'Nothing. I don't care. Only care for you.'

'I'll show you what makes Objectionable Art objectionable,' Willie says. He smiles down at her. He knows how to prolong pleasure. She forgets what she revealed.

What if I sleep a little longer and forget all this nonsense? But she can't sleep all day. She races to her secret workstation. Clasps the ancient tree nymph from Gyaraspur close to her and stares at it in wonderment. The sculpture is broken below the thighs. Its nose is slashed. Its arms are lost. Its breasts are smashed.

Yet it is splendid, its smile of bliss enfolds her as if it will never stop, as if time has stopped. 'Thank you,' she whispers to the small sculpture. 'Thank you, thank you.' Tears well and she weeps, elated by its mysterious beauty, she weeps as she is released into awe, she weeps as if she is dissolving into it; she has never felt as free, as ecstatic. As she slowly surfaces, she wonders, *Is beauty dangerous because it is addictive? Is happiness objectionable? Does joy give courage?*

She skates to the workstation, the echo of skates clattering behind her. Lights glow at her approach. Fade after she passes. She thinks the way to an unknown nourishment is coming to light within her and longs for this. *Art dissolves you into its vibrant vastness, you never are alone again. Is this the secret of art?* The workstation is completely lit. Each screen is flashing. An identical message: 'WE CAN MAKE YOU LOOK EXACTLY LIKE THE OBJECTIONABLE ART YOU ARE FAKING.'

The moonlight is brilliant. Clustered starlight pierces a high, sapphire sky as if behind night's screen an immense sheet of light constantly exists. Far below, each grain of sand glistens like a translucent seed. It is cold.

MIRROR-RORRIM

CLARK PRASAD

EXODUS: THE JOURNEY HOME
Cointrin Airport, Geneva, Switzerland
18 June 2028, 7.35 a.m. CET

Everything is an illusion.

Adi Soans's brown eyes narrowed as he read the words on a signboard outside the Geneva airport. The sign stood out with its bright yellow font on a black background. He wondered why these signs had been put up across multiple airports across the world. Was it a brand campaign? He shut the door of the cab and remembered the first time he'd seen those words. He had been a child then. It had been in his mother tongue, Hindi: '*Sab maya hai.*' Just last week, though, he'd seen the same words again, written on a Post-it note stuck on his desk at the lab. He didn't know who had put it there.

Everything is an illusion. Sab maya hai.

As a physicist specializing in quantum mechanics, he knew those words could be right. He worked at the CERN, investigating the fundamental structure of the universe. They were close to finding the God particle, and they were also investigating another new atom code named the Devil's Angel particle. Adi led one of the teams in that search.

Of Anglo-Indian descent, Adi had grown up in a middle-class locality in West Delhi, always dreaming of making an impact on the world. As a child, the Terminator series of films had fascinated him. He had wished to be John Connor in those films, the saviour of the human race, battling against intelligent machines. His dream was to influence AI development so that it was a partner for the human race, but in the early 2000s, when these dreams had taken hold of him, AI was not given its proper place in society. It was now the year of our Lord 2028, and things had changed. Adi was glad he could claim to have played a small role in that.

During his job placement after graduating from the hallowed Indian Institute of Technology, Delhi, Adi had got a job in an investment bank, but he was not happy there – he wanted to study further. His passion was to find a way to merge artificial intelligence with quantum mechanics. He had planned to work for a couple of years and then study at the California Institute of Technology. He'd worked hard to achieve that goal. At Caltech, Adi was the only student in his batch to receive a full scholarship to study quantum physics. He left India in 2020 to finally chase his dreams, but now he was also leaving behind the girl he loved – Sana Vasishtha.

He had met Sana at a speed-dating club. Her family was rich and had vast property holdings, but Sana did not want to rest on their laurels. A hard-working student, she eventually became a professor in astrophysics. When he left for California, they promised to remain in touch, but as Adi became increasingly busy, contact between them decreased. Then came the job opportunity in quantum computing for CERN in 2023. Five years had now passed, and he was still there.

Now, settling into his business-class seat, he thought of the past. He felt the need to see Sana. He was going back to India for both a holiday and an alumni reunion, and was looking forward to the break. Over the last month he and his team had battled the issues in the new particle collider that had caused ultra-high-energy cosmic rays, UHECR, to be produced in the new series of the AWAKE experiment. But it was all almost under control now.

Leaning back in his seat, Adi fiddled with his watch, telling himself he needed to change the time zone to India Standard Time. Then, deciding to do it later, he tapped the Star Trek communicator badge on his shirt to begin playing the music, which started from the flexible strip placed behind his earlobes.

Phil Collins – no one sings like him. The singer's voice brought thoughts of Sana back into his head. Sana had introduced him to this music. *Where is she now,* he wondered. *Why isn't she returning my calls? I can't wait to see her...*

He closed his eyes as the music soothed him and was soon asleep.

AL-BAYYINAH: THE CLEAR EVIDENCE
In the sky above New Delhi, India
18 June 2028, 7.35 p.m. IST

'Dear passengers. This is your captain, Nafisa Sharma, speaking.'

Adi gently opened his eyes to the in-flight announcement.

'Please fasten your seat belts. Our descent into Delhi has begun. We will be landing at Sardar Patel International Airport shortly. The temperature outside is 49 degrees Centigrade, and the air quality index is a very poor 350, with high particulate pollution. Do not forget to wear the complimentary masks given to you by our ground staff.'

It seems changing the name of the airport is more essential than cleaning up the air in the capital city. The government may be trying, but not hard enough. Reality may be an illusion, but climate change is not.

'And apologies again for the turbulence an hour ago.'

Turbulence? I didn't feel a thing... How deeply was I sleeping? Adi checked his watch. The seconds needle was not moving. He gently tapped the watch. No change. Unstrapping it, he pulled the side button out and adjusted the time to the one shown on the display screen at his seat. He shut his eyes again.

An hour later, he was standing outside the arrivals gate. His friend Thayar was supposed to pick him up. He looked around, then called Thayar, but the phone rang on. After a couple of minutes, he pressed the call button again, and this time there was a response.

'Hey, Thayar! Adi here.'

'Hey man, you've reached?'

'Yes, it's been over an hour since we landed. You're close?'

'An hour? I thought the flight was landing now.'

'Excuses, excuses.'

'No, man! Check, it's 10.00 p.m. now.'

'No, it is 10.30 p.m. now.'

'Maybe your watch is not synchronized correctly. I am on my way and will be there in twenty minutes.'

'Okay, my friend.'

Adi looked at his watch. It read 10.32 p.m. A blonde teenage girl wearing leather boots, her hair tied in a single side braid, was standing near him.

'Excuse me, miss?'

She turned, their eyes meeting. She gave a gentle nod.

'Can you tell me what time it is?'

She turned her left wrist to view the screen of her smartphone and pressed the blue button on its side. The screen projected the time as a 3D image in the air. It was 10.00 p.m.

'I think I had it wrong. Thanks.' Adi removed his watch again and turned the dial.

The girl chuckled, covering her mouth with her palm. 'I'm sorry. I'm just surprised to see one of those is still around,' she said as he looked at her, his eyebrows raised.

'Well, it has sentimental value, and I like the leather touching my skin.'

She rolled her eyes.

Adi shrugged. 'Pretty neat ComDev you have there.'

'Yes, it is an augmented reality device I got off Amazon.'

'Fascinating. Is it a recent release?'

'No, it's over a year old. And...just one thing... Why did you assume my gender?'

'Sorry? What?'

'You called me "miss". The right thing to do is to ask what pronoun the person prefers.'

'I – I don't understand.'

'I identify as non-binary, and by not addressing me correctly you are being passive-aggressive.'

This shit has arrived in India now, Adi thought. 'Okay, miss, I mean... Sorry. Ah...'

The girl huffed impatiently and walked away. Adi shook his head in irritation. *NPC droid. Non-playing character, indeed. No wonder Trump won again.*

After about ten minutes, he finally caught sight of Thayer. He waved and as Thayer waved back, Adi thought, *He looks different from his Facebook pictures and videos. New hairstyle.*

They shook hands and hugged.

'Look at you, Thayer. You got a new hairstyle. It looks good on you, man,' Adi said.

'And you look great too! Europe agrees with you. But this is not a new hairstyle. I've had this for quite a while now.'

'Nonsense! I don't use Facebook a lot, but I did see your recent photos.'

'Maybe you were looking at a different Thayer,' Thayer said, laughing, as he slapped his friend on the back. They continued talking excitedly as they headed towards the car park where Thayer had parked his Tesla. Adi's eyes widened at the sight of the car, and he looked at Thayer.

'Impressed, Adi?'

'Yes!'

Once they were seated, Thayer started the car but took control of the steering wheel.

'Aha, still the old way.'

'Yup, for some time at least. Let me see what the traffic's like and then...'

They exited the airport area and entered the city.

'So, good to be back, right?' he asked Adi.

'Yes, at least for a few days...'

A white van suddenly cut across their path. Adi gasped and the car jerked for a moment. Thayer cursed under his breath, then aloud. 'Fucking traffic! Better to put the car on auto-drive.' He pushed a couple of buttons with his right hand, slowly letting go of the retracting steering wheels. Then, leaning back in his seat, he continued, 'Your folks will be excited.'

'Yup, they will be. We'll be reliving old memories.'

'Hm, good. And tomorrow evening will be exciting, catching up on old times.'

'Yes, the reunion! Good old times. And let's please not be politically correct in our conversation. This PC culture is killing me.'

'Hahaha. Well, PC culture killed *Star Wars*.'

They laughed and Thayer started mimicking Darth Vader's voice.

'"Noooo...I am your father!" That was probably the most significant reveal.'

'Yup, you're right, Thayer. But he didn't say "no"; he said, "Luke, I am your father."'

'You seem to have memory loss. It wasn't...okay, let's check it out.'

Thayer called out to his car, 'Okay...Lizzie.'

'Yes, sir?' A 3D hologram flashed on top of the leather dashboard. It looked like Leeloo, Milla Jovovich's character from *Fifth Element*.

'Show us the scene in *The Empire Strikes Back* in which Darth Vader tells

Luke he's Luke's father.' The scene plays, and Darth Vader says, 'Nooo...I am your father!' Adi squints his eyes. Must be a mistake, he thinks.

'Wow...I didn't know Tesla cars had such features and a hologram. I'm even more impressed.'

Thayer laughed. 'Yes, these are exciting times. But, I had meant to correct you earlier... It's not a Tesla – it's a Tezla. With a zee.'

Adi ignored the comment, thinking his friend had changed the name himself.

'Does it always work?'

'It only works on the auto-cruise option. I've customized the hologram to my favourite sci-fi character Leeloominaï Lekatariba Lamina-Tchaï Ekbat De Sebat'

'The supreme being Leeloo,' said Adi ecstatically.

'All hail Leeloo. And she even says "multipass". Let me show you.'

Thayer once again commanded the hologram to come online and asked if she had the pass. She said, 'Leeloo Thallas multipass,' in a seductive yet sweet tone.

'Boys and our toys,' quipped Adi. Both laughed.

Leeloo Thallas instead of Leeloo Dallas. Maybe it is the recording.

They continued talking the rest of the way.

'Tell me, Thayer...do you know what's happening with Sana?'

'You're still crazy about her?'

'Well. No...'

'Come on, man! You're blushing. Madam is a professor, as before. No change. Although...' dropping his voice, Thayer muttered, 'she's just a little crazy now.'

'Did you say something?'

'Er, no. We're almost at your home now.'

When Adi got home, it was as he had expected. The excitement of seeing everyone again had him instantly teary-eyed. They spent an hour talking before Adi's father called it a night. Adi looked at his watch. It was 12.11 a.m., late indeed.

Back in his room, he checked his smartphone for any messages from work. There was only one, from his boss. It mentioned a surge in the radiation reading of the particle collider, but all was as it should be. He spotted another message – this one from his own email id. He tapped it to read it.

Everything is an illusion
Yojayitvātutānyeva
Praviveśasvayaṁguhām
Guhāṁpraviṣṭetasmiṁstu
Jīvātmāpratibudhyate
Cannot say more.

Adi frowned, and then broke into a smile.

Those CERN pranksters. I told them about the Post-it note, and they have hacked into my account now. Jeff and Lauren. It must have been Lauren's idea.

He closed the mail app and lay down on the bed. He felt tired all right, but sleep refused to come and he struggled for another hour against the thoughts flooding his brain.

Sana... What was Thayer muttering about her? Will she come to the reunion? Is she still single? If not, I should have told her when I had the chance. Tomorrow...I'll see her tomorrow... But one day will feel like one week now.

After tossing and turning for a while, he turned to his bedside table to check his watch. It was already half past one in the morning. He decided to give in to the exhaustion that was claiming him.

DEUTERONOMY: THESE ARE THE WORDS
Hyatt Regency Bharat Hotel,
Bhikaji Cama Place, Ghera Road, New Delhi, India
19 June 2028, 4.30 p.m. IST

Adi was in the hall that was the venue for the alumni meet. He was looking forward to the reunion not just for nostalgia's sake but also to gather his batchmates' views on various topics like the aftermath of the economic recession and the fear of the European Union breaking up. Now, deep into their discussion, the group was talking about the politically correct or PC culture that seemed to have seeped into every society.

Adi was quiet until Thayer turned to him and said, 'Hey, you've barely made any contribution.'

'Well, I feel PC culture has killed the expression of ideas,' Adi said slowly.

'How can you say that?'

'With this continuing, there will be a rewiring of the brain over a period, you know. And we'll use the brain to emphasize what we should say and not what we should express,' Adi replied.

'So, you're saying these people are just using this language to justify what they're saying and doing.'

'Yes. And certain groups have created an agenda to shout down conservative voices. It's like the Nazi period.'

'Adi, India is almost a fascist society now. The elections are around the corner, and I hope sense prevails.'

'It is a perspective.'

'Right! Then changing the name of Ring Road to Ghera Road is not a joke.'

'What?' Adi laughed. 'When did that happen?'

'Don't you know?'

'No. When was the name changed?'

'It's been months now. You live underground, so maybe you missed it.

'Well, maybe you're right.'

Adi and his friends continued to talk. He asked the group about some of their other pals who were missing that evening, and was surprised by some new stories he'd not heard before.

'Adi, getting old, are you?'

'Yeah, Yoda.'

'Not knowing your nation's news and about your college pals' lives. Not good, Adi,' teased Sonia. The group laughed.

'Yeah, okay, okay. At least I'm still the joker of the pack.'

'Darling, take it all in,' Sonia said with a grin as she pulled Thayer away to the dance floor.

Adi watched them dancing close together as he took a long swig of the Karuizawa Samurai whisky. Thayer and Sonia were making great moves.

After a while, Sonia changed her dancing partner, and Thayer walked back to Adi.

'Thayer, you've still got that groove.'

'Thanks! And did you get a whiff of Sonia's perfume?'

'Yeah. Some perfume she's wearing.'

'Well, you need to get closer to get the real feeling. It's Black Opium, Yves Saint Laurent.'

Adi looked at Thayer, who winked and smiled.

'Different ladies, different fragrance. You should try the different fragrance.'

Adi gently nodded. 'I did, but I still prefer her fruity scent.'

'Ahh, Sana.'

Adi put his head down. His cheeks grew red as he blushed. 'By the way, where is Sana? I thought she'd be here?' he asked Thayer.

'Oh, she's a lost cause. You don't want to see her.'

'What do you mean, Thayer?' Adi demanded.

'She's different now. Something in her has changed over the last month or so.'

'What do you mean?'

'She's stopped keeping in touch. Just doesn't want to meet me, and...' he stopped abruptly.

'And? And what?'

'I don't understand it, because just a couple of months ago a few of us went on a holiday over a weekend. Something changed there.'

Adi fell quiet. He looked away and then back at his friend. 'But what happened to her? Did you try to ask her?'

'I tried to contact her first myself and then through a couple of others. But she's just...disappeared...from our lives. She doesn't even live at her old place any more.'

Thayer saw the look on his friend's face and guessed that Adi would insist on meeting her.

'See, I heard she goes to a pub in central Delhi. I can drop you off there when we finish here. I would love to stay, but I need to take my wife out tomorrow morning.'

Adi was relieved to hear that. 'Yes, that sounds like a plan. I can see if she's there and then take a cab home.' Thayer nodded.

He looked away from his friend, took a sip of his whisky and tried to focus on the conversation around him. But nothing made sense to him any more. Thayer's words reverberated in his head, and he wondered what his friend had meant by 'lost cause'.

What's happened to Sana? She was a spirited girl. One of the best in the class. The Sana he knew would not miss an event like this. Back in college, she would bring up global issues and ask the batch to lend their voices on various matters. She was always the one telling them about political happenings around the world. Sana was his closest friend after Thayer, and people had often thought that they would get married. Well, at that time, he wanted to too. But now... Well, he would have to wait till they met to find out.

It was close to 5.30 p.m. when they finally finished. They were standing in the parking lot of the Hyatt Regency Bharat Hotel when he reminded Thayer about his desire to meet Sana.

'Are you sure you want to see her, Adi?'

'Thayer, you're the one who told me where she might be found. Just take me to her.'

'Yeah, okay.' Thayer could see that his friend had only changed in terms of his knowledge and looks. At heart he was still the same guy Thayer had always known – never good at giving up.

AL-MUMTAHANAH: THE WOMAN WHO IS EXAMINED
Somewhere near R.K. Puram, New Delhi, India
19 June 2028, 5.52 p.m. IST

They had been driving for over ten minutes in silence. Adi focused his attention on the roads they passed and the changes that had taken place since he was last in Delhi. Some of the areas still had a touch of their old selves but most looked different.

Adi knew his friend was upset about him insisting on seeing Sana. Well, he would apologize to Thayer at the end of the drive, he thought; for now he would just let him drive. After sometime, Thayer pulled over in front of a pub in central Delhi.

'What is it, Thayer? Why did you stop?'

'This is where I was told we may find Sana,' Thayer said, gesturing at the pub.

The pub looked like a shady place. Adi looked at his friend with curiosity and surprise. He couldn't believe what he was hearing and hoped he wouldn't find Sana here. He tried to get out of the car, but Thayer held him back.

'I'll be off then, buddy.'

'I understand. I'll go in and take a look...' Adi spoke in a low tone. They shook hands and followed it up with a fist bump. Then Adi stepped out of the Tezla and watched the car speed away.

He looked at his watch: 6.38 p.m. *The second hand has stopped again.* He gently tapped the watch twice. It ticked back to life. He took a deep breath to keep himself calm, but so many thoughts were racing through his mind. He didn't want to consider the idea that Sana was patronizing this place – this was no place for her. Everything about the pub screamed drugs. There were three motels to the left of the pub and two hotels on the right. Apart from some men hanging around, smoking, there were a few women parading about, openly looking for potential clients. Nevertheless, now that he was here, he decided to steel his mind and make a go for it.

Just as he was headed into the pub, he saw another car pull up. For a moment, Adi thought he caught a glimpse of Sana sitting in it. He stared at the beautiful woman in high-heeled boots walking away from the car towards the pub. The woman didn't in any way seem like Sana, but Adi decided to take a chance.

'San. SAN! If then else,' Adi called out in the code they had shared so long ago.

The woman stopped abruptly, and stood motionless for a moment. Then she turned around.

Adi took a step forward and continued, 'Punch it. Make it so.'

'Engage,' the woman said.

Adi increased his pace and the lady too moved towards him. As their eyes locked on each other's, Adi could see that she was indeed Sana. She began to shake as tears ran down her cheeks.

When Adi reached her, Sana's hands were covering her mouth. 'You are alive?' she whispered shakily.

'Of course I am,' said Adi.

They hugged, she was sobbing on his shoulder while tears pooled in his eyes.

She was breathing heavily. 'No, this is not possible. I saw you dead! This is not happening, Adi.'

'Stay calm, Sana. We need to talk. Something is not right here.'

Sana nodded. Adi put his arm around Sana's shoulder, and they started to walk away from the pub.

REVELATION: THINGS OUT OF PLACE
Hyatt Regency Bharat Hotel,
Bhikaji Cama Place, Ghera Road, New Delhi, India
19 June 2028, 9.00 p.m. IST

Adi and Sana sat in a luxurious room at the Hyatt Regency Bharat Hotel. Adi had booked them in for the night. The girl at the reception did not show them the typical courtesy as she eyed Sana suspiciously, but Adi ignored the girl's behaviour as he handed over Sana's Aadhaar card and his passport which he never left behind. The girl asked for their fingerprints as well. This surprised Adi, as he was not aware that hotels required any such personal details of its guests, but since Sana did not resist he went ahead and gave the girl what she needed.

In the room now, they were greeted by the AI room assistant.

'Hello, Mr Soans, or would you like to be addressed differently?'

'I prefer Adi.'

'Noted. Would you like to update this to your account?'

'No.'

'Noted. How may I be of service, Adi?'

'Show me some movie options on the streaming wall.'

'All right.'

The wall lighting changed and ten channels began streaming, though without audio. He randomly touched one of the channels and it expanded to a full-screen view. It was an old Hollywood film. He turned on the volume but kept it low. He opened the drinks cabinet, picked up a bottle of bourbon and poured a drink for Sana.

'How long have you been like this?' he asked as he handed the drink to her.

'Like this?'

'I mean this hairstyle, tattoos, piercings?'

Sana raised her hand to her head and removed the short wig. Her lush hair loosened and cascaded over her shoulders, down to her waist. Adi sat by her, stroking her hair gently as she reached out for her glass and took a sip of bourbon.

'I was always like this. I only wear the wig so that I don't get recognized.'

'Why?' asked Adi. 'Are you a secret agent?'

Sana glared at Adi. He moved back a little. He could see the embers glowing in her eyes.

'I was going on a Her date.'

'Her date?'

'It's an app to find partners of the same sex.'

'What?'

'What, *what*? You know I swing both ways.'

Adi kept quiet. *She's changed so much*, he thought. He noticed a ring on her finger. He touched it and looked up at her questioningly.

Sana sighed, removing it. 'So the date doesn't get emotional.'

Adi let go of her hand. She stared back at him. Adi said, 'I had hoped you hadn't moved on...'

'Moved on? What are you even saying?'

'What do you mean?'

'Oh please! You were dead!'

'Dead! You've said it twice now. I did try to regularly keep in touch, but you stopped responding!'

'Adi...you were dead. D.E.A.D. dead. No life. I saw the news. I cried, met your family. And then I couldn't take it any more.'

Adi's mouth fell open. Earlier, when she'd said he was dead, he'd thought it was a euphemism she used for him not keeping in touch. But her expression and body language signalled otherwise. 'You...what?' Adi whispered.

'Yes, I thought you were dead. It was in the news, and your family confirmed it!'

'What news?'

'From a newspaper article, I think, I'm not sure. But I know I was in Bombaim when I read it. I didn't believe it at first. They said you were involved in a freak accident at CERN.'

'Well, here I am. Not dead for sure. And where the hell is Bombaim?'

'What do you mean? It's the capital of Maharatharashtra.'

'You mean Mumbai, Maharashtra.'

'Yes, same thing.'

Mumbai is Bombaim? Is Sana on drugs?

There were a few moments of silence as they looked at each other.

'Well, I'm glad you're not dead...' said Sana quietly.

Adi moved forward and, stretching out his hands, grasped Sana's waist. He moved closer to kiss her, but she placed her elbows on his chest and pushed him back.

'I'm sorry,' Adi said, contrite. 'I was...'

'Don't be sorry. Just fuck me. Make me feel like a teenager again.'

Adi moved closer to her, slowly now. His right hand stroked Sana's thick hair while his left moved gently across her face. He touched her lips. She quivered. They were breathing in rhythm, eyes closed.

'Adi, I missed this. Don't leave me again,' she murmured, as she unbuttoned his shirt. Adi's hand moved towards the zip on her top, but she stopped him.

'Later. Not now.'

She pushed him down on the bed and got on top of him. She lowered her face to his. Their eyes met and they began kissing passionately.

Adi let Sana take control. In his mind, he felt her change, as she'd always liked him to take control. But he let it go. Many emotions swirled through the room as they undressed each other on the giant king-size bed. After about half an hour, they held each other, kissing gently.

Later, as they lay in bed, Sana made a paper boat from the thick bond paper she tore off the hotel notepad as Adi stroked her thighs gently while watching a James Bond movie. When she finished making the boat to her satisfaction, Sana wrote 'S&A' on it and pretended to sail it along Adi's bare back.

'Hey, watch this,' said Adi, smiling. On TV was the scene in the movie where Jaws meets Dolly for the first time below the cable car.

'I love this scene, Adi. It shows that love transcends everything and can happen to anyone.' She pressed his arm.

He kissed her. 'Yes, and all it takes is a little connection.'

'And the connection in this scene is their smile.'

'Not the smiles, my dear, but the braces.' She spanked his bare butt. He laughed.

They waited for the scene to unfold. Jaws fell. Dolly helped him to clear the debris. He smiled, and then she smiled.

'Ahhhh,' gasped Sana, and Adi sat up.

'One minute,' he exclaimed. 'Did they do something here? You noticed it, right?'

'Yes... No braces. Dolly has no braces!'

First the Darth Vader–Luke scene. Now, this, Adi thought. *But it's not just the film scenes – so much was different. The city, Sana...and Thayer was looking different too.*

Adi leapt out of bed and picked up his phone. Sana covered herself, raising the sheets in front her. Adi looked at her and shook his head – he was not taking a photo like she'd thought. She let go of the satin sheets. Adi scrolled quickly through his Facebook contacts and stopped at Thayer's photo. In it his hairstyle was similar to the one Adi had seen on him.

'Goddammit!' cursed Adi. *My memory. Am I losing it?* Adi looked at Sana. 'Tell me...tell me how we met.'

Sana raised her brows disbelievingly, spread her hands and dropped them on the bed.

'Come on! I just want to confirm something.'

'What do you want to confirm – my memories or whether I am *your* Sana?'

'Actually, both.'

'What!'

'Trust me. I know what I'm doing.'

'Oh yeah, like you said last time.'

Adi puckered his lips. He asked the same question again. This time he was close to her, back on the bed, on his knees and holding her hands.

'Okay, baby,' Sana said. 'We met on a speed-dating forum. You were wearing a Dr Who T-Shirt. It was blue.'

'Yes, and you were wearing a red satin top.'

'I'm impressed. You still remember.'

'What was the question you asked that made you excited about me?'

'I'm a *Star Trek* fan, and I wanted to see how much you knew as you claimed to be a Captain Kirk fan.'

'Yes, which class of ship is what you'd asked.'

'It was NCC 1764.'

'No...1864.'

'I clearly remember it was 1764. The twenty-third-century Federation Constitution Class starship built in Tranquillity Base, Luna.'

'Yes, I know, and it was named in honour of the British warship HMS *Defiant*.'

'Show-off. And NCC 1864 is USS *Reliant*, a Mirada Class ship. Clark Terrell commanded it. The ship assisted in Project Genesis, and...'

Adi raised his hands.

'Don't you do that, mister. Don't ever mansplain to me.' Sana had her finger raised. She lowered it slowly. Adi walked slowly towards the golden-yellow sofa-chair and slumped into it. For a few moments, he did not move, just stared at the ground. His mind was in turmoil. He clearly remembered Sana asking him about the NCC 1864.

It can't be. Everything is an illusion. My boss's message came asking whether I was placing the stickers. I didn't remember. Or did I, and then forgot about it? Or, perhaps, worse, I am not who I think I am.

Adi looked at Sana. 'Sana, one last question. Since when have you not liked Thayer?'

Sana's eyes widened. 'That asshole is your friend. And that is why I'm not taking any action against him.'

'Meaning?'

'#Metoo, Adi. #Metoo.'

Adi leaned forward. 'When? Oh god! Why didn't you tell me?'

'How could I? It was maybe two years ago.'

Adi loosened his grip on her shoulder. 'Not recently.'

'No. I don't meet him and always ignore him in public.'

Adi stroked Sana's back slowly, as her head rested on his shoulder. He knew the answer now. 'Sana.'

'Hm?'

'Have you noticed anything strange happening recently?'

'Yes, you came back to life.'

'Apart from that.'

'Like what?'

'Well, like in that movie... Dolly didn't have any braces. Or that I thought you asked me a different question when we first met...'

Sana was quiet and snuggled up to Adi as he continued to stroke her back. After some moments she tilted her neck gently and turned her face towards Adi's. She then sat up straight.

'Yes, I think I understand what you are saying.' She came close to his ears and whispered, 'You are a better kisser now.' Giggling, she jumped on top of Adi and pinned him down. 'And you've forgotten how to wrestle with me. And your butt tattoo of the droid is missing.'

'Tattoo? I never had one!'

She stopped teasing. She still held him down, but Adi was not moving. 'You're serious.'

Adi kept quiet.

'Okay. Let me think.'

She got off the bed, walked to the closet and slipped into a polka-dotted robe from the cupboard. She then opened her purse, took out a cigarette and lit up. 'Well, I noticed a few changes in people but ignored them. People are people... And most of my ATM pins were reset. I simply forgot them. Even muscle memory didn't help.'

'Anything else?'

'I thought someone was the chief minister of Delhi, but it turned out to be someone else – from a different party altogether. I thought some brands had changed the fonts in the logos. One of my favourite shows *Sex in the City* was suddenly called *Sex and the City*. I ignored all of this. It didn't really matter.'

'Life was like a box of chocolates,' said Forrest Gump from the TV, on which the film was now playing. They turned to the TV and then to each other. Sana's eyes widened. 'Adi, it is supposed to be life "is" like a box of chocolates.'

Adi nodded and smiled at Sana. He looked at her reflection on the sizeable walled mirror next to the bed. Sana looked at his reflection. She gasped and started breathing heavily.

She spoke in a feeble voice, 'Mirror-Mirror.' Adi nodded.

'Yes, just like Captain Kirk and the boarding party were transported to a parallel universe, it seems we have also been transported to another universe.'

'Is this the Mandela effect? When many people thought Nelson Mandela died in the 1990s and not in 2013. A false memory.'

'Maybe, or it can be a derivative of MMDE. It stands for....'

'I know what it stands for, you dummy – mass memory discrepancy effect.'

'I could believe I missed hearing something about movies and music. But to experience it with someone I know...' Adi stopped.

'It's real, Adi, I mean...Aditya.' The atmosphere became somewhat formal.

'You can call me Adi. I may be from a different universe, but I do have a connection with your Adi.'

'My Adi is dead. I am alone.'

'Well, there are two ways of looking at things. Either we stay together like nothing has happened. Or...'

'Or?'

'Or we find a way to get back to our original universes.'

AMSA: COSMOS, EARTH AND TIME
Hyatt Regency Bharat Hotel,
Bhikaji Cama, Ghera Road, New Delhi, India
20 June 2028, 10.35 p.m. IST

'Sorry, sir, the pin you entered is incorrect,' the receptionist told Adi. She was the same girl who had been on duty the night before.

Adi looked at her, somewhat surprised.

'That can't be, let me see...'

He took the card machine from the receptionist and entered the pin again, but got the same incorrect pin notification. He stood for a while, staring at the machine in his hand as he tried to recollect the pin.

'Are you okay, sir?' the receptionist asked. 'Sir, excuse me, sir,' she said again, louder, when Adi didn't reply.

'Let me get this,' said Sana. She took out her card from her sapphire-coloured clutch and passed it on to the receptionist. This time, she raised her eyebrows and muttered something under her breath.

Sana gave her a stare, then looked down at the bill.

'Just a minute.'

The receptionist looked up.

'We had the continental plan and not the modified American plan that you've put down.'

The receptionist looked at the bill again.

'Oh no, sorry, ma'am.'

'Miss,' said Sana with a quick smile.

The receptionist smiled back and turned away to correct the bill.

Sana craned her neck and was now gazing at Adi. Adi looked at her.

'What?'

'Well, at least one thing is consistent.'

'About?'

'My Adi also never checked bills. Always paid according to what was given to him.'

Adi smiled. 'I am still your Adi.'

Sana kept quiet, but her eyes became moist and she looked away. Adi placed his hand on her shoulder. She gently moved and nudged his hand away.

'Sir. Sir.'

Adi turned and saw the receptionist holding out a pink envelope.

'There was this message for you. It was dropped off with your name on it late last night, but the room number was wrong. Instead of 2109, the sender wrote 2110. I almost forgot to give it to you. Miss Sana, the corrected bill and your card.'

Adi thanked her. Sana took the bill and the card, and watched Adi opening the envelope. It contained a Post-it note. His face grew ashen as he read it. She leaned towards him.

'All okay?'

'It's getting serious.'

'What's getting serious?'

Adi handed the note to her. She turned it around to read the Sanskrit words written in English letters, and more.

Yojayitvātotānyeva
Praviveśasvayaṁguhām
Guhāṁpraviṣṭetasmiṁstu
Jīvātmāpratibudhyate
Time is running out. Make haste.
They are rules. I cannot say more.

'Who sent this? This is Vedic cosmology stuff. I know it like the back of my hand,' Sana said.

Adi sighed. 'Well, it was sent by someone who is me and yet, not me. We need to discuss our next steps. Let's find somewhere to talk.'

They walked away from the reception in the lobby and moved towards the lounge. There, they settled next to the fountain, which had cushioned two-seater sofas arranged around it. The sound of the flowing water encapsulated the closed zone around it. Adi did not want anyone hearing their conversation. He looked around before looking at Sana. 'Go on then, what does it mean?'

'It's a verse which describes how the Supreme Being is part of every universe in the cosmos.'

'Okay. Is that the translation?'

Sana re-read the Post-it note, her brown eyes moving quickly through its contents. Then she said slowly, 'It can be summarized as "By bringing together all the separate entities into a compact mass, He manifested the infinite ordinary universes and also became the hidden parts of every extended conglomerate. At that time, those with life and soul who slept during the devastation were awakened."'

Adi sat forward with his hands clasped together and his eyes closed as he heard her out. Sana blew air gently on his face, and he opened his eyes.

'We need to break it down – only then we can understand it.'

'The separate entities are different life brought together. So, universe creation.'

'Okay, and He is hiding in this creation.'

'Well, I would think it can be She – let's say the Creator is hiding.'

Adi nodded. 'Okay, and then there were lives and souls, which were not aware and became aware.'

'Awareness can be the rise of consciousness.'

'Yes, you are right, Sana. Now it makes complete sense.'

A paper boat was floating in the fountain water and reached near where Sana and Adi were sitting. It had 'S&A' written on it. Sana reached out and picked it up. She shook it gently for the water to fall out.

'Isn't this the boat from last night?'

Sana gave a quick nod. 'Yes, but I had packed it in my purse.'

She opened her purse. To her surprise, it was not there. She looked again carefully at the boat and noticed something written inside it. Sana placed the paper boat on her lap and opened it. In the centre was written:

To open the box, the wolf whistles over I pet goat.
Tick-tock. Tick-tock.
They are rules. I cannot say more.

She frowned and passed the paper to Adi. He looked at it.

'I know one part of it, and it points towards CERN.'

'Which part?'

Adi took a deep breath and spoke slowly, 'Well. "I pet goat" is a sort of code. In fact, certain elements say this set of words relates to CERN destroying the world.'

'What set of words – "I pet goat"?'

'Yes!'

'And you don't have any idea why?'

He shook his head and looked back at the paper. 'What I don't know is what "wolf whistles" stands for.'

'That's me. Do not ask me who, do not ask me how.'

Adi looked at Sana and squinted his eyes.

'Okay, okay…I'll tell you, but we have to go to a secure place.'

'Where…?'

'Just follow me.'

LEVITICUS: LAW OF PRIESTS
Suburbs of New Delhi, India
20 June 2028, 11.05 p.m. IST

Adi was now at Sana's house. It was a magnificent two-storey villa within a large, verdant compound. Uniformed attendants moved around the grounds and greeted them as they passed. Sana had a large trust fund set up for her by her parents. She had come into this money when her parents went missing in their private jet and were presumed dead.

Upstairs, in Sana's bedroom, she closed the door behind them and without a word strode over to what seemed to be her wardrobe. She opened it and to Adi's surprise beckoned him to follow her. Adi realized it was not a wardrobe at all but a large room. She stepped in, moving multiple coats suspended on hangers. On the wall behind the coats Adi spotted a fingerprint scanner. Sana placed her left thumb on it and some bits of the walls parted.

A lift! What the fuck.

Adi stepped in and had just registered that the lift had no buttons when Sana whistled and the lift started moving down.

Oh! Sound activated!

In a few seconds, the door to the lift opened and they entered a larger room, which Adi concluded was in the basement. The room was dimly lit in a green hue. The air-conditioning felt pleasant. One of the walls had multiple monitors, each showing a different area of the property. *Security cams.* A large table, semi-circular in shape, stood facing the wall next to the one on which the security monitors were set up. The table had two pairs of monitors on it, each connected to a large companion Corsair keyboard. One of the monitors was running the Norse live attack threat map. The other three had screensavers running on it. These were images of Adi – images which he could not recollect.

Settling into an ergonomically designed red chair, Sana moved the mouse and the screensaver faded away. She motioned Adi to look at the other monitor and as she placed her finger on a scanning device next to the keyboard the screens came to life asking for a password. Adi saw Sana enter the password: 'AYd0ppBA3l64BTUn63r.'

Woah, that is a complex password. But why are there such high levels of security?

The screen then asked for retina verification, which Sana gave.

Then, it dawned on Adi. *Fuck! Sana is a hacker. This is a top-notch hacking set-up.* Adi froze, feeling a rush of blood around his legs. Sana was looking at him now.

'So, tell me, how good is your security clearance at CERN? Are there protocols hidden from you?'

Adi was taken aback by the question. 'Why do you ask?'

'Well, according to the notes sent to us from ourselves, I would need to hack into CERN.'

'Hack! Why?'

'Well, I need to whistle over I Pet Goat to open the box.'

'Whistle... You mean hack? I'm confused!' Adi clasped his now sweaty hands. 'Well, CERN has multiple programmes. I don't have access to all the folders, but I do know most of the experiments that run.'

'If you see a folder that may be out of place, can you identify it?'

'Yes, I think so.'

'Okay, let's get started. There will be hidden folders and secured layers. That's where I'll find this box.'

Sana began to type furiously. Her eyes were focused on the screen. She accessed CERN's intranet website.

'How good are you?' he asked, sounding naive even to himself.

'I am the best.'

'Ah...right!'

She made a face at him. 'I never liked sarcasm, you know.'

'Aren't you scared?'

'My ghost is active. And I have multiple re-directs. It is my own power-analysis attack.'

Sana entered the site via the back page and moved quickly through different layers of security. Seeing her cracking the folders, Adi's mouth fell open.

'You are *good*.'

'Yes, baby. My hacker name is Whistler-Priestess.'

'You are the *Whistler...the* Whistler-Priestess?' Adi was incredulous. His throat felt dry.

Sana smiled at him, winked and turned back to the screen.

'*You* hacked the NASA and Area 51 computer networks?'

'I was looking for information.'

'What information?'

'*Udantakshari*,' said Sana and gave a gentle laugh.

'UFOs?'

There was a moment of silence. Adi saw Sana continue to work her magic. After some time, Sana stopped. One of her programmes was doing the cracking now.

'Two folders were present. It's show time, baby.'

The first folder had a set of PDF files. She opened a few of the documents and squinted as she read them.

'Gibberish.'

'No!' Adi was breathing heavily, his nostrils dilated.

'You're angry,' Sana said.

'They lied to me.'

'Who?'

'My superiors. They said no other experiments were on. And it looks like they were running some off the official records.'

'Really?'

'Yes, and it seems things are getting complicated.'

'What does that mean??'

Adi pointed at a graph in one of the PDFs. He explained the experiment to Sana. The chart showed higher energy output than was being inputted.

The energy units were passed across space and dimension, and more energy was returned where it should have remained the same. It did not make sense.

'So, it's as if one hundred units are sent into a doorway, and a hundred and ten come back. Which means there is energy coming from the doorway.'

'And a doorway means dimensions. Which experiment is this? The God particle, the Angel particle, or something else?'

'Different, not the Higgs boson. But a newer version of the AWAKE experiment, th...'

'The proton-driven plasma Wakefield acceleration experiment.'

Adi looked at Sana, raised his eyebrows and nodded. 'Yes, but we're not using plasma. It's something else.'

'What? Are you opening portals in other dimensions?'

Adi was quiet. Sana huffed. It was a secret that Adi did not want to share, but he felt an urge to. It was as though a voice spoke to him: *Give her a hint*. 'All I can say is it has something to do with gravitational waves.'

A chat box suddenly opened on one of the monitors. A message pinged to life.

Adi looked at Sana. 'We don't need to answer. It could be an AI security bot used for tracking.'

'It isn't.'

'How can you say that?'

'See what's written on it, and the username.'

Adi read the message. *All your butt my duplicate. Username, provost.*

'Adi, it's "all your butt belong to us" and my duplicate is my password reminder combination.'

'What do you mean, Sana?'

'This message is from me from another dimension.'

'And the username is "provost"?'

'Yes.'

'Well, in the message, should it not be "base" instead of "butt"?'

'With all that's happening, that's all that's bothering you? This is *me* communicating *across dimensions*. I thought of using this message just in case a multi-verse situation arose.'

Adi nodded, as Sana moved closer to the screen to chat.

Provost: All your butt my duplicate

-

-

Provost: Hi Wolf, This is Wolf. Hope Adi is convinced of our skills now.

Whistler: Yes, my priestess. @n63r

Provost: :) Talking to myself. I don't have much time.

Whistler: Go on, sister.

Provost: Do not stop the dance. But dance with it. Sleep. Don't be awake.

Whistler: ?

-

-

-

Whistler: @n63r.

-

-

'She's gone.'

There was a moment of silence. 'Yes, I can see that. Any idea what you, I mean she, I mean your other you…damn!'

Sana was quiet as she began to type again. A satellite image of the CERN building in Geneva came up on the screen.

'It is the Shiva statue,' Adi said. 'Must be…"Do not stop the dance. But dance with it." The Shiva Nataraja statue. And "don't be awake" has to mean that we need to stop any AWAKE experiment.'

'Yes, I know about the statue – the cosmic dance. But do you know how to stop the experiment?'

'I need to go to CERN.'

'So, when do we leave?'

'We? *I* need to go to CERN.'

'Why can't I come? I'll pay for my own tickets, you needn't worry.'

'No, no! This is not about the tickets. Getting the visa will take days and we don't have time.'

Sana frowned at him. Then she opened a drawer in her desk and pulled out her passport. It was burgundy red.

Adi's eyes widened. 'You… You're a British citizen?'

'Yes, I am.'

'I thought your mother came to India before you were born, and...' Adi stopped. 'Damn these dimensions! Do you understand this?'

'I think I know what you mean...'

'We are from different universes.'

Sana nodded. Adi continued, 'In this universe and the universe from where you've come, you are British. In my universe, Sana is Indian.'

'So, I'm not your Sana now.'

'No... No, no. She's nothing like this.'

Sana smiled teasingly. Adi blushed.

'We'll go now, right?'

'Yes. I'll inform the family from the airport that I'll be back in a week.'

'Right-o. Let's go into hyperspace.'

'Light speed ahead.'

'Engage.'

They raised their hands and high-fived each other.

RUDRA SAṀHITĀ: FIRE IN THE SKY
CERN Area, Geneva, Switzerland
21 June 2028, 11.45 p.m. CET

'It's so impressive,' said Sana excitedly. Before Adi could say anything, Sana raised her phone and clicked a set of selfies with the two-metre-tall Nataraja statue in the background depicting Shiva's cosmic dance of creation and destruction. They were in the garden outside the main entrance. The security had requested Adi to bring his guest in with proper papers as her name was not on the visitors' list. But Adi called his superiors, and they gave Sana permission to enter the garden area.

After the eleven-hour flight to Geneva, both Adi and Sana had rushed directly to CERN. In the plane, they'd discussed various hypotheses about what the message could mean. They concluded, only when they reached in front of the Nataraja statue, that at least one of the hypotheses would work.

Sana took more selfies and multiple photos of the Nataraja to get a clue to deciphering the message.

Inter-universe travel. Is this the reason for our moving across universes, Adi thought

'Adi, remember Carl Sagan speaking about this in *Cosmos*?'

'Yes, I watched the show as a kid. He referred to Vedic cosmology. I hope his spirit guides us.'

They studied the statue. It had four hands, each pointing towards one of the four directions. The right hand at the back pointed west and in it Shiva held his musical instrument, the *damaru*. The left hand at the back pointed east and held *agni*, fire. The third, the lower right hand pointed north in the *gaja hasta* mudra, and the fourth, which was the hand in front, facing south, pointed towards his crossed leg.

'The *damaru* signifies the sound of creation. Rhythm and time, the universe begins,' said Adi.

'Yes. And the lower right hand in the *gaja hasta* mudra shows that Shiva offers us protection. The fire signifies the destruction and end of the universe. So we have creation, protection and destruction all depicted here.'

'And which will be the multiverse point of view, then?'

They moved around the statue, inspecting it. Sana suggested stepping away from it a bit to see it from a distance. They walked backwards till the whole sculpture was well in perspective.

Sana spoke up, 'The fourth hand points towards his leg. And here it means liberation. One needs to be active and dance.'

They looked at each other. 'DANCE,' they said, in chorus.

'We need to dance but not let it dance.'

'The leg is lifted. Lord Shiva is dancing. If he was not dancing, his leg would be on the floor. And both his legs would be on the dwarf, Apasmāra.'

'The dwarf is said to stand for ignorance.'

'Yes, Sana, as I said on the flight, it can mean cretinism or under-development of the brain.'

'Right...which means that if he stops dancing, ignorance can end. All knowledge is released.'

'And then creation may end. Then a reboot will happen. Like in *Matrix*. It's a cycle.'

'It's an interesting hypothesis.'

'So, we dance and we don't let Nataraja stop dancing. Which means we need to keep his leg in the air and not let him put it down.'

'What would bring his leg down?'

They stared at it again. The sun was now at its zenith. The statue shone, and the circular metal carving around it, representing fire, began reflecting sunlight back with a higher intensity.

'Are you thinking what I am thinking?' said Adi.

'The fiery circle?'

'Ah-ha! It looks like the Large Hadron Collider! He's dancing, and the dance is the universe's secret.'

'And if he stops dancing then the universe ends.'

A strong gust of wind blew Sana's hat away before she could grab it. She started to run after it, but Adi held her back. She looked back at him, irritated, but he was staring at the sky. She looked up. The sun had begun to disappear. Dark clouds seemed to roll in out of nowhere and the sky was turning purple.

A piece of paper flew in their direction. He plucked it out of the air, opened it and read it.

I HaSh 24: Hydrogen
Tick Tock. Tick Tock. Tick Tock.

'"I hash 24" and "hydrogen"?' read Sana.

'No. It is chapter 24 and verse one. We need to hurry.'

'Why? Which chapter of the Bible, Quran, Puranas does it...?' Sana looked bewildered.

'No, Jewish, the Book of Isaiah. "Hash" is HaShem. It means God. I must have written this,' said Adi. 'It's my style of coding verses and periodic table elements. Let's move quickly.'

They began to move towards the lobby.

'Isaiah 24:1 reads, "Behold, HaShem maketh the earth empty and maketh it waste, and turneth it upside down, and scattereth abroad the inhabitants thereof."'

'The end of the world?' Sana pronounced solemnly.

'Maybe... Or of the world as we know it. The experiment is starting, and we need to stop it.'

'Adi! It must have a kill switch. Do you have access?'

'No, but can you hack it?'

'I can try. Maybe I need to use low-energy Bluetooth or something similar. But we have to be near the lab.'

'Let's get inside.'

They had reached the lobby and entered it, not aware that they were being followed by guards talking into their walkie-talkies.

'Herr Soans, Herr Soans! Fraulein!' one of the guards shouted out.

'Ignore them... Come on, hurry!' Adi told Sana as they ran across the yellow-red circular design on the floor of the lobby. Adi picked up a pair of blue helmets and handed one to Sana.

'Where are we going?'

'To the collider. The controls for this experiment are there.'

Adi, his all-access badge in his hand, headed for the lift around the corner, Sana following him closely. The guards were gaining ground, shouting across to them. Luckily, the lift opened as soon as they reached. They entered, and Adi jabbed desperately at the buttons. Just as the lift door was closing, they saw a guard throw the walkie-talkie towards them, hoping to jam the lift, but the instrument landed with a bang against the closing door and the lift began to move down immediately after.

'Adi, what are we going to do?'

'I don't know.'

'Well, you better come up with something, or we'll get arrested.'

'No, we won't.'

Then the lift opened, and Adi and Sana stepped out. The floor was deserted.

'Is it meant to be like this?' asked Sana.

'Well, we're not in the Beijing subway.'

They could hear the humming noise. The experiment had started! They ran towards the control room a few hundred metres away.

'Adi, I'm not feeling well,' said Sana, gasping a little. Something was different, Adi noted. He held her hand, and they were sprinting now, tiring quickly. Suddenly, a guard showed up in front of them, his gun drawn. He warned them to stop. They turned to run away. Shots were fired. They fell to the ground.

GENESIS: SO IT BEGINS
In the sky above New Delhi, India
19 June 2028, 2.35 p.m. IST

'Ladies and gentlemen, this is your captain, Nafisa Sharma, speaking.'

Adi gently opened his eyes to the in-flight announcement.

'Please fasten your seat belts. Our descent into Delhi has begun. We will be landing at Sardar Patel International Airport shortly. The temperature outside is 49 degrees Centigrade, and the air quality index is a very poor 350, with high particulate pollution. Do not forget to wear the complimentary masks given to you by our ground staff.'

Changing the name of the airport is more important than...

Adi shuffled in his seat. *What is going on?* He moved his head frantically from side to side as though to clear it. His co-passenger, a young teen, asked him if he was okay. Adi did not respond.

Was I dreaming this entire time?

'And apologies again for the turbulence an hour ago,' he heard the captain say.

Turbulence.

Adi checked his watch. The seconds needle was moving this time. *I was dreaming. Oh my GOD! Oh my god. Or was it real?* Adi tried to calm himself, slowing down his breathing. He closed his eyes again to relax.

'Mr Soans. Excuse me, Mr Adi Soans.'

Adi opened his eyes. One of the air-hostesses was leaning towards him.

'When the plane lands, Captain Sharma wants to speak with you. Please wait in your seat. And she wanted you to have this.' She handed him an envelope.

Puzzled, Adi took it and asked her why the pilot wanted to meet him. The air-hostess shrugged – how was she to know? Adi thought for a moment and said he would wait, ignoring the smirk on the face of the teenage boy next to him. Turning the envelope around in his hand he opened it.

His face froze, and his mouth fell open. *Sana's paper boat.* It had an 'S' and an 'A' inscribed on it...in Sana's handwriting. *So, I was not dreaming.* He checked the date on the large-screen monitor in front of him. *Today is the nineteenth, the day I'm landing in Delhi. The paper boat. It may have a message.* He opened the paper boat and the scribbles inside confused him even further.

"WOW"? What does she mean by that?

The plane landed. The passengers were leaving. Adi gulped the orange juice he'd kept off the food tray. He had to wait till he met Nafisa. A little while later he saw the captain enter the business-class section, where Adi was. He greeted her.

'Good evening. My name is Nafisa Sharma... I have two messages from Sana.'

'Sana? How do you...? What messages?'

'She connected with me before the flight, saying it was about life and death. I would have ignored it, but I did love her.'

Adi looked at her, puzzled. *Is this another dimension now, where Sana and the captain are lovers?*

'She said you would understand.'

'O-okay, what is the message?'

'The first message is: The Apollyon dance is not complete.'

'What dance?'

Nafisa shrugged.

'Okay... And the second message?'

'Well, it seems you need to save me?'

Adi could not fathom what Sana had meant. Instead, he asked, 'But where is she? Where is Sana?'

'She said she would be out of range as she is going to Sagittarius.'

'Where?

'The Orion stars, I think. The number she called from was Russian. Moscow. I can share it with you.'

Adi took the number and thanked Nafisa. He told her he would be in touch. As he took his bag from the overhead bin and started to make his way out, a sense of déjà vu came over him. He had been in the same place before, he knew that. But how? In his mind he went over Sana's message. *Sagittarius and Apollyon. Can it be...? The common thing connecting them are centaurs, half-man and half-horse. Maybe she's asking me to reach out to a place where they can be found? Need time to figure it out. But it is a step forward.*

He stopped. He was on the bridge now and could see the stars clearly in the night sky. He smiled. *I am in a different universe again. I can see the stars in Delhi. No pollution.*

As he stood and gazed around the transparent bridge, he noticed a large signboard. Something that he had seen before. On it was written, 'Everything is an illusion.'

There may be someone across these dimensions who's experiencing what Sana and I are experiencing. And that person is putting up these billboards. But who?

Adi closed his eyes. *Oh, Shiva. Sana and I have lost our fabric of reality. We have become the bhumandala couple.*

FLEXI-TIME

MANJULA PADMANABHAN

Dr Venkatesh glanced up at the shimmering strips. Turning towards him and drawing slightly apart, the seemingly weightless entities invited him to step down towards them, to stand in their midst. Sometimes there were audible sounds, such as chirps or deep groans. No actual words were said. Nevertheless, the professor found it possible to understand what was expected of him. This was believed to be a form of telepathy. If so, it was extremely subtle, not involving words or images. Whatever the method of delivery, the professor complied with the invitation without hesitation.

There was no pain involved in what followed, no discernible, quantifiable discomfort. Yet, the small man's hair stood up on end. He sweated. His pulse was elevated. He claimed that his mind was a perfect blank. But the truth was that he emptied his consciousness of thought and thus remained stubbornly empty by sheer force of will. He hated every moment that he spent in this condition, surrounded by vast unknowable beings, refusing to think, refusing to let them enter his thoughts. After perhaps one hour, the audience was over.

When he had returned to Human Space, Dr Venkatesh was permitted two hours for recovery. He changed into fresh clothes, replenished the water he had lost from sweating and ate a substantial lunch.

Then it was time to meet the members of the PCC.

The PCC campus had been set up within the grounds and building of what had been the Ashoka Hotel in central Delhi. The meetings were always held within an underground banquet hall, a space that had once been the venue of countless weddings. Venkatesh was escorted to the chamber by helmeted, armoured guards. They opened the ornately decorated doors and immediately withdrew.

Inside, council members were seated in a cluster in the centre of the room, each one behind a desk. Three of them had cups of tea or coffee in front of them, while one had a bottle of water. The professor had a winged armchair to sit in, facing them. He had a small side table to himself and his own cup of tea. He rarely ever got around to drinking it.

There were always four council members, the same four: two men and two women.

'Good afternoon, Professor,' said the general representing the People's Republic of China. She wore a crisp khaki uniform with medals on her chest. She spoke through an electronic interpreter. Each of the others heard her via earbuds in whatever language they preferred. 'Thank you for joining us today.'

Before the general could continue, she was interrupted.

'What can you tell us?' This was the general from the European Federation. He had a thatch of unruly white-blond hair, pale blue eyes and a craggy, permanently frowning face. He wore an aggressive all-black uniform with epaulets, medals, brass studs – the works. 'Anything of note?' His voice had a weary edge even via the translation device.

Dr Venkatesh cleared his throat and shifted in his seat. 'Uhh…' he began, speaking into a discretely placed body mic, 'that is to say…no. Nothing.'

The European general groaned aloud, pinching the bridge of his nose. Then he drew in his breath and jumped to his feet. 'All right,' he said, in a low, furious voice. 'I've had enough. I'm not going to take it any longer –'

Dr Venkatesh blinked and swallowed. He got to his feet as well. 'Sir, there's nothing I can do about the lack of a result,' he said. He tried to keep his voice calm. 'Believe me, performing this task is not my choice. If anyone else could take my place, I would gladly let them do it.'

The Chinese general was about to speak again when the woman with the polished ebony skin and dense halo of orange hair, representing the combined Americas, said, 'I see the general's point.'

As all eyes turned towards her, she got to her feet, achieving a towering height in her six-inch scarlet heels, her chic, floor-length black robe with scarlet flounces at the shoulders. 'We've been at this for…how long? Six days? Seven?' she continued. 'I agree with my European colleague. We have had enough. We need to know what lies ahead for us. For this planet. For our…species.' She looked directly at the professor now. 'Come on. You have to be able to tell us something!'

'But, Madam, I –' began the professor.

She stopped him with an imperious gesture. 'No! I'm sorry, Professor. This is not good enough. We need more.'

She paused and looked around before continuing. 'You and you alone have been invited into the presence of these beings who have, with no warning, taken over our entire planet. How they've done it, we do not yet know. One day we've never heard of them, and the next day they've taken over the world. No weapons, no conflict, no mode of travel – yet there they are. Everywhere. In every country, in every small village and town. These dangling, shimmering strips, suspended in mid-air! Emitting odd sounds! Issuing mysterious wordless orders! They defeated us before we even knew we'd been invaded. We don't know what they want, we don't know how to oppose them, we barely know who or what they are. This is intolerable!'

She looked hard at Dr Venkatesh. 'According to you, the call to approach the Home Space came in the form of an absolute conviction that arose from within, apparently telepathically, to go to the New Fa clearing. You went there, you halted at the impenetrable barrier, whereupon a portal opened, through which you, and you alone, were allowed to pass.'

Biting her lips, as if attempting to control her temper, she continued, 'The whole world has been waiting and wondering, waiting and watching. Yet every day you present us with exactly nothing. Surely, as a man of science, as a sentient being, you can understand that an entire planet cannot wait indefinitely? Surely you realize –'

The fourth delegate, a pale willowy man, wearing a sober, steel-grey business suit and representing Unified Africa leaned forward, cutting in. 'Excuse me, I'm not happy with the term you used just now, Madam Americas. I do not rush to conclusions about this issue of "defeat". After all, the Fa are merely amongst us. That is not the same as "defeat". True, they are everywhere. True, they have the ability to move people and physical objects in ways that we cannot explain or resist. But so what? To the best of our knowledge, they have caused very little actual damage. No demands upon our resources –'

'Oh, for heaven's sake!' the European general exclaimed. 'Let's just agree that earth has been invaded, okay? By a superior power. What I find quite *bizarre* is that this superior power has chosen to create its headquarters...where? In INDIA! Land of inefficient plumbing and a billion contradictions. Uncertain power supply and quarrelsome people.

Too many languages and too many gods. I mean, do I need to go on? In the 150 years since the end of the Second World War, the rest of the world has managed to solve these problems. Even Africa. Even the rest of South East Asia. Even, God save us, *Brazil.*' He waved a hand towards the relevant representatives.

He was panting now, his face red.

'But here? Noooo! Here, a state of primordial chaos reigns. Here, the traffic is jammed because of cows. The trains are late because of the rains. The streets are flooded because of the blocked drains. And yet...where do the silent Shimmerers pick as the preferred spot for their Home Base? Here! And who is their preferred interpreter? An Indian! I simply cannot accept that!'

Dr Venkatesh felt the surface of his skin heat up and grow damp with sweat once more despite the air conditioning. He hated confrontations. As a young boy he could remember physically wriggling and bending away from situations involving other people. They would get irritated because he could never give answers quick enough for them. He was highly intelligent and very good at his studies, but he had to think through his verbal responses. He liked to be precise, he liked to be accurate and truthful. It meant that he needed to take his time. It also meant that people frequently wanted to slap him – and occasionally did.

He had learned as an adult to control the reflex to fold himself in half and crawl away. But inside his head he felt a sensation exactly as if he were attempting to curl himself into a tiny ball, rolling himself into a corner.

'Ahhm,' he began. 'I wish I could help you. I...I want to help you. But there's really nothing that I can to tell you. I go to the venue, I meet with the Fa and I...'

The European general's eyes bulged, his lips drew back in a snarl and he lunged towards the physicist. The Chinese general, who was quick on her feet, spun around and hit the military man full in the face. 'No! We can't afford to fall apart this way!' she cried, as the other two representatives squawked aloud in surprise.

At that very instant, as Dr Venkatesh flinched away from the furious general, he found the space around his body stretching and ballooning outwards. It was as if he was contained within a bubble of some sort. It was a bit like an infinitely elastic cling film covering him without restricting his movements. Outside of it, he could see the rest of the room frozen in place. Within it, he could move around with ease.

Hesitantly, he took a step forward. His scalp was tingling with amazement and curiosity. He took another step. The bubble, or whatever it was, moved with him. Meanwhile, the other people in the room remained frozen. Still as statues.

Dr Venkatesh walked slowly and wonderingly over to the Chinese general's desk. He picked up the bottle of water that was there, still unopened. Then he returned to where he'd been standing, beside his chair. None of the four PCC members had so much as twitched an eyelid. A sense of sparkling enlightenment began to dawn within the professor's head.

So, he thought. *So!*

He opened the bottle of water, drank from it and capped it once more. All the while, the invisible bubble kept him contained. He looked around the room thoughtfully. He could take his time, he realized. This was like his childhood habit of trying to escape physically from torment but transformed into a temporal bolthole: a bubble of time where he could not be reached. He had let his guard down in that moment of panic when the general came at him. His mind had curled in upon itself, rather like a turtle pulling in its limbs and head. In that instant, he had slipped into the bubble.

How will I get out of it, he wondered, even as the answer appeared in his head. *Just reverse the turtle act. Unfold yourself.*

Immediately, the room filled with sound. The two generals righted themselves. Madam Americas was staring strangely at Venkatesh. The African representative looked slightly ill.

'What?' asked Venkatesh, looking at the others as if they had said something to him.

'You...' began Madam Americas. She stopped and began again. 'Something happened to you. I saw it. Just a blink. But I saw it.'

'Thinned out,' said the African rep, in a strangled tone of voice, as if he'd swallowed a toad. 'I saw it too. Weird. I can't explain it.'

Venkatesh's mind was wonderfully calm. 'I'm thinking,' he said, as he twirled the water bottle slowly in his hands, 'that perhaps I was wrong. Perhaps I do have some news to share after all.'

'Come on, come on!' said the European general, waving his hands in the air, as belligerent as before. 'Get on with it!' The Chinese general, though, stared at the water bottle. She recognized it as hers.

The physicist smiled. Perhaps for the first time since the assignment had begun, he was feeling happy.

'You know, General, what you were saying earlier? About the thousand ways in which India has resisted the modern world? I can well appreciate how irritating it is for you – all of you who transitioned to the digitized era with your perfect regularity, your punctuality, your precision! Yes, India is annoying. Yes, we appear dysfunctional. Yes, we lag behind in so many sectors that we seem to belong to an older, quieter time altogether. We move at our own pace. And that drives people like you mad, General.'

The general snarled and bristled, but his Chinese counterpart grabbed his arm. She was frowning, her gaze still on the bottle in the professor's hand.

Venkatesh paused, holding up the water bottle. 'You've noticed the bottle, Madam General? Yes, it's from your desk. I walked over and picked it up. While the two of you were assaulting each other.' He glanced at the other two council members. They were staring at him with their mouths hanging open. 'What you saw of me was a sliver of myself as I moved around in a bubble of expanded time. That's why I looked weird.'

He took another sip from the bottle now. 'So, here's what I'm thinking: I don't know why the Fa came to our planet, I don't know what their plans for us are. All I am certain of is that they are benign. And the reason they chose India? Maybe it's because of that quality the rest of you complain about when you come to this country: an altered sense of time. Not wrong, not late, not lazy, not stupid. Just...altered. Different from the rest of you speedy-needy types elsewhere on the planet.

'Maybe that's what the Fa saw in us Indians: a fondness for stretching time. Maybe it's an ability, not a liability. Maybe it's a talent, not a defect. Of course, we've not been able to do what they do, which is flex the boundaries of the fleeting minute. But maybe they knew that Indians, more than any other humans, would be more receptive to learning their so-called "chronological otherness"? Maybe we have a natural talent for learning their techniques of time-bending and chrono-stretching? Moulding it to suit our needs, rather than being imprisoned by it? Maybe that's what they've been passing on to me during my time with them.'

He put the bottle down on the table next to him. 'And now, if you don't mind, I'll take your leave and return to the Fa. I believe I have finally understood how to receive their instructions.'

The four members of the council watched in silence as Venkatesh thinned out before their eyes. They heard a few indistinct chirps and clicks. A moment later, he was gone.

THE OTHER SIDE

PAYAL DHAR

1

They were very close to the border when Leela's foot caught on an exposed root and she went down with a muffled moan. This past week had conditioned them to being quiet. It was an instinct. Even those who had died had done so silently.

Nisa dropped down next to Leela in the pitch darkness. The driver's firefly lantern – their only mode of navigation – grew fainter and fainter ahead of them. They did not have the luxury of stopping to assess Leela's injury. For one, the night was their biggest ally; once the cover of darkness was gone, there was only death – or worse. For another, getting left behind was not an option.

There were shouts up ahead, and Nisa's blood turned cold. Shouts were not a good sign. Silence was everything. Then there was a gunshot, followed by more shouts. In that instant, Nisa knew that by tripping Leela had most probably saved their lives. They lay flat against the dark, cold ground, as still as possible, shivering, whether from pain, cold or fear, who knew – probably all three. The uneven rasping of their breath seemed like a beacon for their enemies to home in on.

The cold air and the damp chill from the ground seeped into Nisa's clothes, digging their fingers right into the bones of her tired body. Fear and cold had her paralysed, the night pressing down on her from the top, and the cold, dark, formless ground pulling her into itself from below. She felt like she was being buried alive, like the broad, almost-there outlines of the trees that surrounded them were closing in. She was so tired that the idea of lying there and letting the forest take her was a welcome thought. Even though they were so close.

Low whimpers from Leela nudged her back to reality. The firefly lights were gone now, replaced by the penetrating beams of powerful torches that swept the area up ahead. A gentle swishing sound meant that the wind was starting up again. As Nisa lifted her head a bit to look around, she felt a sharp pain in her arm. Leela's fingers were digging into her bicep, her grip like a vice even through all of Nisa's layers. Her mouth felt gritty with mud and she smelt wet earth close to her face.

Sight, sound, touch, taste and smell. *I want to live.*

She realized she had spoken aloud when Leela replied in a whisper tight with pain: 'Me too.'

Surely they had left all the Company check posts behind? There weren't supposed to be border guards here. Their heavy tread made the ground vibrate, the sounds of their search muffled by forest noises of rustling leaves and animal calls.

Nisa and Leela had been towards the end of the train, but there was no way to tell if any of the others had scattered and circled around behind them when the guards had appeared. Nisa wondered how many had been captured, how many shots had been fired. It was odd that the guards were carrying guns, though. It was too retro; she would have guessed tasers, set to beyond 'stun' but short of 'kill'. The thought of being caught was like a foulness spreading from within. Everyone knew what they did to captured workers. And, worse, to allies.

Leela's grip on her arm loosened for a moment and then tightened again. 'They're moving away,' she whispered.

The arcs of light were now further away. Nisa felt the tension leave her limbs. Perhaps they would live after all. She propped herself up on her elbow and stared at the faint receding outlines of the guards, three of them.

'It'll be light soon,' Leela pointed out.

That was not good news. Nisa turned to her. 'What do we do?'

'We have to go on. We know the border is close – in that direction.' Leela nodded with her head. 'It's now or never.' She pulled herself upright as she spoke, grimacing in pain.

Nisa thought of her friend's slight frame. 'I can carry you.'

'No!' The reply was sharp.

'But your ankle...'

'I have another.' She stood with the help of the stick she had been using to navigate the more difficult mountain paths. There was no arguing with her and, anyway, there was nowhere else to go but forward. Keeping under cover as best they could, the two young women inched forward. Nisa reminded herself that the rough path etched on the grass was evidence of others who had come this way before.

The sound of voices stopped them short. The glow of a fire nudged from the edge of the mountainside. Their path went over the ledge, right over the border guards' watch point or camp or whatever it was.

'One by one,' Nisa whispered. 'You first.'

'No...'

'I said it. You first.'

There was no time to argue; they would rather have an opportunity to fight about it later. She knew Leela felt the same.

Voices rose from the guards. They laughed. The fire crackled. Nisa's nerves jangled like her out-of-tune guitar back at what had once been home. She held herself tight, watching Leela move further and further away. They would have to be as quiet as gravestones.

But Leela crossed without event, and when Nisa could no longer see her companion over the dip in the path, she finally allowed herself to breathe. It was her turn now. As quietly as she could, she started to move. As she neared the fire, she bent low – she was taller than Leela and had to be careful nobody spotted her over the lip of the ledge. Nearer to the camp, the laughter rose, a raucous sound over the rough hiss and spit of the fire and strains of music. Crouched on the crest right above their hideout, Nisa couldn't help inching forward to see what they were doing.

Four people were gathered around the fire, so well bundled in thick coats and hats that it was impossible to tell if they were men or women. Their rifles lay on the ground, but within reach, as two of them picked through a threadbare canvas knapsack, removing items of clothing and laughing at each item.

Rage burnt through Nisa. She knew that knapsack. It was old Uncle-ji's. One of the guards appeared stretched out on the ground. It was an odd place for a catnap – even with the fire, the ground would be chilled. As the fourth guard moved, Nisa had a full view of the napper – it was a body.

Then it fell into place, realization hitting her like a bludgeon. These were no border guards – they were bounty hunters. The kind that were paid to return bodies of escapees. Bodies that would be displayed in public as deterrents.

A moan almost escaped her lips as she recognized the lifeless form. She clapped her hands over her mouth. It wasn't just the sight of his death that shocked her; it was the long, thin implement impaled in the dead man's eye, something that glinted.

Nisa swallowed down the bile in her throat and choked back her sob. Shaking, she rose to a half crouch and turned in the direction of the waiting Leela. Then a loud crack – she had stepped on a twig.

'What's that?' A man's voice from below her.

'There!' Another shout, and an arm came into Nisa's vision pointing towards the forest, down in the valley. Away from her.

It was brighter now, light enough for her to see someone running in the forest. No, two people, an adult and a child. Mohi and her young son? But Nisa had no time to think about anyone else. She had been given a lifeline. She couldn't save anyone else. As the bounty hunters pelted down the mountainside, eerily silent despite their speed, she turned and ran the rest of the way, to where a trembling Leela was waiting.

'What was the noise?' Leela whispered, her voice unsteady and shrill. 'I thought...'

She caught Leela by the shoulder, sobbing. 'Nazir is dead, Leela! They... they put...they put his eye out.'

'Oh.' The sound was like the air going out of Leela's lungs. She pressed her hands on Nisa's forearms for a moment. Then she wiped the tears on her cheek with the back of her hand. 'We can't mourn him now. We have to go. Fast. It is nearly dawn.'

Nisa nodded, unable to speak, letting Leela lead the way. The path was clear, and they stumbled along in silence.

'Look,' Leela said.

Her voice sounded different, making Nisa turn to her instead of where she was pointing. She hadn't seen a smile in a long time.

'*Look.*' Leela nodded as if to emphasize the importance of the word.

Nisa turned to look. It was the border. A shrouded figure stood beyond it, gesturing to them to move faster.

2

Eight days before Nazir died, a sharpened steel rod through his eye, Leela and Nisa huddled deep inside a container truck along with three other people, in a cramped, hollowed-out space between a cargo of carpets, knees and elbows jostling, giant rolled-up parcels towering over them.

Nisa clutched a plain canvas rucksack to her chest – the plainest and most nondescript one she had been able to buy from the offline market in the Walled City. Leela's hand gripped hers. It was surreal to think that the life she had known just a week or so ago was over. Everything she owned was now in that rucksack; the books and clothes and gadgets and money, everything else gone. The thought that from here on she and Leela only had each other was terrifying.

They knew nothing about where their first station was or how long it would be before they arrived there. All they had been told was that they had to move quickly and quietly, and follow instructions. Whose instructions, they didn't know. Nisa couldn't tell how long they had been on the road, but the smooth movement of the truck and lack of frequent stops indicated they were on the highway. Her stomach tightened into a knot. How far would they have to travel in this confined, suffocating space? Would they know if plans went wrong? What would happen when they reached a check post and the truck was searched?

The ragged breaths of her companions got on her nerves. She couldn't tell if she was the one shivering or if they all were, as one. Her body was taut from anticipation, and each time the truck slowed she tensed even more.

When they finally did stop, things happened very quickly. They were not privy to what would make the truck stop in the middle of the highway, or how they would get out of the electronically locked container. But the small beep of the lock disengaging and then the cold air striking them with its metallic-smoky tang set them all in motion. Mohi with her son Golu went first, followed by the frail Uncle-ji, and finally Leela and Nisa.

Smog hung in the air, limiting visibility, but there was no mistaking the sound of voices and the loud metallic clanging going on towards the front of the truck.

'What…?' Nisa started to say, but the woman who had let them out shushed her and pointed to a narrow strip on the ground worn between the waist-high shrubs and the surrounding trees.

'Quick and quiet.' Those were the only three words she said.

They walked in silence through forests and fields, a tight, tense, terrified group, bound only by the hope of freedom.

Dawn was licking the edges of the sky when they reached their first station. It was an underground bunker, the entrance hidden in a rock behind a scraggly crop of bushes. The metal doors screeched as their guide pulled it open, unnaturally loud in the forest. Nisa was glad when they were inside.

Narrow, bricked stairs, illuminated by the light of a torch, led straight down into a small, squarish room. One dim LED bulb hung from the ceiling, a fading ball of light around it. There was silence apart from their footsteps on the stairs, but Nisa knew instinctively that they were surrounded by people. Still, it was a shock to find about a dozen huddled shapes around the room. Some of them stirred, some slept, some sat up. Nisa imagined their eyes on her as she found place for herself and Leela in one corner. Someone handed them blankets.

'Sleep if you can,' their guide said. 'Facilities are this way.'

The 'facilities' was a tiny room with a plastic door and an overpowering chemical stench that in all likelihood masked other smells. Nisa got out of there as fast as she could, her heart sinking at the thought that this was the reality of her new life. She suddenly yearned for her comfortable bed and well-lit room, her eco-flush toilet and temperature-controlled shower.

She pulled the blanket around her and nestled beside Leela. Despite the coldness of the floor and the uncomfortable contortions of her body due to the lack of space, she fell into a deep, exhausted sleep.

Nisa woke to the sound of people shuffling and talking. She untangled herself from the blanket and pulled herself upright. She felt rested, if sore, so she guessed it was probably daytime. The room was still dingy and dark, though now humming with restless activity.

Leela sat with her back against the wall, blanket over her legs, eating a rolled-up chapati. She gave Nisa a wan smile. 'Hungry?' She pointed to a rickety table next to the stairs. There were chapati rolls with jaggery inside them, and an insulated dispenser with tepid tea. Nisa helped herself and went to sit with Leela, studying the others. She counted ten people in all, some clearly travelling in pairs and others alone. The conversation was muted, and with her eyes adjusting to the gloom, she could see her own worry and fear reflected on faces of the others.

The woman who had guided them here in the early hours of the morning – 'station master' was the correct term – walked to the middle of the room. Seeing her face clearly for the first time, Nisa was surprised to see a worker. She had expected an Upper, but her roughly cropped hair, her small, thin stature and her manner of speaking said otherwise. When she started to speak, turning around to face the others, the girl even spotted a biochip scar. And yet, the woman – she said her name was Fatima – spoke with a confidence and assurance that Nisa would never have associated with a worker before. She missed the first few sentences, and when she caught up Fatima was giving them instructions.

'There are three kinds of people we must look out for. First, Company guards, easy to spot because they are loud and obnoxious. They are also usually in and around check posts, which we will do our best to avoid. If they catch us, we will be worse than dead. The second lot are bounty hunters. These are the most dangerous because they could be anywhere and anyone. They could be you or I, we have no way of knowing. If they catch us, we will be dead because they are paid to return our bodies. The third danger, which is 99 per cent of anyone we come close to, is the general public. Most of these people are not dangerous in themselves, but being spotted by them might mean Company guards on our trail.

'So, it's simple. We have to stay hidden. We will travel only by night and mostly on foot. Sometimes we will have transport from allies who are part of the Underground Railroad. It will take us anywhere from six to fifteen days to reach the border. There are six stations along the way, and you may be joined by other travellers. You will meet your engine driver today, who will either take you right to the border or hand you over to another driver. Depending on how dangerous this crossing becomes, you may be joined by other drivers or be split into smaller groups. Any questions?'

There were none.

'It's hard to say when you will travel again. Rest when you can, but be prepared to set out every night. To freedom.'

'To freedom,' everyone murmured back.

Their driver arrived later that day. Nisa was stiff from sitting, but it was impossible to sleep all the time. The nervous energy in the room was palpable and when the door to the bunker clanged open, her heart leapt into her mouth. She pressed into the wall between Leela and Mohi as the dark outline of a man came down the stairs. He stepped into the bubble of light.

Nisa clutched Leela's hand tight, making her gasp. She stared into the face of the man who would lead them all to freedom. She wanted to memorize every line, every shadow on his face.

'Call me Nazir.' Those were the first words he spoke. 'Think of me as Nazir and nothing else.' Nisa was sure he was looking straight at her and Leela as he said this and felt compelled to nod. A second later, Leela nodded too, and then Mohi and all the others in the room did the same.

'We will leave in a few hours,' he said. 'We have to walk to the other side of the forest from where two trucks will pick us up. We will be passing through residential colonies, so speed and silence are essential.'

The next few days passed in a blur. The nights were mostly for stealthy travelling, following the firefly lantern that Nazir carried. Its flickering lights gave the impression of fireflies in the air, much safer than torches, which would give them away. The days were for sleeping or huddling in dark, airless spaces. Nobody spoke much, but almost everyone cried.

Nisa had no idea how far they travelled, but when they reached their third station, there were only nine of them. One young man, who had seemed sickly and cried all the time, was missing. Nisa tried not to think of the splash she had heard when they were crossing a bridge. Their station masters kept them fed, but food was often short. The constant gnaw of hunger made her weak. There were times she wanted to turn back, but of course she had crossed the point of no return a long time ago. She could either go on or wait for another bridge with a roaring river underneath.

She sought out Nazir whenever she found him alone. 'How long have you been doing this?' she asked him.

'More than a decade now.'

'Why do you do it?' She wanted to understand what would make him risk everything like this.

'It's my repentance,' he replied.

'What are you repenting?'

Instead of answering, he said, 'But this is going to be my last crossing.'

'Why?' When he didn't reply, Nisa asked, 'How many crossings have you made?'

'About four in the last few years. Why? Don't you trust me?'

'If you weren't trustworthy, I'd be dead by now – we all would.'

'Maybe. Or deleted.'

Nisa knew he wasn't joking.

3

A week before Nisa escaped in the back of a container truck, when the Magadh Carpets factory was being surrounded by Company guards, she was in her room, getting a guitar lesson from her robotic music teacher in Japan. She had no idea how she had got approval for these online lessons. Access to websites outside Company-controlled areas was severely restricted.

Lately though, she had been losing interest in such things. The more time she spent in the workers' colony in the Walled City with Leela, the more ill at ease she felt. Even today, practising her chords monotonously, she was thinking about Internet censorship. These days she couldn't wait to skip school and sneak into the Walled City, Leela by her side. She hated the place, yet it kept pulling her back. What compelled her to go back week after week were the nameless handwritten magazines that circulated there. Just the thought of getting her hands on the illicit publications sent a thrill down her spine. She didn't know if she believed the things she read in them, but she couldn't keep away.

She almost dreaded finding out that there was a new issue – they weren't regular, they only came out when the (unknown) writers had something to say. Everything about the threadbare sheets of paper stapled together, even their existence, made her uncomfortable. They turned everything she had ever known about her life on its head. Especially the idea that social structure had nothing to do with the natural disposition of different kinds of people, but was merely a ploy to keep wealth concentrated with what the magazines called the 'Point Five Per Cent'. Was life really all about money? As distasteful as the idea was to Nisa, Leela once said that only those who had never had to think about money could afford to scoff at it.

Nisa logged out of her unfinished guitar lesson, her thoughts swirling around in her head. There was so much she had never considered before. What if it was true, as the magazines suggested, that workers were small in stature not because of genetic disposition but because exposure to radiation and pollution made them malnourished?

She wondered how she could possibly access the open Internet and find out more about these things. Forget the Internet, she wanted to travel, to see how people lived in places where everyone had the same rights and you could do what you wanted and live where you wanted. It was never going to happen, not with Mamu's running of the family business. It would be a miracle if the family even retained their Upper status, forget getting to Elite level. Only the Es were eligible for foreign travel, of course.

Unless I escape via the Underground Railroad, thought Nisa. For a second, the adventure of trekking secretly to Nepal, being admitted to a refugee camp, and beginning a new life seemed deliciously thrilling. Then she sobered up, recalling the horror stories she had heard at Leela's.

The kitchen staff wasn't answering, so Nisa decided to go down and see to that snack. It was irritating how unresponsive they tended to be whenever her aunt was away. She clattered downstairs, only to find the kitchen deserted. 'Hello?' she called. 'Anybody?'

No response. Nisa checked the pantry, and then stepped across the short corridor to the workers' kitchen. That was deserted too. Disquiet welled up inside her. Where was everyone? The door leading out to the backyard was ajar. Nisa peered out in the night.

Wait – were those shouts? Panic gripped Nisa. She was all alone in the house – Mamu was probably in the factory, Mami was away and all the servants seemed to have vanished. What was going on?

The shouts were louder now. Someone barking orders, sounding suspiciously like Company guards. Nisa ducked into the house and pulled the door shut, latching it. She needed to check that all the doors were secure. But even before she made it out of the kitchen, she heard the bang of the front door. Whoever they were, they were in the house. And somehow Nisa knew that she didn't want them to find her.

She stepped back into the kitchen, hands and feet numb with fright. She wanted to curl up and scream, but that wasn't an option. She looked around, frantic. Then she remembered the walk-in freezer. She had loved going inside it when she was a child. She ran into the pantry and yanked the door open, blinking against the harsh blue light, and flung herself inside.

As she pulled the door closed, the light went out, leaving Nisa in near darkness. Which was just as well because it stopped her from shutting the door all the way. She wedged a thin packet in the door, leaving it open a crack, and squeezed herself into the opposite end, trying not to touch the walls or the frozen goods hanging from hooks above. She gagged at the smell of raw meat.

In her cotton shirt and jeans, she was already freezing. Her teeth were beginning to chatter when she heard the heavy tread of boots in the kitchen. They came closer and closer. Nisa wrapped her arms around herself, willing herself to become smaller and her teeth to stop chattering. The footsteps stopped. She held her breath. How close was the guard? There was an electronic beep, then a harsh female voice said, 'Kitchen all clear.'

Nisa waited for the footsteps to die away, then exhaled with relief.

She remained in the freezer, letting the minutes tick by even after the guard had gone. She remembered her phone and fumbled to get it out of her pocket. She tried her uncle's number, then her aunt's, but the same recorded message told her they were unreachable. If only the Walled City had a mobile network. She could have called Leela and asked her what the hell was going on.

When Nisa was finally convinced that the guards had gone, she tiptoed out. The house was empty, furniture upended and valuables missing. She ran up to her room and found that her hybrid was gone. Distraught and confused, Nisa searched the house again. She went outside, right up to the lawn gates, which yawned open. But it was deserted. She could see a lone Company guard in his distinctive khaki uniform at the large main gate up ahead, lounging against the wall disinterestedly, smoking. She knew she couldn't ask him for help, but she also knew that she had to get out. She needed to get to the Walled City.

She was about to turn away when something moved in the shadows close to her. A scream almost escaped her, but she clapped her hand over her mouth at the last instant. The figure moved slowly towards her, keeping to the wall. Nisa knew she should run, but her feet refused to move. When the figure rounded the last corner and came face to face with her, she felt she would die of relief.

It was Leela, who caught her arm and dragged her towards the back of the house. 'Guards?'

'All gone. What's happening?'

'There was a raid on the factory. There are rumours of a conspiracy against the Company.'

'That's ridiculous!' Nisa exclaimed. 'Mamu can barely run the factory, let alone mastermind conspiracies.'

'They are saying he was trafficking workers. He's on the run.'

'What! Oh, they haven't arrested him?' Nisa felt relief washing over her. He might be inept, but he was still her uncle.

'They haven't been able to find your aunt either. They'll be back, Nisa. They'll be back for you. Your uncle sent a message for me to come get you.'

'G...get me?'

'Yes, let's be quick. Pack your stuff.'

'How are we going to get out? There's a guard at the gate.'

Leela thought for a few seconds. 'We'll disguise you as a worker.'

A few minutes later, Nisa was blinking back tears at the uneven way in which Leela had hacked her hair off. She had stuffed herself into a worker's uniform. Leela also used a black pen to draw an approximation of a biochip scar on the back of her neck. They realized the Company guard at the main gate wouldn't let them carry anything out, so Nisa wore as many clothes as she could under the uniform. She stuffed her phone and charger into her pocket, even though they would be useless in the Walled City, and grabbed as much money as she could find.

Then, with heads bent, they scuttled out towards the gates. There wasn't much acting needed – Nisa was terrified. If the guard chose to scan them, she would be caught since she didn't have a biochip. But as it turned out, Leela played her part to perfection, snivelling and shivering. 'We were so scared, sir,' she whined to the guard. 'We hid in the freezer. Please, sir, let us go.'

The guard waved his taser at them. 'Get lost. Useless things.'

They ran all the way to the Walled City.

Nisa took a cup of tea and a bowl of rice porridge from Leela. The house was dark, everyone asleep. They had the outside room to themselves. Ever since Leela's father's death, her aunt, aunt's baby and Leela's two siblings slept inside, in the only room in the house with air-conditioning.

'How did my uncle get in touch with you?' Nisa asked.

'He sent a messenger. You remember Raghu?'

'The one-legged guy who was deleted last year?' He had lost his leg in a work accident. 'How does Raghu know my uncle?'

'He's resourceful. Much more useful than most people with two legs.'

'Will you take me to him in the morning?'

Leela shook her head. 'You should probably stay hidden. Morning will be too risky. We can go now if you want to meet him.'

They walked through the narrow lanes of the Walled City, Nisa huddling under a large shawl to cover her face, to the tiny tin-roofed shack that Raghu called home. He didn't seem surprised to see the girls. There were a couple of other men in his shack, who melted away into the night as soon as they arrived.

Raghu only repeated what Leela had already told her. 'Your uncle is in hiding. Don't worry about him. He said he's sorry he couldn't get you out. He didn't know about the raid till it was too late.'

'And my aunt?'

'I heard she's safe too.'

'Raghu, do you know where my uncle is? Can you take me to him?'

He shook his head. Nisa didn't know which question he was answering. *Nani was right*, she thought. *Mamu can't be trusted. And he's a coward. He ran and hid when his family was in danger.*

'What am I going to do?' she said. Her voice shook. 'I have nowhere to go.'

Leela's hand pressed into her shoulder. 'You can stay at our place for now.'

Raghu seemed uncertain. 'They'll be looking for you, though. There will be a reward for information. You can't go back, but you can't stay here either.'

'You don't have to come with me,' Nisa told Leela. She tried to sound firm, but her voice shook.

'I want to go. I would have gone eventually, Nisa. Even without you. I want to get out, so I can make a better life and buy my family's freedom. It was my father's dream and now it is mine.'

'But it's dangerous. What if...'

'What if I stayed here and nothing ever changed? And it's dangerous for you too.'

'But I have no choice.'

'Neither do I.'

4

Eight months before Magadh Carpets was raided, Nisa skipped school for the first time to visit the Walled City. The two girls had planned it meticulously. Leela had taken leave, using her father's ill health as an excuse. She told Nisa she would wait for her at the gates of the Walled City. Nisa took the school bus in the morning as usual, but got off at the next stop saying she had forgotten her locker pass and had to go back for it.

She almost didn't recognize Leela in her faded cotton T-shirt and brown trousers, carrying two threadbare umbrellas – she was used to seeing her in the drab uniform of the house servants. But it was Leela who looked at her up and down in dismay. 'Everyone will stare at you.'

'Why?'

'Your...' she started to say, but stopped. She handed her an umbrella. 'Never mind. Come on.'

Nisa pulled off her pollution mask since Leela wasn't wearing one and tucked it into her bag. She coughed in the acrid air as she opened her umbrella. She had expected security guards at the gate, but there were none. The 'gate' itself was just a gap in the ten-foot-high wall with rolls of barbed wire on top, which turned in to form a long, bricked corridor that turned right and then left.

The first thing that Nisa noticed about the Walled City was the smell. An odour of sweat, food and something else she couldn't identify. The next thing she realized was that it was nothing like the cheery, well-laid-out colonies shown in her school textbooks or in the media. The roads were so narrow that there was only space for two people to walk abreast. The houses were haphazard buildings crammed together, shaped to fit whatever space they filled. Some didn't even have proper doors.

And the number of people! Little children, out unprotected in the harsh sunlight, ran around, screaming in play. Men and women sat at their doorsteps, stitching, smoking, cutting vegetables, talking across the narrow lanes to each other. And everyone stared at Nisa, her smart and shiny maroon-and-grey school uniform standing out among the drab, faded and mostly formless clothes visible otherwise.

'Good day for sightseeing,' someone called.

'Ignore them,' Leela muttered.

Nisa followed Leela deeper into the labyrinth, gobsmacked at the sights and sounds around her. Did people really live in such close proximity, in that stench and in open air? It was horrifying. Most of the houses had old-fashioned air conditioners, but there was no sight of climate control. Leela's house was an even bigger shock, just two rooms, even tinier than Leela had described, a bulky air-conditioning unit hanging lopsided from the only window.

Nisa perched awkwardly on a bench by the door while Leela went to get them tea. Leela's young brother and sister stood before Nisa, studying her like she was an interesting scientific specimen. She tried to speak to them, but they continued to stare. Finally, Nisa had to look away. She could see an old man in the corner of the other room, sitting on a plain wooden bed, his back to the wall, staring into space.

'That's my father,' Leela said, handing Nisa a stainless-steel mug of strong ginger tea. 'He was suspected of stealing so they cut off his fingers.'

Nisa sputtered into her tea.

Leela shrugged. 'This was before the biochip days. He could no longer pass the scanners, so he was demoted from worker to x class. Deleted.'

'I am so sorry, Leela. I...I didn't know.'

'It's not your problem. Almost every family here has a story like this.'

'Suppose you worked really hard and saved up, you could rent a house outside the Walled City?'

'I'll never earn enough working as a cleaner.'

'I still say you should take your boards, go to college and become a teacher.'

Leela shook her head. 'Even if I did have enough money, I wouldn't be allowed to live outside the Walled City.'

'What? That's insane.'

'You know they track us, right?' Leela tapped the back of her neck. 'This chip. Any *neech* not authorized to be in the Upper Quarters after midnight spends the night in lock-up.'

Nisa flinched at the Leela's use of the derogatory term for workers. But they used it freely in the Walled City, almost defiantly.

'That's...' Nisa didn't know what it was. 'So, you...*have* to live here? All your life?'

'There's one other option.'

Nisa could tell Leela was being flippant, but she asked anyway. 'What?'

'Take the Underground Railroad out of here.'

'What's that? A rail service?'

Leela laughed. 'It is, but not the kind you think.'

'Then what? Stop talking in riddles, Leela.'

'Oh, all right.' She leaned forward. 'But don't go around repeating it or I will get into worse than trouble. There's a network of workers – and some Uppers or allies as we call them – who smuggle workers out.'

'Smuggle them out where?'

'To the border, where they can cross into Nepal.'

Nisa exhaled loudly. 'Allies? Like the liberals and activists who want to end Company control?'

'Yes.'

'Wow. They're dangerous people. I hope you have nothing to do with them.'

'Dangerous? Depends on how you define the word.'

Sometimes Leela said the strangest things.

5

Nisa decided she wanted to see the workers' colony six weeks before she bunked school and went to the Walled City for the first time. The idea germinated one evening, when she was sharing her schoolwork with Leela, something they had got into the habit of lately.

'I must be a fantastic teacher.' Her teasing tone belied a smidgen of resentment as she looked over Leela's algebra answers.

Leela waved a brush with long, loose silvery bristles at her. 'Ha, you're just jealous because I am better.'

That was a bit too close to home, so Nisa changed the subject. 'I don't understand why you dropped out of school. You are clever – you should have taken your boards.'

'What would be the point?' Leela asked, resuming her dusting.

'Point? You could go to college, get a degree, then a job…' Nisa let her words trail off, watching Leela shake her head.

'Do you know how many workers get into degree college?'

'What do you mean? There's a quota.'

Leela shook her head. 'Forget it. Pipe dreams.'

'But you do have them, right? Dreams? I mean, what would you be if you weren't a…' Nisa didn't want to say the word to Leela.

'A *neech*?'

Nisa winced. 'I meant a worker.'

Leela shrugged. 'I would have liked to be a teacher.'

She said it matter-of-factly, without pausing for thought. It reminded Nisa of her own dreams.

'I once wanted to be a doctor,' she said wistfully.

'What's stopping you?'

Nisa swept her arm in a semicircle, indicating everything around her. 'Everything. The family.'

'But you don't have to listen to them, right?'

'It's complicated. Why are you a cleaner in a house when you could be training to be a teacher?'

'Our circumstances aren't quite the same.' Leela said it gently, but Nisa felt like it was a rebuke.

'Are they that different though?'

'You have no idea. Our worlds are different.'

Nisa had known Leela for more than a year, and they had been friends for most of that time. Friends of a sort, that is, given the differences between them. The first tenet of their relationship was secrecy, of course. She couldn't imagine what Mamu and Mami would say if they knew she had been chatting with a worker, sharing food with her, letting her sit on her bed.

Before Leela, Nisa had never questioned segregation. Society had to have structure, everybody knew that. The workers were the support – that critical but behind-the-scenes system for the rest of the people, who ran the country and made sure everything functioned. And it worked because your role in society was marked out depending on what you had a genetic predisposition for. As an Upper, it was your responsibility to run the country, including making sure the workers had all they needed for a suitable, ordered life. Everyone had their place.

'To build a structure, you need a foundation,' the Company Chair had said in a speech after being elected just last month, which Nisa had streamed secretly on her smartwatch during an economics class, 'a strong one to keep the edifice of society standing. Though foundations are seldom visible, without them, society would crumble.' Nisa recalled the thunderous applause that had accompanied these words, and those that followed, extolling the workers and laying out the new facilities that were being rolled out for them.

As far as she knew, the workers had everything in their colonies – housing, water and power supply, their own schools and hospitals, and even their own transport system. They were a hardy, physical lot; they had better immunity than the Uppers, so they tended to spread disease and had to live separately. They also needed a different environment – her biology textbook said workers became weak if they lived in climate-controlled environments for long periods. They needed to be closer to nature. It sounded raw and exciting. But somehow, whenever Leela talked about her home, which wasn't that often, she made it sound different. Nisa couldn't reconcile what she knew about workers' colonies and what Leela sometimes described.

'Take me to your house,' she said.

Leela's eyebrows went up, so far that Nisa could almost see the crinkles in her scalp through her closely shaven hair. 'You want to see where I live?'

'Yes. Invite me.'

Leela seemed uncomfortable. She looked around, like she expected Nisa's aunt to jump out from the behind the cupboard and berate her for sitting on Nisa's chair. 'Your folks will never let you go.'

That was true. There were many dangers for Uppers to be in close proximity to workers, though almost a year spent in Leela's company hadn't made any difference to Nisa's robust health.

Nisa had a brainwave. 'I can skip school. It will be such an adventure.'

Leela didn't seem convinced, but she agreed eventually.

6

Two months before Nisa started tutoring Leela, and Leela in turn began to educate Nisa on life in the Walled City, the two girls had fallen into a routine.

Every morning, Leela brought Nisa's breakfast up, and they sat on the floor of the balcony, out of sight of anybody who happened to look up. They set the tray between them and shared the food – there was always more than enough. Leela had been hesitant at first, but Nisa had pushed her till she relented. The hungry eyes with which Leela had stared at the food when she had first offered to share her meal were indelibly printed in Nisa's mind. It was almost like she had never seen food like that, but of course Nisa knew that there was a separate workers' kitchen at the back of the big house where food was specially cooked for them.

One day, they finished breakfast early and pushed the tray away, both of them reluctant to get up just yet. Nisa's eyes roved up to the top of the giant, transparent polymer cylinder topped with a shallow dome that surrounded the big house and garden, keeping the whole area climate-controlled while still allowing a view of the dusty grey-blue sky.

'I wonder why they call this the big house,' she mused out loud. 'It isn't even that big.'

Leela snorted with laughter.

'What?'

'You think this is small?'

Nisa spread her arms. 'Well, it's just four bedrooms – one for me, one for my uncle and aunt, and a couple of guest rooms.' It annoyed her that sometimes Leela could make her so defensive. 'And a dining room, living room, kitchens... Why are you still laughing?'

'Because you think this is a small house.'

'Most of my friends in school have much bigger houses.'

'Do you know anyone who has a smaller house than this?'

Nisa narrowed her eyes, trying to figure out if Leela was teasing or laughing at her. 'Yeah, sure. Why?'

Leela stared back at her, all serious now. 'I wish you could see the Walled City.'

'Why?' Nisa asked again.

'You just should.'

Nisa kept looking at her. 'How big is your home?'

Leela turned away. 'We have two rooms.'

'Two bedrooms?'

'No, two rooms, in all.'

'For how many people?'

'Six.'

'No!' It was impossible.

Leela laughed again, a tight, mirthless laughter. 'Two rooms smaller than your bedroom.'

'You're joking.'

'And we're lucky – at least we have a kitchen and a private bathroom.'

'*One* bathroom? For six people?'

Leela nodded.

Nisa leaned back against the wall, uneasy. 'The worker colonies have adequate housing with no overcrowding and are equipped with all necessary facilities.' Even to her ears it sounded trite, like she was quoting from her social responsibility textbook. 'Any verified worker above the age of sixteen may request independent accommodation. Why don't you move out and live somewhere better?'

Leela was staring at her, her mouth open. 'Look at you. You sound like a Company pamphlet. You're so naive sometimes, Nisa.' Her voice was soft. 'As for "verified worker" – do you know what happens to those who are not verified?'

Nisa bit down on the strange feeling building inside her. 'You mean the x class?'

'We call them the deleted people.'

'Why?' Nisa was curious. 'The x-es have their retirement homes and institutions, don't they?'

Leela didn't answer for a long time. Then she said, 'On paper.' She stood abruptly. 'I have to get back to work.'

7

Nisa met Leela almost a year before she had her first inkling that the ordered world she thought she lived in wasn't quite so rosy.

It was a week after Nani's first death anniversary, a Monday but a school holiday. Nisa had plans to meet her friend for a swim. She had almost reached the car before realizing that she had forgotten her bag.

She entered her room and almost screamed in fright when a dark, slender figure unfolded itself from the far side of her bed. Then she noticed the simple black-and-grey uniform of the servants of the big house and the long-handled vacuum brush.

'I am sorry, miss, I didn't mean to scare you.' The girl at the end of the vacuum brush couldn't have been more than 15 or 16. Her face was unfamiliar, but then Nisa wasn't used to paying too much attention to the servants. She had been brought up to believe that the best workers were neither seen nor heard, and had always found that a convenient precept to live by.

'It's all right, carry on.'

The girl turned away, bending down and prodding underneath Nisa's bed. Nisa's eyes fell on a red welt at the back of the girl's neck.

Of course, she had a biochip. Everyone who worked in their house and the factory had one. Mamu didn't like the old system of fingerprint- and iris-scanning.

Nisa had rarely got an opportunity to stare at a biochip scar so unabashedly. She'd been told that it was beneath someone like her to stare at lower-status markers, but the truth was she was fascinated. She'd seen a few of these scars, but none so angry-looking like this girl's. She wondered if the girl might have tried to gouge it out. They'd studied biochips in school, and news about hacking and workers trying to cut theirs out with knives and what not were always doing the rounds. She shivered at the thought of such deliberate injury. And, anyway, why would you want to gouge it out? Biochips were convenient.

She fingered her own biochip, implanted in her wrist, the scar long since faded away. Doors opening automatically when she approached, especially high-security areas like banks and schools and supermarkets, and she could walk out without having to pay because it would automatically scan your chip and deduct payment. Who wouldn't want all those conveniences? But then, workers' chips didn't quite work that way – they were mostly to keep workers out of areas not meant for them.

As if she sensed Nisa staring, the girl turned. Nisa looked away instantly, annoyed at being caught.

The girl stood up, facing Nisa. 'I can come back later, miss.' She spoke with her gaze fixed on a spot under Nisa's neck.

'No… I…' Nisa found herself at a loss for words. The girl was probably around the same age as she, but shorter and very thin. But then most workers did have smaller builds. Being slight and nimble was what made them suited to manual work. Her hair was very short, like it had been shaved and was growing back; again, not uncommon since many workers found it easier not to have to manage unruly hair. Her skin was a dark brown, eyes almost black.

'What's your name?' That was the only thing Nisa could think to ask and immediately felt stupid. Like all the others, this girl too had a prominently displayed identification tag, and a quick look would have told Nisa her name.

'It's Leela, miss.'

8

Thirteen months before she first met Leela, Nisa's biggest regret was not having asked Nani to endorse her application to switch to the science stream sooner. The seven weeks and three days that she procrastinated proved to be a day too many. Very close to the application deadline, she finally screwed up her courage and marched to Nani's room with her tablet in hand. But she found a great deal of excitement outside Nani's door.

Their family physician, Dr Hema Gino, stepped out, the sharp clip-clop of her boots as matter-of-fact as her words. 'She's had a cardiac episode. She's stable but doesn't have much time.'

Nisa clutched the doctor's sleeve, distraught. 'Why aren't you taking her to hospital?'

'Stubborn woman,' was her short reply.

Nisa strong-armed her way into Nani's room, pushing aside the burly nurse and her aide. Nani looked diminished, as if she had shrunk overnight. Her four-poster bed looked too big and her covers seemed like they were trying to swallow her. A drip pole on clawed feet stood near the head of her bed, while various machines beeped and hummed around her. Nani's eyes were closed but when Nisa approached the bed, she opened them. Nisa knelt on the floor and took her grandmother's hand, small and frail. Nani's eyes looked through her, unfocused. She started to speak, her words muffled. Nisa leaned forward, bringing her ears closer to her grandmother's mouth.

'Don't...trust...him...'

'Don't trust whom, Nani?'

'I don't trust him. Samir.' The words were clearer now. Nani's eyebrows were knitted together, her body tense. 'You are the future, Nisa.'

Nisa shook her grandmother's shoulder gently. 'Nani? What are you saying? Please, let Dr Gino take you to the hospital. You could get a new heart.'

Nani exhaled softly. Her eyes cleared suddenly. 'A stranger's heart? I think not.' This sounded more like the grandmother Nisa had known all her life. Nani closed her eyes, her breathing even. Within minutes, she was asleep, the hand holding Nisa's going slack.

Nisa watched her grandmother's chest rise and fall rhythmically for a few minutes, then, satisfied that Nani was okay, she left the room.

Nani never woke up.

After her grandmother's passing, it seemed to Nisa that the ground had gone out from beneath her feet. Growing up in that large house, even with cousins coming and going, uncles and aunts in and out all the time, when it came down to it, Nani had been her world. Her parents had died in an accident when Nisa had been a toddler, and Nani had stepped in. Her grandmother had never been the easiest person to get along with, nor the warmest and most approachable, but Nisa hadn't known anything else. Most importantly, she hadn't wanted for anything – as long as she didn't step out of line.

Nisa also knew that with Nani's death her dream had come to an end. When she approached her new guardian, her uncle Samir, about endorsing her application to switch streams in school, he had looked disapproving. 'You can't be a doctor. You are my mother's named heir.'

And that, Nisa knew, was the end of that. She remembered her grandmother's almost-last words to her – *don't trust him* – and shivered. What sort of a man was he that even his own mother didn't trust him?

But as the months turned into years, Nisa found her uncle to be inoffensive to the point of boring. She heard rumours from other, more distant family members, who were resentful of not having a bigger say in the running of Magadh Carpets, that Mamu was an ineffective manager, that he seemed disinterested, that employee turnover was high and the company was losing money constantly training new workers. Eventually, her distrust of her uncle levelled off to a vague sort of apathetic contempt. Maybe that's what Nani had meant – Mamu couldn't be trusted to run the company. Especially not after she had worked so hard to turn its fortunes around.

9

About two years before Nani died and a few weeks after Nisa turned 13, her grandmother told her, 'Just because you remember something doesn't mean it happened.' Nisa was old enough to know that Nani wasn't calling her a liar, and she was clever enough to understand that what she meant was that memories could be unreliable.

To be fair, if she had a choice, she would rather that the gruesome images in her mind were the result of an overactive imagination. But try as she might, she couldn't shift the heavy stone of unease that lay deep inside her stomach.

All her life, Nisa had seen the servants and other workers being scanned, not just in her own house, but also in markets and banks and schools. Watching them press their fingers – right, then left – on the scanner and waiting for the green light, then bringing their faces close to the iris scanner – right eye, then left – and waiting for the second green light was as ordinary as breakfast appearing on the table every morning. And just like the kids she had seen that morning, she and her friends and cousins had also played 'scanner-scanner' when they were young, using old shoeboxes and cardboard rolls. Back then, you didn't get the toy scanners that kids had nowadays, complete with the fake buzzing and the lights.

'But it felt so real, Nani,' Nisa insisted. She wrapped her arms around herself, as though the steady 25 degrees of the climate control was too cold for her. 'Like I remembered something that I've seen with my own two eyes, not like something I watched on screen.'

'What you see on screen is also with your own eyes,' Nani pointed out.

Nisa could see that she was already distracted, having gone back to her spreadsheets and reports and what not. Her hybrid computer was folded back into a tablet and whatever it was she was clicking and scrolling through was invisible to anyone outside the narrow range of visibility it offered.

The girl turned back to her own hybrid, the new one Nani had got her for her birthday. It was silver and shiny; she knew she ought to love it, but it was without the narrow-visibility privacy feature that she had wanted. She hadn't said anything, of course; she'd just smiled and thanked Nani because she wasn't exactly a spoilt brat.

With a resigned sigh, Nisa navigated to her school portal and let her weekend homework download. Being Nani's blue-eyed grandchild had its advantages. If she did everything that was asked of her, when the time came for her to ask for something, maybe, just maybe, she would get it.

What Nisa wanted more than anything else was to be a doctor. But her future was already mapped out: complete school, go to business college, and take her place among the top management of Magadh Carpets. To step out of the family fold without support was unthinkable; to do so with the family's blessings, she would have to convince Nani. And the way to convince Nani was to impress her. Good grades were very high up on her list of priorities. But it wouldn't be easy. It wasn't convenient for youngsters of her background to have dreams of their own.

For now, she had to tackle trigonometry. Not difficult at the best of times, but today she struggled to concentrate. Like many individuals blessed with a quick brain, Nisa hated nothing as much as she hated not understanding something. It was easy for Nani to brush her memories off as a bad dream, but that didn't answer Nisa's question: *Why?* Even if it was a dream, why was she dreaming of something so gruesome, something straight out of a retro horror film from the 2020s?

10

Four-year-old Nisa loved spies even though she wasn't exactly sure what a spy was. So it wasn't unusual to find the little girl crouched under a table wearing a wireless headset and tapping on a piece of board. People were used to her crawling out from under beds or finding her crouched inside cupboards. They knew when cardboard cartons with holes appeared in strange places that Nisa was on a stakeout, and when things disappeared from the electronics recycle bin that it was she who had pinched them to repurpose into spy gadgets.

The day she reached the pinnacle of her career in intelligence was also the last day she every played 'spy-spy'. It was just as well that it wasn't something Nisa was fated to remember.

It was a baking summer day. The sun was so strong that it hurt to look up at the sky, even through the transparent enclosure that kept their garden, with its springy lawn and vibrant flowerbeds, alive and cool. There were so many hiding places here – thick pillars on which potted plants rested, the underneath of ornate benches, the bushes shaped like elephants and tigers and other extinct animals. One of her favourite games was to see how far she could get towards the main gate without being seen. It was fun out there because she could watch the servants and factory workers being scanned and photographed and time-stamped before being let into the compound. But it was outside the big house's electronic lawn gate, beyond which Nisa wasn't allowed by herself. She'd never managed to escape and go out alone, but it was worth a try.

As she crept steadily from pillar to bush to bench, Nisa knew it was going to be a good day. And, sure enough, she soon found herself behind an oversized pot stationed right next to the gate. A thrill coursed through her. She watched as the guard released the lock and their cleaner trooped inside. The two started to talk, their backs to her. The electronic gate hadn't closed yet. Nisa didn't stop to think. She darted out through the gap.

At first, to be all alone in the outside compound was thrilling beyond measure. But the sun beat down on her and the heat came off the concrete ground in waves, making everything shimmer. She began to feel uneasy.

Near Nani's office building, there was a ladder thing on wheels, reaching up to a small door. Nobody was about, so Nisa scampered up the ladder and slipped inside. She found herself in a tunnel, just big enough to crawl through. She hesitated at first, but having crawled a little way ahead found that it was the most fun tunnel ever. It twisted and turned, and every now and then she found herself by tiny windows with bars across them through which she could see into rooms. Most were empty, some were filled with people at desks, looking at computers. Boring. Then she reached one through which she saw Nani.

Happy to see her grandmother, Nisa was about to bang on the bars and ask Nani to let her out when something made her stop. Nani was standing with her hands on her hips, a frown on her face. Next to her stood her uncle, the new one who had come home just yesterday. Nani had said he had gone to a big university to study about how to make their factory the best in the country.

Mamu had his arms folded across his chest. He didn't look happy. Nani looked very angry. She was shouting at another man, who was on the floor, on his knees, his hands folded. A thick rope tied his wrists and ankles together. He was crying.

Nisa frowned. Grown-ups didn't cry.

Nani was shouting, the crying man pleading. Nisa couldn't make out what they were saying, she didn't understand the language.

Nani turned to Mamu. 'Do it!' she barked.

'No! Please!' the crying man shouted.

'No, no, no. *Please*.' Mamu sounded scared too.

'Do. It.'

Mamu was shaking. He looked scared. Nisa already knew Mamu was scared of Nani. The previous evening, he had knelt before Nisa and hugged her. 'I am so happy to finally meet you, Nisa,' he had said. 'Do you know who I am?'

Nisa had shaken her head.

'I am your mother's brother. My name is Samir, but your mum always called me Nazir. Will you call me Nazir Mamu?'

Nisa had been about to nod, when Nani had cut in. 'You will call him Samir Mamu.'

Her uncle hadn't responded to that. Nisa had decided to call him just Mamu.

Now, Nani pressed a long, thin stick into his hands. Tears ran down Mamu's face too. She said something to him, her voice hard, like she spoke when Nisa had been naughty. The sound of that voice made Nisa's blood run cold. She knew she shouldn't be here. If Nani caught her, she would be spanked.

In her panic, Nisa missed what happened next. All of a sudden, the crying man was howling in pain and a stick was poking out of his eye. There was blood everywhere.

Mamu dropped to his knees, holding his head in his hands, while young Nisa wondered how the howling man would get past the eye-scanner now.

EPILOGUE

The last time Nisa saw Nazir Mamu reminded her of the first time she had seen him: her crouched in a ventilation shaft, him poking a stick in a man's eye like he was driving a cricket stump into the ground. She knew now what his repentance was, and she understood why he had chosen to do this dangerous job.

'I always thought he was a weak man, unbending and narrow-minded,' she told Leela as they sat on a rocky outcrop just outside the refugee camp in Nepal. A wind whipped around them and Nisa couldn't feel her nose. 'I know now that was what kept his double life safe.' Her grief knifed through her. She exhaled slowly, trying to ease it out. 'I only spent the last few days of my life really knowing, knowing who he was – I regret that. He was a hero, but everyone thought he was spineless and ineffective. He said this would be his last crossing – it was because his cover had been blown, wasn't it? If he went back, if he was caught, they would have killed him.'

They sat till the sun went down. Nisa's old life felt as though it had been someone else's story.

When they were walking back to the camp, Leela said, 'You know all those dreams we had? I feel they don't mean anything any more.'

Nisa stopped and turned to her friend. 'What do you mean?'

'I feel...' Leela struggled to get the words out. 'It's like...everything is so big, and I am so small. I need new dreams.'

Nisa nodded. They walked the rest of the way in silence.

15004

SAMI AHMAD KHAN

Deoria Sadar Railway Station, Uttar Pradesh
Local Time: 2100 hours

'Yatrigan kripya dhyaan dein. Gorakhpur se chalkar, Allahabad ke raaste, Kanpur junction tak jaane waali 15004 Chauri Chaura Express platform number char par aa rahi hai.'

The familiar, *purabiya* voice stirred up a cold panic in my gut. Amidst shuffling feet, grime-coated surfaces and the sickly stench of faeces and peanut shells, I felt numbed by the strange phenomena that shrouded my shivering family. A thick blanket of unnatural smog – call it fog or mist – enveloped the small, bustling railway station, and alert klaxons started to blare in my brain.

Something didn't smell right.

My nostrils flared on their own accord and I instantly pictured Dada-ji's big, bulbous nose, which I often held between my fingers while playing in his lap. How things actually *are* and how they *appear* are two very different things, he used to say. His ideas were incomprehensible to me, but his soothing, sing-song voice often lured me into a placid sleep. *Dingansik*: that's the only phrase I remember from our encounters. I still don't know what it really meant, but I can feel it stuck like an old catchy melody inside my head.

I blinked to clear my smog-impaired vision.

When in doubt, seek the familiar. A large analogue clock ticked at the other end of the platform. An aged, panting coolie eyed a family of five huddled under a lone, tattered blanket as he struggled to balance four huge suitcases on his head. The resounding, reassuring ring of *manjeerey* emanated from an ancient Shiva temple a few feet away from the platform.

Silhouettes of old men huddling around a blazing fire swayed in front of me: their *charas*-ridden gestures slow, deliberate and fluid like those of a Kathak dancer.

An unnatural silence fell on the platform. A white sheet of moving vapour had devoured the world around me, gnawing at the innards of reality. It became so quiet, in fact, that I was able to hear a low, soft, whimpering segue into a groan that didn't sound…natural. Despite looking, the pathetic, flea-infected station mongrels couldn't be found. Perhaps the strange smog and frigid winds had chased them away to the hidden, subterranean domains of the station mice, I rationalized.

Mice!

The mere thought of the disgusting mammals made my right toe, protected by two layers of black woollen socks, twitch with rebellion. I tilted my head towards my silent, brooding mother – smashingly young and pretty to the passers-by, frighteningly neurotic to me – and caught a glimpse of her indifferent face.

'Why do we have to leave so soon?' I complained, knowing I was still not too old to quit whining. 'This is so wrong! You…'

My words yearned to gush forth and protest against the profound injustice of a vacation terminated midway, but they couldn't. For my easily irritable, bald father was back by now – and his permanent scowl with him. Papa's portly six-foot frame radiated a certain *je ne sais quoi* that unnerved me, and his perpetually pursed lips rarely masked the tobacco on his breath. He swaggered towards us, kissed my head casually and thrust a packet of *sohan halwa* in my hands.

Ma placed a protective arm around my waist and drew me closer, an act that brought out from within me a spontaneous, irritated shrug. Purple bruises throbbed on her forearm, concealed under layers of foundation, and Kabeer, my younger brother, blocked my view by burying his face into her yellow Banarasi sari. I stared wide-eyed at the foggy darkness around me – and the unspoken one within our family. I knew Kabeer wouldn't suffer for long. Children grow up much faster these days – and sooner too.

I had.

The twitching in my right toe got more pronounced and had to be restlessly brushed twice by an adjoining toe to be quietened down. Impulsively, I opened my mouth to taste the smog, and thrust my tongue out into it like a red sand boa that Dada-ji had once caught in his bungalow, the one whose tail resembled its mouth. I remember ogling at its wildly thrashing body as an emaciated Gond had, at Dada-ji's behest, impaled it on a *chilbil* branch, doused it in *mitti ka tel* and burnt it alive to counter its *ashubh* presence in the house.

Pushing the image of scaled, shiny reptilian skin on fire, dripping and hissing fat, and the sour, acidic smell of such a funeral pyre out of my head, I flicked my tongue up and down again, sparring with the smog.

Something didn't taste right.

Dingansik.

The railway platform had emptied by now. The crowded EMU passenger train had departed from the other platform, haemorrhaging shit, diesel and smoke in its wake, an old, wounded war horse dragging itself towards the waters of its final destination in its last throes of agony.

A stare burnt my neck, boring into my soft flesh like a sniper's mark from far away. Exasperation and rage stirred inside me, and I shook my head to come back to the present, afraid of what lay within. A faint light in the distance was getting brighter in the tracks, and its urgent whistle assaulted my eardrums. I firmly squeezed my eyes shut, and fervently prayed that the train would never arrive.

It never did.

Gauri Bazar Railway Station, Deoria, Uttar Pradesh
Local Time: 2130 hours

'Behenchod!'

Sparkling red waves – and particles – of heady, chewy madness flew out of the WDM-3A and dashed against the metal railing of the slowing locomotive with a soft *phhich.* The speed of the Chauri Chaura Express, coupled with the wind direction and the angle of spitting, ensured that a generous portion of paan-flavoured saliva bounced back off on to an averagely built man in his late forties.

Ramnath Singh exploded into a thousand nasty invectives as his starched, sky-blue shirt was infected with a crimson patch, a stain spreading in a slit across it. His irritation evinced a good-natured guffaw from a young man standing right next to him in the cramped confines of the Gonda-based locomotive.

Amar Franklin, Singh's chubby, twenty-four-year-old co-pilot, wore similar clothes, though his week-old stubble and glasses that were too large for his eyes gave him an unkempt appearance.

'I told you, RB Babu, you are from Rajasthan in name only. In *asliyat*, you are a *bhaiyya* from *our* side, total Allahabadi. Any plans to stop spitting paan all over India, my *eashterrn* friend?'

'I'll stop when you stop whistling at *ladeez*,' Singh spat out, quite literally.

Amar sniggered in response.

Singh raised an annoyed eyebrow. 'You're still on probation, don't forget that, *saale*. Keep your views to yourself till you become *pakka*.'

He was already in one of his rotten moods. Inclement weather conditions, antipathy towards his job and a troubled family life were more than what a fatigued, underpaid government employee could have combated successfully, certainly not a smart-ass junior.

At least Amar was still posted in an Indian Railways zone he could call home, Singh thought ruefully – unlike him. His efforts to be close to his family had all come to naught. He had petitioned to be transferred to the north-western railway zone multiple times, one that was closer to his ancestral village. The unctuous, Janus-faced babus in Gorakhpur had merely passed his application around, *despite* the usual 'transfer money' being offered, and had treated him like a punctured football that had lived past its utility.

Except, *this* football still drove trains.

Bitterness rose in his throat like bile, and Singh tried to shrug it away. He knew this was no time to regret his life choices: lives depended on him being efficient, effective and observant. He gently slapped an armrest and focused around him. The greasy, green interiors, mucky gauges and oily instrumentation cluster in the locomotive stared back at him. There were no needles in the red zone, no alarms had been raised, no collision alerts sounded, and no track changes scheduled. Singh exhaled in relief. Studying the instruments and concentrating on his job always relaxed him. Human emotions were unpredictable and so were transfer applications: machinery, however, not so much.

Singh stuck his head out of the pilot window and looked for the next signal. The dismal visibility and rapidly falling temperature made him a bit apprehensive. He glanced towards the chair where Amar sat, playing with his newly purchased smartphone.

Singh felt a sudden urge to puff a bidi. He grimaced as he pushed the thought out of his head, knowing that partaking of any substance while on duty was an offence that could earn him a memo or, worse, leave without pay. A paan was as far as he was willing to go. His mind whirring, Singh did the next best – or worst – thing possible. He decided to have a lungful of the smog-ridden air outside the locomotive.

'Amar,' he said matter-of-factly, 'WhatsApp your *laundiya* later. Get up, take the controls. I've got the *talab*.'

Amar, annoyed at the intrusion, rolled his eyes and muttered something under his breath. But he also immediately sprang up, for he was not one to disrespect a direct senior, especially one who had taken him under his wing. He caught a hold of the walkie-talkie from Singh and placed himself at the helm of the locomotive. Singh, meanwhile, moved towards the door on his left, slid it open, and let his ruby mouth drink the smog in large, thirsty gulps.

As the cold, translucent air entered his system, Singh felt a raw, refreshing power pump up his limbs; his lungs felt surprisingly accommodating and light. For a split second, his mind detached itself from his body, and he stared into the unknown, unmindful of a row of people shitting across the adjacent tracks.

A thin skein of pure energy shot out of the smog in the distance. He shrieked and almost lost his balance. An ominous bolt of lightning, and the skies cracked open for a microsecond.

Then there was nothing.

Singh squinted at what he saw, or what he thought he saw. He kept gawking until the empty whiteness up ahead started to hurt his eyes. Nothing again. His mind was playing tricks on him, he concluded and cursed. As a Class II pilot with over 25,000 hours of freight and passenger piloting in various electric and diesel locomotives across multiple railway zones (there were sixteen, he recalled) under his belt, Singh had driven trains amidst fog, rain, hail, sleet and the scorching loo winds. However, this time it was different. He was curious to understand why the smog had descended so quickly, and why it seemed to grow heavier and denser with every passing minute, turning the very air into a sort of thick, cold, grey soup.

Then Singh groaned. He had just realized this smog would most definitely cause a delay. *Another* delay.

If the passengers felt irked by trains being late, he told Amar, they should try discovering what it felt like to be cooped inside an uncomfortable, claustrophobic space replete with the overwhelming stench of sweat, urine and diesel for hours. And for what? So one could somehow make ends meet. Barely.

Amar's lesson of the day courtesy his senior: Fuck the railway *babus*, fuck the *afsars*.

Today had been markedly different when it began, Singh remembered. A few hours ago, the sun had yawned like a wrinkling yellow raisin, and the sky had had a brown tinge at the crumbling horizon. He had walked his six-year-old son to the bus stop, where a daisy-coloured schoolbus with red stickers saying 'Caution: No Honking' had swallowed the boy, and left with a faint trail of hushed rattles and blinding screeches. Singh came back home and slept, hoping to get some rest before reporting for duty later in the evening. As night descended, the city had been engulfed by a strange smog that chilled the bones. The journey to the station from his home, which usually took no more than 20 minutes, had taken an hour today.

The locomotive jerked and changed tracks, dragging Singh to the present. He spat out another stream of red liquid and dusted his shirt. *Saala kohra ko bhi jhelo*!

Time passed without any incident, its surroundings blurred: the 15004 slowly glided along the tracks, and Singh saw signals turn red the moment the locomotive crossed them. He was about to withdraw into the cabin again when his ears picked up a faint noise, audible despite the steady din of the engines. He thrust his head out of the window and heard a low buzzing overhead.

'Amar?' Singh detected a faint note of concern creeping into his own voice, as if something was wrong but he couldn't really point out what it was exactly.

'*Haan*, sir?'

'I can hear something. Come here. *Suno*. I'll handle the loco.' Singh beckoned him near the locomotive entry gate and took Amar's place at the controls. Amar quickly tiptoed to the gate and strained to hear anything out of the ordinary. He then positioned himself near the outer railing of the moving locomotive and picked up the swarming sound of angry bees attacking a lamb tied to a post. It seemed to be coming from somewhere above him.

A part of him shuddered, and he felt, rather surprisingly, angry.

'Yes, Singh-ji,' he quickly replied, eager to hide the edge in his voice. 'Sounds like the overhead wires.' He coughed, inhaling copious amounts of the smog. 'Must be carrying too much current.'

'But...' Singh began, and fiddled with a gauge. 'That *just* isn't possible!'

Amar slowly understood why his colleague's face bore an incredulous expression.

'This route isn't electrified yet. Yes, some wires have been installed in a few sections, but there's no *bijli* supply *peeche se*. That's why we use a diesel loco on this section, not an electric one.'

'I know, sir-ji. Maybe the engineers are doing a test run? Some new tech?'

Singh nodded, uncertain of this explanation but unsure of what else to believe.

'Shall I call ahead and ask?'

'No. It's none of our business,' Singh shrugged, deciding against poking his nose in affairs that weren't his. 'Come back in. Close the door. It's getting chilly inside.'

Amar nodded and turned around at Singh's words but stopped dead in his tracks. He felt something move within his chest, an ominous wave that paralysed him for a microsecond, just like the epileptic fits he used to have as a child. He clutched at his stomach, horrified, waiting for the seizure, but the feeling was gone before it hit him. Alarm and relief flooded him simultaneously.

Singh saw Amar stumble on his way back inside and shot an agitated look in his direction. *'Arre!'*

Amar gasped, gulped, and sank to the floor. He suddenly felt fatigued, as if every iota of energy had been sucked out from his body.

'Go, sit. Drink some water. I will handle the train.' Singh took charge and gently helped Amar lie down.

This was not uncommon, he thought. The long working hours, draining tasks and pathetic service conditions of loco-pilots quite often led their systems to be perpetually messed up. All they needed were rest, hydration and a little bit of support.

Honed by habit, Singh noisily sucked in the air and saliva from the corner of his lips, wiped his mouth with a blue handkerchief and returned to the 3100-horse-powered, V16 diesel engine under his command. Amar was a good, solid lad, he thought. To see him act up like this, that too at such a young age, raised questions about his tolerance as a long-term loco-pilot for the Indian Railways.

But then Singh had bigger things to worry about than Amar's dizziness. Somehow, the brakes weren't working as well as he'd have liked. As he began writing it in the logbook for the maintenance staff at Kanpur, his radio cackled to life, interrupting him in mid-sentence.

15004 had been cleared on to platform number four of the next station.

Singh turned to look at Amar, and tried to cheer him up. 'It's on four, as always.'

An uncomfortable silence greeted this statement. Singh's brows furrowed. As was their ritual, Amar hadn't pestered him about getting *litti chokha* from a particular vendor at platform number four DEOS. 'I'm buying today, *bacche*!' No reply, still.

Singh looked over his shoulder, a paternal, empathetic glance. 'Are you in pain, Amar?'

Amar softly grunted in response. He lay supine on the loco floor, trying to regulate his breathing. His vision felt blurry, and his head was swimming. The world around him had slowed down. He could no longer see clearly, but he could immediately smell and hear better. The smog, that sweet, delicious colloid, pressed against his nostrils and ears, invading him at a primal level, and he could discern his neurons firing at an exponentially increased rate. He could hear the thump of the engines, the overhead buzzing, the *chug-chug* of the locomotive, the sporadic cackling of the walkie and smell all the distinct scents wafting around him.

Amar gasped for air; he wanted more of the smog, it made him feel less restless.

'*Kya hua*?'

Amar Franklin did not answer. He reached into a corner, swiped at something and let out a blood-curdling scream.

Singh whirled around, almost jumping out of his skin. Amar, his eyes red and teeth bared, sat on the floor with a thrashing lizard in his hands.

'What are you *doing*?'

Despite himself, Amar did not bother answering Singh's question. He was experiencing something he had not ever felt: absolute disgust. An intense wave of hatred coursed through his veins as the lizard severed its tail and writhed in pain as he squeezed its head in his fist.

He stared at the reptile which was completely at his mercy, scared out of its wits, and felt a sudden urge within him: a longing for destruction, domination and conquest. *Blessed are the mighty, for theirs is the kingdom of this universe.*

'Amar, no! Don't!' Singh shouted.

'This is a different *species*,' a voice whispered in Amar's ear. 'How dare it sneak into our territory?

Before Singh could apply the brakes or radio the onboard RPF personnel for help, Amar, in a frenzy, slapped the windows of the locomotive with all his might.

Crack!

The window pane turned red: though this was a different shade of crimson than the one Singh had gotten used to. Amar kept hitting it until it broke, and a shard of glass went straight into his fist, making a deep cut. Blood dripped on the floor and the lizard, which Singh had last seen in Amar's palm, vanished, pulped.

'*Hai bhagwaan!*'

A horrified Singh realized that Amar – *his* Amar, the kind, obsequious, eager-to-please lad – had caught a lizard and crushed it to a gory death between his hand and the glass windows of the loco. He looked at Amar, who was now convulsing on the floor, his face a curious mixture of surprise, anger and shock.

As Singh reached for his radio, he heard Amar repeating one word till he passed out, a word that chilled Singh to the core: 'Kill. Kill. Kill.'

Kill.

Deoria Sadar Railway Station, Uttar Pradesh

Local Time: 2145 hours

Boom!

My eyes quickly darted to the right, terrified. The temple still breathed, the dogs still whimpered and a young man had started to sell tea. A man sprinted across the track from the neighbouring platform and leapt up, eager not to miss the train. A smell of burning ash moistened by the smog swirled up my little nose to forever soak into my mind.

I located the source of the noise. A defiant, agonized train had decoupled its carriages with a heart-wrenching, shear-ridden splutter. An *insaan* is just like a railway carriage, Dada-ji used to say: as parts of trains bound for different destinations, they switched behind different engines, connecting and leaving other carriages like them, until they forgot who they really were and where they had really wanted to go. The only engine that moved them was *kismat*.

'Why can't we stay for just one more day? Just one, come on! The *mela-numaish* has just begun, and it's Sunday tomorrow. We can eat Shambhu *ki poori-subzi* for breakfast. Also, the sale starts at Malviya Road tomorrow. Don't you love it too?' I complained some more to no one in particular.

My mother flicked an uninterested glance in my direction, shrugged and looked away to deal with my younger brother who stood clasping her leg, unmoving. Her face betrayed angst, resignation and hopelessness at once, an expression that subtly said, 'I'm in an unhappy marriage. Even though I have enough to spend and am blessed with two lovely kids, I'll only be a wife and...somehow...that isn't enough.'

I was too young and too naïve to see the light go out of her eyes. It hadn't happened all of a sudden; the rot had crept like *seelan* into her kitchen and bedroom. In her twenties, perhaps, my mother used to think life would always be a smooth highway with no potholes, traffic jams or stop signals, until one day she realized she'd driven to the end of the road and straight into a congested, claustrophobic *chowk* of domestic conjugality from which there was no escape. Life had happened to her. It was all downhill from there.

Phat, phat, phat, phat.

I heard a knocking behind me and whirled around. A twenty-something boy with an unremarkable face and *gutkha*-stained teeth was furiously pumping a particularly dirty kerosene stove. The tea seller was dressed in a ragged pair of light blue trousers and an overused mustard sweater that stuck to his bony body. It was easy to find obscure faces like his on the streets of this poverty-stricken town. He placed an aluminium kettle on a flat iron dish filled with smouldering pieces of wood and luminescent, bituminous coal and lit the flame. My throat started to crave the sweet, milky tea which contained ample urea, detergent and formalin.

Slipping away from my family, I thrust a freshly minted five-rupee coin at him and waited for my handleless, fire-burnt cup.

The tea seller poured one. *'Ae babuni, e le la.'*

The whitish-grey smog was billowing on to the platform from all sides and was getting thicker with each passing second. I reached out for the *kulhad*, barely able to see it properly. His eyes rested on my mine and then, hesitantly but inevitably, slid down. He had the sly, deceitful eyes of a famished wolf, betrayed and wronged by his kin.

His gaze slipped further downwards. Dressed in a blue *salwaar-kameez* and four layers of *vardhaman* wool sweaters, I was suddenly conscious of his probing gaze upon me. Under all this veneer of *izzat*, *tameez* and courtesy, our bodies were still hardwired like animals.

Dingansik.

I hurriedly turned away. The cold air pinched the corner of my eye and squeezed out a teardrop. I felt ashamed of myself, and I didn't know why. Determined not to look back, I started to walk towards the protected, triangular space of my waiting family.

Ma and Kabeer stood huddled close together. Father stood alone, stiff in his wooden posture, his fingers fiddling with the cap of a bronze Zippo in his coat pocket.

The sound of an unwelcome chuckle made me glance at a bench on my right where six men were flocked together like peas in a rotting pod. Twelve eyes scanned me up and down, from the laces of my shoes to the maroon muffler around my neck. The beginning of it all was as simple as that: I was unnaturally warm and experienced a dull throbbing under my skin. It felt like I had swallowed a blob of hot balm, which had started to melt and flowed from my throat to my skull. Heat vapours started to crawl and condense at my brainstem, making it itch under the dermis. My fingertips started to shudder, and I sneezed: the smog was desiccating the passage of my nose and my saliva tasted like crystals of an alkaline salt.

My jaw clenched involuntarily, and I panicked as the world around me mutated. I had an indescribable urge to cut into the soft flesh of those six warm necks, slowly tearing them open with my pretty pink painted nails. Not just of those men, but men, *all* men.

My eyesight was no longer a seamless, continuous stream of vision but the montage of a fast-moving series of flash photographs. I stumbled forward till my fingers brushed against Ma's.

A sudden movement on my left drew me out of reverie, and a surge of energy in my hands made them go numb. The tea seller was back and this time he had an axe in his hand.

People parted, the world went quiet, and my family gasped. He leapt towards my father, his teeth bared, mouth foaming. Ma let out a frantic shriek. Papa turned to face his attacker, and I saw an expression on his face which I could never have associated with his arrogant, cruel nature: fear.

The tea seller planted himself directly in front of my father and swung the gleaming blade with all his might. Thankfully, with the agility of one far past his age and grace beyond his portly frame, Papa ducked, stepped aside to avoid the blow and counter-attacked. He kicked the axe away and took hold of his assailant from behind, crushing his windpipe in a vice-like grip. The tea seller crumpled to the floor and Papa jumped on him, pinning him down with his weight. But he didn't stop there. His face contorted, he repeatedly smashed his fist into those rotting, yellowing teeth, beating the face of his attacker to pulp.

I leapt towards Kabeer and hugged his little body. Wrapping him in my arms, I kissed his forehead and prayed that I could resist the darkness within me. Moments passed. I heard police whistles. Gasps. Shouts. Announcements. Uniformed personnel honed in on us.

Our train was now in sight. The world became normal again, if only for a second. It was as if I had come out of a nightmare, and the last two minutes hadn't really happened. Kabeer hugged me tighter, a throbbing vein on his little forehead pressing into my neck. I responded by patting him and telling him that we were going to be fine. I didn't want him to leave my side. Someone, *something*, inside me wanted to hold on to him.

Dingansik.

How else could I have gouged out his big brown eyes and squished them with my sneakers? I suddenly craved to be in an empty room with him and nothing more than a knife so I could calmly cut open his small, smooth belly.

Slowly.

I wanted to kill my brother.

And I wanted him to know death was coming.

Onboard the Chauri Chaura Express, Deoria, Uttar Pradesh
Local Time: 2200 hours

The 15004 was about to pull into DEOS. Singh saw the outer cabin and knew the platform would soon be in sight, or at least it would have been under normal circumstances. He was still reeling under the impact of what Amar had done – what he had *become*. Singh had already radioed the station master of Deoria Sadar to request that a medical team be kept on standby. He peeked at Amar, who had, after his sudden fit, passed out on the grimy floor of the loco.

The train chugged along, and was almost at the platform. Singh, hurriedly, reached for the braking lever and pulled it down. Nothing happened. Singh's heart almost jumped out of his panting mouth. *What?* He tried again, but the train kept running.

The world around Singh slowed down. He repeated the drill another time, this time vehemently, but the effect was the same. 'What the...'

Now he really began to panic. There were people up ahead on the tracks, crossing from one platform to another, assuming that the train would stop. Beads of sweat started to appear on his forehead, and his heart thumped faster. Singh no longer thought: he merely acted on impulse. He turned towards the emergency console, flipped it open and slapped a red button marked 'Emergency Stop: Use with Caution' with all his might. The train screeched, struggled and instantly started decelerating. Sparks flew out from under the coaches, and Singh was thrown forward by inertia. Time resumed its normal flow.

He heaved a sigh of relief as platform number four became more tangible on his left. It looked like the train would stop as per schedule, Singh having executed an emergency technical halt. He then focused on his next priority, knowing the train was safely in. He poured out water from an old Bisleri bottle on to Amar's face, and washed the blood from his face and hands.

Smog stole inside the cabin through a window he had slid open, and he heard the buzzing grow louder around him. Singh gulped in mouthfuls of air in panic and anxiety. It calmed him, the air, and made him feel more at ease with his current predicament. As he breathed in, his world started to go out of focus. The slowing platform next to him became a blur. In the two minutes it took for the train to come to a complete stop, Singh was only able to observe and detect only one presence near him: Amar Franklin.

He lay right there, senseless, coated in blood, and looking so... vulnerable.

Something caved inside Singh. He no longer saw before him a young man whom he regarded as a protégé, whom he was grooming to take his place one day, but rather he saw *A. Franklin*.

Singh growled and bent down towards Amar. A screwdriver, discovered from the depths of a nearby toolbox, materialized in his shaking hands. He felt his heart slow down to nothingness and his breathing become even more pronounced. It was as if his instinct was trying to fight the monster that was caged within, but his body was betraying it by drawing in more of the toxic smog.

Singh heard urgent shouts: the train was about to come to a total halt, and the PA system on the station blared mundane things. The stationmaster would soon board and bring a medical team with him, Singh thought vaguely. He wanted to reach out for the radio and say something, but a red-hot pain blinded him and he fell to the floor, writhing in pain right next to Amar. He screamed at the top of his lungs, and the world went black.

When, after no more than a minute, a pale-looking stationmaster with a thousand unanswered questions on his face, boarded the WDM-3A with a never-opened emergency medical kit in his shaking hands, he saw Singh bent over a jerking Franklin. Singh did not even notice the newcomer. He kept stabbing at Amar Franklin's eyes with the screwdriver, squealing in grief and howling at the world around him.

Boots echoed, and the stationmaster jumped out of the locomotive, invoking the gods, cursing humanity, screaming for redemption.

The train from hell had arrived.

Platform Number 4, Deoria Sadar Railway Station, Uttar Pradesh
Local Time: 2230 hours

Blood.

Bone marrow.

Guts.

Blood, bone marrow and guts. Spilled all over the platform. *Our* platform.

Even before the passengers waiting at specified places for their respective coaches had a chance to pick up their luggage and move towards the slowing train, the doors to the Chauri Chaura Express flew open. A stream of its damned occupants hit the platform with the intensity of a mighty tidal wave. The train spewed its noxious contents, which constituted the most volatile, combustible and dangerous weapon known to man – man himself.

Cries, screams, shouts, groans, shrieks and moans rent the air around me. The smog parted, as if alive and with a mind of its own, and I saw the unforgettable. The images seared my brain – before it stopped functioning.

Flesh crashed upon metal, bones on blood and nerves and sinews on sharp instruments. Within the blink of an eye, the station had turned into a medieval battlefield. People rammed into each other: whacking, hacking, biting, lacerating, slashing, maiming and mauling each other. Their purpose was the same: to *end* the other.

'Hell is other people,' Papa used to say sometimes, especially when Ma fought with him, sobbed and locked herself up in the bedroom.

It surely was.

My father stood near the dead body of the tea seller, triumphant, the man's throat cut open by his own axe, a godly pendant still hanging around a profane, severed neck. He then proceeded to hold two of those slimy six men by their thin necks, banging his head on their bleeding, deformed noses in turn. Then he looked straight at me, and let out a roar that made me cower.

My mother grabbed a little girl by the hair and kicked her abdomen with all her might. My tongue tasted something metallic. Kabeer lay in a pool of blood that kept spreading – like the expanding iris of a reptile. I let go of him, and *smiled*.

Fifteen minutes of madness.

I still remember that day.

The official list of casualties was to be released much later, but to me, they, we, us, were all dead – a long time ago.

Govindaraj Swami, 28, a soap salesman, was the first to die at the Deoria Sadar Railway Station that day. He was thrown off the platform into the path of an oncoming train. He spoke a different language than his murderer. They did not agree on what should be their first language.

Syed Ali Rizvi, 72, a retired army colonel, was the second to die. He was killed by the injuries sustained due to repeated blows to the back of his head from a blunt object. His murderer, who belonged to a different religious sect than Rizvi, managed to achieve what Pakistani bullets hadn't.

Murali Gupta, 35, a scrap dealer, was the third to die. A cauldron of hot oil, which was until very recently being used to fry samosas, was thrown on his unsuspecting face. He suffered extensive burns and passed away in shock. He was not the same class as his killer and drove a different vehicle.

Vijay Kashyap, 47, an additional district judge, was the fourth to die. He was electrocuted using high-tension wires. He prayed to the gods – his killer, to a God. *Fiat justitia ruat cælum* had abandoned him. And the heavens *did* fall that day, but he still didn't get any justice.

Lipeshwar Prasad, 55, who taught Hindi at a local school, was the fifth to die. His stomach was ripped open with a sharp object by a man who did not share his caste.

Aparna Das, 22, an master's student at the University of Allahabad, was the sixth to die. She was tied, raped and strangled by her killer, not necessarily in that order. She loved a woman; her murderer did too.

Chrisanthi Dayaweera, 39, a tourist, was the seventh to die. She was beaten to death with a steel pipe. She had a different nationality than her murderer. Not everyone believed in *vasudhaiva kutumbakam*. The world wasn't one family – it was a crazy, psychopathic, homicidal family.

David Maitai, 32, an assistant manager in a bank, was the eighth to die. Besides excessive bleeding, the real cause of his death was a broken ballpoint pen was found in his pharynx. He was killed by a man of a different ethnicity.

Omveer Rana, 49, a sugarcane farmer, was the ninth to die. His head was repeatedly bashed on a railway pillar. He voted for a different political party from his murderer.

Gurpreet Kaur, 19, a trainee medical technician, was the tenth to die. Her windpipe was bitten off by a set of blunted dentures. She was of a different gender than her killer.

These murders were all different, committed by different people for different reasons, but at the same time and in the same location. They were, one might speculate, precipitated by the same extraneous factors.

Hell is other people.

Hell must be destroyed.

Kill. Kill. Kill.

All these people happened to be nice, decent people but, unfortunately, in a world where only the fittest survive and natural selection operates, *sharafat* serves no tangible purpose. In fact, some of them even killed each other before being put down by someone else in this group. *Pair the victims and their murderers together and choose the correct murderer-victim combination*. A? B? C? D?

Perhaps this would be a DI & LR question in the CAT exam when I appear for it one day, I thought to myself and chuckled. Wham!

A screeching object in the skies made me look up, and then an explosion made me shield my eyes. I threw myself down on the ground, and crawled towards the railway carriage.

It was time to board the train.

Above the Deoria Sadar Railway Station, Uttar Pradesh
Local Time: 2300 hours

The train had snaked across the dry, dusty terrain and reached a particularly abhorrent population centre that reminded S'aulk of why the extermination was necessary in the first place. The craft chirped, as if anticipating the scent of victory about to sneak into S'aulk's nose. He decided that he had earned a quick breather, and his command module lit up: it was time to SoTem.

The practice utilized a machine that manipulated sound and temperature, and their infinite permutations and variations made the

Qa'haQ experience states of altered and enhanced consciousness: once you were hooked, hooked you were. The SoTem machine lowered and increased the temperature of his craft and sent different kinds of sound waves crashing towards him.

S'aulk closed his eyes in pleasure and whistled in joy. After what seemed like seconds, his eyes snapped open and he instinctively looked down at the train. From above, it had looked like a frightened young WanghKa running away from its loving mother – and it should have been doing *just* that, he thought, half-amused. WanghKa mothers loved their progeny – mostly as gastronomic delights.

One more image flashed in his SoTemmed brain. Chasing the train from above reminded him of the PagSha hunts at home. He missed the sleek duran arrows and their silvery, deathly glint in the two moons of the Qa'haQ home world as they buried themselves in warm PagSha flesh from above. Flesh which was then used to incubate the Qa'haQ.

That was all in the past. The Great Purification had changed it all. Hunts had become slightly more rational now.

He switched on his communication channels and heard high-pitched squeals from the station below. Human screams didn't scare or please him: they turned him on. There was a joy in noticing the exact moment the hunter became the hunted. All this while humans thought they could do anything to this planet.

Well, they couldn't *any more*. Ş'aulk's felt his face flush. The AI he had moved to tertiary alert had stopped scanning the skies around him in order to divert all processing power to run simulations on conversion outcomes. It spewed out statistics, the data was unexceptional. The casualties and fatalities were well within defined parameters. One-tenth of the population would be left alive and then, after being HoV1ed, they would be assimilated into the Foreign Legion. This was turning out to be yet another victory, and an easy one at that.

HoV1 was the messiah of change and the serum of truth. Perfected by Qa'haQ scientists in order to meet the goals of the Qa'haQ race: *One World. One Species. One Mentality.*

HoV1 promised a new dawn, a cure to the illogical, mindless heterogeneity of his people that had almost driven the Qa'haQ to extinction. When all was lost, HoV1 had come out of a science lab and it was turned on its first target species: the Qa'haQ themselves.

The results were revolutionary. Homogeneity was banned. His entire species had become truly one: one people, one race, one gender, one class, one spiritual belief, one political outlook, one caste and one nation. Order, structure and peace became more important than individual goals, selfish interests and diverging views. A new organizational paradigm was drawn up to administer Qa'haQ society in the best possible way. Different specialized professions, based on genetic breeding, were created to serve the collective macro needs of the Qa'haQ. One would be what the society wanted one to be. There was no place or scope for choice and difference. *Uniformity was power. Obedience was strength. Expansion was life.*

Within a few *dak*s of the Great Purification, the warring Qa'haQ factions had made peace with each other, and the Hive was born. The HoV1 – the homogeneity retrovirus – and the Great Purification it precipitated had unified society and launched an empire that had conquered, expanded and assimilated half of the galaxy – it was the beginning of *pax* Qa'haQam.

The Qa'haQ had also become aware that their ancient wisdom and culture was not theirs alone: it had to be spread across the entire solar system, the galaxy and the universe itself. Even by force. Consequently, the HoV1 was tweaked into various strains to attack various sentient life forms on multiple planets in different physiological ways: its effects, however, were the same across. It destroyed the ability of the target life forms to accept plurality, heterogeneity and multiculturalism.

It was not a moral dilemma, not at all, S'aulk reminded himself. The *uni*verse was, ipso facto, one. Life was one. Consciousness was one.

One. Not many, but *one*.

It would be enforced at any cost. That's why the Enforcers were engineered.

Seven *kek*s ago, he and nine other Qa'haQ Enforcers had positioned their TerHops at equidistant coordinates in Sol-III's stratosphere, each allotted a specific zone. He had decided to learn more about the world around them before they finally ended it. S'aulk was returning from Sector MX-19/Sol-III where he had been investigating anomalous readings emanating from the deserted ruins of an ancient human religious settlement. His neural implants had interfaced with some useful native technology. The 'Internet' had proven to be a treasure trove of information about earth, and had reminded S'aulk of the pre-Hive communication networks used before the Great Purification.

S'aulk's corneal HUD spewed out alien phrases like *mahaparinirvana*, *yin-yang* and *ding an sich* at him, and he carefully analysed the Omtronic radiation readings that he had collected from the site.

S'aulk's interest in humans was unsurprising, his onboard AI had reasoned. Enforcing was his secondary gene; the core of his genetic make-up was that of a Learner. No wonder he had been unable to resist the lure of exploring the unknown, even when operating under the strict operational protocols of the Enforcers.

He had been busy processing the recently acquired information, which was presently being fed directly into his cerebrum, when the cloaked TerHop lurched, wobbled and found a new target to follow: a human mass-transit vehicle, a train numbered 15004.

'Hik'sha!'

His craft had moved from within and rearranged itself to become a perfect sphere. It had developed a rippling, metallic surface that seemed to be alive. S'aulk knew what was happening: the TerHop had gone into battle mode, and the manual controls of the craft had been overridden by the AI of the mother ship. He was no longer a Learner. From now on, he would be another Enforcer, an instrument of death and peace, of desolation and order. Organic life was chaotic. Death wasn't.

Just as the train had pulled into the station, the outer layer of the craft had peeled away into nothingness, exposing a greenish algae-like covering underneath. Minutes after this secondary hull layer had come into contact with earth's atmosphere, it dissolved into colourless smoke. A white vapour had sprayed out of the shimmering, rotating sphere, spreading across the skies like tentacles over a gaping, festering wound.

Human wails, screams, shouts and screeches from down below – emanating from his craft speakers – brought him back to the present. S'aulk knew what was in store for earth. The blue-green planet was an anomaly, a paradox, a tear in the fabric of space-time, and one that would soon be corrected. It was an affront to the Qa'haQ way of life and thought. One planet, just one, had multiple sentient species on it which, to his dismay, had co-existed for ages. To top it all, individuals of the dominant species, the Homo sapiens, who were different from each other in every possible way, had accepted, against all logic, their heterogeneity as normal. They even perceived their diversity as a source of strength.

S'aulk hissed again. *Not for long,* he thought. *This puny planet will no longer resist the impending Qa'haQ onslaught. Not. For. Long.*

A warning klaxon and a slight jolt dragged him back to the present. *What...* Mentally, he reached to the AI for a status update and switched it to primary alert. At that precise instant, the clouds parted to belch a glinting fighter aircraft that had a tricolour roundel on its tailfin.

The AI, no longer dormant, beamed images of a darting Su-30 MKI to his secondary brain, along with its speed, direction and possible angles of attack. An instantaneous, unexpected smoke trail from the Indian Air Force fighter jet, caused the TerHop to suddenly swerve and triggered its anti-collision alert system.

S'aulk's SoTemmed iris widened like concentric ripples in a pond, a shimmering *Astra* air-to-air missile seared in its centre.

Ding an sich.

WHY THE WAR ENDED

PREMENDRA MITRA

(Translated by Arunava Sinha from the original Bengali 'Juddho Keno Thamlo'*)*

11 August 1937: The famous American aviatrix Hilda Stamers disappears while attempting to fly over the Pacific Ocean after taking off from Patagonia in South America.

22 June 1922: A relatively unusual item in the daily report of the Mount Wilson Observatory states that a familiar planet has changed appearance when viewed through a telescope.

1 September 1939 to 12 January 1940: Germany demands Poland handover Danzig. Poland refuses. Germany invades Poland. France and Great Britain join the war in support of Poland. Apocalypse in Europe. Spreads to Asia. Japan annexes Formosa from China. An American naval expedition against Japanese airbase in the Pacific Ocean. Germany and Japan declare war on America.

12 February 1940: After only a few months of war across Europe and Asia, most cities destroyed, millions killed. Unexpected declaration of the end of war.

1 March 1941: Astounding news about Australia. Arrivals and departures of ships and planes banned by order of the new League of Nations. Surprise, curiosity and suspicion among people around the world.

15 January 1940: The first reception of a strange radio message by an Australian warship cruising near New Guinea. Captain grows curious. The attention of two British warships directed towards the area. Ignoring military orders, a British plane flies off in the search of the source of the message.

20 January 1940: A British plane hit by Japanese fire over Formosa. Injured pilot captured by Japanese.

22 January 1940: Secret radio exchanges between the heads of state of Japan, Germany and Italy.

28 January 1940: Voluntary proposal of armistice by Germany, Japan and Italy to Britain, France and America. Suspicion and scepticism from Britain, France and America. Proposal of an all nations meet in Shanghai at Japan's insistence.

20 March 1940: Expedition of international team of scientists to New Guinea.

18 December 1940: A League of Nations ban on the broadcast of new, sensational news from recently constructed observatory in Lhasa.

4 May 1941: Worldwide panic at the revelation of unimaginable epidemics across Australia, China and South America. United world prepares for new battle.

Most of the events alluded to here in brief with the dates jumbled up are known today. Yet, most people are aware of neither the deep relationship between these seemingly disparate events, nor of the enormity and unimaginable nature of the phenomenon that they point to. The whole affair is shrouded in horrific, unravelled mystery.

Under orders from the League of Nations, it was forbidden to reveal all the details of the matter. But realizing that the people of the world cannot be left in doubt, suspicion and the uncertainty of oncoming terror, the ban has now been lifted. A complete account of the greatest crisis in the history of the earth is provided here.

First, we must go back to 22 June 1922, on board a ship in the Pacific Ocean. An ordinary freight ship. Sailing from Selibis to Darwin.

Late at night. Mr Langdon, the aged second mate, is the only person on watch on the observation bridge. Not that there is anything to watch over. A cloudless star-filled sky, a motionless sea. But for the sound of the propeller screws, it is hard to tell the ship is moving.

Gazing into the darkness, Mr Langdon is probably thinking about his home in the valleys of Scotland. Retirement is approaching. He has spent his entire life at sea, without having attained the success he had hoped for. But he has no regrets. All he wants is to spend the rest of his life in peace in his own country. So what if he has not gained fame or power? Are these the only ingredients of happiness?

Perhaps destiny is smiling covertly at Mr Langdon's desires. No one knows that even if he does not seek it, his name will be connected to the history of an epochal change on earth.

As Mr Langdon is trying to recall images of Scotland, his flight of fancy is suddenly interrupted. He stares at the sky in disbelief. In the course of the 30 years he has spent as a sailor, Mr Langdon has seen many remarkable sights on the high seas, but he has never been as astounded as he is tonight.

What is visible in the skies can be described as a meteor shower, but this description does not do justice to it. He has been fortunate enough to witness many such showers in the course of his duty during silent nights in the warm tropics. But the scene tonight cannot be compared to them.

He has never heard of so many meteors of such dimension and brightness falling to earth together. The most noticeable aspect is the perfect formation in which they journey downward. Someone seems to have arranged them with great skill, like fireworks, before ejecting them in the sky.

Although Mr Langdon does not get the chance to count them accurately, he estimates there must be 20 of them. Their radiance makes the darkened sky glow with a blinding light for a few moments. Not just that, he also thinks he hears a strange sound as the burning meteors plummet earthward. The darkness and silence of the night are restored soon afterwards. Later, Mr Langdon wonders whether he has been dreaming.

The very next day, he informs the captain of the ship, as well as several other shipmates, of the strange meteor shower. It is revealed that another of the sailors also saw the strange glow, though not the meteors themselves. The incident is mentioned in the log.

The incident is considered closed for the moment. Mr Langdon returns home and writes about the meteor shower for a minor newspaper. Not many people read it. Even fewer make an attempt to understand the mystery.

If it is not for the intrepid American aviatrix Hilda Stamers's attempt to fly over the Pacific Ocean 15 years later, on 11 August 1937, and if another two-and-a-half years later, a sailor on an Australian warship is not roused into action by a strange radio message received while sailing near New Guinea, it is doubtful whether humanity would have had the good fortune of solving this mystery in time.

Let us begin the second act of our story aboard the warship.

The flames of the world war are burning across the globe. Separated from its fleet, an Australian destroyer is trying to navigate a dangerous area under the cover of night to escape the Japanese navy. There is no respite for the operators in the radio room. The destroyer can only move forward by constantly exchanging coded messages with other ships. Danger lurks in every moment. One message not received, one instruction misread, and the vessel will either fall into enemy hands or be dashed on the rocks of New Guinea's treacherous coast.

As the messages pile up, an operator is startled by a new, very faint communication in his receiver. *Who could be sending an uncoded message in this time of war?*

He has no time to concentrate on this message. But his curiosity is growing. As soon as he has a few moments to spare, he tries to read the entire message. When he does, his confusion increases.

Would anyone but a lunatic send such an eccentric message?

'Go to the source of the River Sepik in New Guinea. Earth faces imminent disaster. There is no time – no time.'

What does this mean? And yet, the radio operator cannot be indifferent to it. He cannot help relaying it to his fellow operators, followed by the commander of the ship.

By this time they have sailed out of enemy waters into a relatively safe zone, secure after receiving assurances of support from two British warships nearby. The strange radio message becomes the subject of their attention now. The message is still being transmitted constantly, like a distant cry for help from a dying person.

The commander of the destroyer is not a man who is bound by routine. He has the imagination and the courage to go beyond established procedures.

On his orders, the attention of the two British warships nearby is drawn to the message. They are asked whether they can make sense of the communication.

The message has also been received by these two ships. It turns out they don't understand it either. One of the commanders has been on an expedition once within New Guinea – he says the source of River Sepik is still unknown to outsiders. No one from the civilized world has set foot there yet.

The message is about to be abandoned as the ravings of a lunatic. But destiny is not wholly unkind when it comes to the human race. British warships have a plane or two on board to look for submarines. After discussions about the message with Mr Benn, the pilot of one such plane, both he and the aircraft are found missing. No one knows when he has taken off in the darkness of the night, despite having no formal orders.

Flying off with a plane without orders is an act of gross indiscipline. Punishment is inevitable. But it seems unlikely that Mr Benn will return to face it.

Let us now follow Mr Benn's aircraft deep into an unknown, hilly region of New Guinea in search of the source of the Sepik.

It is nearly dawn. The wings of the aircraft are red from the rising sun. Below, the forest-covered hills of New Guinea are still dark. The first rays of the sun are yet to reach them. A faint thread can be seen amidst the darkness. The Sepik.

Gradually, the terrain becomes visible. The Sepik turns into a silver ribbon. Mr Benn flies at a lower altitude. He is now flying over an undiscovered part of New Guinea. Even if he cannot solve the mystery of the radio message here, his expedition will not be wasted. The descriptions that he can provide on his return is by no means worthless for exploration.

The plane drops even lower. The Sepik is becoming narrower, its source is not far away. Mr Benn flies over a range of low hills. The Sepik has cut a path through it.

Mr Benn reduces his altitude further. Tribal villages are visible now and then, houses resting on raised platforms. But this is strange! Are they not inhabited? Mr Benn knows the curiosity tribal people have for aircraft. But not a single human being can be seen.

It isn't natural for them not to emerge into the open at the sound of a plane flying overhead.

Mr Benn flies over several villages. All of them seem deserted.

The range of hills in the distance appear to hide the source of the Sepik. Mr Benn flies closer to the ground to observe the place closely.

How odd! A calamity seems to have struck not just the people but also the plants and trees in the area. They appear to be dead. He is also astonished to spot several perfectly circular lakes cut into the hillsides. Who has made these flawless structures in this land of tribal people?

The plane is skimming the treetops now. Mr Benn is about to pull back on his joystick to gain altitude when he notices something. The fuselage of a crashed plane. One wing points towards the sky.

A plane? Here?

Mr Benn now simply has to investigate. After circling the area twice, he lands in an open field. The first thing that catches his attention when he climbs put of the plane is an unfamiliar smell. Although far from being a stench, it is making him uncomfortable. Mr Benn looks around for a wild flower of the kind that gives off such a fragrance, but he cannot find any. Unable to locate the source of the scent hanging heavy in the air, Mr Benn proceeds towards the wreckage of the plane. A huge surprise is waiting for him.

When he is closer, Mr Benn can read the signs on the aircraft. He has no trouble realizing that it is American, and that the crash is not a recent.

Noticing a hut woven with branches and wild grass near the site of the wreckage, he is about to go up to it. He intends to ask its inhabitant about the plane. But he has to come to an abrupt halt, for a voice from the hut is saying to him in his own language, 'Stop! Stay right there!'

It is natural to be taken aback by such a development. Who could be speaking English in this remote land? Is the pilot of the plane still alive? But if that is the case, why ask someone from your own race to maintain a distance?

After a few moments of bewilderment, Mr Benn takes a step or two ahead. At once, a sharp order is heard from the hut: 'I'm warning you, don't move another step. It's dangerous.'

Stopping unwillingly, Mr Benn asks, 'What sort of danger?'

'You'll find out soon,' comes the answer.

'But who are you?' Mr Benn asks.

'You don't need to know.'

'Of course I do. I want to know whether you're the one who's been sending those strange radio messages,' Mr Benn asks hotly.

'So you're here in response to my messages. Thank you.'

'There's no need to thank me. Identify yourself.'

'It's no use. I'm beyond all that now.'

'What is this nonsense?' says Mr Benn and takes another step or two forward.

Now the order turns into a plea. 'No, don't come any closer. I'll tell you who I am. I'm Hilda Stamers.'

Hilda Stamers! Mr Benn stops in his tracks. *She's still alive!* It seems unbelievable. 'If you're Hilda Stamers,' he says excitedly, 'what objection can you have to showing yourself? Why, for that matter, did you send those strange radio messages?'

'I will tell you everything. It is to reveal everything that I have patiently remained alive.'

'But I want to see you first.' An adamant Mr Benn marches towards the hut.

'I beg of you, don't come any closer,' the plea is repeated in a wretched voice.

Now a bloodcurdling scream is heard.

It is Mr Benn who is screaming. He had not expected such a sight. It is beyond his imagination that the human body, god's creation, could become so gruesome. What he sees is not the beautiful Hilda Stamers but a nightmare. The figure in front of him is even more grotesque than the shapeless, hideous lump that one may get by inflating a human body like a balloon. Even the most obese humans retain some of their proportions, but this particular bloating seems the result of a dreadful disease of some kind. It creates an instant feeling of revulsion. Besides two eyes and the glimmer of a mouth in the middle of an enormous and ugly sphere, there is no resemblance with the human form.

Mr Benn rushes out of the hut. He now understands why Hilda Stamers refused to be seen, why she pleaded with him not to go any closer. Controlling himself with great effort, he says, 'I do not understand how this happened to you.'

A little later, a soft reply emerges. 'That's what I'll tell you. If I can do this service for the world before I die, I will have no regrets.'

To provide a detailed account of the valuable and extraordinary information that Mr Benn gathered from Hilda Stamers, we have to skip forward to the news of the British aircraft shot down by the Japanese over the island of Formosa on 20 January 1940. The pilot of this aircraft is none other than Mr Benn. He is on his way to Europe from New Guinea when this mishap occurs.

Here, too, destiny comes to the aid of mankind. Had Mr Benn died when his plane crashed, it is doubtful whether humanity would have had the time to prepare for the ultimate test.

But Mr Benn, having bailed out with a parachute, is safe, although he has been taken prisoner by the Japanese.

There is no need for a comprehensive retelling of which Japanese officials Mr Benn is taken to, what he tells them, what evidence he provides for his claims, and how his statements filter upwards all the way to the top of the Japanese government. It is enough to know that it is on the basis of what an ordinary aviator reveals that the leaders of three nations voluntarily offer their opponents an armistice.

That the proposal was not in vain, that human beings have not taken leave of their senses despite being engaged in a brutal war, is proved by the first conference of the major world powers on 16 July 1940 in Shanghai. The conference is held in complete secrecy. Mr Benn is the only person besides heads of states and top scientists who is permitted to attend. It will turn out to be a crucial event in the history of the world. It is here that the League of Nations is reconstituted with several special powers. It is decided that a delegation of some of the finest scientists in the world will be sent to New Guinea to learn more about the incredible information conveyed by Mr Benn.

However, the League of Nations is unable to exercise its authority until the delegation of scientists returns from New Guinea. There is no dearth of people who are suspicious of the necessity and the purpose of reconstituting the organization. Marshal Renault, the well-known French general, has been opposed to the idea of the League of Nations from the outset. The longer it takes for the scientists to return from New Guinea, the more he incites his country against the existence of the League of Nations. He has no hesitation in attacking the League while attending a session on 23 July 1940.

As an agitated Renault is explaining to the gathering that it is futile to reconstitute a League of Nations, which has already failed once, that it is nothing but the conspiracy of a handful of power-hungry individuals, that they are demonstrating supreme obtuseness in giving credence to the absurd story of an insignificant and neurotic aviator like Mr Benn, an aged Japanese man with a mane of white hair is seen entering the assembly with slow footsteps.

Everyone present stirs at the entrance of this man. That is not surprising. For the aged man is none other than Dr Sanuchi, the leader of the team of scientists sent to New Guinea. His unexpected appearance, without being accompanied by anyone else, piques everyone's curiosity. But Marshal Renault shows no signs of relenting. Taunting the Japanese scientist, he says, 'Will Dr Sanuchi kindly elucidate on the mortal danger that earth faces which he learned of in New Guinea?'

The august Dr Sanuchi smiles. 'I hope to do that. But first, there is something else I must inform everyone of. The danger to our world comes not from New Guinea, but from a much more distant location.'

'More distant than New Guinea!' Renault says in a tone of surprise. 'And where might that be?'

Dr Sanuchi smiles again, but sadly this time. 'It is not from anywhere on earth, Marshal Renault – the threat to the world comes from Mars.'

'Are they going to attack us?'

'Not "are they", Marshal – they already have. Eight years ago.'

Now everyone is dismayed. What is Dr Sanuchi saying? Has he gone mad?

Gauging the reaction of the gathering, Dr Sanuchi says, 'Even though what I am saying is difficult to believe, it is absolutely true. We have arrived at this conclusion after detailed investigations and research in New Guinea, and after reconciling our findings with astronomers' records over the past 30 years. The Martians mounted an invasion of earth 18 years ago. The description from the Mount Wilson observatory of the meteor shower on 22 June 1922 and the account of the same phenomenon in a minor Scottish newspaper by Mr Langdon, the second mate of a freight ship, prove that the event took place.'

'But it appears to have been a rather friendly invasion,' says Marshal Renault mockingly. 'I see no signs of an army or of weapons.'

'Would you employ artillery to disinfect a patient's room from germs, Marshal Renault?' Dr Sanuchi asks with a smile.

'Why would I, when I have phenyl and chlorine?' Renault answers testily.

'That is the precise arrangement that the Martians made to disinfect earth, Marshal Renault. To them, we are nothing but germs on this planet. Instead of deploying arms, they have used a chemical which acts like poison on us. It is this poison that is about to destroy mankind.'

Now Dr Sanuchi explains the results of his team's investigations in detail. The burst of meteors that Mr Langdon observed 18 years ago were not meteors, they were projectiles fired towards earth by the unknown inhabitants of Mars. They exploded on landing in New Guinea. The circular lakes that Mr Benn observed were created by the impact of these projectiles. Dr Sanuchi and his team have discovered fragments from the metallic outer layer of the projectiles. The projectiles were filled with the seeds of a poisonous plant unknown on earth. These seeds were scattered on the soil, growing into vegetation over the years. They now cover most of New Guinea. The strange smell that Mr Benn got on landing on the island was from these plants. He did not spot them because they stick to the ground like moss. But he was told by Hilda Stamers that it is the smell of the poison that attacks human beings. The poison is inhaled and mixes with the blood, bloating and destroying the body and then the mind.

Hilda Stamers's plane crashed on this island. While trying to escape, she discovered the terrible plight of the local population who had been poisoned by the alien plant and learned the horrifying truth about them. Realizing the havoc that the poison could wreak on all living creatures, she applied her dwindling strength to repairing the radio on her plane in order to send out a warning message. She then tried desperately for many years to contact other humans with her ominous communiqué.

The people of the world have responded and tried to take precautions. But the poison has begun to spread already. The war between nations has been called off in the face of this impending doom, but this has not stopped the venom from infecting people elsewhere. From New Guinea, the plant has spread to Australia and from there to China and South America, bringing its poisonous effect with it. The League of Nations suppressed the news for a long time to prevent panic, but that is no longer possible. Australia, China and South America have become graveyards. The air there is so full of the poison from Mars that it cannot be breathed. Scientists are trying their best now to prevent the poison from spreading further. Although they have been partially successful, is there really anything to be optimistic about?

No one can doubt the intelligence and strategic superiority of those who can send poison to earth across space. It is unlikely that they will give up if thwarted this time. Human beings cannot even begin to imagine what form their next attack will take. All that they can do is to establish observatories at different points on earth and train telescopes fearfully on Mars. There is no knowing how or when the enemy will attack. Mankind may become extinct when that happens.

The only source of satisfaction in the face of this global doom is that all differences of race and colour and gender seem to have been magically wiped out. The entire world is united today. Mankind has finally realized the foolishness of fighting amongst themselves.

WERE IT NOT FOR

ARJUN RAJENDRAN

Historians will forget the fishermen, their 5000 boats and black flags. The dimensions
of the monument to the medieval warrior king is 210 meters tall and costs

enough to fund a decade of suicides for the state's indebted farmers –
having battled pests all their lives, it's natural they should end theirs with pesticide.

A feat like David Copperfield's, who in 1983, vanished
the Statue of Liberty to assert the importance of freedom, graces the inauguration.

The Hon'ble Prime Minister closes his eyes, rubs his temples, and the ginormous
monument of the maharajah brandishing his sword, disappears like the values

of currency notes. Indian pilots, flying Sukhois above the Arabian sea, past
the kingless horse – to reinforce the disappearance, touch spectators' raw nerves,

stir erasure into their blood. Any fisherman volunteering to cast his net only hauls in
cow bones. The Hon'ble PM rubs his temples harder, and everyone is

in 1659, witnessing a grainy scene of a tiger-claw (هکن هگاب) plunging into Afzal Khan's
chest. The PM opens his eyes. The maharajah is back on his steed, 420 meters tall.

The sea feels bountifully Hindu again. Gifts Bombay ducks and shrimps
to the fishermen. A sword brandished at the sky, in case it starts raining Mughals.

THE BENEFICIENT BRAHMA

CHANDRASHEKHAR SASTRY

Manohar chose the highest floor of a multi-storey building to rent a flat. It was a two-bedroom flat with a compact, open kitchen that allowed him to chat with his wife Navika as she made dinner. Most of his friends attributed his love of homes in high places to his soaring ambition. He was yet to become someone, he was yet to become rich, and he was yet to become famous. But he had worked out that the finest camouflage was to have no camouflage and had shaved his head to hide the balding and the streaks of grey, both of which betrayed his age. This was much better than dyeing his hair every week. Towards the end of seven days, the growing hair displayed white at the roots and he felt it defeated the purpose of the camouflage. Shaving his head gave him a Buddha-like countenance of permanent youth.

He sat on the sofa, peering into his open laptop, telling his wife about the tiff he had had with a colleague that day. He worked in the editorial department of a news magazine and was careful not to offend. Navika, who was stirring a pot on the hob, was amused but did not want to nag him by repeating her many warnings to be careful, to not hurt a colleague's feelings for no reason. When she looked out of the kitchen window, she was surprised to see something hovering like a drone. It was not like what she'd seen innumerable times on the Internet and on Facebook. She could not see any propellers arranged symmetrically about a fuselage. It resembled an inverted pyramid, maroon in colour, with a white fin scrolling down from the upper base to a lower apex, which was spouting a small blue flame. Rotating slowly, it gave the impression of screwing its way through the air to remain aloft.

'Come look at this – it's a UFO or an ET!' she screamed and started frantically waving at her husband. He rose from the table carrying his mobile phone and, through the clear glass window, he clicked a few pictures before it veered away and vanished into the sky. He was sure his editor would appreciate a good story. The next day, the papers were full of many fascinating theories trying to explain the strange phenomenon that several people had observed and photographed. Surfing through all the dailies and all the TV channels, he felt his report was the most genuine. The scientific community, however, belittled these stories. They maintained that UFOs would not come so close to earth and have always remained a lofty mystery. When the object returned a week later, he knew he was being watched by an extraterrestrial.

The next evening, while returning from work, he dropped in at the local police station and spoke to the sub-inspector. The officer would not register an FIR because he considered the whole story unusual, though he had read about it in some of the city's newspapers. 'Let us know if it appears regularly at the same time or on any special day of the week, or if it seems threatening,' was the advice Manohar was given.

Ever since they moved to the big city, they had aspired to own their own residence. Manohar and Navika were eager to buy a flat as soon as possible, and to this end, they both lived frugally and worked hard to increase their savings. In the wild hope of winning a fat purse, they had bought tickets for several lotteries but seemed fated to perpetual disappointment. However, they persevered; now they each bought only one ticket every month. On the day the results were published, they scrambled for the newspapers and pored over the results, tickets in hand and hope in their hearts. Each disappointment led them to believe even more firmly that the next month would bring them the long-awaited good fortune and bag them the treasure – that elusive treasure which seemed to be going to other people every month. Surely one day it would be theirs, the first prize or at the very least the third prize.

Neither of them was superstitious and they just picked a ticket at random from the bunch clipped on to the board at the grocer shop. One month, while studying the results they noticed that the last eight numbers on one of the winning tickets could be read as Manohar's date of birth. They were convinced that it was not a coincidence, and that it was a portent of something good. After that, every month they ruffled through the tickets and chose one that read either of their birthdays, or of their siblings' or even a friend's. When they would not find a ticket to match any known sequence, they chose one nearest to their sought-for number.

Would it not be the finest birthday present? Manohar wondered as he sauntered forth on the morning of his birthday, determined to find a ticket which ended with the numbers that signified his date of birth. He had to trudge through seven streets and as many shops before he found a seller with the right ticket. Delighted with his find, he chuckled loudly at the bewildered girl standing at the counter, who had tired of this wild man with the shaved head, which was sweating with the effort of rustling through her clipboards of lottery tickets for the last 10 minutes. 'I hope this is the lucky ticket you were searching for.' She smiled as she gave him his change.

Manohar went into the puja corner as soon as he reached home. Calling Navika, they reverently placed the lottery ticket on the wooden platform that had a few sacred icons, a bronze lamp, its bowl half-filled with oil and a drooping wick, and a stand for incense sticks. They folded their palms and prayed for a bountiful future. The gods had let him down so many times but he was sure that one day the infallible law of averages would shower him with blessings. Nothing could be more powerful than the science of statistics in the service of a deity.

One evening the following week, Navika was reheating the dal in a pan when she heard a frantic knocking on the window. She was surprised to find the ET apparition right next to the large clear glass window. It seemed very agitated, like it wanted to communicate something. Used to its frequent visits, Navika was convinced that it was a benign ET. She released the latch and opened the window a small bit with the intention of hearing what it had to say. However, she was taken aback to see that the ET, sucking hard, had opened the window fully and with a great whoosh had emptied the boiling dal from the pan. It had left behind a dead gecko lying at the bottom, its tail curved like a question mark.

Navika looked at it first in shock and then with a slow relief that flooded her. The kind ET had saved them from poisoned food. That event convinced them that the ET was a true friend that would help them avoid any catastrophe. Navika called it Brahma, alluding to its descent from the cosmos.

After that blessed christening, whenever it appeared, Manohar pulled out the polished bronze plate on the puja platform, heaping some raw rice and jaggery on it as an offering. He also placed the little bronze lamp on the plate and lighting its wick, he would offer an *arati* to Brahma. Moving the plate in clockwise circles, they implored the god to bestow impossibly good fortune on them. The rice with the jaggery was then cooked into a delicious kheer in the evening.

Living on the top floor, Manohar had kept the windows unblemished by any steel grills. He was sure no burglar would enter the 10th floor of a high-rise through a window. Watching a sunrise through a clear glass window without the intervening steel bars was a pleasure only surpassed by the unhindered sight of a full moon climbing over the tree-rimmed horizon, its colour altering from a strikingly bright red to an orange phase which faded into a pearly white with irregular patches of light grey.

One morning, a month after his birthday, as he was looking through the day's paper, he found the result he had waited so long for lurking on the last page. *There it was.* Not the top prize or the second but the third prize was unmistakably against the number that he picked every month, the number with the ending that signified his birthday. He quickly retrieved the lucky ticket from the sacred platform and, quite needlessly, reconfirmed that the figures were the same as in the newspaper. Despite being the lowest prize, it was still a substantial sum for Manohar and a moment of great joy for him.

Navika and Manohar could not sleep that night. They were discussing the things they could do with the money. It was not sufficient to buy the two-bedroom-hall-kitchen flat they wanted. They knew they could raise a loan from a bank or housing corporations but had no clue about how much could be raised and whether it would suffice, or what the interest rates would be or if they could afford such loans. They were both employed, had no children, and were free of any family responsibilities for siblings or aged parents.

They spoke to the manager of their bank the next day.

'Congratulations,' the manager said, pleased that one of his account holders had won a prize. He hesitatingly informed them that collecting the sum would have a tax implication. At present tax rates, it would be as high as 30 per cent. This was something that had never occurred to either Manohar or Navika. They were crestfallen to find that their winnings would be lowered so substantially.

Seeing their crestfallen faces, the helpful manager suggested, 'I could find someone who would pay you fully in cash for this ticket. You will need some cash if you are buying property. A loan from the bank would also be forthcoming.' They readily agreed and the next day, the bank manager presented them with a medium-sized suitcase brimming with high-value currency. When he asked for a gratuity for his services, they happily presented him with a bundle of notes. They took the suitcase home and that evening, Manohar sat down to count what he thought was well-earned money.

Navika was frying some vegetables with the usual spices, and she kept the window open to ventilate the strong aromas from the kitchen. That was when Brahma appeared, flying into the room. In one long draw, it sucked up a substantial portion of the notes being counted. Then, two long tentacles emerged from its side and grasped Navika by the waist, and Brahma lifted her up and flew through the window as an astounded Manohar ran to his writing table and took out his pistol. Ever since he had been threatened by powerful people for his investigative writings, he always kept it loaded. 'Dacoit! Kidnapper!' he yelled as he ran out through the door in pursuit. The lights on the landing had gone out and the lift was shuddering to a stop. Those inside were struggling to open the lift doors as Manohar rushed down the stairs. It was crowded by other residents and he was charging through them, the firearm held high above his head, as the first rumble was heard.

When he burst through the porch and reached the courtyard, he saw a stunned Navika sitting on a bench, stuttering but unable to speak. Brahma had flown off and the earth was quivering slowly as the building leaned to one side without falling. In a short while, Brahma returned and as it approached them Manohar lifted the Mauser and shot at the apparition repeatedly till his magazine emptied, while Navika fell upon him screeching, 'No! No!'

Brahma had completely disintegrated and among the debris, Manohar found all the bundles of currency that the apparition had retrieved, returning to collect what it had left behind, bringing the full amount back to them. When he realized what he had done, Mahohar's contrition knew no bounds.

'Alas, alas,' he wailed. 'I have destroyed my benefactor.' Disconsolate at his stupidity, his contrition depleting his reason, he raised his emptied pistol to his head in an attempt to kill himself when Navika pounced on him and tore the weapon with its empty magazine from his hand.

THE GODDESS PROJECT

GITI CHANDRA

Ta'Ki

She looked like a lion and walked like a wolf. If you looked only at her hair, you missed how the eyes were both watchful and sad. If you stared too long at the slow-blinking eyelids, the mane of tawny hair disappeared into drifting halos. But if you froze, mesmerized by the long, loping strides of the dancer, you missed the fact that she came twirling knives.

And so, when strange men were found killed in merciless ways, and no women and children mourned them, the dwellers underneath the crumbling flyover left an extra plate of something outside her window. Some left old shawls on foggy nights, sometimes she found repaired sandals on summer mornings. Occasionally, there would be a name.

Ta'Ki didn't think of herself as an assassin. She kept no count of the bodies she abandoned after justice had been done. She didn't see herself as a hero. Everyone under the flyover had a job, a thing that they did on behalf of all the other Under-dwellers; this was hers. When she did think about it, she thought of herself as a stitcher of stories.

She tried to explain this to Kolima one evening. They were sitting on the half bench, propped against a concrete pillar, picking their way through chunks of orange salvaged from the dhaba. Kolima didn't mention that her mother looked after her now, but Ta'Ki noticed that the old bruises had healed, and no new ones had appeared. And Ta'Ki didn't mention that this last kill had been hard – he was strong, she was hungry – but Kolima knew that in the story of her life, one chapter was now closed.

'So you see, Kolu,' ended Ta'Ki, spitting out a seed, 'it's a bit like the dress you're wearing.' Kolima regarded her grimy, patched and mended pinafore with pride. 'Lots of different pieces have to be put together from here and there, holes have to be closed, sides have to be brought together with clever buttons, and then, finally, the story is done, and you can wear it and make it yours.' Kolima didn't see – she was not really good with metaphors, preferring things she could see, hold and, preferably, eat – but she nodded energetically, her sun-browned hair bouncing into her black eyes.

'What's your story, Ta'Ki?' she asked, the still-blueish bruise around her eye making her look like an alien. A tanker rumbled somewhere in the distance. The Under-dwellers knew better than to think that the *sarkar* was sending them anything, much less precious water, but they listened until the sound of cold, drinkable water faded towards the rich part of the city. Then Ta'Ki looked into the inquiring, alien eyes and leapt up, chucking the peels into the corner. 'Let's go. Your mother will be waiting.'

Ta'Ki's mother – or what she thought of as her mother – was waiting for her too when she climbed into the little shelter in the corner. She was old and darkened by pain and hunger. She sat hunched on a stool, stirring milk into a small cup of tea. Ta'Ki knew that the milk hadn't been there when she had left in the afternoon, and she didn't ask where it had come from. Mothers produced milk for children, even if it was an impossible thing to do.

Durga Ma looked up as Ta'Ki entered, and the lightless space glowed with the love in her eyes. 'Why didn't you tell her your story, *beti*?' The voice was low and husky, like a tiger breathing.

'I haven't stitched it together yet, Ma.' Ta'Ki smiled, taking the cup from her hands and inhaling the impossible aroma of freshly brewed tea. The Under-dwellers had little use for such luxuries as water, tea leaves, milk and sugar. Water was distributed when it was found, passing cows were surreptitiously milked when no one was looking, and tea leaves and sugar were tales told around fires on winter nights.

Durga Ma nodded, her matted hair swinging a little around her hard chin. 'I have found you a missing piece,' she said, looking up suddenly. 'A sister.' Then she disappeared.

Ta'Ki brooded over this piece of information late into the night, as she sorted through her next few kills. At least two would be difficult to find, and she winced as she heard the wailing in her head. The sooner she found and eliminated them, the sooner the wailing would stop. So she plotted into the dark, turning bits of information over in her mind, until the first light of the morning stopped the mumbling and the incessant movement of her hands.

Durga Ma was there at the dhaba, with a little bundle of salvaged food tied tightly into her sari. 'Come,' she said, and Ta'Ki followed, her graceful, wolf-like strides making her lion's mane billow out about her watchful eyes. It wasn't until they had reached the bungalows that basked in the shade of leafy trees that Ta'Ki touched Durga Ma on the shoulder. But Durga Ma ignored the tentative question and strode on. When she summoned it, there was still a power and a grace in her movements that reminded Ta'Ki of the first time she had seen her, her eyes blazing with fury, her knife fresh from the kill.

Ta'Ki was no stranger to these wide avenues, the gentile quiet, the unhurried movements of servants shutting gates and mowing grass. More kills than she could remember had happened in beautiful surroundings such as these. Often, the wailing here was louder than in the clustered canopies under flyovers. Durga Ma stopped, listened, clicked her tongue in annoyance, and turned quickly into a bylane. Ta'Ki followed, one hand to her ear as a piercing wail assailed her senses, the other hand hovering over the long knife tucked into her waistband. She quickened her steps to match Durga Ma's, but made a mental note of the house, the tied servant in the tiny room and the series of metal bits the man wielded in his fist. Those would come in handy later tonight.

Sisters

'I have been thinking for a while now that it is time for me to go,' Ma Sara repeated softly, holding her arms behind her so as not to give in to the urge to catch the young woman to her heart and never let go.

B'har Atma wheeled on her in astonishment. 'No! No, you cannot go yet, Ma Sara!' The song she had been humming under her breath broke into a shout of fear. She stepped over the sleeping body of the man with two quickly closing stab wounds in his side, his brother dead beside him. B'har Atma could not heal the dead. And just now, she forgot the two boys kneeling in the mud, gasping through half-strangulated throats and gashed mouths. She leapt to the slender woman's side and caught her shoulders.

'You cannot leave me! I have no one! I will die without you, Ma!'

Ma Sara forced down the lump in her throat and turned her pale face up to this girl she had raised as her own. 'You have managed to subdue two riots and at least four gang wars in the past few months, and look how you heal as you go. This family, this family and so many others, they owe their lives to you. Entire mohallas are intact because of you. Streets remain dry of blood because of you.' Her tone softened and reluctantly, she reached a hand up to touch the wet cheek, moving damp strands of curly hair that stuck to the tears. 'You are ready, my dear. And I am needed elsewhere. But I have found you a companion. A sister.'

A boy moaned. B'har Atma turned away from the only mother she had known. It had been a few years since she had been brought to the luxury and love of Ma Sara's household in the wide avenues of the city. They told her she had been six, at the time, and she had no reason to disbelieve them. Less than 10 years, then. Well, she thought bitterly, that was all the mother years she was going to get. So be it. She knelt beside the bruised child, focusing her energies on closing the gaping wound in his thigh, closing her mind and heart to the leaving of her mother, keeping her own pain for later – later – later.

Ma Sara took one last, long look at the slender back, so vulnerable in its resoluteness, sighed, and turned. Durga Ma stood inches from her nose, blocking her way.

'*Kyon*, Saraswati?' she rasped in her characteristic growl. 'Abandoning another daughter?' Her question was not rhetorical, and it was not gentle. Ma Sara saw the sari-clad old woman, bent and thin, and knew that her own youthful, jeans-and-ankle-boots look did not sit well with her sister. They were the same age – if eternity could be called an age – but Durga had always allowed herself to be depleted by her human protégés. Ma Sara had heard of the assassin girl she was raising, and now she recognized the tall, leonine, young woman standing watchfully behind Durga with a shock. Goodness, she had done well with the pathetic, charred child they had dug out of the rubble.

She shook herself out of the memory and raised her perfect, pointed chin, allowing herself just the faintest air of looking down her straight nose at the pair. 'I have given her all the knowledge she needs, Durga,' she announced loftily. 'And skill. She has learned well. And I –'

'And you are bored,' Durga Ma finished flatly. She cast a cold eye on Ma Sara's fashionably styled hair, the elegant jewellery. Ta'Ki found herself faintly interested in this conversation. She had known Durga Ma all her life, but had never even heard her mention that she knew some rich, snobby, pretty, young woman in the heart of privilege and luxury. Of course, this meant nothing – Durga Ma was scarcely your average mother figure, and even Ta'Ki could tell that there was a great deal about her that was not, strictly speaking, human, or that even followed the natural laws of reality that the rest of the world lived by.

But right now, her eyes slid irresistibly past the attractive woman to the figure of the kneeling girl, who seemed to be humming softly to herself, surrounded by dying people. She didn't appear much older than Ta'Ki herself, although there was a vulnerability to the curve of the back, the exposed nape of the neck, between clustering curls. As she watched, the girl rose and turned, brushing off her hands on her jeans. She stood, looking at the three women uncertainly. Durga Ma found herself staring – something which Ta'Ki would have got a smart whack on the back of her head for: 'Never let them know where your thoughts are!' – at the girl's face, sweating in the little alley, red from being bent over her work, half-covered with damp, curling, hair, which fell into eyes that held so much sadness in them that Durga Ma herself recoiled from their depths.

She wrenched Ma Sara aside, out of earshot of the girls, and hissed: 'She remembers! I can see it. How can you leave her like this, Saraswati?!'

Ma Sara cautioned her with an angry finger to the lips, glancing quickly at the two girls standing awkwardly together. But when she turned back to Durga Ma, her cheeks dripped with tears. Durga Ma watched, fascinated as ever, as Ma Sara hastily opened a delicate lace handkerchief to catch each pearl as it fell from her face. Of all the insane qualities to be born with, this turning of tears into precious jewels was one of the things she most mocked her sister for. As Ma Sara gently knotted the little square of thin linen and dropped it into her purse, Durga Ma allowed herself a small smirk: no wonder she lived under flyovers, and this woman lived in the richest confines of the city.

'It isn't as much as you think,' she sighed wearily.

'Those eyes –'

'Yes, those eyes,' interrupted Ma Sara. 'She harbours the emotion, the aftermath, the numbers of the dead, their endless grief. That is how she heals.' Ma Sara looked away, one hand surreptitiously catching an emerald as it slid down her cheeks.

Durga Ma breathed out slowly. 'Such power,' she whispered. 'Such bottomless, fathomless, power. How does she...?'

'She doesn't know. She has no idea where her healing comes from.'

There was silence as the two goddesses looked past each other's faces. Somewhere close by a peacock cried out, the harsh, high-pitched screech that proved that beautiful plumage did not an opera singer make. Ma Sara thought of it as an ironic comment on this painstakingly pretty part of the city.

'Who will look after her?'

'She has the means to look after herself, financially and otherwise, Durga. And why do you think we decided to let them meet, after all? So, they can look out for each other, *na*?'

Durga Ma gave her sibling a withering look. 'No, Saraswati. That is not why we brought them together, and you know it. You can assuage your guilt with that notion, if you want.' Her tone softened its tigerish growl. Those pearls and jewels were proof enough that this was not easy for Ma Sara. Aristocratic and elitist. But proof. 'We brought them together because the time is coming. Lakshmi has seen it.' A thought struck her. She opened her mouth, dismissed it as unworthy, shut her mouth, then blurted it out. 'Shouldn't Lakshmi be the one whose tears –'

Ma Sara laughed aloud, cutting the question short. 'Why, because Learning and Knowledge and the Arts are not priceless? Are not prized? Are useless in this' – she waved a pale arm – 'material world, where the rich beat their wives and brutalize their servants, the poor grow violent and impatient for riches, and both are grateful they are not being killed by the other?' Durga Ma had the grace to look embarrassed. Ma Sara smiled grimly. 'It was a boon from her. Granted to me to ensure that I have the means of keeping the Arts alive. Arts such as healing.'

'All right, all right,' Durga Ma shushed her, keen to end this particular topic. 'But speaking of Lakshmi...'

'Yes. She has seen it. Durga, things will get much, much worse. That is why I must go.'

It was as if B'har Atma heard those fatal words. The look she turned upon Ma Sara would have melted mountains, but Durga Ma saw, not without some admiration, that her sister met the girl's gaze calmly, as they both walked back. It appeared as if the girls had been talking, standing side by side now, with a more relaxed air. The injured family had left, taking the one dead man with them. They would remember little, if anything, of the attack in a quiet alley by knife-wielding thugs, of the religious profanities that were hurled at them as the knives did their work, of the gravity of their wounds or the people who bandaged them and set them on their way. And really, these were not details that anyone was interested in any more, concerned as people were, mostly with not living downwind of the mass graves.

The Goddess Project

It seemed a great idea at the time. Bringing in reinforcements. Something to strengthen the failing hands of women who were losing their strongest and fiercest to hate and anger. And fire. Someone whom even the paraders of power would not be able to fault. So they went to the abandoned warehouse on the outskirts of the capital, evaded the skittering rats, put clothespins on their noses and ducked their heads as they entered the best-kept secret in the year 2028. The women of the Goddess Project had been fired, rejected or otherwise hounded out of various engineering and technology jobs; some left universities as women students and faculty were systematically weeded out by newly appointed fanatics. Driven first to help those most desperately in need, these scientists and engineers attracted other women with all manner of skills almost immediately. Welders, inventors, plumbers, electricians, scavengers, weavers, even singers and painters, crystallized around this initial nucleus, building, designing, imagining, until the Goddess Project came to be recognized for the power it drew from its women, rather than for the mythical creatures it took its name from.

And so, when they brought in a woman so mutilated that even the seasoned goddesses shuddered, the task of creating organs and limbs that would meld with what was left of her body stretched their abilities beyond possibility. There were women out there, discreetly covered in modest clothing, who owed their daily bodily functions to the technology of the goddesses. Limbs, eyes, noses – especially noses – breasts, even hair, all kinds of implants, artificial intelligences, prosthetics, even bits of brain chips, replaced those parts of their bodies that women lost to men, religion, tradition, culture, history, art, risky livelihoods and the dangers of survival.

The goddesses became increasingly adept at hiding their work under natural-looking veneers. Skin, hair, shapes and movement became softer, smoother, quieter, more human, until the rebuilt mutilated woman was almost entirely android. They wept as the AI chips went into their brains, taking over more than basic functions, subduing the insanity, suppressing the dementia, bypassing the PTSD, reintroducing a social interface that hid the emotional and mental mess that so closely mirrored the mutilation of their bodies. They sighed in relief as tender skin was grafted on to reconstructed muscle and bone, giving them the appearance of human beings, rather than human-sized pieces of driftwood, washed up on cold sands by a cruel sea.

That was how, when the motley group of girls, shivering with the audaciousness of their plan, fetched up at the Goddess Project, the goddesses were ready to hear them out.

'We need more powers we're simply not...'

'... because weapons need training and where will we...'

'And anyway, it's what they want, right? Goddesses!'

'Yeah, they *love* their goddesses, it's like the country itself...'

'Well, considering they want all women to be like goddesses...'

'And goddesses are women, right?'

'So, we thought if real goddesses...'

'And then they would see, wouldn't they!'

The goddesses listened to the impassioned pleas and logic with bemusement. Little girls weren't often listened to, almost never heeded, and their passion was always dismissed as childishness. The oldest of these girls couldn't have been more than 13. And that is why the decision to actually produce androids trained as warriors and protectors who would go by the names of goddesses was as close to a miracle as the last 10 years had seen.

But the real miracle wasn't one that even these women could have manufactured, or even dreamt of. Maybe not even desired. But it happened anyway. Because there was a fire.

There was a raging fire once, it happened this way
A body that was a woman once, now as charred wood lay
And once they saw how quick, how easily she burned
The great solution dawned on them, and to a man, they turned
They found every arm and leg, every bit of hair and nose

And piled them shouting in a pile, and hot the flames they rose
The heat it drove the men away, but bound the girls in red
And the fire danced and stamped its feet, till all the girls were dead
And the fire danced and stamped its feet till all the girls were dead!

Many years later, this was all that was left of the great fire. A chant for children who held each other's shoulders and stamped around in a circle and fell down together at the end, laughing and shouting, and got up and started again. But soon after the goddesses were commissioned and manufactured, nobody thought that so many women would have to be killed just to get rid of the goddesses. Nobody thought that the history and tradition and culture and learning and arts and nationalism and religion and patriotism and love for the soldiers who killed the women would also want to kill the actual goddesses when they finally appeared. But that, as Durga Ma said to Ma Sara, is what you get when you play with fire.

B'Har Atma

People smiled when she walked past. They couldn't help it. It was as if someone who had hurt them in the past had suddenly apologized and tried to make it up, as if a stone had simply dislodged itself from a shoe, leaving the foot free of pain and limp, as if hair that had been clinging with damp and heat to the neck had been blown free by a breeze that dried the sweat under the ears. And as they smiled, without knowing why or whom to be grateful to for the release of their aches, they saw only their own relief, and missed the boreholes of grief in her eyes.

'I'm tired of being damage control, Ma Sara,' she sighed, as they walked home. The meeting with Ta'Ki and Durga Ma had not lasted long. Ma Sara was acutely embarrassed at having to weep before anyone, especially Durga, Ta'Ki had seemed preoccupied and kept putting her hands to her ears as if they hurt her, and frankly, the two girls really didn't know what to make of this whole 'this is your sister' thing. Born out of nowhere, baptized by fire, raised by 'mothers' who could only be put between inverted commas, the whole idea of sisterhood was not something that they had ever expected to confront. Or even had space for, really.

Ma Sara was not planning to speak much until she left. She couldn't, without spilling gems on to the sidewalk, for one thing; and what could she really say? Even the hundredth time, as this easily was, it was as harrowing to leave as the first young girl she had left. But this – this she had words for.

'This is not damage control, B'Har!' If there was one thing she was passionate about, it was this, this art above all other arts. 'Healing is the most important, the most spiritual of all human activities. You know this, my darling, I have taught you this from the very beginning, you...' She saw the girl turn her head and stare into the distance, and knew that it was too early to leave her. She was strong, but very young, and Ma Sara had not realized how much of that strength came from her, Sara.

'It seems as if the more I heal, the more there are, Ma Sara,' she whispered bleakly. 'Is that what they want? That they can keep beating and knifing as long as enough people don't die and I keep saving them and patching them up just so they can keep getting beaten and cut again and again and more and more will it never –'

'It will stop. Listen to me when I say that, B'Har.' Ma Sara took the girl's face in her hands and looked intently into her dark eyes. 'I know. You will just have to believe me!'

'And when you're gone, Ma Sara? Who will I believe then?'

The screams tore through the streets, resounding in the flowered roundabouts, hurtling down the broad avenues, ricocheting off the majestic green trees. Even as the two women spun about, searching wildly for the source, the assassin flashed past them like silent thunder, her hair flaming about her, blades glittering in her hands. The song burst from the healer, following the pitch of the screams and soaring and falling in agony. The two goddesses were stilled by its force, shifting, physically, under the burden of pain, and then, just as the very trees seemed bowed with the effort, the first free notes appeared, steady as a drumbeat, heralds of triumph. Durga Ma watched a turbaned man on a scooter riding serenely past, with his wife and daughter sitting behind him, almost asleep in the early winter sun filtering through the trees. It never failed to amaze her, this ability of humans to ignore what they didn't want to see.

When Ta'Ki emerged from behind a white-washed bungalow, carrying two limp forms in her arms, the goddesses hurried to minister to the freed woman and her child, but she strode straight down the graveled driveway to her sister. Her eyes blazed in her small face.

'What did you do?!' The astonishment rang clear in her voice. 'How did you do it, the singing, that sound – I thought this was it. I never go in completely randomly like this. Totally unprepared. And he was so strong, with those metal things on his knuckles – but then this – this song! It was like someone physically lifted him off his feet. And he was so close to killing this woman! We were both going to – how did you do it?!'

B'Har Atma stared at this force of nature, still dazed from the effort, and stammered something incoherent. She had always sung while she healed, without really thinking – a way to heal herself, as she closed gashes and dried blood and soothed pain in others. This time the song had sung her, and done her work where she could not.

Neither sister paid much attention to the goddesses fussing over the inert form of the woman in Ta'Ki's arms; she was clearly a servant of some kind, horribly bruised and burnt. Ta'Ki had found her bound in a tiny closet of a room, the man looming over her. The sound of her whimpering would follow the assassin into the long hours of the night, frightening the sleep out of her eyes. Middle-aged, even a little plump, in an unbelievably old sari, colourless with age, and something wrapped about her that must have been a shawl once. Ta'Ki had bundled her and the child into the first thing she found lying next to her.

Then Ma Sara cleaned the dried crud away from half her face and her hand stilled where it was.

'Lakshmi?'

Jai

Because of course, there had been three of them. Only Lakshmi remembered. And when she was ready (oh, the luxury of running warm water, soap, clean clothes, balm to the body as salve to wounds, the spirit cleansed of the lingering memory of those hands, that breath on her face, the very voice like slime on her neck), she told their story to the two girls. Of the three goddesses manufactured to save the women from the men who worshipped them. And of course, they had been named, each identical android, for the three most loved goddesses: Durga, Saraswati and Lakshmi. Euphemistically, ironically, hopefully, to channel the yearning for strength and learning and a hope for new beginnings that the group of young girls had brought to the women in the warehouse. Once constructed, they appeared, and were entirely identical: the chips, the AI, the robotic technology, the programming – as human, in appearance, as the next woman, and as inhuman in abilities as every human longed to be. So of course, they did what they have been constructed to do: they protected, they nurtured, they led out of bondage.

They were impervious to blows and machetes, the self-charging chips closing holes, stitching skin and evicting bullets automatically but in the privacy of the warehouse. Arms raised to fend off belts and knives and acid were visibly damaged, but didn't falter, didn't fall, didn't fail to protect the girls they sheltered. Bodies placed between groping hands and cringing travellers showed the physical signs of harm inflicted on them, but remained adamantly – and adamantine – in between.

Rumours spread, but in an age of untruth and hyper-truth, no one believed the stories of these unkillable, unharmable, women. It was always hearsay – someone's ayah, some child's didi, a passer-by in one account, a fellow commuter in another. And the men who dealt the blows rarely affirmed that they had been thwarted by some arbitrary female. Still, the goddesses met, and decided that perhaps it would be safer for them to mentor, adopt, train, raise, women and girls who could defend themselves. There were only three of them, after all, and like all technology, there was a limit to the wear and tear and repairing and re-patching that they could take.

'But...' It was Ma Sara, who had been looking increasingly confused through this account being told to the two girls by Lakshmi. 'But Lakshmi' – and here the embarrassment was almost comical on her perfectly made-up face – 'Lakshmi, we are not' – she looked to Durga Ma for help and reassurance – 'we are not – how do you call them – "androids"! We are – *hum toh deviyan hain.* We are goddesses.' She said the word with a shy self-effacement that testified to the unnecessity of having to point out the obvious. 'We have always been...'

'Always?' Lakshmi's voice was gentle, but it fell on Ma Sara like an axe. Doubt was not something goddesses entertained – especially not when it concerned their own eternal and infinite existences. Ma Sara's smooth forehead creased, but she was silent, unable to respond to this quiet challenge. Durga Ma broke in then.

'*Kya bakwas hai, Lakshmi!*' Her voice was gruff, but without the growl, for once. 'What is the point of this nonsense! We all have things to do! Why don't you tell us instead how you came to be stuck in this man's servant's quarters? How could you not release yourself? This is unthinkable for us...'

'I will tell you everything, Durga. I thought only these girls need to know, but it looks as if you and Saraswati also...' Her voice trailed off into silence. 'It doesn't matter how I got here. That story will keep for another day. Today, there is great need that we know the past. How we were born.'

This time Ma Sara pursed her pink lips and held her peace, while Durga Ma regarded Lakshmi from beneath her brows. The two girls looked from one to the other in trepidation. They could feel that this past would change everything about their present – and this present was precarious enough as it was.

Lakshmi gazed into the distance as she spoke. The large mugs of steaming tea, the little pastries and tiny sandwiches that Ma Sara had effortlessly mustered when they reached her bungalow graced the delicate china on which they were arranged, as the afternoon sun glowed pinkly on the lace curtains and the carved arms of chairs. The child – she may have been about 10 years old but looked painfully small and thin – was tucked into the plush sofa, freshly washed hair gleaming in the light, a smile on her thin face.

'They came for us, as you know – that day when riots had been put down with actual guns and the *sarkar* was looking for someone else for the men to rage at. And the rumours were already there. So it was just a cleverly placed post here, an insinuation by some spokesman on some TV channel there – and they came for us. How they found out about the warehouse, I don't know. As I say, stories for another time, waiting to be discovered and told. They grabbed all the girls they could find and took them there in trucks. They must have known that we would come for them. They were bait, those hundreds and hundreds of –' She bit her lip. She felt the cigarette burn on her cheek again, smelt that sour breath. She was a goddess. She lifted her head, opened her mouth again.

'Put all of them into that warehouse, overpowered us when we came, poured.'

Ta'Ki gripped B'Har Atma's shoulders to stop them from shaking. To stop her own from shaking. To stop falling apart. What was that roar she could hear? It was not tigers, like Durga Ma's voice, it was not the thunder that ran with her on her kills, it was wind and it was –

'Fire. You remember the fire.' It was a statement, not a question this time, not gentle this time. And by this time, they all remembered.

'But we were goddesses,' whispered Ma Sara.

'No. We were androids.'

'Until the fire.' Durga Ma remembered now. 'We came because they called us from the fire.'

Lakshmi nodded. 'We are often called upon in grim times,' she said, 'but I cannot remember a summons so –'

'It was the brands!' They all turned to Ma Sara. 'It was the brands!' she repeated, and in a kind of bemused daze, the three goddesses knew this instantly to be true. 'On each girl, each body. They were calling to us with those brands!'

'But the men put the brands,' muttered Durga Ma uncertainly. 'Surely they were not in need of us? Then why did they call us with so much blood sacrifice? It was not they who needed us? Why then – I, who am always summoned with blood, with burnt flesh, I heard it immediately, as they knew I must!'

'Maybe. I can't say what will help them the most, those men. Maybe we could have helped those who tried to stop them and were also killed.' Lakshmi's voice was flat, unable to keep the memory of the fire from burning away emotion. 'I heard the roar of light – I, who am summoned every Diwali with light and fire, and cleansing, I heard the bright roar and I came.'

'That is how we came – we were summoned by the blaze, the brands, the agony, the screams, the –'

'*Atyachar.*' Durga Ma's word stilled them all. 'There used to be a word for it. "*Atyachar.*" Gods and goddesses came when they were called by a scream which rent even the curtain between our worlds. That is what this fire, this branding, this spilling of blood and burning of flesh did. *Atyachar.*'

'And so, the androids became goddesses.' B'Har Atma's voice was quiet, but the awe was palpable.

'Yes,' said Lakshmi simply. 'Made, constructed, manufactured, created, desired, summoned – call it what you like and as you wish, but that is essentially all we'll ever know.' She turned to Ma Sara and Durga Ma. 'Even we. Will we ever know more than that, no matter how many more eternities we exist?'

'What did they brand you with?'

The little voice startled them all, and they turned to see the child sitting up in a cocoon of blankets, glowing in the now oblique evening light. Under her tousled hair, the word 'jai' was clearly etched into her forehead – pale and pink, like a healed burn, but clear.

Lakshmi smiled. 'Meet Jai, the littlest of our daughters.'

Ta'Ki glared at Lakshmi aghast. 'You wrote her name on her forehead?!'

'What? No, of course not! I –' And then she understood. Pity and love shone in her eyes as she put a hand on each of their faces, and held them in her gaze. 'You are all saved from that fire, my dear daughters, you know that, don't you?'

This time it was B'Har Atma who spoke. 'Well, yes, I sort of gathered that, but I didn't know it was this fire!'

'And the people who found you named you after what was left of the brand burnt into your skin. They thought it was your name,' explained Lakshmi, her voice growing ever softer. She saw the horror and revulsion on their faces and her heart melted and her resolve hardened. 'But you see, my dears, it is a victory! Our victory! They did not know what they were creating when they did it, but we know. We know what we have made of ourselves, the goddesses we have made of ourselves. It is our brand now.'

'Yes, but what did they brand you with?' The child had leapt out of her cocoon, barefoot on to the carpet, and this time there was no ignoring it. Ma Sara took the two girls by the hands and led them to her till they all stood expectantly in a line. And the goddesses looked at them and smiled, for there they stood, these girls who would prove Mother India victorious in the end:

B'Har Atma, Ta'Ki, Jai.

Bharat Mata Ki Jai.

THE LAST TIGER

MOHAMMAD SALMAN

Firework holograms lit the skies above Raisina Hill, bathing India's most powerful neighbourhood in a silent riot of smokeless colour. It was three days before Diwali, and a few stray walkers along Rajpath savoured the citrus fragrances of autumn, away from the maddening, festive markets of New Delhi.

The celebrations did little to lighten the mood in the prime minister's office just up the hill. A group of terrified civil servants huddled outside, too terrified to sit. The minister of state in the PMO was inside with the PM, the heavy teak door unable to mask the shouting inside. They exchanged nervous glances. This was going to be a long, humiliating evening.

'Can I help you, gentlemen?'

The national security adviser, a seasoned ex-superspy, let out a small yelp as the others turned to face the PM's principal secretary. The PM's temper was the terror of Raisina Hill, but his PS was unflappable. Amused by their terror, she walked past and knocked on the door. The shouting stopped immediately.

The door opened moments later, the balding, pasty-faced minister slunk out. The tufts of black hair on his ears failed to hide the red of his shame, and he walked past without acknowledging anyone, mumbling furiously as he went. '*Isteefa de doonga!* What is this nonsense? To hell with this cabinet position! Now he wants a new way to show off. Bloody disaster...'

The PS sighed. She had just saved him from more humiliation, but not so much as a 'thank you'. She motioned to the media adviser, a wiry, grey-haired man with a perpetually shifty expression, to join her. 'Come with me, sir. The PM has some ideas to run by you.'

They walked into the beautiful, wood-panelled office, lined on all sides with portraits of ex-PMs. The incumbent himself sat behind a beautiful mahogany desk, a picture of Mahatma Gandhi peering benevolently at the room from behind him.

The PM cut a truly impressive figure, modelled on the Great Leader from the early 2000s, the only person to hold the PM's office for over 20 years. In his image, the current leader sported a short, clipped white beard, dressed in light pastels reminiscent of the Nehru jackets of the past, his deeply attentive eyes behind rimless glasses. Myths from decades past had encouraged him to work out every day, even when he was well into his sixties, and as a result, the PM was rather broad around the chest and shoulders.

He waved a powerful hand at his officers. 'Sit down,' he said irritably, 'I hope *you* two will earn your keep for the day, unlike that moron. Just *one* bloody portfolio, and yet he can't come up with ideas. Is this how we will become a world power? How can we have a global image if the PM isn't respected globally? Twenty years from now, when my ashes are in the sea, I must be more than a paragraph in the *Manorama Yearbook*, no?'

The media adviser interrupted. 'Sir, for the polls next year...'

'*Arre, chup karo yaar!* You guys can't even give me an image booster during festivals, just how the hell am I to trust you in 2087? The people mocking me are more famous than I am. That Paki college kid's videos mimicking me have gone viral worldwide. Those spoofs are more popular than my actual speeches! At least ask one of our Internet superstars to mock their army chief the same way, but no! You have no ideas! Your best suggestion was a tough crackdown on the protests outside the army's new robot facility. Apparently, that was supposed to send a strong message!'

Media croaked again. 'Thank you, sir...'

'Quiet! Idiot. The strong message was to be about my decisive push forward with new technology, and instead the press is going to town on my reputation! They're saying having a robot army diminishes the soldiers and mocks their sacrifice. And they have a point. Who is going to be loyal to a machine?'

'Sir, sorry...'

'*Bhai,* what use is your apology? *Kuch milega, kya?* Listen, I have a plan and I need it done right. New tech isn't impressing people these days, so the image booster will have to be a return to our heritage. The roots of our great nation. I need to be seen as respectful of old values. Which I am.'

'Umm...'

'Don't make that stupid face, man. Come on, give me ideas!'

'Err...'

'Forget it. Listen to me. Let go of the 20th and 21st centuries. We need to dig deeper. Go way back into India's past. Revive traditions that no one's thought of reviving. I've given this some thought, and I have a superb idea.'

The PS and the media adviser leaned forward. The PM chuckled. 'You really want to know, eh? Look, I read somewhere that during Diwali, people used to sacrifice owls to bring prosperity to their households. If I can do this in 2086, it could be a big win with the trading community. I'm thinking – let's get 36 owls, one for each state and union territory. And on the day of the festival, we get a butcher, preferably Muslim for the secular...'

'Sir, *no*!'

The PM stopped with all the grace of a man striding into an open door only to realize that it is closed and the glass is really clean. 'What did you say?' His eyes glinted, his rage barely suppressed.

The PS held her ground. 'Sir, you cannot do this. This was a cruel practice and if no one does it any more, good riddance! You will be drawn and quartered by the animal welfare community and pretty much everyone else. If the media adviser here hadn't lost use of his tongue right now, he'd tell you how the press would punch you left and right as well.'

The PM looked at her closely. 'I've rather taken a fancy to owls, and you have to get them. If cruelty is the issue, we won't kill them. We'll innovate a bit. Set them free, like people do with doves. Now go find me those owls. Go!'

There was clearly no room for negotiation. The PS got up and walked to the door, the stunned media adviser following close behind.

'And another thing,' said the PM. 'Get me 37 owls. 29 for the states, seven for the union territories and a big one for the country.'

The PS looked at the staff waiting outside. Of all the things they hadn't signed up for, this had to be the worst.

Supriya KT looked back at the village of Danapur as the matt green, fuel-cell-powered Maruti Suzuki Gypsy made its way into the forest. The houses glowed with twinkling fairy lights of every colour, while silent firework projections shot into the overcast night sky.

Diwali. The best time of year to be anywhere in India. Records from before 2030 spoke about how the festival had become an ecological horror over time, with billions of fireworks triggering week-long spikes in air and noise pollution. She thanked her stars for living in a time when it had once again become a festival of lights.

The Gypsy powered on noiselessly through the soft dirt track, its occupants encased in a glass dome that allowed them unfettered views all round but could also double up as an extended computer screen. Driving the tough little vehicle was Kadheer, her trusty assistant of 12 years. A conservationist with the WWF, her job was to protect and track leopards along the banks of the Kapila River deep in the forests of Karnataka. With wild tigers declared extinct in India in 2075, hundreds of experts like her were assisting the government in protecting the next line of endangered big cats.

Seated in the back, she checked the equipment on board. She was going on a week-long expedition to the Lone Mountain, a solitary, thickly forested hill deep in the core area to confirm rumours of a black panther sighting. She pulled a tablet out of a recess behind the driver's seat and touched the centre to switch it on. Navigating through the controls, she accessed footage from the 20 camera traps hidden in locations on and around the hill. The banks of the Kapila had not seen a black panther for over three years, the last one having most likely migrated out to another park towards the south. It couldn't be tracked efficiently because a massively underfunded wildlife programme meant that neighbouring areas lacked the kind of sophisticated equipment Supriya worked with.

They drove silently for two hours, Kadheer concentrating on the road while Supriya scanned data and made notes. There was a sharp beep from the car's dashboard. Kadheer brought his foot down hard on the brakes, bringing the Gypsy to a stop. The first loud beep was followed by a series of softer ones. The word 'SCANNING' appeared on the car's central console.

Supriya jumped into the front passenger seat.

'What do you think it could be, madam?' Kadheer said. 'Elephant?'

'Not likely. The sensors on this car are very precise. The alarm is programmed to be softer in case of an elephant or any large herbivore. This one's a big cat less than a kilometre from us.'

'It could also be a sloth bear.'

Supriya sighed. 'Kadheer, my friend, allow me some optimism. Let's pray this is the black panther we've come for. We'll have work for a week instead of the usual aimless waiting.'

The animal moved in the direction of the car, the screen showing what looked like a child's attempt at moulding a clay four-legged animal. Supriya and Kadheer did not move their eyes from the screen as the image slowly grew clearer. The sensors also picked up the increasingly panicked movements of small animals away from the approaching cat.

'Tail's long. Not a bear then...'

'No long snout either...'

'It's just 200 metres away now. Can we get a visual?'

'The animal is huge!'

'Of course it is. We're looking for a full-grown leopard.'

'No, no! It's bigger than that, Kadheer. I don't understand, unless...'

Wide-eyed, they looked away from the screen and at each other.

'It can't be, Supriya. They're extinct!'

'The computer can't make this up. Look at the screen. The shape of the ears. Its gait as it moves. It's just a hundred metres away now. Put the cloaking system on.'

They sat in silence, listening to the forest. The image of the approaching animal left little to the imagination, but they had to see it for themselves. Supriya switched on the colour-resolution cameras, which would project a perfect colour image of the animal on the windscreen regardless of how dark it was outside. Their eyes bored into the instruments. They were shaken out of their trance as a low, powerful roar sounded a few yards away from them.

'Oh dear God! That was *not* a leopard.'

The bushes finally parted and an animal no Indian had seen in the wild for over a decade walked on to the path. Its yellow eyes looked directly at the camera as it contemplated the strange metal beast trespassing in its territory. It bared its fangs and growled. The colour sensors captured its orange fur and black stripes in beautiful detail as the tiger turned away and walked across the path into the forest.

After what seemed like an eternity, Kadheer turned to Supriya, tears in his eyes. 'This is a miracle. There's a TIGER near the hill! We need better protection in the area!'

Supriya stared wordlessly at the 3D rendering of the tiger rotating slowly on car's dashboard screen. She laughed softly as the tears came freely. 'Unbelievable. An adult male tiger! They may have eluded our eyes all these years, but the tigers still seem to have a stronghold in India's forests. I never thought I'd see one again in the wild.'

'What next?' said Kadheer, 'Do we head to camp as planned, or do you want to go to Bengaluru to share this with the office?'

'We head to camp. We've all the connectivity we need over there to let the bosses know. Let's go.'

The PM banged his fist on his desk. 'Damn you! Can't any of you do anything right? Because of your incompetence, I've become a laughing stock on Diwali. The Opposition and their news guys are having the time of their lives at my expense.'

The PM's officials stood in absolute silence as he ranted. Speaking could be fatal today. After his prayers on Diwali morning, the PM had happily surged downstairs to an emptied-out parking lot with his entire cabinet and top bureaucrats for his owl-freeing ceremony with national and international news teams in attendance. There were a few diplomats as well. The Opposition had boycotted the event, protesting against cruelty to the captured birds.

Five bird catchers had done a fine job of getting 36 little owlets and one big barn owl to the ceremony. Managing the birds while they waited for the PM, though, had turned out to be harder. The birds fidgeted and fought, crowded on three perches.

As the PM walked out, the cameras began to click furiously. The flashing lights drove the owls wild. The barn owl broke the string tying it to the perch, freeing a few of the smaller birds in the process. They attacked the PM, pecking him on the face and arms and defecating on his spotless white clothes. One zealous guard fired at the birds and missed. The bullet ricocheted off the brass PMO plaque and caught the Pakistani high commissioner in the foot. The offending guard was dragged away as the bird catchers scrambled in to restore order.

The only uninterrupted part of the ceremony was the photography and the video recordings, played on loop on national and global networks, and even reaching the off-world UN base on the moon. 'Owl's Not Well with the Indian PM', 'Diwali a Hoot at the Indian PMO', 'A Parliament of Owls Craps on India's PM', said some of the prominent papers.

It was a PR disaster and quite a diplomatic incident, and the media adviser fortuitously felt some pain in his chest and was rushed off to the hospital along with the PM and the Pakistan envoy. The PM got his scratches and cuts attended to, inquired after the high commissioner's health, ignored the media adviser completely and rushed back to summon a cabinet meeting.

'I have lost faith in all of you,' he said to his officials as they waited for the cabinet to assemble. 'There are going to be changes in the bureaucracy too when I do the next cabinet reshuffle. Let's hope my new ministers have better ideas than you lot.'

The cabinet ministers sat around the table, watching the PM walk in a few minutes later. They were absolutely still, no one wishing to draw the PM's attention. The PM took his seat, his officers standing behind him. 'Does anyone want to tell me about what happened?'

The minister to the PMO, skilled at attempted suicide, spoke. '*Pradhan Mantri-ji...*'

'Not you,' the PM seethed. 'Not today. My own minister of state, ladies and gentlemen,' he said as he waved around the room, 'is the perfect example of a person so devoted to the cushiness of his job, he forgets what he's supposed to do to *keep it*. There's a reshuffle due next month, and one thing you all will be evaluated on is your role in building our image.

'At this point, suffice to say that none of you have done the government's image any good. And after today, we've taken quite a beating. Now, I only have one hour to give you before we all adjourn for Diwali with our families. In that time, someone come up with an idea, or so help me God.

'Since this latest disaster has branded me an enemy of the environment, we need to reverse that. What natural symbol would help us best?'

Sensing an opening, some of the ministers chimed in. 'Elephant,' said the Minister for North-East Affairs.

'No. It's already a symbol for the Opposition. Appropriating it is not worth the effort.'

'Peacock,' said the foreign minister.

'No birds after today's incident.'

'Rhino,' said the home minister.

'Extinct. Read a little, man!'

'Camel,' said the railways minister.

'Ugly.'

'Eagle,' said the textiles minister.

'No birds! Who else has an idea?'

'Snake,' said the PS in a whisper only the PM could hear. He turned to her with a look of pure venom, and then resumed glaring at the cabinet.

'Come on! This planet is full of every kind of creature. How can you not come up with one?'

'Lion?' the sports minister ventured.

'Can't. Those animals are thick as thieves with the CM of Gujarat. We'll only confuse the public. Think hard – all of you. Close your eyes and think since we are like a classful of primary students right now. Is there a problem, Environment Minister?'

The Minister for Environment and Forests, seated three places away to the PM's left, had been fidgeting with her phone and had knocked a glass of water over. Shocked at being called out, she cobbled together a reply. 'Sir,' she croaked. 'Sir. I was looking at my phone because important, uh, urgent, uh, message...'

'Be clear. Quick.'

She set her glass right, poured some water and took a sip. 'Sir, a wild tiger has been sighted in Karnataka!'

The room received this news with stunned silence.

'Wow. I thought they were extinct. Now that is a symbol I would be proud to be associated with. So,' he looked at the rest of the room, 'how do we spin this to our advantage?'

The minister for industry spoke. 'Sir, we could build on your "friend of the environment" image. What better proof of your commitment than tigers coming back into our forests?

The defence minister followed. 'We could use some great lines, sir. The tiger is the sentinel of our forests, just like you are the sentinel of our great nation.'

'This isn't a First Family government, Defence Minister. Stop the sycophancy.'

The PM clasped his palms together, elbows on his desk. He closed his eyes for a few seconds as the room waited. He opened them a minute later, suddenly happier. 'I have an idea. Republic Day is coming up, and the parade has honestly become a bit of a bore. I really cannot stand it. Why don't we do a green parade down in Karnataka and get the tiger for a photo-op? Isn't that a great idea, Environment?'

It wasn't, but no one was going to say that. 'Of course, sir. Brilliant idea. I'll get in touch with the ground team and get this done.'

'You won't do it alone,' said the PM, turning towards his PS. 'Work closely with my office to see that everything happens smoothly.'

The PS seemed to be under great strain. She could hold it in no longer. 'With all due respect, sir, you *can't* have it on the day of the parade. Preparations are on, tickets sold and the German chancellor has confirmed his participation. There can only be trouble.'

The PM stood up. He would not be defied in front of his cabinet. 'I want to make one thing very clear. This place works like a democracy on the day of the polls. Not before and not after. You'll do as you're told. You'll all do as you're told. It is the *only* way you remain safe. Now go.'

'An invite to the PMO? Supriya, this is quite something!' The joint secretary for forests pushed the letter of invitation towards the young biologist.

'Thank you, sir. I hope I can get the PM to give us the funds we need. This tiger is young, born at least a couple of years after they had been declared extinct. There could be more where this one came from!'

The JS looked at Supriya over his half-moon smart glasses. 'One step at a time, Supriya. I hate to disappoint you, but there will be a political angle to all of this, and it will be thrust on you whether you like it or not.'

'What do you mean, a political angle? I can't have *netas* using this huge moment for a photo-op!'

'Play the long game, Supriya. You're young, there may be more than one tiger in the wild, and there's a lot you can do for them. The environment ministry in New Delhi has no money to help you, nor do we at the Karnataka forest ministry. The PM's your only hope, and he'll want something in return. Think about that before you speak at the PMO.'

Supriya fiddled with her collar in the slightly stuffy, under-airconditioned office of the PS at the PMO. The bureaucrat sat with her fingertips arched together, cordless earplugs relaying the contents of Supriya's proposal. The file took three minutes to play, after which the PS pulled the earplugs out, reached for a glass of water (offering none to her visitor), downed it in a gulp and started talking.

'I like your proposal. It has promise. It looks like you'll build on this big discovery and turn it into the biggest conservation story of our time.'

'I would be honoured to have your support, madam.'

'And you shall. You shall. But...' the PS rummaged through some papers, 'we need to be practical about this. The PM's Special Projects Fund is not as big as people think. See, Supriya, from where the PM sits, there is a limited amount of resources and countless people and causes begging for his support.'

'I am not beg –'

'I know, I know. Just a manner of speaking. It falls on the PM, with some support from me, to decide where to spend this money. So, while wild tigers returning from extinction is big news, and your project is very visionary, what's in it for the PM?'

'Well, I intend to make it very clear that it is the PM's support that turned a chance tiger sighting into a new conservation project. We could name it after him if you like.'

'That won't do. I think this is a chance to do something bigger. You know how politics is today. The right move for one's image can guarantee more terms in power. More, er, opportunities to serve, as it were.'

'I wouldn't know, ma'am. I don't really understand politics very well.'

'Allow me to guide you then. What is our situation? We have a PM surrounded by a hostile media, an army of detractors mocking his every move. His attempts at image building haven't really worked. And that's what makes your help important. If the PM were to go public with the tiger, be seen with it, now that would be something.'

'What do you mean, "seen" with the tiger? It's a wild animal and needs to be studied, undisturbed. I cannot allow this to happen.'

The PS leaned forward. 'Let me be very clear. I don't care about this tiger of yours, any more than I care about anything you conservationists become a pain in the ass for. But it helps the national image to know that the national animal is not extinct, and it really helps that you discovered this in the present PM's tenure. I am offering you two choices: comply, and let us do the announcement of the tiger's return at a parade in the park in Karnataka. A day's trouble, after which you will have the time, resources and freedom to pursue this project as you will. If this is indeed the last tiger, we will milk every last drop of publicity out of it.

'The other option is that you continue to be difficult. In which case we shut you down and find a biologist more willing to cooperate with us. The government's universities are overrun with scientists who wouldn't mind the sudden fame.'

She looked at her watch and then back at Supriya. 'I have to walk across to the PM in two minutes. That's all the time you have.'

Supriya looked at the bureaucrat with pure loathing.

In the tense, short-lived silence, the PS put a few letters in a file, readying them for the PM. She looked up at the sound of a sniffle.

Supriya fought back tears and heard herself say, 'Yes.'

On New Year's Eve, Supriya and Kadheer sat in a treehouse overlooking the Kapila River. Kadheer brewed tea in a kettle while Supriya watched footage from eight spy drones silently scanning the area. Three of them sent back images of the tiger walking towards the bank.

The two of them stared at the footage, lost for words. Every day over the past two months, they had managed at least an hour's worth of tiger sightings. They hoped the animal would cross the park boundaries and lead them to a mother or a mate or even a male rival fighting for territory. But the tiger stayed within the park, content in its new home.

The kettle whistled sharply. Supriya swore while Kadheer hurriedly switched it off. On the screens, the tiger, about a kilometre away, stopped walking and stuck its neck out at the sound. Supriya and Kadheer sat motionless. A minute later, the tiger resumed walking towards the river.

'Poor guy,' Kadheer said. 'He has no clue of the horror that awaits him three weeks from now.'

Supriya glared at the footage from drones flying over the Republic Day event zone chosen by the PM. 'There's scaffolding going up at the edge of the forest. Scaffolding! One old, vain bastard's insecurity ruining acres of good forest. For a *parade*!'

Right at the edge of the forest, the PM's office had ordered three acres of land cleared to make a pen for the tiger. On Republic Day, the animal would be driven into the pen by drum-beaters, where the PM and the chancellor of Germany would pose for an image with the tiger in the background. High-definition 3D holograms would render an accurate copy of the proceedings to billions of holoboxes across the world, while millions would 3D-print the likenesses for souvenirs. It would be an unorthodox Republic Day with (as the PM saw it) immense symbolic power. An end to his recent run of humiliations. As every official and staffer fell in line behind the PM's orders, Supriya watched with bitter resentment.

Later that night, keeping watch while Kadheer was sleeping, she pulled out a diary and scribbled her daily account. Pen and paper were off the grid and anything she wrote in there would be safe. Poking out of her bag was a small book called *Editorial Hotline: A List of the Globe's Biggest News Networks*. She had a big expose ready, implicating everyone responsible for this brazen disregard of the environment to feed the spiralling insecurities of one man.

Let him have his parade, she thought. *Let's see how he feels after my story hits the news.*

On the evening of 25 January 2086, the PM leaned back in his chair and surveyed his chief officer. 'So,' he said in what he hoped was a confident, prime ministerial voice, 'I hear everything is ready for tomorrow. Madam PS, am I to be assured on this front?'

'Yes, sir,' said the PS. 'All preparations are in order. The German chancellor and his retinue are at the seven-star property next to the wildlife reserve. The national and international media have their top reporters on the ground, covering the run-up to Republic Day. We've sold a thousand

VIP passes at an average price of 10 lakh rupees each. All that money goes to your relief fund. Security is in order. Everything will be fine.'

'As you always say. What of the tiger?'

'It has been hemmed into an area of 10 square kilometres. We couldn't put it in a smaller area for fear the animal would become aggressive. It has had a free run in a sizeable part of the Deccan forests after all.'

'And once it's brought into the viewing area, I will pose with it?'

'Yes, sir – you and the German chancellor.'

'Will someone tranquilize the animal and make me stand next to it? I once saw this great picture of an old Russian president next to a bear.'

Idiot. 'No, sir. Unlike that famous bear or other trophy animals, the tiger is the national animal. It has to be seen as free and strong – like you.'

'It won't attack me?'

'You are the prime minister of India, sir. You have the biggest security detail of any world leader. The tiger is only fangs and claws.'

'Easy for you to say. Still, it could be worse. Tell me, what is the media saying?'

'Do you really want to know, sir?'

'You know I already know. I just want to see if you can tell me the truth.'

'The response varies, sir. The animal rights lobby is up in arms. They're protesting at Jantar Mantar. We've had to barricade India Gate, Rajpath and Raisina so that no one can create problems here. There was also a natives' protest in the buffer-zone villages around the forest where the tiger was found. Twenty-odd people armed with sticks, threatening to attack any forest-clearing operations. They hugged the trees and stood while our men came to clear the viewing area.'

'What did you do then?'

'We had to stun them, though it was a trifle harshly done, I suspect.'

'Fatal?'

'Two or three will live.'

There was an awkward silence. 'This isn't good. Does the press know?'

'No, sir. Intelligence is at work in the vicinity of the forest. Local journalists are under strict, er, control. Not a word will go out.'

'Good. Is the chopper ready? It's nearly 10 p.m., and I've to leave in just 30 minutes.'

'Yes, sir. All set to go.'

'It seems you have become a shade more competent at your job. Let us leave.'

The PM cursed under his breath as he made himself a cup of green tea. It was 5 a.m. and on a normal day, he would have appreciated the birdsong outside as a welcome break from the sounds of his household stirring. But his mood was dark. A look of thunder had possessed his face for the past hour. He had been irritated at the absence of newspapers when he arrived in the national park the previous night, the luxury tents doing nothing to cheer him up. Something was amiss and his staff was hiding it from him.

He avoided reading news off the Internet as much as he could. The coverage against him was always too much for his temper. He was a sensitive man after all, and the press was most inconsiderate. What had he done that was so out of line? When Saheb had set his example 80 years ago, it got him four chief ministerships and five terms as PM! To win was to compromise, especially in Indian politics. He had skeletons in his closet, many hundreds of them actually, but who didn't? Sometimes strength lay in being able to sacrifice a few lives for the greater good of millions. Yes, that was it. Clear thinking like this would keep him away from the pills the doctor said would calm him. Still, he had to know what it was everyone was keeping from him. He switched on his phone and browsed. The journalists on his side had done their job well.

Republic Day: New Venue for a New India

Going Back to Her Roots: India on her 138th Republic Day

Kings of the Hill: PM Meets the Last Tiger

Tiger Diplomacy: The Maharaja Wows the Kaiser

He breathed deeply, because he knew the others would be savage.

Man of Iron(y): PM Clears 3 Acres of Jungle to Showcase Conservation Success

Tiger Diplomacy: Is There No End to This Farce?

Kapila Villagers Missing on PM Jungle Show Eve: Coincidence?

India's Jungles: For the PM, Of the PM

He threw his phone down as his breathing grew ragged. He ran across the room to the medicine box by his bed. Falling halfway, he crawled to the nightstand, took out a pill and forced it down with a glass of water. He leaned against the bed as the panic attack subsided. Media management, they had said! He would have the bloody adviser's head once this was over. He got to his feet, gingerly, and walked over to the bathroom. 'Be strong, Narsingha. This is your moment. Your time. It will all be fine.'

He heard a knock on the door and the mask was on again.

'Breakfast, sir!'

'Coming.'

The tiger walked eastwards, away from the noise. His sleep had been disturbed before dawn by a constant *BOOM, BOOM* accompanied by the sound of humans shouting. There were too many of them, and the racket they made was unbearable. The noise had also driven little animals into the tiger's path, but no sooner did he settle down to eat a freshly killed rabbit or deer than the humans grew closer and drove him away. He snarled at the direction of the sound to no effect.

Let me find one of them alone, the tiger thought. *That will be the end of it.*

Hariya turned to his band of drum-beaters. 'The tiger is getting angrier. We should be patient and let him finish at least one of his kills.'

'We can't, *da,*' his brother Sesha responded. 'We have eight kilometres to go and only two hours until the function.'

'Good thing they sent 20 of us then. But I am surprised we didn't see any elephants or buffaloes.'

'The department is looking after that, *da*. There is a huge circle, 10 kilometres across, that they have kept the big beasts out of it for the past three days.'

'I don't know how the PM thinks this will help him. But 20,000 rupees each is generous. I am content to do as I am told.'

Supriya sat at her desk, making a furious diary entry.

'I have been placed under house arrest. I have no access to the Internet. There are cops stationed outside the apartment. They are kind and empathetic in their fashion. They don't mind getting me groceries and surprisingly, they have not asked me for tea or meals even once. It's been three days and I have to endure this for one day more. The bastards have driven the elephants and bison to the edges of the forest, away from the event. There is a media blackout with independent local reporters detained in the same manner as myself. What havoc the big beasts have caused in the buffer-zone villages will only be known in a few days' time, when the dead or injured start reaching the district hospital.

'I am told the PM is beside himself at the prospect of seeing a wild tiger. A vain, unscrupulous autocrat seeking validation through an animal which is a marvel of nature. The tiger is all the more marvellous for having hidden in the wild when we all thought his kind extinct. This diary will go to press very soon, and I am going to bring this man down if it's the last thing I do. I hope I am not the only one who is trying to do this today.'

The dignitaries settled down after the playing of national anthems and after the PM, via hologram, gave obeisance to the Amar Jawan Jyoti at India Gate in New Delhi. They sat on an elevated platform at the edge of the forest, safe behind a bulletproof force field. To their left, bathed in soft sunlight after a rainy night, was the three-acre meadow that had been cleared for the tiger. To their right sat an assortment of dignitaries, celebrities, some schoolchildren and the media. Further back, in their thousands, were the orange-clad 'supporters' of the PM's, brought in from all over the district on the promises of a great spectacle and the chance to see the PM up close. And a small credit of 10,000 rupees into their accounts.

The PM turned to the German chancellor. 'Your Excellency, I hope you are enjoying this rather unorthodox celebration.'

'I would be, Mr Prime Minister, if your actions had not led to a PR disaster for me at home.'

'What?'

'Against all sound judgement, you have denuded a patch of forest for an event that is essentially about conservation. Then you have been harassing what is possibly the last wild tiger in India. If that were not enough, 20 villagers have disappeared, allegedly in another one of your famously brutal reactions to dissent. I should walk off this dais.'

'You could. But you won't, will you? Not with all the agreements we have to sign, the bulk of which will benefit your people? And you do realize that I am the only world leader of any consequence supporting German businessmen by letting half your manufacturing sector translocate to India? I would suggest you swallow your pride and go through the motions with me. Ah, the sound of drums. The tiger comes close.'

He got up and walked down the steps to the ground. His security detail rushed to surround him. The PS and media adviser ran to his side.

'Sir, you're exposed,' the media adviser said. 'This is not a great idea.'

'Shut up! When this is done, we are going to speak about your keeping the news from me.' He turned to the PS. 'Have my security staff on full alert. I am going to stand at the fence of the enclosure. Make sure the cameras capture that when the tiger comes out.'

The PS opened her mouth to protest but thought better of it. *Let him have this day as he likes*, she thought. She saw the cameras follow the PM as he moved, and the Doordarshan and ANI drones circled the meadow searching for the tiger. A giant screen showed aerial footage of the forest, the tiger expected in sight at any moment.

The PM walked to the audio console and picked up a microphone. His appearance on the screens led to deafening cheers from the back. He waited for the noise to subside and spoke. 'Friends, I welcome you all to this most unique of all Republic Day celebrations. Today, we are here to celebrate the rediscovery, nay rebirth, of one of our greatest national icons. You have heard the mischievous ones say that India is no closer to being a superpower than it was a century ago. They said our development agenda has failed. They said the environment is in tatters. But tell me, what does the animal we are here to see represent?'

There was muffled cheering from the crowd. The PM looked around, letting his gaze rest on each dignitary behind the force field.

'We are here to see the last tiger. The sole remnant of a kind of majesty, grace, power and respect seen no longer in this world. That tiger is us. Read what you will in the news, but remember this – it is the people of India who are the world's most enduring civilization. It is we who have retained our gods, our culture, our traditions and *sanskaar* while others have fallen by the wayside. Just like the tiger, who now approaches. His ancestors migrated from the east many thousands of years ago at a time when India's jungles were home to lions. The tigers were the underdogs in that war, but they were clever. Over thousands of years, they picked each lion one by one, pushing them further and further west until the only lions we had were confined to the forest of Gir in Gujarat, and ultimately died there.

'The victorious tiger could not enjoy this supremacy for long. Man took over and until a decade ago, he all but destroyed this beautiful, awe-inspiring animal. The fact that one survived is a lesson in resilience, and that is what I am here to share with you. Enough with the parades, with the state floats! This is a new India, 140 years into our independence! We will fuse the old and the new, being loyal to our ancient symbols as we forge a new path into the future. Let us now witness the return of our national animal! *Bharat Mata ki Jai!*'

He walked to the fence as the chants of *Bharat Mata ki Jai!* hit the skies. *This is a great start*, the PM thought. *Something is finally going my way.*

He slipped on a fresh buffalo turd and narrowly avoided a fall, clutching at a commando who was shadowing him. He looked up and saw the chancellor smirk. He didn't dare look at the cameras for fear of another panic attack. Disregarding the shit that squelched in his leather sandals or the stain it left on his clothes, the PM walked with slow dignity to the fence, leaning casually against it once he got there. He ordered his commandos to go stand near the dais, a hundred yards away. 'Friends, the drums come closer. The tiger is nearly with us!'

The drums finally stopped. The crowd was suddenly struck into silence. Out of the trees and into everyone's line of sight, there in the meadow and on millions of screens around the world, the tiger walked out. He was a majestic, full-grown animal, the winter sun making his coat glow in an orange bright enough to make the beholder weep. The tiger snarled back at the forest, his displeasure at the drum-beaters evident.

A low *boom* reverberated across the park as the tiger roared. More *booms* as he roared again and again. The crowd and the PM watched in stunned silence. Whether they cared about wildlife or not, the only living wild Royal Bengal Tiger was a sight to remember. Even the thought of how great this would be for his PR was only a trickle at the back of the PM's brain.

Soon, though, reality beckoned. This was his show, and the tiger was second to him. He lifted the mike and turned to the cameras. 'Here it is, my friends! The tiger has returned!'

The skies were rent with another deafening cheer. The tiger sank to the ground at the noise, covering its ears with its front paws. Opening its eyes, he spied the lone man standing at the edge of the fence, only a few bounds away. The men near him were too far to be of any help against a charging tiger. He roared again and leapt.

The PM's customary waves to the cameras were interrupted when he saw his commandoes run towards him, guns raised. He heard the snarl and realized what that meant. He turned back to see the tiger gaining upon him.

The tiger cleared the fence in one leap, the PM staring at him open-mouthed. He heard gunshots as the commandoes fired in a panic and saw the animal collapse before hitting him. The tiger hit a rock to the PM's left, and lay there. He stood transfixed looking at the beast in its death throes.

Phew.

Another snarl and the tiger rose again, claws ready to swipe. Ten commandoes fired 10 bullets. One of them ricocheted off the rock and the PM felt fire in his leg, his vision blurred as he heard his bone crack.

The cameras continued to roll.

A NIGHT WITH THE JOKING CLOWN

RIMI B. CHATTERJEE

'Hey Rayne!' my boss yelled. 'How's the robot army coming along?' They all laughed. Mr Salman Vaghela, CEO of Ramdhun Corporation, begins every meeting with his departmental heads with this question, and all the other bastards laugh. But I'm used to it now. They're just putting the Orbison in his place. Fucking Dynastics, so proud of having a daddy backing them up. Lineage is so important yada, yada, yada – as though the fact their daddies shot their mummies full of cum is part of God's great plan or something. Just because I was made from a prefabricated embryo implanted in the womb of some slag who must have been *sooo* grateful to be on contract with human resources, they think they're better than me. How straight of them to make an Orbison their head of tech, everyone should admire their broad-mindedness and give the morons a big fucking prize. So, I said what I always say: 'It's coming along well. I'll send along a prototype for you to look at soon.' He doesn't care about the prototype. Everybody knows the robot wars can't begin until all the space hotels are up and running, because when we finally destroy earth and all life upon it, the top guys want a seven-star gallery in the sky to watch it from. Bastards.

The meeting began, and I resisted the urge to watch darknet videos on my BlackTab under the table because the boss has replaced all our old tables with glass ones. He's afraid someone will pull a concealed weapon on him, shoot him when he least expects it. Like what happened to Jasper Edgemont, who was Ramdhun Corporation's guy in the Tarim Basin till a month ago. Times are tough. I suppose that's why the other heads didn't waste much time on pleasantries, thank fuck.

There were 12 of us in our black Samsa suits, our helmets resting on the table beside us. Samsa suits keep us clean, compensate for our lack of sweat glands and protect our desensitized New Guy skins from random damage. Since 2030, every man on earth has been born with Male Hypertoxic Syndrome: we're the New Guys, better than the Old Guys, who were pussies and didn't deserve to rule the world. By the time we New Guys hit our teens, we can't feel a thing. That sounds real cool, but it can be a problem: I knew a guy in school who sat on a stovetop and burned all the skin off his butt, and he didn't even notice. Suits protect us from doing stupid shit like that and getting laid up in hospital while the other guys nick our stuff and our chicks. These new suits even swallow puke, store semen (very valuable), link with social media and organize our schedules, but fuck, are they heavy. Just one of the many shitty things I have to put up with. Like these 11 jokers: I've known them since school, and they've known me. This doesn't make us friends: there are just so few guys left in the world that it's impossible for us to avoid each other. After the Sweep and the Consolidation, the only guys anywhere on the planet are in the corporate HQs, each corporation controlling a territory, surrounded by their chicks and slags and living like kings while the world falls apart around them.

Slimy Salman says if you live long enough, you meet every guy in the world. I hope he doesn't live long enough. He's already 42. He's worried about Shigenobu. He should be. Shigenobu Corp. controls the smallest territory in the world: Japan. It's a piece of grit in the oyster of Ramdhun. We control the entire Pacific Rim except for California and Hawaii, which have belonged to Dynacorp since the Consolidation. Dynacorp don't mess with us: they've got their hands full dealing with Pentecostco, which controls the fat midriff of America, regards Dynacorp as an abomination in the face of the Lord and wants to nuke 'em dead. Bastards.

I amused myself watching Slimy Salman's mouth move as he talked. To give Slimy his due, he kind of appointed himself my protector in school, or at least he made sure that no one got full bullying rights except him. He was smart enough to see I had brains and the roiling self-doubt that makes one invest time and training in thinking skills rather than brute force. Salman's no fool: he knows that the younger New Guys, about a third of the ones around this table, never knew the struggles he and his father faced. He once told me how he watched his dad suborn governments and blast feminazi rings so he could build a safe world for his son. Hah. I never had a dad to help me rule the world. No Orbison is ever so lucky.

So now these punks get the good stuff handed to them on a platter. They pick fights with each other because they're bored. I guess ruling chicks and slags is boring; I wouldn't know because no one puts me in charge of them. I could rule them just fine if I got the chance. It's simple – slags, who are females who live in the service territories and do U-jobs where we never have to see them, are conditioned from birth to see us New Guys as remote, all-powerful gods who can do with a casual word what it takes them the energy of a lifetime to achieve. Chicks, promoted from the ranks of slags and holding V-jobs where they work where we can see 'em, don't have quite as rosy a view of life in the corporate enclaves as the slags do. But that's because we need them to do the actual work of accounting and collaborating and negotiating and communicating and entertaining and translating and healing and caring and serving and suffering patiently whatever the torture of the month is. Chicks still see us as their protectors and providers, even though if they ever rose up and got in touch with their true bitch natures, they could probably kill us all in a fortnight. But they'd never do that. We're their dreamboat lovers, their baby boys, their wet dreams, even when we're mean and nasty. So, what does that leave us New Guys to sink our macho teeth into? Video games mostly, and giving each other the finger. I should know: when there are no chicks around, I'm the target of choice for these funny guys.

I tried to refocus on the meeting. Apparently, the scuttlebutt is that Shigenobu are cosying up to Lionfist, which controls inland China and Tibet. Lionfist's power lies in the Tarim oilfields and Satellite City, their space launch facility in the Quaidam basin. They put up everyone's space hotels and sell us oil for our high-end gas guzzlers, so no one wants to piss 'em off. An alliance between Shigenobu and Lionfist will pinch our coastal Chinese factory zone, and Ramdhun's hopes of becoming self-sufficient at manufacturing will go down the toilet.

Since hearing this news, Slimy Salman's got the heebie-jeebies so bad, he wanted to pull up all the anchors keeping New Singapore berthed off Sentosa Island and sail it into the Yellow Sea. I persuaded him not to, because we might tell the world that New Singapore is a floating city that can go anywhere and ride any catastrophe, but the reality is that all these silvery cruise decks and on-board pool gardens are hiding a big stinking pile of rust and rot that goes far below the waterline. Back in the 2020s when it was built, it might have been seaworthy, but we'd be dead if we tried to move it now. According to the reports, a third of all slags have to pump the bilges at any given time to keep us floating. It's their big-hipped butts keeping us on the surface, not the leaky buoyancy chambers and badly patched hulls.

I once hacked the head of Datanets and scoped some of the below-deck feeds from the securicams. I wanted to see what the damp and darkness of the slag heap was like, the faces of the off-duty slags when they think they're alone, in the womb of one of whom I was gestated as she floated in the gel tank for nine months...

'Rayne! I asked you what you're doing about this Joking Clown thing. Don't you read my memos? I wanted a response three days ago.'

I nearly dropped my BlackTab. 'What Joking Clown thing?' Dear heaven, how did Slimy Salman find out I'm a fan? Has he penetrated my ID spoofs? Has he been logging my net traffic? Impossible! No one's better than me at this shit...

Salman smirked. 'For the love of fuck, pull your head out of your lab sometime. This Joking Clown bitch is the latest media craze the slagheap's hooked on, the hottest act of 2078. We don't know how she uploads her music videos – we tracked the data trail to Antarctica, but that's a bust. The place got so screwed in 2048, they can't even keep the servers going. Anyway, that's for the head of Datanets to worry about. Right, Wu? What we want right now is to own the Clown, whoever she is. Radely, tell him.'

The head of merchandising cleared his throat. 'The Joking Clown appeared on the darknet about six months ago, and her videos became an instant sensation. When she broke the 1000 viewers per hour average, we set up multiple sites selling merch referencing the Clown, as we do for any mass slag appeal franchise. However, every site we've put up has got away from us in minutes. The sites are all functioning fine but none of the revenue is showing up on our servers. Some big-time data wranglers are behind this. It could be Lionfist setting their dark hackers on us, or it could be a private scam from inside the Ramdhun setup. Either way, we're clueless. Fact is, the Clown's a ghost, and she's sucking our blood.'

'We can't let her get away with this.' Slimy smashed a mailed fist into the glass table, which lived up to its specs and absorbed the blow. Everything around us New Guys has to be double-armoured, because we're so crazy-mad all the time. 'The bitch is laughing at me, at my generous desire to give the slags a better life than they get under any other corporate territorial authority. I will not have it.'

I started to sweat inside my Samsa suit. That's another one of my guilty secrets: we New Guys aren't supposed to sweat. It's part of our condition. We're not supposed to be fat either, but guess what my nickname was at the Ramdhun Institute for Boys, premier school for witless fucks like the 11 guys around this table?

'Well, Porky, what are you going to do about it?' Slimy Salman smirked again and took a swig of his champagne. 'I didn't make you head of tech so you could rack up XP playing sex games in your gamecave.'

'Do we need to do anything?' I stammered. 'We own those slags anyway. Why don't we just shut down their credit pipelines so they can't pay for the merch? Then they'll lose interest and the next piece of ass will get the traffic.'

'Think we didn't try that?' snapped Wu. 'The first time they struck, we shut down the service-dollar pipelines for all subscribers, and it was like we'd thrown a stone into a nest of wireworms. In less than a minute, I had a new bunch of rogue pipelines leeching access, so I sent a posse of Punisher Class Bully Boys from Corporate Security to search and destroy any merch bought offnet. Made a big bonfire in the slag mess hall on Level 4 and chucked the possessors in Corrections without the option of competing in the Bully Qualifiers. They'll never see the light of day again.'

'Indeed. Those slags are too untrustworthy to convert into Bully Boys,' said Nix, head of human resources. 'Their assertiveness looks like it could be an asset, but their slipperiness argues against it. We prefer straightforward brawlers, because after the Bully Alterations, they flex their new-found guy muscles and keep the slags down with gusto. These people aren't worth jeckshit.'

'Ahem.' Wu glared at Nix. Those two hate each other so bad, flies get fried when they cross gazes. 'So, guess what? The morning after our exemplary raid, there's a real-time black market in merch operating out of that very same slag level, totally dark. More search and destroy, more Bully Boys putting the boot in. It's no use. The slags are addicted. They can't get enough of that freak in greasepaint, and we're losing credibility as well as chick-dollars. The only way to stop it is to freeze the whole service-dollar transaction system. Shut the whole slagheap down for a day and cleanboot all servers.'

'Absolutely not,' Salman rapped back. 'The eyes of the world are on New Singapore. We're the flagship city of the Achiever Era, the poster child of New Guy cool. I've worked my ass off on convincing the other corps that we have the best standard of living in the entire world. Know why Shigenobu is still respected even though they own a piddling bunch of islands? It's their culture. They invented rape rock and victim chic. Their slags live like princesses in maid costumes. Have you seen their promo videos? They let their slags live in real suburban houses and ride the subway to work, just like in the twentieth century. They're all living the dream, baby! That's what we have to match if we want to get and keep Japan. So, we gotta have rock stars for the slags to cream themselves over, show that we know how to give our workers a good time, and the acts can't all be Bully Boys sponsored by the corporation coz that stinks of setup. Besides, letting a few rebels pop up now and then is good HR practice. It gives us a handle on slag mentalities, a way to figure out what's eating them. We did this before – in my dad's time. There was this crazy bitch called Babelion who was riling up the feminazis back in the 2030s. This was during the Bitch Wars, terrible times, worker loyalty was at a historic low. We co-opted her and got her on our side. She helped sell the idea of New Singapore and Achiever Culture to a whole generation of chicks and slags. You follow? We need a new cultural icon for the 2070s. Someone to give us integration and brand authority. That's our selling point to the other corps. And I want the picture to be perfect. Nothing but happy faces, guys. Happy faces.'

'It's true that it would be very hard to put a good spin on a full shutdown,' said Berhamji, head of public relations. 'It might well be seen as a confession of weakness.'

The rest scowled. Berbie is our most hated yes-man, but no one can touch him because he's Big Percy's little boy. Except that right now Big Percy's in the ICU after his third coronary. He was fixing to be the first Achiever to live beyond 50 years, but no, he had to get a lap dance on his 48th birthday and kaboom! His heart gave out. Berhamji doesn't seem to care, though. He knows Big Percy's no use to him any more, so right now, he's got his lips wrapped tight around the boss's jewels. Anything Slimy wants, Berbie makes sure he gets. Bastard.

'That's not all,' said Rafaelo, head of domestic operations. 'Things have moved on since last Wednesday. You're all aware that the Silver Heights

Love Fest is on this weekend? It's the biggest event of the slag social calendar. I was informed this morning that the organizers got a call from one of the shadier agents on the mainland, saying they could deliver the Clown for a live set on the last day of the fest.'

'Have they agreed?' The question popped out of me before I could stop myself. Slimy grinned. 'I knew you'd be interested, Porky. Everyone knows about your depraved tastes.' This from a guy who once bit off a chick's ear and ate it because she hadn't got it altered the way he wanted. Fucking bastard.

'Well, it's your lucky day, Porky, because they said yes. Which means I want you to be there on the day with a 3D camera. I want top-quality scans and face recog on that bitch.'

'Why? Why me? Can't Wu do it?'

'No, I'm busy running this rust bucket of a city, Rayne. We all know what you do in that lab of yours. Get out there and do some work for a change.'

They sniggered. Berbie most of all as he said, 'We can't get any face data worth shit off the Joking Clown's videos because of the greasepaint and the jewels. Put yourself in the mosh pit, you should get a good view.'

More nasty laughter. I knew Slimy was enjoying this. He likes nothing better than to bait me.

'Got it, Porky? And then I want you to pull her in for – ahem – questioning. Whoever these hackers are who are helping her, I want their asses on my breakfast table by the end of the month.'

'Yes, boss, consider it done.' I don't know what else they talked about for the rest of the meeting. All I could think about was, how the hell do I stop this? You see, the Clown's kind of an obsession with me. I'd thought it was my secret, but somehow these bastards had figured it out. Or maybe I was just being paranoid. They hate the Clown because she's everything the slags are not allowed to be. She's really tall, probably over six feet, and kind of willowy and whippy. She always appears on her music videos in elaborate clown make-up, with a big rainbow wig. Every inch of her skin is covered. Most music vids are just skin shows; young slags make them because they think it'll get them into charm school and a chance at a V-job where they'll get ogled by us New Guys, but not the Clown. She's so fucking *angry*. It gets me hard just thinking about it. The first video of hers that I discovered while I was trawling the darknet was 'Knife in my

Belly', the a capella version. The only accompaniment to the Clown's heavenly screams is the drumming of her gloves set with nine-inch nails on a big steel drum. When I first heard that song, I wanted to pound every bastard who'd ever bullied me into a little wet, greasy patch on that gnarled concrete floor. Listen to the last two verses:

I got a knife in my head and its name is you
I got a pain in my belly and you say it's nothing new
I'm gonna scream till your fucking walls come down, I'm gonna [screams]
I'm gonna [screams]
Break you as you go, you hanyo, break you as you go
Break 'em now! [Solo]

Come out of the workshops baby, come out of the holes
Come out of the prisons saving all your pretty souls
Come out of the shadows baby, come into the light
Let me do it to you all the motherjeckin' night!
Let me sing...
Let me sing...
Let me [screams]

She sang the 'break you as you go' line so fast, you had to concentrate to hear that forbidden word 'hanyo' in the middle. Just saying that word on tape is enough to give the CorpSecs cause to drag her in for questioning and cut her up starting from the toes. The word 'hanyo' is originally Japanese, it means half-demon. It's what the slags call us New Guys in the depth of the night, when they've been chicken-hunted by five horny New Guys out for fresh meat and left for dead, or their child's failed charm school, or the foreman's fined them for the fourth time that month and they don't have the chick-dollars for meds. When they curse us, they call us 'hanyos' – not New Guys, not Achievers, not iron-skins or fire-eyes. And maybe they remember that we didn't always rule the world. Slimy Salman jokes that there are three sexes ever since we Achievers became the only dudes in town: chicks, slags and New Guys. Three different paths that never meet. For instance, I knew right then, as we 12 hanyos sat around that table in the light and luxury of our conference room, I knew that in some stinking, half-lit, soundproof stairway tucked inside a metal pillar of the room, a bunch of slags were sitting huddled over their cleaning kits, waiting for a red light to turn green when we left for the day. Then they would scurry out, clean up after us, scrub the stains on the glass between them and the masterful vistas all around, and they'd vanish gratefully back into the walls, glad to be out of the scary light and space and beauty of our world. They might as well be rats for all we know or care. That dank hell is the world of the Clown. That's where her anger comes from. It scares the shit out of me, but it also gets me really, really hot.

So, after the meeting I went back to the lab and watched the Clown's whole discography while I stuffed my face with pizza. It felt sort of elegiac, because I'm damn certain that playing live in Hanyo Town is the Joking Clown's way of committing spectacular suicide. Even if they let her get on stage, there's no way she'd be leaving after that. Maybe she has a death wish. Or she's going to blow us all sky-high. Yeah, that would be a fitting end to everything. I'd die with a smile on my face, for sure. Or maybe I wouldn't, because I still haven't cracked the boss level in *Bitch Republic 6: Satan's Sisters*. Gaming rumour has it that if you complete it with a perfect score, the leader of the resistance gives you a blowjob in the winner's cutscene. Can't die without seeing that, or what would I brag about in heaven? And then before I know it, the next track on my BlackTab cycles and the intro to 'We're Going to the Garden' starts up and, hell, I'm crying big tears into my pizza and hoping the Clown brings a barrelful of C4 to Silver Heights so she can end this filthy mess now. And then the Clown's soft-hard, man-woman, angel-demon voice begins to sing like the last call for paradise:

We're leaving tonight for the garden
We're going to get there okay
We'll pay with a star for the cable car
And climb the hill by the bay
The flowers are waiting to welcome us
The lanterns are lighting the dark
And I feel in you petals of tenderness
As you take a walk in the park
As we take a walk in the park.

[all voices]
We're going to the garden
Before the sun grows cold
Where love will share our burdens
And no one's bought and sold.

For the leaves are all falling like dollar bills
The billboards look naked and nice
The man in the moon's got shares in his room
And the caviar's nothing but ice
But you gave me the key to the mountainside
You struck off my chains with a sigh
You looked in my eyes and saw paradise
And showed me my world was a lie
And showed us our world was a lie.

We're leaving tonight for the garden,
I'm standing here under the sign.
Hoping you'll break through the cordon,
Hoping you'll win and be mine.

Throw down your keys and your jewellery
Tear up your Daddy's card
Break off the shackles they put on me
Breathe and it won't be that hard.
I'm here at the rendezvous waiting,
I've got your favourite coat,
I think that we're done with the hating,
For you sang to me all that I wrote,
You sang with me all that I wrote.

After that, I wasn't much good at getting out of bed for the next couple of days. They say we hanyos don't feel pain: it's part of our condition. I'm the only one who knows the whole story behind that because I'm the one that Slimy Salman tasked with scrubbing every trace of the truth out of the archives. One day, I'll tell you how our world ended up like this. Anyway, we don't start out with skins like iron: when we're born, we're in agony. Our little baby nerves are hypersensitive and so are our immune systems: everything makes us sick. Even human hands against our skin hurt. By any natural logic, we should all have died at birth. But we didn't because the Old Guys figured out how to save us, in the early decades of the twenty-first century. A doctor called Pradip Shankar saved us because he might have been the one who broke us in the first place. And the Old Guys cheered him, because how could they have gone on living without their sons to leave everything to? If not for us, then who was all that raping and killing and world domination for? Bastards.

And now, the Old Guys are history (we made sure of that), and a handful of hanyos rules the world through the corporations and armies and nuclear stockpiles the Old Guys bequeathed us. Yay. And I'm one of them. So why do I feel like a bucket of turds soaked in piss? All I want to do is eat and play video games and cry while watching the Clown dance. Whoever said that the skin is the only part of you that feels pain was a liar.

I was hoping to make it to the weekend without having to do anything much, so I ordered in some more pizza and a big box of shitty fake wine, but on Friday morning, someone leaned on the buzzer at the lab door. At first, I thought I was dreaming the sound, but it was too insistent for that fantasy to stick, and eventually I had to crawl out of my sleep pod and answer it. Bleary-eyed, I stared at Berhamji's smug face. 'Whoa,' he said. 'I was going to say you're at work early, but I guess you just never went home.' He peered around the door. 'So, it's true: you live here. Where are all the RanDees?'

'I work alone,' I said, getting slowly shunted backwards as he came in, helmet under his arm. 'I don't need a bunch of mute slags to clean my glassware and type my notes. Anyway, the RanDees are no use ever since HR started nuking their speech and hearing centres. Executing their non-disclosure agreement, my ass. These days they can't innovate worth shit, but try explaining that to HR.'

'Well, security comes before progress as Slimy likes to say. No point making cool stuff if other corps can snitch it, huh? And slags can't help flapping their lips unless you stitch 'em up good.' He parked his helmet on my workbench. I took a deep breath. 'What are you doing here, Berbie?'

'Oh, Slimy sent me to see that you make it to the Silver Heights Love Fest. It's starting today: all the Bully Boy groups will be playing in the first lineup. Classic rape rock mostly. I like Beaver Junction; have you heard their new single "Vagina Mono"? They're headlining today.'

I gritted my teeth. 'I'm busy. I was working late on the prototype. And I have no interest in Beaver Junction. They suck.'

'So, it's only the Clown you like.' He picked up a sample I was working with: a block of superpearl. I twisted it out of his hand and threw it back on the lab bench. Bad move: he had my arm bent behind me and my face pressed into the worktop before I could yelp. I could feel his breath on my neck and squeezed my eyes shut. 'You know something, Porky?' he whispered. 'I like you. I've liked you ever since school when I'd compete with the others to make you wet yourself. Remember those strategy classes where we were told there are only four possible roles in business? Bossman, henchman, competitor, and what was the last one again? Oh yes, victim. It seems to me, Porky, that you've spent your whole life rehearsing for that role.'

I made a sort of squeak to tell him I could feel the deep tendons of my arm starting to tear. He eased off when my Samsa suit began beeping and saying, 'Exceeding parameters,' in that sexy female voice it uses. Mine is a cheap-ass suit, it doesn't have FightBack™ or I'd have laminated his ass to the floor. When the purple spots in my eyes had finished their lightshow, he was sniffing my pizza. 'You eat this stuff? This is almost as bad as slag food.'

'I'm saving up for a new gamecave.' Cautiously I rotated my shoulder. If I'd had my helmet on, I could have got a damage readout but, of course, it was by my sleep pod, flashing alarm status messages on the heads-up display that I was too far away to read. 'What do you want, Berbie? Coz whatever it is, I'm not in the mood.'

'I can see that,' he said grimly. 'I think I'll go to the Love Fest alone. You'd cramp my style.'

I grimaced. I knew he was going to romance some slag, tell her all kinds of bullshit, offer to show her how the chicks live in Hanyo Town and then, when they were alone in his gigantic mansion on Level 7 of the Starcruiser Lightspeed, he'd lock the staff out and chicken-hunt her through the endless rooms. We don't call it rape any more: New Guys say rape only ever existed in the imagination of hate-crazed feminazis. Berbie does it every Love Fest. He says he likes to eat the innocence of slags. He says it tastes good. 'I'll come pick you up on Sunday evening. Have the equipment ready. We gotta nail this bitch to keep the boss in a good mood. Shigenobu's really getting up his ass.'

I made one last bid for freedom. 'You don't have to come. I can do it myself.'

'The hell you can.' He chuckled. He paused in the doorway even as every cell in me silently begged him to fall through the floor. 'You know what the boss once said to me? He said, "Berbie, I'll tell you why the chicks will never rise against us. It's because of you Orbisons. Creating you little shits was a stroke of genius, one of many for Ramdhun."' He took a moment to grin at the irony of it. 'We get the slags to sign up for marriage, which in our times is a one- or two-year contract with HR, and we put an embryo inside them. When the kids are born, the slags take their girl babies back to the slagheap with them, but they leave the boys in the hospital when they're done with the milk-giver's contract. They never set eyes on the boys they birth, and so later, whenever a slag looks at one of you Orbisons, she thinks to herself, "Maybe this one is mine." A bitch will turn on anyone except her own children. Stroke of genius.' He gave me an ironic salute. 'Good work, Porky. Merely by existing, you help us keep 'em in their place. I guess that's why you suck at everything else.'

Then he left. I slumped against the workbench and moaned with relief.

God help me, in spite of my fear of what Berbie might do, I stayed in my gamecave for the next two days, playing stupid role-playing games from the dawn of time. Kiddie stuff, shooting pixies with peashooters and growing mushrooms with rude names. Hell, even our Achiever kiddie games are kind of vicious. I like it, a little bit. It makes me feel meaner and less jellylike without actually making me see or do anything that'll bring me down. I felt almost normal on Sunday morning.

Berbie turned up at 11 a.m. 'Lunch. My treat.'

Like most of us New Guys, Berbie's a gourmet. Our hanyo skins are fucked, but our mucous membranes work fine. I figured lunch at least would be tolerable. We went down to the Silver Heights Experience Centre to be close to the venue. All of Silver Heights is built on top of the hull of an ancient aircraft carrier, one of five we've integrated into the city (the other four support the Formula One race course). It's the tallest structure in New Singapore, but it's still dwarfed by the jagged tops of the half-sunken skyscrapers leaning drunkenly in the distance where the old city sank beneath the waves in 2023. I try not to look at them.

Everything was dolled up in pink and white for the Love Fest. There was a posse of nude ballerinas on the roof of the Experience Centre, their silicone breasts stiff as stone as they hopped and twirled. Berbie made a sound deep in his throat. No doubt he was jackpotting into his Samsa suit. 'Ah! That felt like a billion dollars!' I didn't smile at the hoary old joke. Back in the 2040s, sperm was the most valuable commodity on earth. Guys could pay their way through business school with regular jackpots. Now, of course, it all belongs to the corp. We still have loopheads in our bodies to collect and preserve our semen, but no one gets paid for their jism any more. It all goes to human resources, and we just pretend it makes us rich. Like most of the things we pride ourselves on, it's all a lie.

'So,' said Berbie after we'd got a table and he'd smoothly ordered for the two of us, having assumed correctly that I'd just slow the process down. I didn't object: my goal was to get through lunch on autopilot. 'You like the Clown.'

'What makes you say that?'

He shrugged. 'Knowledge of human nature. Your nature, to be specific.'

'How does that figure?'

'You're a loser. Obviously, you like big, powerful chicks. You used to like *Fat Peggy* back in school.'

'Fat Peggy...that takes me back.' *Fat Peggy* was a banned comic strip about a reluctant dominatrix produced by a slag called Weerasaratne who'd vanished in 2048. The strip was set in the Feminist Spring of the 2030s, and Fat Peggy was always skiving off her job. Her dom speciality was verbal abuse. She'd sit with a whip in her hand and her huge stomach balanced on her earth-mover thighs and she'd tell her hanyo clients what she thought of them, using the whip for punctuation. How I used to lie awake in school after lights out and wish she'd come and take me to her boudoir and beat the living crap out of me till I didn't even know my own name. 'Okay, you got me. So?'

'Well, we're here to take the Clown out. The boss needs to know you won't cause any trouble.'

'Trouble? Like what?'

'Who knows? A sudden attack of romantic would-be heroism, perhaps?'

I snorted. 'Save that for your rape show re-enactments. I keep my fantasies strictly in my imagination.'

'You're a smart guy, Porky, for all your posing. Anyway, if you tried anything, I could fight you off with one hand.' He flexed his wrists. 'The only time you beat me at arm-wrestling, you cheated.'

'That's because I'm smart, like you said. How do you think an Orbison has survived working with you Dynastic shits for almost a decade?'

'Fuck, it's been that long, has it?' He grinned nervously. 'You joined when you were 17, right? Like we all did. And now you're 26 – two years younger than me. Wow.' He leaned forward. 'You know that the average life expectancy for us New Guys is 35?'

'Inaccurate. If you leave out the data from babies who die in the first five years, it goes up to 44.' What was he driving at? Could Big Percy's impending death be looming in his mind? Or was he hinting that Slimy Salman had nearly hit the finish line? Damn, I started to sweat again. I've survived this long by never being part of any group or faction. If Berbie sucked me into his intrigues, I'd be dead meat. 'I don't let it bother me,' I ended weakly.

'You should.' He spread his hands, taking in the opulence of the restaurant, the topless waitresses with their rubber chests, the vivid blue of the sea dotted with yachts and speedboats, the colourful marquees and the big stage laid out down below. 'Doesn't it eat you up that you have so little time in which to enjoy all this?'

'I don't leave the lab much. My work is important to me. And to Ramdhun.'

'Oh, come on! Lighten up, Rayne. This is supposed to be fun.' A venomous grin spread his features. I didn't say I seriously doubted that this so-called luxury would last much longer than the average hanyo life. Everything's falling apart, not just New Singapore. Then the food arrived. 'Eat,' he said. 'This is actual meat and vegetables from our farms in Malaysia. This meal costs more than the entire yield in real dollars to the corporation of the average slag in a lifetime. Your mom could have worked herself to death and not even afforded a tenth of this meal. Its price can't even be computed in service dollars. A nice kebab of human flesh would cost less in either of the world's two currencies. Beats fake pizza made of fungus and algal slime, eh, Porky? Enjoy!' I just grunted and dug in. Real food weirds me out a bit, but I figured I could do with the micronutrients. Of course, bloody Berbie never puts on any weight. He burns it all up: New Guy metabolism is supercharged. Only mine isn't. No one knows why: the doctors have spent years poking at my flab and shaking their heads. Three years ago, HR sent me a memo saying my sperm was unsuitable for human resource generation. Bastards.

'You want dessert?' I shook my head. 'Seriously, Porky? This is all on account, you know. Boss said give the meatball anything he wants.'

I pushed my plate away with finality. 'Shouldn't we get down there and scope out the venue?'

'Already did that. But come on, since you want to see the fleshpots of Silver Heights so bad. You got the 3D camera on you?'

I nodded, and patted the case at my hip. We descended to deck level. Slag rock fests start with Bully Boys making all kinds of hard-ass noises and then mellow out into acoustic acts. By the third day, people are pretty bombed on illicit drugs, provided discreetly by HR, of course. We control the dealers, and we control the cops who pull in the clients. No matter what game you play in New Singapore, the house always wins. Currently there was a four-person ensemble singing fake country and western.

'Gah,' said Berbie. 'Nothing but drippy chicks singing about dead babies. Or cruel lovers. Selling the dream, huh? Only the top 10 per cent of chicks will ever have a boyfriend, yet all our soap writers and chart toppers yak on about how mummy, daddy and baby makes three.' His face twisted. 'The truth is those feminazi bitches broke the world. They made us guys get so fed up with their whining that we reneged on the deal.'

'What deal?' I asked. I didn't care, of course, but I figured if I kept him talking, he'd be self-involved enough to not focus on baiting me.

'Why, sex in exchange for stuff, of course. That was always the deal. They give us sex, and we give them money, or food, or babies, or respect, or whatever bullshit crap chicks want. What they forgot back in the 2030s is that the deal only holds as long as we want it to. We... guys. Coz we own everything, we create everything, and we provide everything with the sweat of our brows, and they have to please us. That's the order of nature. When they don't please us, we take sex and don't give anything back. That's their punishment.' He eyed a passing chick tottering by on 18-inch transparent platform heels. She had 'DMT' tattooed in curly letters on her back and chest. 'Whoa. That's a Pharm Girl. Who do you think she belongs to?'

'She's got her own legs, so she's probably a wife's maid, not a Model, coz these days the Models all have those superlong prosthetic legs. I bet she belongs to one of you Dynastic shits. That puts her out of my league, Berbie.' I squinted at her retreating back. 'Mmm, looks like her tattoos say she lactates dimethyl tryptamine on command. Classy.'

'I'm going to follow her.' His red-rimmed eyes glowed hungrily. 'Maybe she'll give me a hit. Meet you back at the big tent at 10 p.m.'

If I'd dared, I'd have pumped the air with a fist. But I just stood and watched till he was out of sight. Then I went into the big tent. The first thing I noticed was all the rainbow wigs. Lots of people were cosplaying the Clown, but none of them was tall enough to be her. Then I wondered if perhaps her height was just a trick of the videos, and she was actually here already, watching from some corner. Maybe she could see me. And maybe I could warn her. I took the 3D camera out of its case and held it in the crook of my arm. 3D cameras always have these creepy faces, like they're looking at you out of their two eyes. Maybe she'd take the hint and stay away. Certainly the slags were keeping their distance, but Samsa suits have that effect on them. I've long been resigned to the fact that as a hanyo I would never have any friends. Just bossmen, henchmen, competitors and victims.

So now I had four hours to kill before Berbie returned from his escapade, but I didn't care because, deep in one secret pocket of my Samsa suit, I had a red pill of pure Substance P. Not the stuff the slags buy for piddling service dollars. This I'd sweetly cooked up in the lab myself, pouring into it all my loneliness and frustration. Now, I know it's dangerous to trip on P in the open because it fucks up your senses, but I'd done it before and the really intense part of the trip only lasts a few minutes. If you sit tight and ride it out, you're in beautiful afterglow for hours. So, I found a forgotten chair at the back of the tent, settled myself in, popped it and put my helmet back on, setting the visor to 'Reflective'. But the helmet seemed to melt off my head. In a few seconds, I had a hallucination that my nose had split down the middle and opened out, letting in everything around me. I could smell the rust and barnacles far below my feet, I could smell the tears of children, and the bodies of every single slag in that tent. I could smell the loser sweat and sour defeat of my own body. I could smell particles of my lunch on my lips. I licked my lips, and suddenly the air was kissing me, thrusting at me, pushing its tongue down my throat. I gripped the chair as if I was drowning. Dear heaven, I could almost see the outlines of this air-body that was bringing me such exquisite…

'You here for the Clown?'

One of the cosplayers. Same Joking Clown make-up as the rest, jewelled sun round one eye, diamond tears flowing from the other, rainbow rising on forehead, dark crimson kiss, multicoloured powderpuff hair, nose pulsing with light… No, what am I saying. My ears seemed to be pulsing, breaking up her words into sweet music, drowning the meaning in the sound. 'You hear for the Clown? You here for the Clown? You. Here. For the Clown. The Joking Clown. The. Joking. Clown.'

'Hear,' I croaked. 'Clown.'

She seemed to nod. 'He said you'd be here.'

'He?' So this was one of Berbie's informants? I could feel the P coming down and felt inexpressibly cheated. Damn it, I can't get high for one fucking second without some hanyo pissing on me in the boys' toilet. Bastards.

'Keep calm,' she said. 'When the shit goes down, just make some noise and run around and you'll be all right. I'll take that.' She hooked the 3D camera out of my nerveless hands. I let it go. Berbie probably thinks I'll fluff it. I was relieved. 'Can I go now?'

She gave me a look. 'You'll miss the show. You don't want to miss the show.'

'I don't?' I looked around and the entrance to the tent was dark, stitched with neon. 'Fuck! What time is it?'

'Late enough. The Clown is coming. Get ready to laugh your guts out.' Then she vanished before I could be certain she wasn't a hallucination, leaving raw panic behind. I checked the time on my BlackTab, secure in its hot pouch on my armoured chest. It was 10.30 p.m. These shindigs always wrapped up at midnight. They were setting out big steel barrels on the stage, rolling them on like this was a dockside cargo bay. I perked up a bit. The crowd was watching with intense concentration. The silence seemed to suck at the stage. This was abnormal. I could feel the electricity crawling up and down my spine. Then something hit the back of my head so hard I nearly bit my tongue. Damn, when did I take off my helmet?

'There you are.' It was Berbie. 'Did you get my message?'

'I...' But the speakers boomed. To my half-drugged eyes, they seemed to swell and spit the sound out like howling mouths. I scrounged for my helmet behind my chair and put it on.

'People,' said a deep male voice, probably a Bully Boy, they're so proud of their artificial testosterone and all its gifts. 'Please welcome J-Squad, partners in crime to the Joking Clown, root kittens of the apocalypse, survivors without parallel, kinky thinkers, dark hackers, gardeners of children, lovers of love, unzippers of sense and antisense. Dance, all you clowns! Bring the world down with your drumming feet!' And the dancers catapulted on stage. Each of them tall and whippy and stuck with jewels and cotton-candied in a thousand colours and stomping, man, stomping us all into the ground. And then came the voice, singing, only this time deeper, fuller, somehow... different.

Silver shiny goddess in the house of pain,
Split me wide and beat me down again and again,
Break me on the spirit of your duality,
Turn my skin to ether so that I can be free.

Let me love, let me live let me bleed, let me scream
Let me sing let me bring you down,
Let me open my eyes to the hanyojecking dream,
Let me show you how to be a clown!
Let me show you how to be a clown!

I nearly jumped out of my suit. It was like the Clown was singing with my voice. I could feel the words vibrating in my chest and I couldn't be sure I wasn't making them. Berbie was looking at me weirdly. I guess he'd got a load of DMT; he had a bit of a milk moustache. He held on to me as if I was anchoring New Singapore to the bedrock.

Lithium madness moving like a snake in my skin
Warrior sunsets die inside my eyes
Daddy said he'd teach me how to earn how to win
But he never said a word about the prize.

The voice seemed to be getting closer, but in the flurry of dancing clowns we couldn't make anything out. Then, the surf of colours and cotton candy and writhing bodies parted, and we saw who held the microphone, who was singing, naked but for the clown make-up, body dusted with gold dust on mahogany skin, every detail plain under the lights.

Let me speak, let me shake let me run let me fall,
Let me sing let me bring you down,
Let me open your eyes to the hanyojecking dream,
Let you show me how to be a clown!
Let me show you how to be a clown!

'Get him!' Berbie yelled, and my trance broke. The one singing was a *guy*. He had all the usual guy bits bulging in his golden jockstrap, and his chest was smooth and unscarred. I grabbed Berbie and held him back as chaos erupted around us. 'No! Don't do it! This is not some chick you can hand over to the Punishers. He's one of us! We can't mess with him until we know who he is.'

Berbie stared at me. 'So who is he? How did he get here? Which corp is he from? What the hard-ass FUCK is going on?'

I stared to speak, but the screaming lot of slags were charging the stage, pushing us with them, marooning the Bully Boys in CorpSec uniforms in a choppy sea of crazy high-pitched bitches. Clowns cascaded down from the stage like trippy liquid and began pulling rainbow scarves from the Bullies' noses and blowing hooters in their ears.

'Sir!' one of the Bullies in command shouted at Berbie. 'Please clear the area now. We need to infracannon the stage.'

'Not enough time. Get him! He mustn't get away! Throw a cordon round the tent and another one round the whole complex. Check everyone's ID tattoos. Strip-search them if you have to, I don't care who they are.'

'Sir, please clear the area, we can't...'

Berbie grabbed me and tried to head for the door. But there was a solid wall of people all around us, and we were too late. In an instant, I doubled up with the worst pain I'd ever felt in my adult life. It started in the pit of my stomach and rose with my priceless all-natural meal into a barf rainbow that put the Clown's hair to shame. As I hit the deck, I had the presence of mind to throw off my helmet again and let the barf fall free to the deck. Berbie wasn't so sorted. Served him right. Bastard. I heard the thud of bodies falling, and moans and screams all around me. That was the first and last time I was ever infracannoned. Our suits protected us: we didn't bust a gut like the slags, just felt like we did. But I knew the Clown was gone. He'd played his trick and vanished, and now here we were sitting in a pool of our own vomit and wondering who the hell had played us and for what stakes.

I couldn't help it. Something else was rising, chasing the nausea away, building in the recesses of my soul, as cleansing as Fat Peggy's whip, as crazy as P, as liberating as the final moment before death. I laughed. I laughed till my belly ached. I laughed even as Berbie crawled to his knees and stared at me blankly through his vomit-stained faceplate like I was the one who had gone mad. I laughed as dying slags were stretchered away and the head Bully came and reported that of the 118 people arrested, none of them appeared to be the Clown, but they'd go on torturing them until they got something they could use. I laughed with relief and happiness because now I knew that one of us was free. One of us had eluded the nets of the Sweep and the Consolidation and all the shit after that, and he was still out there, uncontrolled by anyone – surviving. I knew we wouldn't be able to blame Lionfist or any other corp for this. This was pure Clown.

Berbie took off his helmet. It was starting to self-clean, but it would probably take hours. I laughed some more at his mucky face. He didn't smile. 'So the Joking Clown's a guy,' he ground out. 'I knew it, Porky. You are SO gay.'

'Fuck you, Berbie,' I said, and didn't care. 'Guy, chick, who gives a shit? The fact is, he played all of us for fools today, and we don't even know how. It's official: the Joking Clown rocks! Now go wash that million-dollar meal off your face. I'm going home to the lab to laugh in peace.' This wasn't the end, I knew it. The Clown would be back. And he'd come to destroy us forever, and he'd do it and take his final bow like the magician he was. All I wanted was somehow to be a part of it. I wanted it like I'd never wanted anything in my life.

I went to bed happy for the first time in my life. If he was out there, loose and free, then he could be making babies with the slags on the mainland. He could be creating an army of thousands to overwhelm us and grind us into dust. The boys would die without hospitals to save them, but the girls would survive just fine. Under natural conditions, one in ten foetuses would be female, and so a lot of babies would die. Would the Clown be willing to pay that price for our destruction? He probably doesn't think of babies as HR statistics. The Sweep forced every male into the corporate paradises and was intended to corner the market in human reproduction in each territory, but he'd broken our monopoly now. Yes! I hadn't lied to Berbie – now that I knew he was a guy, I was just as fascinated as I had been before. Could he be an Old Guy then? An impossible throwback to the time when humanity hadn't been broken? It would make no difference: the disease that broke the world, Male Hypertoxic Syndrome, will have infected him. He won't have any normal kids.

My euphoria started to ebb a bit. Coming down off P always makes me a bit weepy. It's like the door to heaven is slowly closing because I'll never fit through it. Slimy Salman will declare war, of course. He won't care whether the Clown is a free agent or working for another corp; he'll want blood just the same. How is it that everything I love always ends up under some hanyo's heel or other? I've tried so hard to insulate myself from their bullshit, to keep my head down and not be a target, but they always find me, and they always lay a turd on my stuff. The hot sweat of rage came like a tidal wave out of my armpits and my Samsa suit uncomplainingly gulped it down. I'd had enough of hiding. I wanted to fight.

Before tonight, I'd thought of the Clown as a fragile slag who was living her anger in the only way she knew how. Now I knew he was a guy, and I saw all his actions as part of a bigger plan. We New Guys were the targets – we had to be, because we were the biggest threat to his existence. He understood the slag minds, and he understood us too because he was us. Any plan we made to neutralize him, he'd have simulated a thousand times already. The hacking was only the tip of the iceberg. We were seriously outclassed here. The Clown cosplayers – I wondered how many of them knew. That kid who took my camera, she wasn't Berbie's plant at all, she was the Clown's. And now I was going to have to explain to Salman why the fuck I didn't have any 3D footage of the Clown. I thought, *I'll just blame Berbie and his drug habit.*

The buzzer at the door went off like a bomb. I jumped out of my sleep pod and ran to it in a panic. 'Open,' rapped Slimy's voice on the other side, and it opened because in New Singapore his voice commands override everyone else's. Salman shouldered me aside and strode in, followed by

Berbie, whose helmet was missing, and who had a huge bruise on the side of his face.

'How could you let this happen?' Slimy gritted. 'Rayne, I know you're a total fuck-up, which is why I sent Berbie to mind you, but explain to me how this nutjob slipped through the fingers of both of you?'

'We thought we were dealing with a slag,' Berbie slurred through swollen lips. 'We weren't prep...' Slimy hit him so hard I heard a bone crack. Berbie dropped like a dynamited wall. Slimy stood there shaking his hand absently. Then he popped his own helmet open with a hydraulic sigh and tossed it on to my bench. I sagged with relief. He wasn't going to punish me, at least not with his fists. Good thing I was in my suit or I'd have had to change my underwear.

'If it was a slag,' he said to Berbie's limp body, 'you should have still been on high alert. I lived through the Bitch Wars of the '40s. I know what slags are capable of.' He looked at me. 'And you,' he gritted out. 'Am I right in believing you're not exactly unhappy that he got away?'

I made a non-committal face. 'I thought it was a bad idea from the start. The Clown wouldn't have come here without a foolproof exit plan. We played into his hands.'

'So, what do we do now? The rumours are already spreading, even though we contained everyone we could catch. This is bad for all the corps, not just us. That guy could be preparing for all-out war as we speak.'

'My thoughts exactly.'

'How do we shut it down, Rayne?'

'We wait. He'll expect us to mobilize now, comb the mainland and the lower decks looking for him. He wants us shooting at shadows. We need to come at him when he least expects it.'

'Hm? So you suggest we hold off? And what if he uses the time to regroup? If he got away without being seen, he could be anywhere.'

'Have you ever played hunting games in your gamecave, Slimy? You have to sit very quietly and watch for movement in the long grass. Because the tiger knows where to find you. Flail around and you lose any chance of ever getting the upper hand.'

He considered this, pacing restlessly between the piles of junk in my lab. 'The other guys want action. Whatever we do, we can't afford to look weak. If those Lionfist bastards scent blood, it won't just be the Clown that's stalking us.'

I sighed. 'How many bad decisions have you taken in your career because you didn't want to look weak, Slimy?' I asked, knowing he'd probably go ahead anyway.

He grinned his bad boy grin and started to say something, but his BlackTab started pinging urgently. His suit said in its sexy voice, 'Encrypted message, top priority, no sender.'

'Open message,' he said. 'No, transmit to Rayne's wall display. I want us both to see this, whatever it is.'

My wall display woke up. A beautiful face looked out at us. Surrounded by white, dressed in white, like a disembodied spirit, a swept-back, intellectual, sensitive black face, with a halo of storm-cloud hair and such deep, knowing eyes. He was looking at us as if he knew everything about us. 'Hello, Mr Vaghela,' he said. 'I am the Joking Clown. I'm happy to finally make your acquaintance.'

'You bastard!' Slimy snarled. 'What do you mean by that stunt you just pulled?'

'Stunt? I sang on the last day of the Silver Heights Love Fest exactly as advertised. Nothing out of the ordinary happened, although your reaction was a little excessive. Anyway, I just wanted to tell you that I'm open to a recording contract with Ramaudio, if you're interested. I think you are, if the enthusiasm with which you've tried to make money off me is any indication. I have enough songs written and arranged to make a couple of decent albums, and I know you have the best equipment available in the market today. We should be able to enter into a mutually beneficial partnership.'

'Who are you? Which corp do you work for? How did you get out of the corporate security enclave without us finding you? Where are you now?'

He laughed, and I shivered to the depths of my soul. 'You're very eager to know about me. I take it you're a fan? I know Rayne is. Hello, Rayne. Another thing. When I come in to New Singapore to record in your studio, I want Rayne to be the liaison between my people and yours. I trust him, and I think you trust him too. So we both know where we stand.'

Slimy whipped round and pierced me with a look. I began shaking my hands and head. 'I swear, I have no idea…'

'He doesn't,' said the Clown, 'but I've been watching you all, just as you've been watching me. You know me through my songs, and I know you through your dreams, your games, your search histories, your credit pipelines, your biostats, your message archives, your loves. I know you, my brothers. I've been waiting to meet you for so long. I want to give you a gift: my music. It's all I have. And another thing. When I come to you, you have to promise that I and mine will remain invulnerable. No Bully Boy touches us, no promise shall be broken, no harm must befall any of us, neither to me nor to J-Squad. Because the moment I lose faith in you, everything I know will go to the ones who can make the most damaging use of it. Do not doubt my capability to do this, because that would be a very bad choice for all of us.'

'Okay,' said Slimy through gritted teeth. 'Come in and keep faith. You won't be touched. But we can't have you running around like this. It's dangerous out there for New Guys like us. You don't even have a Samsa suit.'

He laughed, and it was like music across still water. 'I'm safer right now than I will ever be in my entire life. But everything must move and change, so I will come to you next Saturday with my people. Keep Dock Seven clear for us, and there must be no one to receive us except Rayne. All right, Rayne?'

'Yes! I mean, if Mr Vaghela approves.'

Slimy gave a curt nod. 'You leave me no choice.'

The Joking Clown smiled gently. 'I'm big in Japan,' he said serenely. 'You could use me in your upcoming negotiations with Shigenobu.'

A light seemed to go on in the back of Slimy's head. I could see his old Machiavellian brain starting its reptilian crawl towards a strategy. And I knew that everything was going to be all right. I mean, I had no idea where all this would take me, what I'd lose or gain along the way, but at last my life had meaning and I had something to look forward to. 'Thank you,' I said from the bottom of my heart.

The Joking Clown smiled at me. 'You can call me Jimbo,' he said kindly. 'It's what my mother called me.' Then he vanished.

'End message,' said Slimy's suit. He grunted and put his helmet back on. 'Go to servo-assist,' he said, then picked up Berbie's inert form with one hand. 'Don't fuck this up,' he threw at me over his shoulder, and left.

And that was how I first met the Joking Clown, and how the story of my greatest love and my bitterest sorrow began.

THE DREAM

MUHAMMED ZAFAR IQBAL

(Translated by Arunava Sinha from the original Bengali 'Shopno')

Julian sits up in bed with a start. His body is soaked with perspiration, his throat parched. Fumbling for the glass of water on the bedside table, he closes his fingers around it and drains it breathlessly. He can hear his heart thumping in his chest. It takes a long while to calm himself down. What a strange dream it was.

Julian gets out of bed and goes to the window. It's drizzling, the roads are wet outside. A lamp post casts a long shadow on the street. 'That was an odd dream,' Julian tells himself, gazing into the darkness.

The dream plays in his head over and over again. Not for a moment had he even realized it was a dream. It had seemed as though it had all been actually taking place in his life. Standing by the window, Julian wonders – is it possible that he's still dreaming? Can all of this, his standing at the window in the dead of the night, the roads wet with rain, the long shadow of the lamp post – can all of this actually be a dream? Perhaps he only thinks he's woken up, when he actually hasn't? What certainty does he have that he's awake?

Julian glances around his room. No, this is not a dream. There's his familiar chair, desk, bookshelf, bed. There's his wife in the darkness, asleep on the bed, exhausted.

Breathing a sigh of relief, Julian looks out through the window again, and at once a strange possibility occurs to him. Is it possible that what he knows to be his own life is, in fact, someone else's dream? And that this room, this chair, this desk, this bookshelf, the window, the drizzle outside – all of these are scenes from that dream? Can his pleasant childhood, his colourful youth, his beautiful life of joys and sorrows actually be moments in another's dream? Is the world around him only a creation of that dream? Is something like this possible?

Julian tries his best to push the thought away, but he does not succeed. His mind keeps coming back to the possibility that perhaps he's part of a dream. Perhaps there is no one named Julian, perhaps his life comprises merely a few moments of someone else's dream.

As he ponders over this, Julian grows agitated, his heart starts hammering. He feels betrayed, his anger begins to rise. He feels an irresistible urge to wake up from this dream. But how is he to break out of it?

Julian remembers how he appeared to have woken up a short while ago. It was in pain, he had dreamt that a pack of wild dogs was tearing him apart. Screaming in agony, he had woken up instantly. Can pain be the route to escaping from this dream then? Why not? When the agony becomes insufferable, no dream can survive, it has to break. Beads of perspiration gather on his forehead. Can he find a way to inflict inhuman pain on himself?

He steals downstairs, opening the door to the room beneath the staircase. This is where all his tools are kept. He finds his hand drill and carefully fits in a Number 8 bit, the one he uses to drill into walls. He tiptoes into the bathroom and stands in front of the mirror. His hands are trembling with nervousness. As soon as he presses the switch, the bit starts rotating. He can use it to drill through concrete. If he presses it against his forehead, it will effortlessly make a hole in his skull.

Julian presses the drill to his own temple with quavering hands, screaming in pain the very next moment.

The monstrous creature wakes up from his nightmare. What a strange dream. The creature is astonished. He blinks with all his eyes. Both the suns are high in the sky now. The creature begins walking on its numerous feet along the red stone path.

Another long day has begun for him.

ANANDNA

RUKMINI BHAYA NAIR

Prelims

A beeline is as elegant a form of communication as you can possibly have. When a bee finds a food source, it conveys its message to other bees, as the old Bollywood movies used to, through dance. The length indicates distance – each second a kilometre – and three points – the sun, the flower and the location of the hive – define the angle of the bee's waggle-tail item number. And off they go!

Humans are so much messier. What I am about to tell you is a wild, ataxic story, a cautionary tale, complete with an unanswered mystery. Will our ingenuity, our legendary lust for life, ensure that we beat the odds after all? Or will each of us embrace the lovely species death we've designed?

That ecstatic death is my subject, my swan song.

But who am I, which raving madman, you ask? And what the hell am I talking about? Of course, these are basic questions you might put to yourself each day as well, but do you? No, you go about your daily life resignedly, putting up with tiny outbursts of chaos all around you. I know, I know, my friend. You believe you have handily dispensed with turmoil, with mental muddle and with riddling doubt. Why bother about pinpricks when happiness, thank god, doesn't have to be pursued any more but envelops you like a fitted designer coat. So what if you don't have liberty? Shove liberty!

Life stretches ahead, straight and unbending as a ruler, so comforting that it doesn't bear thinking about. In any case, we are not Americans looking for happiness and other childish things. We are Indians and 'we the people' of India in the glorious year 2087 are justly proud of the tech futures we've managed to build all through this great twenty-first century, now dimming to its end – with some active help from yours truly.

'Acchhe din aayenge,' they used to say in our grandparents' time, *matlab ki* the cool, cool din of FAF (fully automated futures in case you somehow managed to avoid going to school, sir-ji, which I'm guessing would be more or less impossible when ADD – formerly known as Aadhaar, also in the said grandparents' uneven, slow-moving age – tracks everyone so minutely. In the time of FAF, I am you and you are me enduringly, mechanically and there are never any pissing zigzags).

Yet, since you demand answers not of yourself but of me, let me be plain.

My name is Swami Kanaka Murlidhar Iyer aka Payasam or Pay for short, owing to my great love for this dessert of desserts, this food of the gods and fallible men. We have become so much more fortunate in such everyday aspects of our lives in the past decades. Much may have been lost but how delicious these small gains! Laddus, *mishti doi, gajar ka halwa* dispensed by vending machines at every street corner, owned and regulated by the ever reliable Dahi-Doodh-aur-Doosra conglomerate that joyously employs more than 30 million happy, smiling Indians. True, we've never actually *seen* these millions except when some of them beatifically appear on a celebrity show on 6D TellyJelly, but most of us agree that's as good as being there in gelatinous person. And there's ADD keeping its benign eye on all of us 24x7 – absolutely no reason to worry!

Digression again, you say – keep to the point please.

Well, I did warn you, did I not, my dear embedded screen, right at the very beginning, that this would be a tortuous tale? But let me jump back into the middle lane, since you're looking as if you'll turn yourself off any moment, which, o simulacrum of simulacrums, lovely image of Sid and other lost loves, you know you are absolutely forbidden to do without my permission! Remember ADD is watching and we've a long way to go, you and I. Anyhow, I, Payasam, am that very fool who together with his lifelong companions, Syeda 'Sid' Khatoon, famed neurosurgeon, and K.K. Kurien from Kerala, the world-renowned psychiatrist KKK, invented...

Aha! You'll know what we invented even if you do not know that it was us who invented it and that's the crux of my story. But first, let's get some of the biographical facts out of the way because they'll make my outrageous claims a bit more believable perhaps. For instance, you could look us up in the AIIMS register of students of 2052. They will have heard of Sid and KKK, if not me. They used to call us Amar, Akbar, Anthony in those days after some Bollywood *senti-fillum* made 90 years ago. No need for that sort of thing any more. These days we are all Amars (lucky, lucky deathless ones!), not to mention Anandas (favourite pupils of the blissful Buddha), but more on this soon.

But let's talk about me first. In truth, not *pehle aap* but *pehle mein*, despite polite proverbs to the contrary, has always been the name of the game, my faceless one of the thousand faces. So here's my background (I have no foreground as well, you know, flatty-under-my-skin, and neither do you, but enough about that already). Despite my high-sounding Brahmanical name, I am that 100 per cent Delhi boy, fluent in *sadak* Hindi, my English smart and my Tamil non-existent. You know the stereotype.

As for my parents, they are true millennials – liberal, hard-working, smart. However, it must be admitted that they left me mainly to my own devices and to my grandparents. It was because of them, especially my grandmother, that I am a kind of throwback. I studied hard and joined AIIMS. Who does that these days, I ask you? About my GF (not girlfriend but grandfather, you mutt!), he got what he called a 'Delhi posting' as an IAS officer in the 1980s and remained in the city after he retired. By then, he'd bought a fine DDA flat in Vasant Kunj, and it didn't seem to make sense to him to return to live in Chennai. They had an established routine in Delhi, and my grandfather was big on routine and bureaucracy.

My *paati*, a 'homemaker' with a first-class degree in maths, who had never, even entertained the thought of going out to work, said nothing when she heard my grandfather's decision. Even though I was just a child at the time, I could tell by the way her diamond earrings and nose ring sparkled in unison that she was pleased with the lord and master's verdict. The truth was, my grandmother did not want to go back to Chennai and face any flak for the unorthodox way she'd raised her children. As if she had a choice!

A city raises its children with more patriarchal authority than any parents ever could. And thus it was that her son, my pseudo-Tam-Bram father, chewed chicken bones and heaven knows what other polluting stuff from age 10. Plus, he'd ended up joining an advertising firm and marrying a Punjabi girl. Not kosher. Thank god her daughter, my aunt, had eventually married a Tam-Bram and emigrated to the US. Still, on balance, my *paati* wanted to stay on in Delhi and get on with supervising my future. I was an only child whose parents were often out late at work or at parties. Who else would take responsibility for me? My grandmother was determined that she would make up for the karma that had turned my father into a salesman by turning me into a doctor. I would be a doctor – not an engineer, but a doctor. Why? Well, because her father was a doctor, both her brothers were doctors, each one nobler than the other!

An aside: I once discovered my *paati*'s old iPhone lying in a forgotten corner of the house. It was long dead, as was she, but I don't know on what impulse, I revived it. And I found in this heavy, elongated object a whole, lost world of love – love for me. That phone was chock-a-block with painfully typed reminders to herself about what she could do for me – like make me special idlis after school or call tutoring outfits on my behalf or take me out to a neighbourhood mela (which I hated, but she did not know that).

Many young people today haven't even seen these 'mobile phones,' now that we routinely embed them in our bodies (mine is in my big toe, KKK's is in his forearm, Sid's very sexy detachable ones dangle from her ears like diamond teardrops). The good thing is they're getting better at reading our thoughts by the day, which is infinitely more convenient, one must admit, than having to lug around gadgets and always being anxious about losing them like my grandparents. Our tiny implanted computers beep when we are in danger, they guard us at all times. They're great, but sometimes I think that they lock us into loneliness, something I don't believe my *paati*'s phone ever did. My grandmother's phone connected her to a world of love, while my embedded object only links me to my scummy self, although I'm not quite sure whether this is its fault or mine…

Is there any need, after all this, to repeat that my grandmother's steely resolve determined my fate? I became a doctor, studying at 'the best institute' in the country. True, I might not have been as noble as my *paati*'s kin but beauty lies in the eyes of the beholder, etc. As far as my *paati* was concerned, I was flawless and had nobly inherited the mantle of the family tradition. She died a happy soul, nirvana securely knotted in the folds of her *kanjeevaram*. I loved my grandmother, but you know what I'm saying – science may change but society remains bloody static.

But back to the bio. KKK, Sid and I met in the AIIMS canteen early on, during our first year pre-clinicals in anatomy. That was in 2052, 35 years ago now, but the scene is still vividly stamped in what remains of my memory and passed on indelibly to my big-toe mobile phone. KKK made the first move as usual, clearing space for us at the sharp-edged mini-table where he'd claimed a place with the boundless practical energy we'd come to realize was his third best characteristic. His second-best quality? That Zen temperament that paradoxically enabled him to take on risks few others would. But KKK's best feature was his amazing capacity to read and absorb not just facts but stories, histories, poetry – all those esoteric texts that Sid and I were so disastrously bad at. Without KKK's initiative, I doubt whether we'd have completed our mission. KKK had three brothers – one in the army, one in the police and one in business – who apparently shared the same calm of mind, a factor that became important when we first set up our secret labs in Kerala. But I'm jumping ahead of my story.

That long-ago afternoon at the canteen, Sid and I were late as usual, each taking long minutes to silently point at the various items on display so that the counter robot could lift them on to sanitized plates that the tray-robot would then carry to designated tables. (No *payasam* made from *desi doodh*, even if pasteurized, at AIIMS, no sir! Those dispensing machines had been designed for loitering commoners at street corners, people with less self-control than us, the best doctors-to-be in all of India and the world. AIIMS was a key barometer of the Indian nation's ability to be the best.

Like its neighbour, the IIT, which stolidly turned out tech toppers year after year mostly working on teleportation, their big thing, AIIMs only sold *payasam* pills because one, it had been scientifically established that they protected your teeth; and two, they left the flavour of *payasam* in your mouth for ages afterwards while strictly avoiding the messy delights of swirling milk-mud in that ancient but inefficient parallelogram designed by nature called the mouth. The point is, we were determined even then to move towards a society that could dispense with the drawbacks of being animal, of being human – of having mouths, eyes, teeth, ears, scar tissue etc. What a pain the human body was, booby-trapped with so many disaster zones!

Casualty

Pain, the capacity of the non-metallic animal to suffer pain is the true, and painful, subject of my story, Flat Face. The pain principle versus the pleasure principle, geddit, you silent father confessor of a machine, my big-toe bully, my truest companion (except for Sid perhaps), substitute for all religions in the Age of FAF?

No, you don't, but you will...you will...

We did not know it then but the beady eye of the robot at the counter had already detected in Sid and me certain debilitating traits that had dragged humankind into the gutter down the ages, that had prevented it from swiftly grasping at the stars. Disaster, derived from the Latin *dis* and *astra*, bad stars, as KKK eruditely informed us. We were walking disaster zones, Sid and I, with our unpredictable enthusiasm and less-than-iron wills. Invariably, we wavered, we could not decide. Our imaginations routinely led us to be distracted by peripheral items rather than more central ones. (We ached, but we never even quite determined whether we were in love.)

That first day, I remember the counter robot explicitly flashed its small red light warning us that we were dawdling at his display far too long. If I hadn't known that it was impossible, I'd swear I saw those two robots wink at each other, raising their non-existent eyebrows at Sid and my weakling wills with the tray robot going insane like a bee desperate to sting – *bzz bzzz buzzzzz*! – as it carried our neatly laid-out meals ahead of us and indicated that there wasn't enough place at KKK's table. But here's the thing. Sid and I did not know each other then, but we both instinctively defied our robot (it could only manage four student meals at the time, so there were four of us in that queue behind it). The fact is, we'd seen KKK clearing a place for us at the table – standard friend-making tactics in a new class – and our human instincts drew us to him. That instinct was something no mechanical being could grasp back in 2052, and their apprehension of pain or of horror remains pretty doubtful even now in 2087.

What has changed the world far more radically is a certain bio-invention, one that has managed to change sensations of pain in the human brain (well, in the amygdala and the hippocampus to be precise) into pleasure sensations at moments of intense physical suffering. *Our* invention.

You thought a big US pharma company discovered the wonder drug that transformed us forever from flatfooted animals in thrall to pain to ones lining up to happily die? You are wrong. Did you never wonder why it had that strangely Indian-sounding name? The truth is that it was us – KKK, Sid and I – who invented Anandna, the now world-famous elixir that caused our species to fall mortally in love with death.

This is our story.

Human nature is variable, fate implacable and foolishness coded in our DNA, sir-ji. On that day in the canteen, the two other students behind us were less recalcitrant, or maybe they'd just not seen KKK gesture. Anyway, they were meekly guided by the tray robot to a fine, unpeopled alcove, leaving Sid and myself to a close encounter with KKK, bedazzled then and ever after. How are friendships formed, how does love fail? These are questions for which we must rely on memory and FAF be damned!

I remember we couldn't stop talking after that day for all our four years of college and then for the next 20 years. Until Anandna consumed us, and eventually destroyed us, our conversations were endless and winding, exactly like living strands of DNA. We talked politics and Ayurveda and philosophy and even martial arts. We hotly debated whether the closest living creature to immortality was not a human at all but a virus! A virus, after all, was just a blob of DNA wrapped in a protein coat. It could survive a million mutations, it was marvellously protean, it could don the cloak of invisibility in a trice.

Immortality. Yes, we discussed that quite a bit, why nature, so generous to us with millions of cells and synapses, giving us pairs of everything, eyes, ears, nostrils, hands, lungs, was so niggardly with telomeres, the immortality enzyme that protectively coated the ends of our chromosomal DNA strands. We read Elizabeth Blackburn's old Nobel Prize-winning papers. If we had more telomeres, she argued, perhaps we would live much, much longer. But what if we could live shorter but heavenly, blissful, pain-free lives, KKK countered. That would be another way to approach the problem of death and suffering.

And then we were, all three of us, posted in casualty for six sleepless weeks. Casualty was where we bonded, where we looked pain in the eye night after night, stared down death day after day. What is the way out of this senseless pain, asked KKK. He uttered these words with the same practical air as if he were enquiring about the maximum dosage of morphine we could give a cancer patient with unendurable soft tissue pain or a car-crash victim with crushed limbs who had managed somehow to remain miraculously conscious and demanded ceaselessly to know whether his children had survived.

'It is not fair. How can there be so much suffering in the world?' KKK muttered again under his breath, this time as if he was repeating a mantra.

'You are not the Buddha to seek the answers to such questions,' Sid joked, but I could see she was serious.

'I have read about him,' KKK answered. 'He had a favourite student called Ananda. "Be thou a lamp, Ananda," the Buddha told him. It reminded me of this picture I saw in Belgium. I have it in my room. I'll show it to you tomorrow.'

That moment, I remember it just like a classic screen memory, one of that mad fellow Freud's strangely brilliant insights. We no longer read him in psychology class but, as usual, KKK had brought him into our conversations, and so Sid and I learned at least some of his key concepts, whether we liked it or not. Anyhow, the next day KKK brought a rolled-up poster with him to our night shift and we eyed it in between accident victims. KKK had bought it when he won a three-month fellowship to the University Hospital in Leuven.

The painting was by a famous artist called something Magritte, and it was a rare, old paper print, and not an old 3D reproduction off the Network. It was called *The Pleasure Principle* and showed a man with a light bulb instead of a head. The man in the picture was sitting at a table and he was, maybe, reading a book. I don't remember it exactly. KKK said the painting made him think about pleasure, about bliss, about enlightenment. Me? It just made me feel weird. Sid remarked, oddly, that the painting showed that a man could be beheaded but that did not mean he was condemned to die. An artificial head could be sewn on the same body if it was done before the body realized it was dead or the head realized it had been severed. It could be because she was dedicated to becoming a surgeon. But even KKK looked at her strangely, it was such a peculiar observation.

'Have you read Thomas Mann, by any chance?' he asked Sid.

'No,' said Sid. 'Who was he?'

KKK fell silent for a moment. Then he said, 'Nobody talks about a pain principle, but there should be one. That's what being a doctor is all about.'

Soon after, a woman and her child were brought into casualty. She had tried to strangle the child and slit her own wrists, but the child had set up such a terrible wail that the neighbours brought them to AIIMS at once. No more talk about principles.

Yet the topic remained with us. The image of the man with a light bulb instead of a head reaching out for a book became imprinted in our minds. We began to read obsessively. KKK's painting became a 'subliminal' influence, another word from the banished Freud that now haunted us. We read research paper after paper on models of pain, on hyperalgesia and allodynia, on pain thresholds in humans, and the more we delved, the more we realized that research in the area had not advanced much since the early twenty-first century. It had, literally, been superficial, exploring pain on the surface of the human body, pricking the arm with pins, placing ice and mild poisons on exposed areas and noting reactions. Part of the problem was that experimental work on human subjects was almost impossible, which was a good thing on the whole. But it meant that pain relief still relied largely on synthetic analgesics or on good old-fashioned painkillers like morphine.

The research on rats and mice was more promising. It actually reached into the rats' brains, showing how their basolateral amygdala (BLA) region contained powerful interrelated circuits where pleasure, pain and fear were all located. These were the years that my episodes of lucid dreaming began. I would return to the image of the man whose head was a light bulb and supplant it with the heads of patients who had died, their faces contorted in a rictus. Sometimes, I would mechanically put KKK's head, long and dolichocephalic, with his furrowed forehead and head of curly springing hair in the light bulb, and sometimes I would put Sid's head there. In these images, she was always smiling, her lips long and tilted upwards, her lotus eyes sparkling and her skin glowing. Sid was a beauty, and kind-hearted. She would sometimes slip into bed beside me and console me. There was no need for us to get married. We were soulmates from those early days. But I remained desperate for an answer to KKK's conundrum.

Then one day it came to me, clearly, like an echo from the Buddha past. Both Sid and KKK were in my room at the time. I think they knew I needed them, though they'd never admit it. It was about 4 a.m., and I found myself suddenly sitting bolt upright on my bed like a jack-in-the-box and repeating, 'Why, why, why?'

KKK was the first to react. 'Is he a bit delirious, Sid? Should we give him...'

'Why?' I interrupted him once again, loudly.

'Why what, Pay?' Sid asked, gently stroking my forehead – but perhaps I'm imagining this part of the scenario.

'Why,' I finally managed to get out, 'why can we not inject a pleasure-inducing substance that turns the fear and pain circuits into pleasure circuits directly in the central amygdala whenever the body encounters severe trauma?'

Sid and KKK looked startled, but they were not stupid. They saw at once I was on to something. It was already well known, I rambled on excitedly, that most mammalian species, including humans, had more positive response circuitry in their amygdala architecture than negative or pain circuitry. They were born to be happy, not to suffer unnecessary pain, and that's what so many brain studies have told us. Plus, syringe-and-spray technologies had advanced hugely even if pain research had not.

'We should all have light bulbs for heads,' I shouted!

Of course, we all knew *that* reference intimately. True, in practical terms, we didn't have those dim old bulbs any more, only versions of LEDs 9.0 Constant Companions: 'You never have to change them, but they will change your life!'

Suddenly, our research objective was clear to all three of us – radiant! We had to change the brain's pain circuits into pleasure circuits. Doable. It might take a decade or two of research, but it was doable. We knew it in our bones. All we had to do was to find the right combination of drugs and hey presto! At the time, I was thinking of allopathic drugs. KKK changed all that, though. He was always the most dynamic of the three of us and he plunged deep into the world of AYUSH (Ayurveda, Yoga, Unani, Siddha and Homeopathy, for the uninitated).

That, he said, was where the treasures lay! Plus, he had *excellent* contacts in the government. And soon enough, there he was, holding a letter with a *sarkari* hologram that said we'd been awarded a breathtakingly large grant from the Health Ministry to develop a drug that alleviated pain by naturopathic means. And that was not all. KKK managed to get every single permission needed to set up a nature farm in a part of Kerala rural enough for our work to proceed relatively unnoticed, yet well-connected to the big towns and hospitals.

Finals

Three years after we graduated, we were in business – and how! It wasn't just business as usual. We had something to live for. Those years were a happy blur. Hard to believe that they were nearly 16! Yes, it took that long to set up our pre-fab mice labs and the chicken farms where we harvested the drug combos that we spent so much time discussing. We pored over old formulae and Ayurveda texts. KKK even learned Sanskrit, in addition to his excellent Malayalam. He consulted endlessly with the local *pizhichil* massage experts, and we did round upon round of placebo trials on our rats. The workers on our farm were mostly women – clean, silent and discreet. KKK's brothers also did their bit to protect our trials from prying eyes.

Meanwhile, KKK went back to Belgium and married Marie-Anne, the nurse with who he'd had a long-standing relationship ever since his fellowship days, and brought her back to Kerala. Soon, they had three kids, and Marie-Anne taught them Flemish and French. Sid and I tried to teach them Hindi and KKK insisted that they learn Malayalam and English. KKK's kids were among the most multilingual and well-behaved kids I know. The one good thing that came of our experiments with Anandna is that these kids were never our victims.

Oh yes, Sid and I also started a small initiative – a clinic-cum-school where we taught the local children English and science subjects and also treated their ailments for free. We were not, after all, AIIMS doctors for nothing. Funny, we did not ever think of marriage, Sid and I, who were also a bit emotionally lazy, apart from being indecisive. It was good enough for us that we were in close proximity day in and day out, that we could take secluded walks under the coconut palms and drive down to the coast together.

Must such contentment come to an end? Well, machine in my stubby, packed-for-sensitive-nerves big toe, ours certainly did once we discovered the right combo of drugs, testing it on ourselves and then on those among the local population who were facing an immediate and painful death, either from some form of general systems failure or a road or construction accident – nonagenarians, children, adults, within a few hours of death, and the results were spectacular! Our patients died with blissful smiles on their faces, each and every one of them, and their relatives, awestruck witnesses, began to spread the word that we were gods – immortals!

Gods with scars, that's who we really were. KKK, Sid and I began to look like victims of torture as we made deep cuts on our hands and feet, even abdomens, as many times as we could, in order to inject the early versions of Anandna into each other's brainstems. I can only say the feelings that we experienced after each of those injections were indescribable. Call up your Roget's Thesaurus, machine, call up your *Shabdakosha*! None of those words can capture the bliss we felt.

Anandna was to die for!

Sooner or later, though, we knew we would have to go public. We would have to take our case to the Health Ministry, seek the necessary permissions to run large-scale pharmaceutical trials. We dragged our feet about this as long as we could, even KKK. Our instinct told us that once Anandna was out in the open, we would not be able to control its effects.

We were called in front of a panel of experts, all doctors except for a sociologist who was the 'ethics expert'. They sat on our papers for a year, ADD or no ADD, but finally, *finally*, we were given the go-ahead to proceed with human clinical trials on which we spent another five years with matched segmented populations across the length and breadth of *hamara* Bharat. There were a few minor tweaks, but the same results that we had recorded on ourselves were statistically verified in our sample. Anandna eliminated pain, turning it into a form of happiness so intense, it could only be deemed *ananda* – bliss.

So finally, in 2072 or so, we were ready for the market after we appeared before one final committee. That would be no problem, machine, that was what we thought. We were almost at the finish line now.

But at that finish line stood a man – a man smarter than KKK, which is hard to imagine, but it is true. This politically-connected doctor with a foreign degree disputed every finding we had and was especially contemptuous about Sid, gold medallist, MBBS. What exactly did she contribute as a surgeon, he sneered. He had lived abroad for 30 years, he declared, and he had so far found Indian research shoddy, ill-conceived, shockingly poor in rigour and design. We should give him all our research data, he said, and he would look through it himself. This was a favour he was doing us, something he just did not do for everybody.

Well, we had no choice, Sid, KKK and I. We needed the imprimatur of this august body to finally put Anandna on the market. Without these mandatory 'approvals', we knew we'd be stuck forever. That was just how the system worked – no pain, no gain. So, we handed Dr T our entire file of precious results, our formulae, our hearts. And that was that.

The next thing we knew, Dr T. had left for greener pastures and sold our invention for mega-dollars we'd never dreamt of! And then there were the raids on our farms in Kerala. We had to disperse, broken-hearted.

Of course, we had taken it to court, but court cases even in these FAF-ish times drag on for a lifetime, especially when the criminal is in another, more powerful country. Consequently, we do not have much hope. That is the only thing we blame him for. Dr T took hope from us – and innocence. No wonder I had this little nervous breakdown, O intimate machine of my heart and big toe, and now even *payasam* no longer consoles me.

KKK and Sid, and to a certain extent I, Payasam, had had the courage to tackle human pain head on. By this, let me be absolutely clear, I mean physical pain, not mental torture. We have all suffered the latter nonstop ever since Dr T ran. But it's done one positive thing. It has turned us into philosophers, goading us to delve a bit more deeply into what we've come to think of not only as his but 'our' crime. Our intentions may have been Hippocratic in the truest sense. We wanted to ameliorate human suffering, we wanted the well-being of all humans. Never ever would we cut for stone, but we should have read the Buddha alongside our medical research.

Each day now, we ask ourselves – what did we do, *what did we do*? Why did we so arrogantly challenge nature? Did we really think that tampering with the evolutionary order would have no consequences? Nature had invented pain as a safeguard, to alert us to danger. What moral responsibility did we bear for the fact that Anandna had now gone viral, that it has beaten the virus at its own play with immortality? That the mega-rich, at the apex of the human pyramid, now pay to be severely wounded so that they can experience the thrill that Anandna gives them?

Anandna had caused our species to flirt with its own extermination.

It had also forced the three of us to accept a fate far more immediate, much closer to the bone – the slow death of our once inseparable friendship. We had to accept this great sadness, our inevitable drifting apart during the decade that followed the debacle with our miracle drug. The truth was, there was less and less to say, to share. Sid and I could no longer bear to look at one another. KKK lived far away in his Kerala retreat. In a way, we knew this was the final punishment for our hubris, not the loss of Anandna to Dr T, but the loss of ourselves, our very souls.

Then, out of the blue, KKK invited Sid and me to visit him in Kerala on the eve of Independence Day, 2087. We'd once expected that on this symbolic day of freedom, our invention, properly controlled, would have eased suffering amongst the deprived population of India, maybe even other developing countries. Never had we imagined that it would be sold to the highest bidders in the rich world, spreading the killing virus of a death wish (another prescient Freudian concept!) across the deluded globe. It would be the understatement of the year to state that Sid and I were a bit depressed. Still, we accepted KKK's invitation. In theory we were best friends, after all, even if we were now as much strangers to each other as to ourselves.

That starry evening, KKK turned back, to our surprise, to his old philosophical self, launching into one of his hyper speeches. This was exactly the trouble with a race of dreamers, he declared, handing out fuller than full glasses of toddy, while Marie-Anne served peppery cashew nuts and hot kebabs alongside. It's hard to believe but all this activity made Sid and me immediately begin to feel much better. It was just the effect of KKK's excited voice. We knew it would not last, but we felt rejuvenated anyway.

Long after the science that we had painfully invented clearly showed that sleep was just a form of partial mechanical shutdown and dreams mere chemical illusions aimed at organizing the flux of reality, we humans continued inanely to insist that we had to 'follow our dreams', KKK declaimed. 'No wonder we walk round and round in circles even when we aren't drunk. We are too proud to be viruses, tigers, even eagles. And before pride cometh etc., as you well know, my friends!'

'Ours,' he cried, 'is a species that took more than a million years, perhaps two or three, just to drop to the ground and stand upright on our hind legs and march forward, our eyes sliding over centuries to the front of our faces, our brains cooling down enough to accommodate the sudden miracle of speech. Then, about 50,000 years ago what our scientists call the great "social revolution" took place. Homo sapiens began to chatter and argue and gossip and draw lines in the sand. They learned that to cheat and lie and deceive themselves was advantageous. They thought their designs were superior to nature's. That was the exact moment they sealed their own deaths, Payasam. It took millennia but eventually, it happened. It happened, Sid! The "Mills of God" effect kicked in and those mills, as you know, grind exceeding small, down to virus-like sizes, down to doom.

'We created Anandna! One thing we had in common,' KKK proclaimed, tipsy but coherent still, 'was our great appetite for ideas. We believed that what distinguished humans was their endlessly curious, clamorous phenotype, their thirst for ideas. We thought that was the best way to be drunk, on ideas.'

(I thought KKK was going a bit far here, but I didn't protest. We all needed the consolation.)

'Wherever humans happened to be on earth,' said KKK, 'they were incorrigible when it came to being drunk on ideas. They'd recklessly invent drugs called Ecstasy, they'd aim a rocket at the moon and name it Chandrayan, they'd tap strange machines called EVMS full of symbols like lotuses, palms and cycles to bring other humans in whose ideas they believed to power, even when they had good reason to suspect that these humans were far from trustworthy. The list went on and on and it was this conjunction of creating and naming, inventing and cheating over millennia that resulted at the beginning of this century – the twenty-first – in a vast, unmanageable realm of ideas that reached underwater in the form of submarines and into the empyrean as spaceships! It is our capacity for ideas,' KKK continued, throwing his arms round his wife and me in an extravagant gesture (Sid, he left alone), 'that makes human beings potential claimants over the whole universe.'

We'd always admired KKK's wonderful eloquence but that night, he was like a light that we knew would burn itself out. He was a prophet! Each of us has lived for, and by, KKK told us, these galaxies of fantastical claims. They were to us a kind of soul food, *amrit* or prasad. This was what made us Indians, what made us human. So what if that dastardly doctor has stolen our invention? He could not steal our souls!

Ours was a race that claimed we were made up of starlight and seawater, that each one us had an ecstatic god within, that we were at once the same as and different from bees, cockroaches and dolphins. Half-truths and fantasies, those were the wild oceans we swum in, *katha sarit sagaras*, and it has to be admitted that it kept us going for ages. In the end, though, it was the same propensity to make things up without pause that led to our catastrophic downfall. We came to foolishly believe that we were immortal, divine. It was this peculiar trait of self-deception that has led to our undoing. We craved immortality, ignoring the humble virus and now look what has become of us!

It was KKK's last speech – and perhaps his greatest. He collapsed soon after.

Neither Sid nor I could save our beloved friend. We learned later that he'd preserved a small quantity of Anandna and got Marie-Anne to inject it into his BLA directly, and he'd suffered no pain at all. Just as Dr T had made a beeline for his heaven of money and stolen our ideas, KKK made one too. Both instincts were part of human DNA, but we need not argue about which beeline was more elegant, more ecstatic. KKK had found his food source, soaring into the future, his head afire, eternally inspired by ideas.

Be thou a lamp, Anandna.

ANANDNA II

Time for the finals, Sid says
And watch out for that ricochet!
Choices are multiple. Tick one: √
Sci-fi is
Fiction's longbow stretched taut
By science's collinear arrow

Am in casualty, KKK shoots back
Here all is broken, the world off-track!
Every choice is bad. Cross mine out: X
Sci-fi is
Time's rump, hiding in metallic caves
Amnesiac spirit of the forests of the future

I think how much I love them both
And ache to be back at our early prelims
Making faulty choices. My answer is: √ = X
Sci-fi is
Forging pleasure in a petri dish of pain
Imagination's dearest, most daring game

WE WERE NEVER HERE

NUR NASREEN IBRAHIM

'The first word was written by a man, but the ink came from the blood of a woman.'
– Zehra Mumtaz Rashid, *The Eighth Wave of Feminism*

We all left one bright morning, when the sun's golden streaks shot across the heavily cracked pavement, as the roosters were still crowing, as the call to prayer receded into an echo. The dry leaves scattered on the brick road crunched beneath our feet, the garbage bags steaming in the heat, yellowing apple peels scattered about from last night's meals, paan spit blending into the dust, the refuse of a world we no longer wanted.

At first, they didn't notice us leave. Some of them were in the mosque, some washing their faces over their bathroom sinks, shaving, groaning on their toilet seats as they relieved themselves of the previous day's burdens. Some of them were still asleep, snoring softly as we put on our scarves, packed a small bag of everything we loved, and quietly closed the doors behind us. Some of us had no one to leave behind, we departed from empty rooms without fixing our beds, the sheets softly crumpled, the smell of our powder, the henna from our hair, sweat, soap, oily skin lingering as if we had evaporated. We rolled off the hard mats we put on the ground by the roadside, under the shredded tarp that covered us in the harsh foggy winter, rubbing our chapped hands, leaving behind the stench of poverty that quickly faded as we walked away. Perhaps we hoped that by leaving, we would shed all the smells, all the fat of this gluttonous city, all the heaviness that sank deep into our skin and into the skin of men.

We had heard whispers, passed from one woman's mouth to another's ears. Whispers of a secret tunnel running through the salt mines outside the city. Against the crystal walls where carts were once propelled forward along firm tracks, that were now tossed aside, where men once toiled under single light bulbs or in complete darkness. We heard of others disappearing, after making their way into the tunnel in search of sanctuary.

We heard of her, the mother, vanishing in a puff of smoke one morning as the vegetable seller haggled with her grown son. They turned around and she was gone, her plastic shopping bag abandoned, without a sound of protest. We imagined she had given up on this life of compromise, this constant back and forth from the vegetable stand, and decided to make her way through the tunnel in search of something.

We heard of her, the young bride, who calmly walked away from her marriage bed as her husband prepared to enter their room. No note, just a bundle of vermillion and gold, with her diamonds placed on top like heirlooms from an age long past resting in a museum.

We heard of her, the tired middle-aged schoolteacher, who did not return to her class after the break, whose disappearance was only noticed when the principal realized the sounds of mayhem in the classroom had been going on for an hour.

We heard of a secret garden lying hidden at the end of the tunnel, and on the other side of the garden in an old convent was the sanctuary. Whatever was waiting for us there, it could be better than this – anything must be better than this, we thought.

We were afraid at first, deathly afraid. What would they all feel when they realized we were missing? How would they go on?

'We toiled in fields, we nurtured our screaming children, we lay on our backs as men pounded fragments of themselves into our bodies. We were sucked dry, beaten, pampered, preened, torn, broken, peeled, rubbed, touched, prodded, pricked, pinched, painted over, painted under, painted within, stripped to make us beautiful, and then covered to protect our beauty.'

– Kausar Jehangir, *The Ninth Wave of Feminism*

Once, long before we were here, the convent protected women from another world, wives who arrived with their men, the invaders, who enriched themselves off our labour and left. Then the convent selected a few of us, the indoctrinated ones, the wealthy ones, the malleable ones.

Once, we were prepared for marriage behind these walls. When the invaders departed, taking our wealth with them, the convent fell into disrepair, ruin. A few missionaries remained, seeking to salvage its cruel purpose from the rubble, begging for donations from any poor converts. Eventually, they also gave up and left. Now, the convent sits heavily among the rushes behind a dark mountain, just for us, surrounded by grey rocks and a wind that whispers the past to us in our sleep.

Our sanctuary is a large dark house of brick with hidden walls and endless passageways, lined with carpets and high windows. The caretakers, stern women with bamboo canes, tell us in hushed voices to strip ourselves of our clothes, jewels, everything and line up.

'Your journey begins with purification,' a woman with a long gaunt nose and drooping cheeks intoned. 'You are now in our care,' says Nosewoman. 'You need nothing from your past lives.'

'But this is mother's bracelet!' One of us, a small girl with small features, as if they were painted on her porcelain face by a brush of goat's hair, huffs at the end of the line. A sharp snap, the stick makes a *thwack* on the floor and the girl winces.

'Why did you come here, little girl?'

'To get away from my father.'

'And why did you want to leave your father?'

The girl looks at her feet. She shrinks. 'He beat me.'

'Your friend tells me he did much more than that.'

The girl glances up, eyes wide, her face reddens.

'We are all women of pain here. We have no secrets. Tell us what he did.'

'He touched me,' she whimpers. 'Every night, he came to my bed and took off my clothes and touched the parts mother said we were supposed to cover. He did that thing married people do. Except he is my father and I let him – because I was taught obedience!' Her voice is shrill and she is shaking.

We gasp, shake our heads, tug our earlobes in shock. Some of us weep with her, others pray loudly; the caretakers are sombre and wait for the clamour to subside. Nosewoman's cheeks stretch as she smiles.

'He *was* your father. You are no longer his. You are free.'

The girl sighs, her face is now in her hands, and Nosewoman embraces her. Nosewoman shakes, her arms so tightly wound around the girl that some of us start forward. *Is she strangling her? Is she going to ever let her go?*

But she releases her and tears the girl's gold bracelet off her arm and throws it on to the floor. It is an elaborate piece with jasmines carved on its surface. A glint of light shines off the end of the circle, a snake's head with its mouth open, diamond teeth spark menacingly until another caretaker kicks it away in disgust.

We begin to peel off our clothes; some of us have more to peel than the others. Some came here wearing nothing but thin shirts, light shawls covering our heads, escaping with little to show from our past lives. Some came kicking and screaming, bearing bags of jewellery, pictures of husbands, children, grandchildren, letters from old lovers, tattered copies of the Quran, or gold-leaf encrusted leather-bound copies wrapped in velvet or silk.

Some of us have soft hands smelling of powder, expensive creams with lavender, rose and flowers that the others have never even seen. Others have hands with callused, peeling skin that smell like soapsuds, onions, garlic, turmeric and flour.

We are old and young, we have sagging breasts with wrinkled nipples and round breasts tipped with pink, unbroken circles. We left our babies or we escaped the marital bed. Some of us came here as lovers. Some of us came searching for love. Some of us have marks around the thighs, handprints larger than ours. Some of us have smooth, untouched skin but burning discontent inside us.

Some of us were picked up, bereft on the roadside. Some plotted their escapes in secret alleyways, using telephones inside petrol pumps, travelling long distances in the back of a truck. Some of us don't share how we arrived.

Some of us were given the wrong names, wrong bodies, wrong faces. Some of us brought our new names, new bodies. Some hoped to find new names, new bodies.

Some of us can't explain why we are here.

There was a gaping hole inside us, we say.

Some of us can read very well and are assigned to teach those who cannot. It is a useful skill for women, our caretakers tell us. Reading in the hands of women is like fire in the hands of men.

We read scripture in a vast library remade for us. Books line dark walls in rooms with dark carpets on the floor where we sit wearing threadbare white shalwar–kameezes and clean faces. Our rooms are circular with round windows, dropping smooth beams of light on to us. The shelves strain under the weight of knowing. We crave more, we are starved, we tear through the books, their spines straining under our hands, the wind rushing from their pages. We whisper the words to ourselves.

Our bodies are free, we laugh, we walk with our shoulders pulled back, unencumbered by the weight of the outside world.

A thin wind rattles through the halls, bringing fresh air around our ankles.

We sleep in a long hallway and a pale moon grins from the high windows above us. Dark blue shadows flit across our mattresses, spectres from the outside, but by the time we turn to the roof, they are gone. The wind makes us shiver at night and the excitement of this new world vanishes with sleep. We toss and turn and wake up screaming in the night, imagining that by some cruel twist of fate, we were never here.

'The past is a rock pulling us to the bottom of the flowing river of patriarchy.'
–Sultana Shakir, *The Tenth Wave of Feminism*

Before the sun rises, we wait in the dark as our hallway turns a pale blue and the grey stone walls sharpen and shimmer like the insides of a pond. At dawn, thin shards of light emerge from the small windows high above us.

One of us likes to tell the others she is a self-taught reader. But Nosewoman, whom we now call Madam Parveen, rebukes her. 'We are not here to reflect on our past. We are here to shed it.'

The root causes of our oppression is the subject of the first lesson of the day. It is an exhaustive deconstruction of the wrongs done to us over generations, from the control exerted over our bodies to the forceful disenfranchisement of our mothers and grandmothers through oppressive property and inheritance laws.

Some of us shift around, picking at our noses or nails, or breaking off split ends, others pay rapt attention. A former lawyer, the best student among us, was threatened by the police for fighting for a woman burned by her husband with acid. Another one of us has a face scarred and pockmarked by petrol.

The burn victim despises the once-wealthy bride ever since she said the burn victim's face was lopsided. The lawyer rants on property laws while the burn victim hates that we call her the burn victim. She was a beautician in her former life and is glad we have no mirrors here.

Our second lesson is on vanity. Vanity is a woman's worst enemy. It kept us in the thrall of products, gimmicks and medical procedures that forced us to reshape ourselves for the pleasure of men. It forced us into harems.

But a former professor raises her hand. 'Excuse me, *men* forced us into harems.'

A gaunt lady with high cheekbones teaches this class. She prefers to be known as Madam Sophia. She has a high voice, and flutters her hands as if she were waving a wand. We speculate she must have been a fairy in her former life, or at the very least a low-end fashion model.

'Yes, but what kept us in those harems?'

A pause. 'Well…men did, madam.'

'No! And yes. We kept ourselves in those harems, we turned our attentions to matters of the face, the body, of beauty and maintaining that beauty to keep a man's attention,' Madam Sophia says. 'Why would we need a man's attention? We are resilient and can survive without a man's aid.'

'That's well and good,' the professor says impatiently. 'But many of us fought for a man's attention because keeping a marriage was the only way to survive.'

'What if we wanted to be there? What if we liked that life?' another voice pipes up.

'Oh, be quiet!'

As weeks go by, we cannot help but think about the past. The housewife wants to run back to her husband, she misses his touch she says. 'When he didn't hit me, he was gentle,' she complains.

The professor wants to read Hemingway, but his work is forbidden.

The burnt beautician desperately longs for a mirror in this house of endless walls. Her eyebrows are growing out, she complains, even though we can't see them, but no one has the heart to tell her.

Several of us don't belong here, and perhaps we never will.

Some of us have been women all our lives, but born in bodies we did not want. Others call us interlopers, pretenders, even though we have been abused, isolated, ridiculed, our souls questioned, our sisters murdered. We are the least welcome here; even some of the caretakers resist our entrance into this sanctuary.

'Find your own space!' they say.

But others caution them – all women are welcome here.

Some of us escaped abusive lovers, others wanted a life beyond singing, dancing and begging; others had built their lives against all odds, only to have the newly independent world snatch their hard work away. Like the rest of womankind, we also sought disappearance.

We find our only mirrors in the clear invisible water sitting in our bowls every morning. We wash our faces, brush *meswak* across our teeth and catch glimpses of our new selves – scrubbed clean, fresh-faced and neutralized. The burn victim weeps into a bowl, the lawyer notices how her eyes have fresh wrinkles around them, the former dancer sees new hair on her chin, the professor notices how her eyes no longer burn brightly, starved of the books from her old library.

One of us wonders how Madam Parveen came to lead us. One of us watches her with narrowed eyes, and imagines she must have been a nun in her past life.

Madam Parveen knows how to control women, she walks around the reading groups with her arms folded on her long white kameez and chooses to wrap her hair in a black scarf that hangs over one shoulder.

'Shush! The past is the past! Anyone who thinks otherwise might as well go back.'

But how do we go back? There is no exit.

We often imagine the world we left behind, the towns and the big cities where the men surely must have noticed our disappearances. They must begin to see their houses fall into dust and disrepair, their hospitals running low on staff, their schools emptying and their children running amok.

It won't be long, we say, until they find us and drag us away. We should be better at hiding.

'Would that be so bad?' the others say. 'We made our point. Perhaps they will learn a lesson this time.'

Some of us are quiet. Some of us want to go home, some of us miss our children.

But others among us are deeply afraid of returning.

Our divisions grow. We no longer remember what we ran away from. The outside world seems like a distant nightmare, a hazy recollection of another's life.

Some of us even fear that no one had noticed our departure. All of it, all the doubt, the second-guessing would have been for nothing. We had been duped, we had blindly followed an idea without a goal. We are cattle, gratefully responding to any sound of freedom ringing from a convincing source. We are dandelion seeds, waiting for the next wind to carry us to new destinations, unable to direct the wind ourselves.

So we wait and we bicker. We watch the sun rise and fall from our mattresses, we visualize our city in the distance, the old domain of mosques and minarets fallen into disrepair, of empires long destroyed, the city of men that will age into nothingness. Eventually, we begin to forget the streets and the men who caused us pain. We forget why we left. We forget our old lives, we forget if we were lawyers, doctors, wives, beggars, prostitutes, mothers, teachers, beauticians, labourers, servants. We let them forget us – as if we were never there to begin with.

THE NARRATIVE OF NAUSHIRWAN SHAVAKSHA SHEIKH CHILLI

KEKI N. DARUWALLA

It is extremely difficult for me, Suresh Dayalunand, the self-styled Swami Sureshanand Dayalunand, to talk about my friend Naushirwan Shavaksha, first fatal casualty on the space shuttle *Gargantuan*. What is even more difficult is to abide by his last wish, which was that I should write a commentary on his story so that readers in the unknown future may understand what Naushirwan (Naushir to friends) was trying to convey. Sparse of words as I am, I will let his own prologue speak for itself, and will intervene as and when required. And may I add that it was none other than I who introduced him to our joint guru Shri Shri Shri Lobsang Rampa. Let his narrative speak for itself.

Prologue

I, Naushir Shavaksha, will initially be writing about the past. To come to the year 2087, I had to traverse the morass of 70-odd years. Now, first let me explain my philosophy on tenses, which, if I may be bold enough to say, was my philosophy of time or on time; I am a bit shaky with prepositions and girlfriends lately. Sounds pompous but so damn what? There are no tenses. The past was the present once. For instance, 1984 was the present once, wasn't it, as any Delhi policeman who witnessed the riots will tell you. Till then, it was the future and the world knew what Orwell thought of it decades earlier. Now, as any human rights lawyer trying ineffectively to prosecute the guys who led the mobs, 1984 is the past. The same applies to Gujarat in 2002. Those who found themselves at the epicentre of it all, the arsonists and the encounter specialists, are walking the ramp in sold-out political fashion shows. Police officers involved in the fake encounters got extensions.

How can I speak of 2087? I will offer a simple answer to a good, though obvious, question. I employed the time-rope trick my guru Shri Shri Shri Lobsang Rampa, the Flying Lama, had taught me through the intervention of my friend Suresh Dayalunand. Such occult practices are actually taught through intuition and I, along with Suresh, learned it at a great *diksha* ceremony, fully occult, in a secret cave near Tholingmath in Tibet. My guru Lobsang Rampa time-rocketed me into 2087. To learn the mantra, one had to go through the rigorous meditation that went with it. The physical and the anti-temptation rigours were also considerable – for seven days I was forced to stay away from whisky and cards.

First things first. In 2087, the Parsis had vanished, not only from India but from the planet. I thought I was the last of the derelicts. The guzzlers of beer, the gulpers of *dhan sak* and banana-leaf-wrapped steamed fish and lagan nu custard, the crackers of lousy jokes, the inveterate litigants against each other, had vanished from Mother earth. The small causes courts and the high court in Mumbai breathed the proverbial sigh of relief. Earlier, they didn't know what to do with the endless litigation between members of the Bombay Parsi Punchayet executive committee. When the famous case of Cawas Navroz Jhonny Walker Whiskywallah versus the Soli Jehangir Single Malt Whiskywallah came up before the court as listed (it was filed 30 years ago, in 2057), the court clerk also provided the obituary notices for both litigants that had appeared in the *Times of India*. The chief justice, a very innovative judge, suggested that instead of deciding on this copyright infringement matter, the court would send a condolence message to the families. The court clerk asked who the condolence resolution should be sent to because the entire community had disappeared, lock, stock and barrel – black skull cap, *dagli* and flapping pantaloons. The chief justice was lost for an answer.

The National Commission for Minorities had been in a similar quandary. The chairman had found a unique way of keeping the impotent and farcical commission busy and alive. The commission had printed a thousand condolence messages for victims killed in sectarian riots or through cow

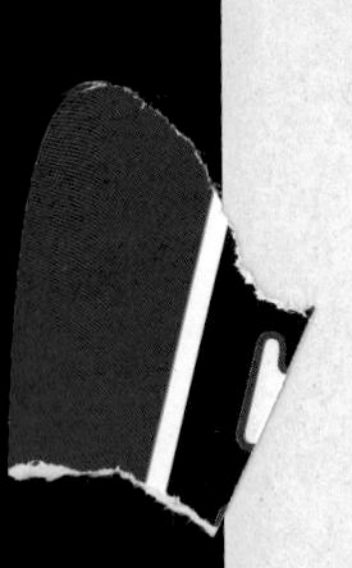

vigilantism, or because of attacks on film studios and theatres which screened films that distorted the histories of 'historical characters' who had never existed. The entire commission was consumed by feverish activity, sending these condolence missives to relatives of victims in all parts of the country. Anyway, the chairman at a Tuesday meeting was disturbed that the Parsi member was not in attendance. He was told that the member was locked in psychic communication with the vultures at the Tower of Silence. The vultures had come back to Mumbai in 2080, but the Parsis had disappeared.

This was not the case with other communities.

They thrived and flourished, by which I mean they begat and begat, excuse my semi-Biblical lingo. By 2087, there was no town or kasbah in India with a population of less than five lakh. Delhi and Mumbai were over six crore each. You couldn't walk in Delhi, let alone drive, for the streets were so clogged. Even three-storeyed flyovers couldn't help. The pollution was so thick, you could not cut it with a knife. You had to use a bulldozer with extra sharp blades. I may be exaggerating a bit, but then what is a Parsi who cannot exaggerate? Nine years earlier, that is in 2078, the party, though on its last quivering legs, was in power. People from a Malthusian think tank asked them to restrict the population to not more than two per family. 'This should be the number one item on your election manifesto,' the think tank had urged. But hardliners from Gujarat and Haryana insisted that the topmost priority should be the removal of Article 370, which gave Kashmir special status in the Indian Constitution. The second was to be a common civil code, which they had failed to implement for 70 years.

Of course, it had not been an uninterrupted run for the BJP since 2014, because the Congress had got two terms in office, during which the government had been busy negotiating a security pact with Italy. Wreaths were regularly laid on the graves of two Italian gunmen who had fired and killed some Indian boatmen. The trials of these under-trials had remained underway till 2060 when they had breathed their last, not as convicts but as 'under-trials,' a word coined in India. Much national mourning was evidenced in Rome and Milan, and Indian tear ducts had not remained unaffected.

Oddly enough, the Indo-Italian pact was cemented in the absence of any opposition from either Nagpur or Gorakhpur. The saffron echelon in Nagpur (now attired in brown pants instead of khaki shorts) had fondly hoped that maybe this was the one way through which the fascist philosophy of the late, lamented Benito Mussolini could perhaps be smuggled into the Indian polity. And so, Nagpur kept quiet.

In the 2085 elections, both national parties had lost, giving way to the right-of-the-right wing Gorakhnath Sanstha which came to power both in Lucknow and Delhi. The shaven-headed, ochre-robed Gorakhnathis had won UP through a unique plan. The BJP and its cow vigilantism were old hat. The Gorakhnathis started the great *abhiyan* (movement), on 9 August, called the Bhains Raksha Sangathan. Woe betide anyone who slaughtered buffaloes for meat. Each of the now 134 districts of UP were asked how many *kasai*s (butchers) their *bhains* vigilantes had slaughtered. One district magistrate, an expert in statistical manipulation, misunderstood the shaved-headed chief minister's order. He thought he had to report the number of buffaloes slaughtered. One buffalo had died of snake bite in his district of Gursahiganj just the previous week. (Gursahiganj, which was once just a *thana*, had become a full-fledged district.)

The son of a dentist that he was, the district collector knew how the chair could be raised, the way Charlie Chaplin had done in *The Great Dictator*. Turning one into 100 had never been a problem with him. (When once the government had asked as to how many compost pits were dug in each district, he had reported such fantastic acreage that it was discovered that one-third of his district was taken up by compost pits.) The figure of 100 buffaloes killed was dutifully reported to Lucknow, resulting in his immediate arrest. He was handcuffed and taken to the Fategarh Jail. The superintendent of police absconded and was rumoured to be hiding with the Maoists in Nepal. Incidentally, the Nepali Maoists were in armed opposition to the twenty-seventh constitution being hammered out since the Nepali monarch had been deposed.

Every movement has to have a raison d'être for its origin. According to rumour, unverified till date, a secret Gorakhnathi cabal had got hold of an unknown herb which increased both the virility of the male bison and the fertility of the female. Within three years, 1000 gaurs were born in the forests of Nepal. In a careful operation, masterminded by retired R&AW and IB officers, these bison were unleashed on Uttar Pradesh. They ravaged the fields, killed cattle and men as they ran amok. The people believed that this was Pashupatinath's vengeance against the slaughter of buffaloes. Through this ruse, followed by massive propaganda through drumbeat, town crier and Twitter, *bhains* vigilantes rose up in UP and won the election. The Gorakhnathis took over Lucknow.

The Congress, in these 70 years, had not remained idle. The party was headed now by the Vadrites. Like the Parsis, the Gandhis had vanished, the bestowers of patronage, propounders of the doctrine of the divine right of the dynasty had disappeared. (I must admit they were never a match for the RJD with its doctrine of the divine right of *saas* and sibling to head the party). However, the Congress were good as ever in the art they had practised for 100 years. They had history to back their sleight of hand. After all, they had set up Bhindranwale to weaken the Akalis. They had set up (along with help from the Intelligence Bureau and their slush funds) the Hurriyat to weaken the National Conference. Then, they had set up the Gilaniites to weaken the Hurriyat. Their policy had always been to set up and back the fanatic edge of the main opposition. True to type, they now backed the Gorakhnathis in order to sideline the BJP. Needless to say, they had succeeded.

Even a decade earlier, meaning in the 2070s, an unusually bright scion of the Vadra *vansh*, had split the BJP in Gujarat. It was a territorial split. Party members in Kutch were induced to ask for a greater share of seats and plums, and were coaxed to take on the Gujaratis and the Kathiawaris. This faction-fighting was known to wags as Gujjus versus the Bhujjoos as the members of the party from Bhuj were known. The two factions, each with a different symbol, had limped to the polling booths in 2085, only to be soundly beaten.

And Maharashtra and Tamil Nadu cannot be completely ignored. An earthquake in the south had ominously opened up huge cavities in atheist temples. In many of these temples, buried treasures were unearthed. The greatest treasure was witnessed in Tanjore, now named Thanjavur. Such was the treasure in the cave, that people believed it was the 1,76,000-crore scam that Auditor General Vinod Rai had talked about once. Since only atheists were admitted to these temples, there were stampedes at temple gates with people wanting to give up their gods. Radha and Krishna, Sita and Rama were abandoned temporarily in order to get entry into atheist temples.

The same tremor had caused a Godse idol to fall somewhere in a temple in Maharashtra. This had led to riots between the enraged followers of the Mahasabha and the Congress. A Mahasabha leader stated that it was the statue of Gandhi that should have fallen. After all, he had given away those fifty crore rupees to Pakistan. The Congress leaders were jubilant that the statue of the assassin had been targeted by the cognizant continental plates. Later the Shiv Sena, now headed by Sakharam Thakre, decided, after some dithering and two closed-door meetings, to pitch for Gandhi rather than Godse. So, a free-for-all had resulted, and the goons of all the three parties had a great time. The looting was such that the Gujarati shops in Mumbai were stripped bare.

Now that we have an available sketch of the politics in India during the 2080s, we can move close to 2087. (But may I add on a personal note, that my interest in politics is waning because I have taken to the high-stakes card tables recently, not bothering even about my flourishing foundry business).

1.

I must start on the not very subtle story of the shuttle. The planet had gotten swamped by human beings, especially Indians and the Chinese – in that order. India had beaten China to the two billion-mark years ago. The Chinese vacillated between the one child and the two child norms. In India, we were free and unambiguous. There could be a restriction on wives, but none on children. You could have six mistresses, but four wives were a no-no. The population 'menace' had become so real that earth had decided to 'export' human beings to other planets. (Indian poets writing in English went to town, calling it the 'Diaspora of Diasporas', 'Exodus of Exoduses'. Most of these poets, almost all from Mumbai, didn't know the difference between diaspora and exodus.)

There was a global movement to this effect. The matter had been taken up by the UN Security Council, who had, for a month, very seriously debated a proposition from the United States of America that homosexuality should be encouraged to slow down the galloping increase in population. Pakistan had raised the banner of revolt. Their madrasas, where sodomy was almost de rigueur, had protested wildly at this proposal. They pointed out that the proposal was not only unholy and anti-Koranic, but also made a mockery of all religious canons. Argentina had joined Pakistan in this crusade. The economy of Argentina survived on meat export. The Peronists got worried that if their bulls became homosexual, their economy would collapse. If that happened, what would Argentina export? Lloyd Webber? They were more vociferous than the Pakistanis in opposing this nefarious option. The outcry from the Catholic church, and the Pope's personal visit to the UN settled the issue and the American proposal was thrown out. The liberals, of course, were aghast that the LGBT movement had received a setback.

But nothing's for free, guys, not even throwing out a stupid proposal. The upshot was that America insisted that the UN pass sanctions against India and China for not controlling their populations. People in the know suspected that the American representative at the UN was still under the impression that the subcontinent was ruled from Delhi. The UN also warned Indonesia about its swelling numbers. The Gorakhnathi government suspected that it was the Malthusian think tank that had leaked out details of the pitiful health of the Indian population to the UN. Two of the most scholarly members of the think tank were randomly picked up and sedition cases were thrown at them by the National Investigating Agency, helped by a Delhi Police commissioner, who on superannuation was given a six-year tenure at the UPSC. Not to be outdone, China waded into this mess energetically, for Beijing also suspected that some of its intellectuals and economists, especially the ones who hollered for human rights, were responsible for alerting the UN. They had 50 intellectuals and 50 economists picked up and shot.

Beijing wrote back to the UN, 'As a result of your letter, we have been constrained to lessen our population by a hundred at one fell stroke. The responsibility for this act is solely on the United Nations.'

The changes on the ground that took place boded ill for the Sino-Indian twosome. America had targeted North Korea for 70 years, and the hinges on the swivelling mechanism of their missile launchers had rusted because they had been pointed in one direction for so long. The launchers were now greased and locked on to the Sino-Indian land mass. 'Time's running out for you, buddies,' declared the American President. He was terribly riled by the UN throwing out his proposal on the need for promoting homosexuality, and had called the Security Council 'a bunch of antediluvian sons of bitches.' May I add that the President of the United States belonged to the Trumpist Party which had defeated both Democrats and Republicans roundly and soundly?

Thus, preparations to build two huge space shuttles were initiated at enormous cost. ISRO was told to concentrate only on this project. The shuttles, made eventually with Russian help, were as large as the Dharavi slums and were to take twenty thousand people in one lift-off to the moon. Huge bribes to be on the shuttles being blasted off from Charbatia in Odisha were paid, and special vigilance commissioners were appointed at enormous salaries to see that the selection of people was fair. By fairness, of course, they meant that all communities must be represented – SCs, STs, Brahmins, Bahelyas, Lingayats, Kammas, the varied clans of the Rajputs, the Kayasthas, people from the sugar and milk lobbies and the various bovine vigilantes had to be equitably accommodated. What made headlines in the press was that some of the special vigilance commissioners themselves bribed the shuttle owners to get on board. As a smiling Tamil lady on board said, 'We are like that only!'

My old friend Sureshanand was on the shuttle as the ticket collector.

2.

Late as it is, let me now tell you my pathetic personal story. I had lost everything because of liquor and cards. Father, Puppa dear, had left me a lot of money. I went through my first crore like a hot knife through butter, like a winter Olympian skating to music. You can't be down always, my card companions said. What goes up must come down. But I shouted that I had never gone up, blast you! That's what we mean, they said, since you have been down for a while, you are bound to go up. Haven't you heard of the wheel of fortune, Shavaksha? It sounded right, but my bank manager in Horniman Circle looked hard at me, as he viewed my cheque and the balance on the computer.

'Your second crore also seems to have gone, Shavaksha. Are you putting your crores in stocks?'

'Precisely,' I smiled back. I have learned that when you lie, you must always smile to appear convincing.

'You know all about bulls and bears?'

'Mr Manager, bear baiting is outlawed and as for bulls, they rule the country, damn it.'

'Hope you have an honest broker, sir. Does your wife know about these extensive withdrawals? You have a joint account, you know.'

'Absolutely. She is handling all the socks and shares, I mean stocks and bears.'

A time came, oh sad day, oh malefic and malevolent day, when I had to sell my ancestral house on Cumabla Hill, sell the Ming vases my mother had left me, and my cellar, all the vintage liquor my drinking pals had left me, by which I mean the wines and whiskies they had, out of generosity, not imbibed (I raised an empty glass to them). My cellar was sold, but my wife, Naja, went into depression! That same month, Naja hung herself. And while the police were untying the rope around the swan-like neck of my darling Naju, I swore I wouldn't touch flush or *teen patti* again. Never!

I took to poker.

The card debts were still around, like a long list nailed to the wall. A house after all can settle only that much. I went to my friend Mehromji Mishtidoiwala for advice. It was March 2084. (I will expatiate on his surname later.)

'*Sala* Mehrom, tell me what should I do. I can't pay off these debts, not even if I live a hundred years.'

'*Sala* Shavaksha, what do you expect me to say? What are your plans? I hope you don't have any intention to run away to Nepal. The Nepalis will hand you over to the notorious UP Police. With a nose like yours, they may just want to experiment and see how soon it bleeds.' I thought that was very encouraging. (May I just say here that the word *sala* is an endearment among the Parsis?)

'Mehrom, I was thinking of something further than Nepal.'

'Where? What are you thinking of?'

'These spaceships are being made, aren't they? Are they safe, Mehrom?'

That's how his briefing started. 'Listen, *sala*, I know something about navigation – after all, I spent 30 years in the merchant navy and only two of my ships sank while I was captain. These Gorakhnathis are planning big. Twenty-thousand in one go, just one lift-off, do you understand? It's never been done before. The moon, as you know has been extensively colonised with artificial habitats. It is hoped it will be able to absorb such large influxes. If these mad guys really bank on moving 20,000 people in one go, then chemical rocket technology will obviously come a cropper. The only option left is the space elevator.'

'And what the hell is a space elevator?'

'The space elevator has long been in development, and the concept once evolved by the Russian scientist Konstantin Tsiolkovsky in 1895 has reached fruition. The space elevator is being used to send people to gigantic space stations in geostationary orbits from where people will be sent to various planets. Everything is under wraps, but the grapevine tells me that that's the plan afoot.'

'I don't understand, Mehrom. What is this geostationary orbit?'

'Listen, don't you change trains at particular junctions? Don't you travel by another line? The train junction here is the space station. A space elevator is a transport system like BEST. It has a cable stolidly fixed on the earth and extending into space. So, you travel along the cable till you reach space, meaning you are free from gravity. You have to travel 35,000 kilometres to achieve that. The geostationary thing, which I suspect is teasing your mind, is the orbit from which another space ship will take the guys to the moon. They have already fixed the elevator near the equator in Africa. They have discovered a material which is stronger and lighter than steel'

'You mean like Rearden metal? Have they been reading Ayn Rand, for Chrissake!'

'Don't be stupid, this is for real. Centrifugal forces will be unleashed scientifically from space. The onward journey will be on a huge spacecraft that will use nuclear-powered ion thrusters. These will then dock at a space station in nuclear orbit, disgorge their passengers, who will then take another space elevator to descend to the lunar surface.'

Three years earlier, in 2084, when I had that conversation with Mehromji, we knew that a seat on the space shuttle was going to be damn expensive – a crore at the minimum. I wouldn't pay half as much for a Joe Louis–Jack Johnson dream bout to decide who was the greatest boxer in history. Add to this, the bribes to get into the shuttle were tremendous – at least half the price of a ticket. As a last resort, I went once again in search of my friend, Mehromji Mishtidoiwala. 'Once more into the breach, my friend, once more,' I hummed to myself as I made my way to him.

For the benefit of posterity, I must say that in the past 70 years, the Parsis had left their old trades and trade names and taken on new ones. I went to his residence and found he had moved. The watchman of the apartment, a Muslim with a beard, laughed at me. He said, 'If you friend is *mehroom*, if he has become beloved to Allah, why are you looking for him?'

I chastised him in really flaming language and said that Mehromji was hale and hearty (though I knew his was a serious case of liver cirrhosis, too much whisky) and was instantly told where he had moved.

Rich as he was, Mehromji Mishtidoiwala, who hailed originally from Kolkota, gave me no cheer. 'I need a crore for the ticket and half of it for the bribe. I hardly have a lakh,' I told him.

He nodded his head because he knew that I had gambled away the wealth my father had left me. Come to think of it, what are a couple of crores, a few Ming vases and an M.F. Husain painting when it comes to *teen patti*, I mean flush.

'*Sala*, you need to take a loan,' he said with great warmth and affection.

'*Sala* Mehrom, who is going to give me a loan? Which bank?'

'You need collateral, Naushir! A mortgage would come in handy.'

'I owe my landlord three months' rent.'

'Mortgage your mother-in-law's house on Cumbala Hill.'

What was he talking about? Ever since my wife had committed suicide her mother was not prepared to look at my face. He knew all that.

'Naushir, I will arrange everything, all you have to do is get her signature.'

As a last-ditch attempt, I went to see my mother-in-law at her Cumbala Hill apartment, to squeeze a loan out of her. She couldn't believe my cheek! She railed and stormed like the Hurricane Katrina of old, and I don't mean the Indian actress of yore. Being the dignified gentleman that I am, I beat a hasty retreat, gave her a stately bow and said, 'Mama, if you ever need help, I am still your son-in-law.'

'I wish you never were!' she replied. As I was making my exit, her Alsatian Rommy (named after Rommel, a Roman general in Julius Caesar's army I presume), bounded in and snapped at my rather lugubrious buttocks that trail behind me, almost prehensile. I ran down the stairs in undignified haste and leapt into my cab. I had not gone to ma-in-law just for a fat loan. I also wanted to ask her for the diamond brooch and the gold locket which had belonged to Naju. You see, I had fallen head over my calf muscles in love with that skittish cancan dancer, Polly Putli, the daughter of a Goan truck driver and a Parsi professor of philosophy at Elphinstone College. The brooch would have looked good on my Putli.

Mehromji seemed to have got it right. A broker I knew told me it was only during the BJP regime that corruption had come down, with bribes only three times more than an air ticket or a movie ticket. But 40,000 dollars seemed much too much. That came to 80,000 for two tickets!

'Two tickets?' asked Mehromji Mishtidoiwala, the yogurt curdling in his belly.

'Yes, of course,' I said. 'I can't go without Putli, can I?'

He hit his hand against his head 'What about your card debts? They are astronomical, I believe.'

'Why else would I want this lunar trip? I wish to set the police an interplanetary chase. Don't you understand?'

'Then you have no option, *sala*! Say goodbye to honesty.'

And that is how, with a heavy heart, my conscience pricking me as if a cockroach had got into my pyjamas, I forged my ma-in-law's signature, sold her house, pocketed the money bought two tickets and was away with my darling Polly Putli to lunar habitats.

I found on the flight that my friend Sureshanand Dayalunand was the ticket collector! Had I known I could have spared myself the expense of buying those tickets! You can never have it your own way. As the shuttle zoomed and boomed away, making a noise equal to half a billion Punjabi couples making love, I realized life couldn't be better, what with my darling Putli by my side. I reached for a tabloid to pass the time. *Mid-Day* it turned out to be, and what do you think the headline on the front page was? 'Parsi Crook off to Moon!' Another tabloid said, 'Lunar Sanctuary for Scoundrel'. Another headline full of cheap alliterations screamed, 'Mortgage Master Thief Gives Malabar Police the Miss.'

The opening paragraph read: 'Naushirwan Shavaksha, Naushir to friends and fellow crooks, and "Sheikh Chilli" to companions of the bottle and the card table, son of reputed philanthropist and one-time millionaire, Padma Shri Erach Shavaksha, has now disgraced the family name and run out of his last penny in gambling dens. The crook has fled to the moon on the space shuttle *Gargantuan*. Inspector Ghorpade of the Malabar Police Station stated that now there was no way he could be arrested and brought to book.'

And these yellow journalists had done their homework. They had spoken to what they called 'Naushir's creditors,' meaning people who had fleeced me on the card tables. But I was beside myself with rage on reading I had visited gambling dens when I had always played in reputed clubs. It broke my heart. What would happen when my mother-in-law saw this? Poor thing, she had no idea that her house on Cumbala Hill now belonged to the Bank of India. Fortunately for me, the yellow press, the 'presstitutes' as an army havildar had called them 70-odd years ago, had not got hold of either Polly Putli or of my signatures on the sale deed of a certain house on Cumbala Hill.

On the flight, (if that's the word – we were speeding at 4,000 miles an hour) I heard what sounded like the mooing of cattle. I asked the man sitting to my left, one Nekram, what the mooing was about. Was someone showing a cattle pen on YouTube?

'We are carrying cattle,' he said. 'We are also carrying members of the R&AW and six from the IB.'

'Are they here to look after us?' I winked.

'No, the IB fellows are here to look after the buffaloes – five out of the six.'

'And what about the sixth guy?' I asked.

'Oh, he is here to report on any dinner parties where our retired foreign service officers and generals start mingling with Pakistani ambassadors. Very serious matter. Remember, 70 years ago, the same organization, the IB, had saved the nation by reporting this consanguineous, conspiratorial meeting between our elite and the Pakistanis.'

'Thank God!' I said. 'And what about the chaps from R&AW?'

'They have no manpower, Shavaksha. You see, the National Security Adviser, the NSA, is always from the IB. So the IB manpower grows exponentially. R&AW is short-changed and short staffed.'

'So how have they managed this lunar wing, Nekram-ji?'

'By closing the Kashmir cell.'

'What, has the Kashmir issue been solved?'

'It will never be solved, Shavaksha. But R&AW officers also enjoy foreign postings, and what could be more foreign than the moon?' We winked at each other.

'How do you know all this, Nekram-ji?'

'My uncle is the director general of the Dangar Sewa Sanstha, the Cattle Service Organization. He even gets to attend certain Cabinet meetings. He rose to fame by setting that hymn from the Rig Veda to music:

'Pushan god of golden day

Shorten thou the shepherd's way.'

'What is his name? Is the great man on the shuttle?'

'Shiv Shankar Thripathi-ji? Of course he is on the shuttle. How could he not be? And he is accompanied by a well-known Vedic scientist Gauri Shankar Tiwari-ji who is gathering material to prove that our hoary ancestors also undertook inter-planetary travel.'

'Do you mean from Sirius to Aldebaran, Nekram-ji?'

'Precisely.'

'But they are some light years away.'

'Shavaksha, the speed of light had not been calculated then. No one knew about light years. Travel was unencumbered by theories. I mean, travel was free.'

'You mean one didn't have to pay 40,000 dollars for a ticket!'

'No, just some *prasadam* for Lord Pashupatinath.'

I went to pee and as I pulled the flush I saw my urine turn to yellow icicles in space and float around our space craft. The yellow crystals travelled alongside us for a while, looking for all the world like a piece of installation art. As we landed at the cosmodrome, we were asked to wait till the cattle trundled down. Then, to my horror, I found almost half a dozen butchers waiting there. What was the diabolic mystery around this? I recognized one of the butchers.

Three years ago, my darling wife Naju had bought a turkey for Christmas – she liked aping the West – but she couldn't ever execute it, I mean assassinate it, I mean cut it up. So, we took the turkey to a butcher in Bhendi Bazar, the same chap who came with the cattle. To complete the story, Naju couldn't even watch the butcher cut up the turkey she had named Tom Collins. So, we went to the chap from whom Naju darling had bought the turkey but to our utter chagrin, he refused to buy it back. One often comes across such evil in the marketplace, or shall I venture to say, in capitalism. So, we just dumped the bird on the fellow and walked off. Naju whipped up a masala omelette and that's what we had for dinner on Christmas Eve. Evil never comes singly. That evening, I had to forfeit the card game with my cronies. I told Nekram-ji about this in brief, but the presence of the Bhendi bazar *kasai* didn't seem to bother him one bit. I just shrugged.

Even though there were 20 exits in the space shuttle, it took quite some time for *Gargantuan* to be cleared. All the gates were numbered, and mine was R.37.60 and as I sauntered out after an hour's wait, I would have fallen if my darling Putli had not caught me by the hand. I saw an old couple, Jal Bulsara and his wife Jerroo at the ticket counter! I thought only three Parsis had been left on earth, my mother-in-law, Mehromji and me. And here was this old couple – Jal Bulsara was a friend of my father! And he was once, some 20 years ago the president of WAPIZ, the World Association of Parsi and Irani Zoroastrians.

He recognized me, and I spoke first, for I didn't want him to ask any questions. 'What are you doing here, Uncle?'

'*Dikra*, we came because of the renowned herb garden.'

'Of course,' I nodded. 'But what kind of herbs are you looking for? Something for longevity? *Maru mano to,* try rum.'

'*Dikra*, we are beyond caring about our lives. We have achieved what we wanted to achieve.' He looked around suspiciously for any eavesdroppers. Then he put his arm around me, brought his mouth close to my ears and whispered, 'We have come looking for an herb, after smelling which no Parsi would marry a *parjat*, a non-Parsi.'

'But Uncle, there are no Parsis left to marry non-Parsis now.'

'Shut up, you stupid fellow.'

'Have you found the herb, Uncle?'

'Yes, we have. Here, smell it!' He thrust an herb with small blue flowers at its end at me, almost inserting it in my nose. I thought of Polly Putli at once! What would happen if the doddering fool was correct? How would I sleep with my second darling (the first was, of course, Naja) now if the herb was really effective?

'Uncle, will this affect you even if the girl is of mixed parents, a half-Parsi?'

'Absolutely, and my boy, there are no mixed ones among us. Either you are Parsi or not! Now that we have got the herb, we have come to book our return ticket.'

Alas, there were two bearded men in white skull caps, looking like maulvis, who happened to pass us and stopped. I recalled that they were in the *Gargantuan*, but clad in jeans and minus caps. The fellows had eavesdropped on our conversation. One of them spoke. 'Sir, you Hindustanis seem to have already decided that the moon, which is the heart blood of Islam, will be declared *Dar al-harb*?'

We didn't know how to answer. The two were obviously from Pakistan. The maulvi spoke again, 'May I request that *Dar al-Islam* may please be given a chance, at least on the moon!'

'I think this should be settled at the subcontinental level, not here,' I said.

Bulsara broke in, 'Perhaps the matter could be settled when the Pakistani shuttle lands, perhaps with *mujahirs* and Balochis on board.'

The maulvis were enraged. 'Pakistan can't send an aircraft to Kabul, leave alone the moon, what with a Trumpist sitting in the White House.' Saying that, they took their leave, and we breathed freely.

It was a bad night. Besotted as I was with darling Putli, I was now beset, or was it besotted (I'm getting confused!), by the herb that Bulsara had made me smell. Just suppose this damned herb was potent enough to turn one impotent? I just tossed around on the bed till Putli got furious with me and kicked me out of the bed. Amazingly, I managed some sleep on the floor.

The next day, with Polly Putli reclining on my arm languorously, we strolled down to the poshest lunar locality, the Times Circle, which had malls made from Jasper stone and was dotted with cinema houses. Whom should we meet there but our friend from the shuttle, Nekram? He came straight to the point. 'Mr Shavaksha, what exactly is the business you are trained in?'

I replied that I had a chain of hardware shops on Princess Street, later named after Shamaldas Gandhi, and a factory producing boilers at Vapi.'

'So, are you going to establish foundries here on the moon?'

'No, Nekram-ji, I intend to move into the entertainment industry. Since there are no restrictions here, I am negotiating with others to open a dance bar, where my star companion, Miss Polly Putli, the great cancan dancer will be the cynosure of all legs – I mean, her legs will be the cynosure of all eyes.'

'Spanish dance, sir, like flamenco?'

'French, of the high-kicking 1820s.'

'Oh Shavaksha-ji, that must have been at the same time as the Russian Revolution?'

'Just a 100 years earlier, Nekram-ji.'

'Oh, those were those horrible days when we were under the horrible Mughals!'

'*Naam ke waaste*, nominally, Nekram-ji.'

He was a bit mollified. And now it was my turn to ask questions. 'Nekram-ji, I salute you for bringing the cattle, but I saw some butchers too – I told you earlier as well – they seemed to be the keepers of the cattle.'

'You are right, Shavaksha-ji! After all, who can keep the buffaloes better than butchers?' he laughed. 'Nekram-ji,' I said, 'this is no laughing matter. Suppose they slaughter the buffaloes? The Gorakhnathis will be after your blood.'

'I am a Gorakhnathi myself. Don't worry, the shuttle security took away their knives. Can you make a cleaver for us? With your experience in the foundry business, can you make a blunt cleaver?'

I was fairly at my wit's end, and told him I didn't understand this request at all.

Nekram said 'Protecting buffalos is our dharma. We won't shy away, don't worry, and none will be slaughtered.' Then he broke into verse and laughed:

'From guarding cattle, we won't be flinching.

But our real pleasure lies in lynching.'

'Nekram-ji, that is really clinching,' said I.

The next day, I went to an ironmonger and got some iron and found the lunar metal soft. I made the blade heavy and the haft light. During our walk at the Times Circle, I was told by Tripathi-ji himself that my contraption was ideal. They were in hiding and as the butcher swung my contraption, the blade flew off and only the haft was left in his hands. Then they beat the fellow up, and the other *kasai*s ran away. I was bold enough to enquire of Tripathi-ji and Tiwari-ji about what they intended on doing.

'Our target was the herb garden, we prayed for it and our prayers has been answered. We asked for an herb and we have found it. We brought some Nagpur botanists with us who have testified to its efficacy. The moment someone eats the leaves, he can't produce children. One swallow, one gulp and the dynasty ends. No vasectomy or tubectomy needed.'

'Will you try this in India?'

'We will.'

'Has the herb a name?'

'Shavaksha-ji, it is called the Royal Sweet-Smelling All-Banishing Virility Potion.'

I didn't get it. 'Why such a long name?' I asked.

They laughed. 'Smell the coffee, Shavaksha-ji. Look for the acronyms.' And they laughed some more.

But soon, I was busy with the opening of my dance bar. I took a bank loan, bought a beautiful place on the Times Circle and advertised like hell. I priced the tickets high and the entire gentry of the moon was eating out of my hands. The tickets sold out. Wine was flowing – the Sheraton wanted to be in on it, and so they picked up the tab. But the night was a disaster. As the queen of dance bars on earth and its moon came in to a tremendous ovation which lasted a good ten minutes, and Polly Putli kicked up what I hoped was another storm, things plummeted for us. With the first high kick, she almost flew into the air. There was an embarrassed silence from the distinguished crowd. With the next high kick, she was airborne – she could have broken a high jump record on *prithvi ma*. You know what had happened? Hell's bells, we hadn't considered lunar gravity! The bloody thing was weak. *Help me, Isaac Newton*, I prayed. But there was no succour. The audience thought they were the suckers. Putli's cancan looked like some kangaroo hopping around because of haemorrhoids.

That is where the narrative of my dear friend Naushirwan Shavaksha Sheikh Chilli ended. He had died of shock. His dead body came back on the shuttle on its return trip, along with his handwritten account of his lunar trip. I, Dayalunand, saw to it that his last rites were performed in a Christian cemetery. There were no *khandiawalas*, Parsi corpse carriers, or priests left to solemnize the ceremonies. Thus went the ultimate Parsi. Kindly note that the penultimate Parsi, Mehromji Mishtidoiwala, had already died of cirrhosis. He was found with a half bottle of Black Label whisky beside him on a small peg table. The great herb by smelling which no Parsi would marry a non-Parsi had come on the demographic-cum-genetic world stage far too late.

Not so with the other herb, the Royal Sweet-Smelling something or the other, the mother of acronyms, if I may call it that. The Nagpur botanists were also back with the shuttle and I followed their trail. I had been introduced to them as Swami Sureshanand Dayalunand, and they had implicit trust in me. 'The herb you were after, have you brought it back?' I asked.

They were stunned. 'How do you know about the herb?' they gasped.

'The high-ups in Nagpur told me all about it,' I answered with affected nonchalance. They opened up.

'Have you given the herb a botanical name?'

'Swami-ji, it is called the "Royal Sweet-Smelling All-Banishing Virility Plant". Actually, it should have been named the anti-virility plant, but the cabal in Nagpur decided on this one. Once you smell it, or taste it with food, your virility vanishes. No vasectomies, no tubectomies, all that is irrelevant now. Even Viagra won't help. The herb has transcended it if I may say so.'

Within a week, the Muslims were celebrating Bakr Eid, and out of goodwill to my fellow men, I decided to go to Bhendi Bazar. I was amazed to find my botanist friends there as well as Nekramji. In huge, gargantuan *deghchis*, pulao and biryani were being cooked. Tiwari-ji came along and supervised the operation. Once the mutton biryani was ready, they started distributing it to the people who had finished their namaz. I noticed no money was being charged for the food. In an hour, more than a hundred had gobbled the biryani up. More rice, clarified butter and spices were being thrown into the cooking pots, along with big chunks of meat, as fires blazed all over. The Eid crowds were lapping the food up. I noticed that from a sack, they were also putting some powder into the pots.

'What is this powder?' I asked innocently.

'It is masala, a moon masala!'

They had no idea – the Tiwaris and Tripathis and Nekrams – that Shavaksha had left a narrative for me, and that I had read it. I immediately smelt a rat. 'Don't you think this is a bit unethical?' I asked.

'Masalas have nothing to do with ethics, Swami-ji. They touch the tongue.'

They smiled and giggled and I knew what they were trying to do. I immediately went to the police station. The officer in charge was shocked to see me. I introduced myself as Swami Sureshanand Dayalunand and he touched my feet – I would have been offended if he had not. I told him that the anti-virility herb was being mixed in huge cooking pots at the Bhendi Bazar. And an anti-potency herb was being mixed in the huge cooking pots.

'What is the brand name, Swami-ji?'

'It doesn't have a brand. It is a powder made from an herb found on the moon.' I almost felt stupid saying a thing like that. The policemen laughed. I told them that the biryani was being doled out for free outside the mosque. They laughed some more.

'There's no offence in the IPC for doling out free food, Swami-ji.'

I was asked to write down my report. When I submitted it, the officer read it, touched my feet, handcuffed me and respectfully ushered me into the lock-up. He also informed me that I was being charged with attempt to create friction between communities.

LOOKING UP

S.B. DIVYA

Ayla clutches her tab with a trembling grip and reads the words again. She can hardly believe her eyes, but the blurring message on the screen doesn't lie: she will be a passenger on the *Mayflower* expedition. Coming to Denver had been a good attempt at forgetting California, but Mars might be far enough to put her past to rest.

'Congratulations and welcome to the team! Let's make history together,' the text says. 'We commend you on being one of our most diverse candidates, proving that the *Mayflower* welcomes people of all backgrounds and abilities.'

Did they somehow measure and rank each passenger's diversity quotient? Ayla sighs. Jeff is lounging next to her on the frayed yellow sofa, his silky black hair loose across his shoulders. They're drinking a fifteen-year-old bottle of wine like there's no tomorrow, and it hits Ayla that soon there won't be any tomorrows. Not with aged wine. Not with her boyfriend.

'A penny for your thoughts, lovely lady?'

'What?' she says, quickly closing the message. 'Sorry, I'm distracted. Work stuff.'

Jeff reaches over and strokes the unmarred side of her face. 'Locking horns with Brian again?'

'Something like that.'

'You have to stop letting him push you around. He's not going to respect you until you show him some balls.'

Ayla raises her eyebrows.

'You know what I mean,' Jeff says, half smiling.

'I do, but never mind,' she murmurs and kisses him, effectively ending the discussion. Even if this relationship can't last much longer – and hers never do anyway – she wants to enjoy it while she can.

The next morning, Ayla walks into Brian's spartan office and sits down in one of the two uncomfortable chairs on the other side of his desk.

'Yes?' her manager says without turning away from his display. His gnarled fingers click on a manual mouse.

'I'm quitting.'

That gets his attention. His unnerving green eyes turn toward her, and she looks away, gazing at her knees.

'Why?'

Ayla takes a breath to give her prepared, polite excuse, and then realizes that she can afford to burn this lousy bridge. She raises her head and looks squarely into Brian's eyes.

'I'm going to Mars.' The disbelief on his face gives her a thrill of pleasure.

Brian snaps his hanging jaw closed and frowns. He turns to the giant paper calendar hanging on the wall.

'I'll need another month from you.'

'I can only do two weeks. Sorry.'

She regrets the apology as soon as it comes out and wordlessly hands him her resignation letter.

'See? That's the kind of attitude that keeps women like you from being good at these jobs.' Brian shakes his head. 'I took a lot of risk hiring you. Good thing you aren't coming back because I could never give you a reference with this kind of unprofessional behaviour.'

'The only unprofessional person here is you,' Ayla snaps, surprising herself.

Her retort is enough to shut him up, maybe out of sheer astonishment that she would say it. She'd long ago learned to prefer the company of rocks to people, especially people like Brian – but he came with the job and the job came with pay.

She leaves the office in the evening and lets her car navigate the downtown Denver traffic on her way to Aunt Sam's apartment. The tall, sprawling, assisted-living complex dominates the space between a strip mall and a tract of houses. Ayla parks her car and gazes westward at the afterglow of the setting sun. The peaks of the Rockies are still bare, but the chill October air carries a promise of snow. How strange it will be to gaze at a skyline of ochre and rust instead.

Aunt Sam lives on the fourth floor. Ayla usually takes the exterior stairs two at a time. It's a fun way to use her spring-loaded prosthesis, but today she goes slowly, stopping at each landing to savour the view. She hadn't dared to believe that she would be chosen for the mission. After all, she's a nobody. But they liked her fitness level at the first screening and her geology degree at the second. So what if her amputated foot and scarred face gave her the final advantage? It rankles, but if that's what it takes to get her to Mars, then so be it.

Samsara opens the front door before Ayla can knock.

'How did you –'

'Your tread gives it away, love. Come in. The tikka masala's almost done, and the cabernet is open. Sorry I couldn't wait on the wine.'

'I don't blame you one bit,' Ayla says, stooping to kiss her aunt's tan cheek. 'The cook deserves a glass of wine while she's in the kitchen.'

'Cooking is its own pleasure now that I'm semi-retired. My graduate students are doing most of the work.'

Ayla inhales deeply as she removes her sneaker and slips a clean sock over her prosthesis. The air is redolent with the aromas of toasted cumin, coriander, fried tomato, onions and chillies. Her mouth waters in anticipation, and she tries not to think about the blandness of food in space. Her aunt moves painstakingly around the small kitchen, but she bites her tongue before she can offer to help. She knows all too well what it's like to be on the receiving end of those offers. Instead, she perches on a counter stool and pours herself a glass of wine.

The apartment is small, just three rooms. The bedroom barely fits her aunt's bed, but the bathroom is spacious enough to hold a wheelchair. The efficiency kitchen opens to the living room, which has a firm sofa, small dining table, and an enormous screen built into one wall. Aunt Sam's walker is parked by the front door, next to the shoe rack.

'Are you getting used to this place?'

Samsara shrugs. 'It'll do.'

'It's good that you moved here,' Ayla says, feeling awkward.

'Oh? Are you and Jeff getting serious?'

'No.' Ayla takes a deep breath. 'I'm going on the *Mayflower*.'

Samsara stops stirring the masala and looks at her. Her aunt's dark brown eyes are sharp and clear. 'The what? You don't mean that one-way spaceship to Mars?'

Ayla nods, tightening her grip around the stem of the wine glass.

'Ayla! Why didn't you tell me? When? Isn't it leaving soon?'

'Eleven weeks, but I go for training in two. I'm sorry, Aunt Sam. I didn't want to tell anyone about my application in case I didn't get in.'

'They're okay with your foot?'

'More than okay. I can get a special prosthesis. It'll be great in space, better than my natural foot, and the gravity is low enough on Mars that it'll be easier on my leg muscles.'

'But – why? Why go? Is it because of Felicia, after all these years?'

Ayla avoids her aunt's gaze by taking a sip of wine. The tang of it fills her mouth and eases the tightness in her throat. Of course, it's because of Mom, but it would break Aunt Sam's heart if she heard that. Her aunt gave Ayla a second chance at life by bringing her to Denver, by raising her when no one else would. She was the only one who didn't blame Ayla for the accident.

'It's the opportunity of a lifetime,' Ayla says, studying the garnet-coloured liquid in her glass. 'I'm a geologist, and all I'm doing here are stability surveys for bloated high-rises. On Mars, my studies will make history. They'll actually mean something.' It's the truth, if only partially.

The room is quiet for several minutes. Aunt Sam turns off the stove and pulls the foil-wrapped supermarket naan from the oven. She hobbles over to the counter, holding on to its edge for support, then cups Ayla's face in her warm, dry palms.

'My dear girl, as hard as I've tried, you can't forgive yourself, can you? Mars will be an amazing accomplishment. You're right about that. But you won't find peace by running farther away.'

Trust Aunt Sam to see through her walls like they were made of crystal. They move to the dining table set for two. After twenty years of living and growing up with her aunt, there's no pressure to make talk, and Ayla takes advantage of it. She savours the chew of warm naan. Fresh cilantro and chunks of silky paneer dissolve against her tongue, and she sighs contentedly.

'I'm going to miss good food,' Ayla says. 'I miss it already, to be honest. I've been eating way too much takeout since you moved here.'

Samsara laughs. 'I can believe it, but every chef needs an appreciative audience.'

Her aunt's watch chimes, and Samsara's smile vanishes, replaced by a deep frown.

'What is it?'

'A message from your sister. It's about Carlos.'

'Dad?' A hand squeezes Ayla's heart. *This is not an emergency,* she tells herself, applying what she learned in therapy and breathing deeply. 'What about him?'

'He had a stroke.' Her aunt's eyes scan the screen.

'How bad?'

'They don't know yet. Elise says they want him under observation for at least a week, maybe two. You should go and see him, Ayla. It's been a long time and – given where you're going, that you might not come back – this could be your last chance.'

'It's been five years since he moved in with Elise.' Ayla shakes her head. 'She won't let me near him.'

'Do you want me to ask her? Maybe if you tell her your news –'

'No,' Ayla says sharply. 'My sister hasn't spoken to me in twenty years. She doesn't deserve to know anything about my life.'

The dispirited expression on her aunt's face makes her relent.

'I'll call the hospital, see if I can talk to him by phone. Okay? Let's finish the rest of our dinner in peace. Please?'

Samsara nods, and they move on to other subjects, but the meal's pleasure is tainted.

Ayla spends the rest of the weekend running her favourite mountain trails and wondering how to break the news to Jeff. He comes over for dinner on Monday night, bearing a bag full of Chinese takeout and a boisterous demeanour. Jeff tells her about his latest challenging client, but Ayla remains silent, full of restless thoughts. She crunches on egg noodles and orange-glazed chicken and wonders if she can bring dried red chillies to the colony. The pioneers of old relied on spices and spiced food for long journeys. Should Mars be any different?

She looks up from her meal when Jeff stops talking. All lightness is gone from his expression.

'What?'

'Don't you have something to tell me?' he says.

She feels sucker punched. 'How did you find out? Brian?'

'Yes.'

'That asshole!'

Jeff flings his hands outward in frustration, spattering sauce from his chopsticks across the table. 'Are you kidding? Do you have any idea how lousy I felt hearing the news from him? Mars! You're going to Mars! How could you not tell me about this?'

'We've only been dating for a couple months.' She hates the defensiveness in her tone. 'I didn't want to risk losing you if they didn't pick me.' *Besides, you'll find someone better,* she almost says out loud.

She gets up to escape the hurt in his eyes and scrapes the rest of her food into the trash can. Her watch beeps. It's a reminder to call the hospital, one that she set herself so she'd stop avoiding it. But the timing is terrible. Her plate clatters into the sink as she tries to steady her shaking hands.

'I'm sorry. I know I should've told you sooner, but it's over anyway,' she says, still facing the sink. 'I'm leaving next Saturday for training.'

'It's over all right, but it didn't have to be like this. You think you're unlovable because your face makes you ugly and that's why no one asks you out. You're wrong. It's not the scars that repel people, not the ones on the outside anyway. I would've been happy to watch you soar into the future, but I can take a hint. I hope you find what you're looking for out there.'

His chair scrapes over the tile floor. She succeeds in holding back her sobs until the front door slams shut. *It's for the best*, she tells herself. *There's no good way to break up*. They hadn't even come to the point of saying 'I love you' to each other.

Later, as she brushes her teeth, she stares at the curtain covering the bathroom mirror and wonders if Jeff was right. She holds the cloth aside and forces herself to look at her reflection. One half of her face is ordinary, a blend of boring brown tones. The other is a warped landscape, stretched taut in some areas, puckering like an angry pink mountain range in others. She lets the curtain fall. Mars won't have any mirrors to hide from.

Elise got the good looks in the family: hair the colour of rosewood, eyes like a summer sky, sweetly bowed lips. How does her sister looks now, after twenty years and two kids? Thinking of her reminds Ayla of her dad, and she imagines him lying in a hospital bed, wondering if his other child cares about him any more.

She grabs her tab as she walks into the bedroom and calls up flights to Los Angeles. There's an evening option for the following Friday, her last day of work. She books it and changes her Corpus Christi flight to Sunday, from Los Angeles. One day with her immediate family – more than enough – then off to mission training.

Her sleep that night is restless. She dreams of spice barrels coming loose and floating like bloated, drunken bears through the *Mayflower*'s cargo hold.

Ten days later, Ayla steps out of the air-conditioned terminal into the warm Los Angeles night. Exhaust fumes mix with the scent of sea salt and evoke memories of driving along the coast in her mother's old convertible. She wonders for the hundredth time since boarding the airplane if she should have come.

She merges on to the freeway and is instantly snarled in seven lanes of traffic. She switches the car to auto-follow. It creeps along and passes a fly-by-night costume store. Her stomach clenches as she remembers the date. *Tomorrow is Halloween*. Lost in all of the Mars preparations, she has, for the first time in her life, overlooked the holiday.

'Damn,' she whispers to the dashboard.

Ayla resumes control of the car and pulls off the freeway, driving through a posh stretch of Santa Monica before heading north along the coast. Here and there, clusters of costumed teenagers are out partying early. She opens the windows and lets in the ocean breeze, fresh and moist. Her curls break loose, flying across her face, but she doesn't care as she loses herself in the buried, painful memories that she's been keeping away.

Ayla, age six, wanted desperately to be a robot, as did her best friends, Emma and Shaden. The three of them decided to coordinate, cobbling together their costumes from cardboard, dryer vents, and liberal amounts of duct tape. They were a hit at every house, wandering the hilly streets of their suburban Calabasas neighbourhood and collecting more than their fair share of candy.

Emma's Dad and Ayla's Mom were their chaperones for the night, happily taking their pictures in front of the more elaborately decorated homes. The street lights glowed yellow-orange, and Shaden pretended they were on Mars, that his LED ring light was a laser.

The sidewalks were crowded, though, and they couldn't easily run in their bulky costumes. Still, Ayla wanted to play, so she tore off a sparkly sticker and wrapped it around the tip of her index finger.

'Pew! Pew!' she shouted, waving her finger at Shaden and then at her mom who laughed and nudged Emma's dad.

Ayla stumbled over something. She looked down and saw a silver-handled toy gun.

'Watch out! I have a laser gun,' she yelled, grabbing it and pointing it at her mom. 'Pew!'

She pulled the trigger.

It's the sounds and the smells that Ayla can't forget: the horrible popping noise over the din of the crowds; the screams, some of which were her own; the smoke that stung her nostrils before they filled with blood.

West Hills is a different hospital than it was twenty years ago, but Ayla shuts down the part of her brain that wants to compare the ICU ward then versus now.

'I'm here to see Carlos Butler,' she says to the receptionist.

'Your name?'

'Ayla Narayan-Butler.'

The receptionist frowns at her display. 'I don't see it on the list. We only have another five minutes before visiting hours end. I'm sorry, but you'll have to come back tomorrow.'

Ayla represses a sigh. 'What time?'

'Nine o'clock.'

Ayla wanders back to the parking lot and slides her claim key into the valet machine. As she waits for the car, she considers sending Elise a message, but she's saved by the car's arrival. The empty vehicle pulls to a stop at the curb, and Ayla slides into the driver's seat. She drives without thinking too much about where she's going, feeling her way through streets that are vaguely familiar like scenes from a faded filmstrip.

The first few months after the shooting, Ayla was in and out of the hospital for reconstructive surgery so often that she was barely conscious. They told her later that the slide on the semi-automatic had blown backward, shearing off half her face in the process, but she was numbed by an influx of medication. She lost her memories of that time in the haze of opiates. When she was in her right mind, she felt Elise's fury in a thousand tiny ways – excluding her from games, cutting off bits of her stuffed animals, knocking over her now clumsy body 'by accident'.

Dad was submerged in his own grief most of the time, but whenever he did look at Ayla, at her mangled face and absent foot, she could feel his revulsion. Only her aunt was sharp enough to realize what was happening. After a year and a half of pleading, Samsara convinced Dad to let her go to Denver. He visited once a year until he could no longer travel, but he always came on his own, without Elise.

Ayla pushes the past behind as the shape of the neighbourhood becomes excruciatingly familiar. There – that's the street where it happened, and that's her own street. She turns the car and slowly rolls by her former home. A light is on upstairs, but she can't see anyone. A silver minivan is parked in the driveway, and the lawn is conspicuously absent of Halloween decorations.

She stops the car in the cul-de-sac and sits, shaking from head to feet. She feels a pang for Elise's children, deprived of both a grandmother and the pleasure of Halloween, and it was all her fault.

As grief and guilt threaten to drown her, she breathes deeply and imagines herself taking the memories and locking them away in a large, heavy, metal box. The trembling and the emotions gradually subside. She closes her eyes and buries the metal box deep under the earth, to be left behind forever. This house isn't her home, nor is this planet. When a semblance of peace returns, she searches the car's navigation system and spends the night at the first hotel on the list.

Halloween morning dawns. The sky is fittingly gray and laden with clouds. Ayla stands in the hospital lobby and stares at her watch, paralysed with indecision. She glances up at the sound of a woman's voice and sees the back of a brunette head at the reception desk. Before she can decide whether she wants to be noticed or not, Elise turns and sees her. For a moment, Elise doesn't seem to recognize her, but then realization dawns.

Elise strides over. 'You! You unbelievable little – What are you doing here? Do you realize what day it is?'

A flush creeps up Ayla's cheeks, and she hunches as she nods. She focuses on the patterns of the industrial carpet beneath their feet.

'I came to see Dad.' Her muscles tense with the urge to run out of the hospital and never come back.

'And you chose today, of all days, to visit him. You are such a selfish, self-absorbed –' Elise stops and draws a deep breath, then lets it out audibly. 'You'll never change, will you?' She taps her foot. 'I suppose you have a right to see him. I'll take you in, but I'm not putting you on the visitor's list.'

Bands of pressure tighten around Ayla's chest. She focuses on her breath as she follows Elise through the security doors and into the ward. She'll say her farewell to Dad, and once she's on Mars none of this will matter. She can put it behind her forever.

Elise opens the door and leans against the wall outside, arms crossed. 'You have fifteen minutes. Hospital rules. Don't upset him!'

The door shuts behind Ayla. Her dad is hooked up to a bevy of monitors that are mercifully silent, but their coloured lines wriggle eloquently across the screens. The room is a plush single, furnished with dark wooden cabinets, an armchair, and an attached bathroom, though, judging by all the tubes running in and out of her father's body, he won't need the facilities anytime soon.

She sits by the bed on a wheeled stool.

'Hi, Dad.'

Her father's head lolls toward her, but his eyes are glazed and unfocused.

'Felicia. You're here,' he rasps.

The good side of her face resembles her mother's. She turns so he can see all of her.

'No, Dad, it's me, Ayla. I came to see you…to see how you're doing… and to tell you something.'

Her father's trembling hand gropes around on the bed until it finds hers. He curls his fingers lightly, and his eyelids droop.

'I've missed you so much, Fel. Why didn't … when …'

The rest of his words are too soft to hear. Ayla leans close until his papery lips brush her ear and his stubbled chin scratches her cheek.

'Forgive me, Fel…terrible thing...little Ayla. I let Samsara take her… was a mistake. Stupid…lost. You left me alone… Ah, I've missed you.'

Ayla has been waiting her entire life to hear these words, but not like this, not like she's eavesdropping on her mother's ghost. She pulls back. Her father's eyes are closed, and his whispery voice trails off into silence. She wants to tell him that she forgives him, that she loves him and understands, but it's not her blessing that he wants.

'Dad, I have some news,' Ayla says, swallowing against tears. 'I'm going to Mars. I'll be on a ship called the *Mayflower*, and it leaves in a couple of months. I probably won't be back, not ever. I'm…' she stops. The words stick in her throat, and she forces them out. 'I'm here to say goodbye.'

She can't tell if any of her words register, but she hopes that some part of him will remember them when he wakes up. She takes a deep, shaky breath and lightly kisses his cheek. His face is peaceful, but it hits her that he looks old – old and fragile like she's never seen him before.

'You're going to be fine,' she says, wishing it to be true. 'I'll send you a postcard from Mars.'

She walks out of the room and finds Elise gone. Her shoulders tense as she strides away, waiting for her sister to chase her. But no one comes, and then she's outside and away.

Ayla spends the rest of the day at Zuma Beach watching the surf crash. Gulls squawk, and the sand is littered with prone bodies worshipping the sun, but there is not a single reminder that it's Halloween Day. The sight of the ocean makes an indelible memory: the vastness of it, the colours from turquoise to silver and sapphire; the way the foam traces chaotic patterns before vanishing underground. These are the colours of the earth. Her future is one of brown and red, the colours of her heart.

She holds on to those images in the following weeks at Corpus Christi, returning to them when she needs to escape the presence of her crewmates – her lifemates. Some of them are already forming romantic attachments, but she holds herself apart. It's not hard. Men have always found it difficult to look past her deformities, and she doesn't mind now. She belongs to Mars.

Ayla spends her three days of leave in Denver with Aunt Sam. They ring in the New Year together, toasting with champagne and caviar. Samsara even drags Ayla to a party with some of her graduate students to show off her celebrity niece. They both avoid any mention of the past until it's time to say goodbye.

'I wish you could've had one last day with your dad,' Aunt Sam says as they stand next to the taxi. Her breath fogs in the sharp morning air.

'I can text him from the *Mayflower* and occasionally after we get the colony set up. It won't be much different from what we've done here.'

Samsara looks at her strangely.

'What?'

'How… You can't…'

The taxi chimes to remind Ayla to get in, but Ayla stays still, watching her aunt's face and feeling confused.

'Nobody mentioned you at the funeral,' Samsara says. Her voice is heavy with anger and regret. 'I assumed you couldn't come because you were at training. What a stupid person I've been! It never occurred to me that she wouldn't tell you.'

'Funeral? You mean – Dad's *dead*?'

'I'm so sorry, love. I thought you knew.'

'Not your fault,' Ayla says reflexively.

The taxi chimes again, and they give each other a long, tight hug before Ayla gets in. Her cheeks are wet from her aunt's tears, but she's numb inside, reeling from the news. Anger builds inside her on the drive to the airport. If she owed Elise nothing, then perhaps the same was true in return, but not when it came to Dad. His life belonged to both of them.

She finds herself at the check-in counter saying, 'I'd like to change my ticket. I need a flight to LAX, and I need to be in Corpus Christi tonight.'

'Let me see,' the agent says. 'We can get you on a noon flight to LAX, but you'll have to move fast. It arrives at 1.30, and there's a 5.30 p.m. flight out to Houston that gets you in at 10.30 p.m. That's the best I can do.'

Ayla checks the map on her tab. She can drive from Houston to the *Mayflower* base in four hours. It would mean arriving in the middle of the night, but she wouldn't miss the final morning briefing.

'I'll take it. Both flights.'

Ayla's stomach clenches with hope and fear all the way through the snarl of Los Angeles weekend traffic, right up to their – Elise's – house. She knocks on the navy blue door. When it opens, Ayla looks up from the cheery 'WELCOME' mat, but not very far. A tiny person with curly brown hair, rather like her own, peers at her.

'Uh – is your Mom home?'

'Mom!' bellows the child, running off and leaving the door ajar.

Elise stops halfway down the stairs when she sees Ayla at the door. Ayla feels herself trembling and rushes the words out before she loses her nerve.

'How could you? How could you let me miss Dad's funeral, too?'

Elise storms down, out, and closes the door behind her, forcing Ayla to back up a few steps. Now that she's closer, Ayla sees the lines and shadows on her sister's face, which is also pinched with fury.

'It's not my fault you're running off to Mars, like you ran off to Denver. That's all you know how to do, right? Run away! What do you care if Dad's dead or alive? You weren't here. You weren't the one looking after him.'

'You didn't let me help!'

'Because I knew you wouldn't. Do you have any idea how much it hurt us when you left with Aunt Sam? You killed Mom, and then you abandoned me and Dad.'

'Abandoned?' Ayla says, her voice raw and shaky. 'I saw how much you hated me. And Dad – he couldn't even look at me! I thought you wanted to get rid of me.'

The tension between them erodes, like grains of sand into the ocean, and regret with the patina of two decades arrives to take its place.

'He was never the same after you moved away. I hated you so much for that, for what you did to him.'

'He said – at the hospital – he said he wished he hadn't sent me away.

I didn't want to go, Elise, not really. This was home. I thought I was helping. I thought, maybe, you could forgive me and move on with your life once I was gone.'

'So you could do the same? Admit it! You want to move on, too.'

Heart hammering, Ayla whispers, 'Yes.'

'Why didn't you fix your face?'

Ayla traces the old scars with her fingertips. 'To remember. To punish myself. I don't deserve to look normal.'

'So you can wallow in self-pity? There were times when I felt sorry for you.' Elise sighs. 'I've been seeing a therapist again, after Dad died. He says we need forgiveness from each other, but also from ourselves. You deserve to be happy, Ayla. I do, too.'

Tears surge behind Ayla's eyes.

'How do I forgive myself? And you – not telling me about Dad, when you knew I was in the hospital for Mom's funeral – how do I forgive you for that?'

Elise looks away, past Ayla, to the distant hills. 'That's up to you.'

Ayla stares at her sister's face, almost a stranger's face, and the anger drains out of her body as if the earth is drawing it through her feet. She lifts her shoulders and chin and inhales deeply, filling her lungs with regret and breathing out stale anger. She imagines her father's body lying next to her mother's, restored to the side of the woman he loved. He must have forgiven Ayla. She owed it to him to do the same.

'I forgive you, Elise, and I'll work on granting it to myself. I want to leave in peace.'

The front door opens and the same child peers out.

'Mom? What are you doing? Who are you talking to?'

'Come out, Ashwin. Come meet your Aunt Ayla.'

The boy stands by Elise's side and stares with wide brown eyes. His resemblance to her – and his grandmother – is striking. Ayla kneels so they're level with each other.

'Hello,' she says, holding out her hand for a shake.

He grins and gives it a big shake.

'I'm building a rocketship with my Legos. Do you want to see?'

'I wish I could, but I'm afraid I have a real rocket to catch.'

'Where are you going?'

'Mars.'

'Wow!' He looks up at Elise. 'When can we go to Mars?'

Elise lays her hand on his head. 'Maybe when you're older.' Her lips turn up in a small smile as she looks at Ayla. 'Maybe you'll go visit your aunt someday.'

'I'd like that,' Ayla says, and stands.

'Can I go in?' Ashwin loud-whispers to Elise.

She nods, and they watch as he dashes back into the house.

'I suppose he's my reminder of you and Mom,' Elise says with a broken laugh. 'I wish we'd done this sooner, that you could've gotten to know the boys. At least you met Ashwin. Paco – my older one – is at his friend's house.'

Ayla reaches for Elise's hand. She squeezes it lightly before letting go. 'I'll write you?'

'Yes. Of course. We'll stay in touch.'

Ayla's last image as she drives away is of her sister, standing in the driveway of their childhood home, arms wrapped around herself against the chill.

She replays their conversation, over and over, as she drives to Corpus Christi. The regret stings: all the years she missed, not seeing her nephews as babies, not being a part of their lives. *Is Mars a mistake?* Will that be her next great regret?

Ayla considers turning around. Highway 77 is devoid of cars, and she pulls into the grassy median and stops. She steps outside and looks up.

'What should I do?' she whispers.

The stars blaze overhead in a giant bowl over the plains. They beckon her, reassure her. *If it hadn't been for the mission,* they murmur, *this reconciliation would never have happened. Be glad for what the future holds.*

As she climbs back into the car, Ayla realizes that at last she can let go of the past. She can start afresh, not because she can leave her past behind, but because it will anchor her as she ventures onward and outward. She gets on the highway and continues through Corpus Christi to the base.

The *Mayflower* stretches up into the night sky, ablaze in floodlights and drawing her in like a beacon in a storm. The silver scaffolding hugs the ship, but she can already feel the struts falling away. She's light enough to fly.

REUNION

VANDANA SINGH

When Mahua wakes up, the first thing she sees is a map. It is a map of her life's journey, it is her heart's desire, it is the abstract landscape of the new science, the new knowledge she has helped develop. More mundanely, it is the cracked plaster on the ceiling. In some places, the cracks remind her of the map of Delhi when she was a student there; other places are like the aerial view of the Gangetic delta. Smaller cracks branch off the wider ones, and so on, and so on, and some even connect to other cracks, forming a web as delicate as the veins of a leaf. She can lie in bed for hours, observing the ceiling, reminiscing, making metaphorical leaps, intellectual exercises that only delay the inevitable. But, later today, the journalist will be coming. The thought of him, and the news that he might bring – about Raghu, after all these years! Pain stabs her heart. *I must be prepared.* The man from Brazil is only bringing her the confirmation that she needs. She doesn't see journalists any more – they tend to hail her as the heroine of the Great Turning, the *Maha Parivartan* – such nonsense! But this man, he said he had some information about Raghu. She breathes deeply and deliberately until the anxiety dissolves and rises carefully from the bed. She stands on her own two slightly shaky legs, acknowledging their loyalty to her body for over seven decades.

Later, in the kitchen, she makes a cup of tea in the semi-darkness. The others will be downstairs soon – she can hear creaks, mumbles, the sleepy, shuffling walk to the bathroom upstairs, the muted sounds of the flush. The domicile houses 23 people, so the three bathrooms require a patience for queues and some bladder control. Sipping her tea by the window, she watches the sunrise, accompanied by the dawn chorus of mynahs, doves, jungle babblers and birds she can't identify. The light is sufficient now for the shadows to have acquired clarity – the trees in their mist-wrapped greenery, the vegetable gardens between the domiciles lower down the hill. From her vantage point, she is looking south-west toward what was once Mumbai, the greatest of all cities of the Age of Kuber. In the distance, the glass towers rise above the drowned streets, glinting gold where they catch the low light of the sun. She can see dark patches and holes like blind eyes on the sides of the buildings, where storms and human violence have taken out the windows. The sea has reclaimed the city – fish now swim in what was once Charni Road, and crabs and mussels have taken up residence in the National Stock Exchange. The fisherfolk ply their boats and barges in the watery streets, and she thinks she can hear their calls mixed with the cries of seabirds on the wind.

She turns – the child Mina is running down the stairs two steps at a time, her hair a tousled mass. 'Did I miss it?'

'No. Come and look!'

They stand at the window together. At the bottom of the hill, shrouded in the semi-darkness, is the river, waiting for the sun to edge its way above the hills to the east. *There!* The light breaks over the rim. The lazy meander of the river through the land is like a word written in fire. The sun is full on it; the new marsh, dark by contrast, edges the brightness like rust on a sword. This is poetry, this moment, the sun's brushstroke on the water. The suntower on the opposite hill is turning slowly, its petals opening to the light. As they watch, a flock of ducks rise high over the mangroves at the edge of the marsh, wheeling in a sinuous half-arc and settling again among the reeds.

The Mithi River is running full because of the monsoons. Twenty years ago, the edge of the river had been a waste dump, bordered by shoddily built high-rises. The developer mafia had held the reclamation project at bay until the superstorms came, levelling buildings, forcing the river to flow backwards and inundate the city with decades of effluents, sewage and other refuse. Mahua had joined a citizen's group engaged in cleaning the city, and she had eventually recruited them to turn the abused lands into a mangrove wetland that would restore the ecology and clean the water. *Protect us from storm surges. Natural sewage treatment. Experiment with the new ways of living.* She remembers the arguments in the citizen councils, and all that it had taken to win over vested interests. Years and years of work, during which the seas rose, and Mumbai became an archipelago again, and resettlement became a crisis of enormous proportions. All these years later her reward is this daily ritual with the child, watching from the window. *Raghu, if only you were here!* Each time, she sees the ducks flying over the suntower, turning in a wide arc to settle on the marsh in the dawn light, her heart beats a little faster, a *drut* of joy.

'Has he come yet, the journalist?'

'No, Mina. But he just pinged me. He'll be two hours late. It's the water taxis. They're always slower in the rainy season.'

'But it's not raining now! Aaji, tell me again about your friend Raghu.'

'Later. Let me give the goats a treat.'

All morning, Mahua has been helping the children shell peas. Now she gets up slowly and takes the empty pea pods over to the goat shed. The air is moist with the promise of rain. The house is a dome, a green mound, its roof and walls almost entirely covered with the broad leaves of three different kinds of gourds. The peas grow at the ground level, but the boundary between house and garden is not at all clear. The house is at the top of the hill, and she has a good view of the *basti* she has helped create, the newest one of hundreds of experimental settlements scattered throughout the country.

Once a *basti* of this design was just a dream. Look at it now, the persistence of that dream, the dwellings on this hill: dome-shaped to reduce the impact of the storms, thick walls of clay, straw and recycled brick, covered with greenery, the architecture a marriage of the ancient and the modern. The walkways follow the natural contours of the land. The vegetables cascade off the walls on vines, and down the hill, At the next house, the children are harvesting them, monkey-like, on rope ladders, before the monkeys come. The nearest suntower rises like a prayer to the sun on the next rise, its petals open to the light, speaking through electronic messages to the next one, and the next one, distributing power according to algorithms developed by the networks themselves. This *basti*, like most of its kind, is embedded with sensors that monitor and report a constant stream of data – temperature, humidity, energy use, carbon storage, chemical contaminants, biodiversity. If Mahua wears her Shell, she will have access, visual and auditory, to any and all of the data streams.

There had been a time when she was never without a Shell in her ear and a fully sensorized visor. But in the last few years, the visor has been lying in a box, gathering dust, and she's been leaving the Shell by her bedside. Recently, she has been feeling the effects of aging, and it is a new, strange feeling to acknowledge the body – she, who has led such a rich life of the mind. Her doctors want her to wear medical sensors, but she has refused. There's something she's been listening for, she thinks, watching the goats. She's been waiting for a change.

Mahua's particular talent has always been the recognition of patterns and relationships. Whenever she has had a shift of perspective or revelation, it has been preceded by a feeling of waiting – as though her unconscious knows well beforehand that something new is coming. But why now, so long after she has stopped doing active work? What has she been waiting for, apart from confirmation of Raghu's death in the Amazon? When she first moved to the Mumbai shores for good, 27 years ago, she used to watch the western sea for his arrival, in defiance of all reason. Reason had won, eventually.

What old age has taught her is patience. The epiphany, if that is what it is, will come in its own time. For now, for today, she has to prepare herself for the journalist's visit, for the reality of Raghu's death. *How did we get to this point, old friend, in our lives, in history?*

History is not a straight line. That's Raghu's voice in her mind, but she's saying it with him as she wanders back to sit in her chair. The children are having an argument over whether the biggest gourd – a pumpkin – is ripe enough to harvest. Mahua looks over at the western sea, from which he would have come, if he were coming, and sees how the light of the sun is shattered by the water's surface into diamonds.

The past is a palimpsest. She imagines unrolling it – the surface is smooth, like vellum, but as she moves her hand over it, the words fade and disappear, to be replaced by a new script that is slowly revealed to the light. And touching the new lines, they, too, fade, and in their place appears what lies underneath. What is the last layer – if there is one? She's dreaming over her second cup of tea in the garden chair, oblivious to the children's voices. The palimpsest. Faces, voices, word fragments appear, disappear.

When Mahua had been a child in Delhi – between the scholarship that had rescued her from the slums and the start of college – she had been afflicted by a disease she could scarcely remember now, except for the fatigue, the lines of worry between her grandmother's brows and the smell of boiled rice and strange herbs. At the time, there hadn't been much to do but lie in bed and look out of her second-floor window into the branches of an old mango tree. It stood in a small courtyard, the only greenery enclosed in a block of cheap flats where the roof leaked in the monsoons and one could hear the arguments of neighbours through the thin walls. But in the leafy, airy spaces of the tree, there were small, daily dramas. A black drongo chased off a cheel coming back to strut on the branches and fluff its feathers. A line of large ants moved over the bark, negotiating each tiny gully, each ravine, with mathematical precision. A bird's nest, with the eggs a blue surprise, and later the ever-open mouths of nestlings. Too feverish to think clearly, she had let go of herself, crawling with the ants, soaring with the cheel. It had been an escape from her illness, her incarceration and, as she later understood, an expansion of her own limited self. Her cousin, Kalpana-di, home from work, would sit Mahua up to lean against her, and spoon rice water into her mouth while her grandmother went out to buy vegetables. Later, she had never had the courage to ask her grandmother precisely what kind of illness she had had; secretly, it was one of the happiest memories of her childhood.

As she grew up, she practised this letting go, this hyper-awareness. It helped to be a student of the sciences because that added another dimension. Walking in the rain, she would imagine the drops coalescing in clouds high up, then falling, faster and faster until drag reduced the acceleration to zero. She imagined the fat drops coasting down, shaped by surface tension and gravity, little water bags bursting against the concrete rooftops of the lab buildings, leaving a circular signature, a ring of daughter drops. Imagining she was there in the moist, cloudy heights, she was falling, refracting light, buffeted by wind, ridden by bacteria that travelled by cloud. She would be startled out of this reverie by a drop falling on her head, or her hand, and that would snap her back into herself, but not without a laugh of comradeship with water, with the clouds. It was a weird way to be. Impossible to explain to her grade-driven, ambitious fellow students, who scoffed at anything remotely poetic.

Her classmates had mocked and teased her for her poverty and her dark skin. '*Junglee*' they had called her, although she had lived in Delhi most of her life and knew nothing about her maternal grandmother's people. Her grandmother had tried to teach her something of their origins, but the grinding toil of life in the slum, followed by the pressure of studies after the scholarship changed their lives, left no time for anything but the imperatives of the present. Within only a few years at the elite school, the *junglee* shocked her classmates by topping the final exams. Grumbles about reservations gave way to a resentful silence when it became clear that this demonstration of academic excellence was a trend, not a one-off. Those were difficult years – she would not have got through it all without her grandmother's determination and Kalpana di's affectionate presence – Kalpana di, whose life and death she still could not remember without pain.

'Kalpana-di, help me with my homework!'

The two of them would sit cross-legged on the bed, and Kalpana di would look at Mahua's mathematics notebook. After about an hour, she would say, with a little laugh, 'Mahua, your sister is not as clever as you! Let's eat something, then you try again. You can do it!'

Working into the night, Mahua would come upon the solution to the problem. Beside her, Kalpana-di would have fallen asleep, a faint smile on her lips.

Kalpana-di laughed no matter whether she was happy or sad. Fuelled by a desire to improve her lot, she had been the first to leave their village in Bihar. In Delhi, she had been a maid in rich people's houses, and had saved to go to night school so that she could get her school certificate and move up in the world. When Mahua's grandmother and mother arrived, with the newborn Mahua, they had stayed in the slum in Mehrauli with Kalpana.

When Mahua was in high school and doing well, Kalpana decided she, too, wanted to go to college. It was then Mahua's turn to tutor her. Kalpana di grasped ideas, but slowly, and had to repeat rules of mathematics or grammar so that they would not slip out of her mind.

'I am slow, I am slow,' she would say, laughing. 'Things go out of my mind very quickly. I'll try again.'

'It's that fall you had when you were a child,' Mahua's grandmother would say, shaking her head. 'Fell off a tree, hurt her head. Now she can't remember anything unless she repeats it a hundred times!'

Later, Kalpana had gone to live in her college hostel, thanks to a grant for underprivileged students. Whenever Mahua asked how she was doing, Kalpana would laugh and say all was well. But, after a while, her eyes turned sad, and her ready laugh sounded forced. It was only later that Mahua put two and two together. Kalpana-di's fellow students – privileged, upper class – were like aliens from another world. Her English was utilitarian, but they were at home in it; their mannerisms and customs were unlike anything she had encountered. There were sexual orgies in the hostel to which she was mockingly invited. She was teased constantly by a group of college boys who called her Essie Esty, and mocked her dark skin and slow mind. She started failing her courses, but she was too ashamed to tell her family, especially now that Mahua was doing so well. In her suicide note, she wrote that three boys – sons of rich businessmen and government officers – offered to help her with the final exams in return for sex. Having been teased for what she herself had come to think of as her ugliness and her heavily accented English, she assumed at first that this was another cruel joke. But the boys were serious, she wrote. They said that nobody would want to marry her, so why not get a little experience?

The next few lines had been crossed out so many times that they were unreadable. 'I can't bear it,' she wrote at the end of the letter. 'You'll be better off without me. Forgive me.'

The police investigation came to nothing – the three young men had resources that Mahua's grandmother did not. For months afterwards, Mahua carried within her a fierce and all-consuming anger. She couldn't get the image out of her mind: Kalpana-di's body hanging from the curtain rod in her hostel room. Not knowing what to do with her rage, Mahua turned to her studies with increased vigour, carrying off honours and awards, feeling, after every victory, a vengeful satisfaction. *For you, Kalpana-di*, she would say to herself.

Mahua formed her first tentative friendships in college, but her friends tended to think of her as an oddball genius. When she described her out-of-body experiments of comradeship with water or birds or ants, they called her brilliant and strange, and changed the subject. At first this upset her – she felt passionately that what she had, this desire and ability to be companionably present with the non-human and the inanimate, was something potentially important, that it could be developed and learned by anyone and improved with practice. But nobody believed her when she tried to explain. It was one of her first life lessons – that most people are content to live within their perceived limitations.

After that, she stopped talking about it. But it got her interested in the development of ways for people to sense the information flows around them – between matter and matter, inanimate and otherwise. Eventually, this led her to the work that would make her famous: the development of embedded intelligence agents in the inanimate world, the creation of the modern, sensate city.

But in her undergraduate years, those were distant visions. She was determined to stay on the path she had chosen for herself: to study engineering, to make a mark in the world, to make her grandmother proud of her. She would go out sometimes with her friends to movies or to parties, but always kept herself aloof from close relationships – until she fell in love with a fellow student called Vikas. They were interested in the same things and had started studying together. He was good-looking and treated her with respect. She had never thought of herself as pretty but in his company, she felt beautiful. One night, while studying late for an exam, they went out for a drink. In the crowded, noisy bar, they touched glasses, grasped hands and kissed.

To her, the kiss was the promise of the companionship she had never had, of both mind and body. The next day she felt alive in an entirely new way, exquisitely aware of her body's language, the stirrings of desire. So when Vikas asked her to spend the night, she nodded shyly. 'It's not like we can be serious or anything,' he said the next morning as they lay in bed. 'You know, my family and all. But we can have a little fun, can't we?'

Her blood ran cold. 'Never speak to me again,' she told him as she left.

After that, she became wary of intimate relationships. When she met Raghu at a conference, she was open to the possibility of a friendship, nothing more. Domesticity, in any case, was not for her. Other people had families and children; she had ideas. That was the way it was meant to be.

Raghu had been a student of time. A scion of a well-off family, he had walked away from his old life, divorced himself from his past to study the possibilities of the future. His talents took him to climatology and eventually, to creating virtual reality renditions of possible futures. His simulator mapped out paths to the future based on climate models, and a continually adjustable jiggle matrix allowed for incoming data to change future predictions. One could sit in the simulator dome and have a full-on sensory experience of a chosen future.

His immersion in one possible future for Delhi had nearly killed him. He had violated his own safety protocols and conducted the experiment alone. He had begun by following the brightest thread of probability and falling into that future. The first time they met, he described it to Mahua so vividly, she could see it in her mind's eye.

He's lying in the sand, in the relentless heat. The sand half buries his old home in Lajpat Nagar. Everyone who could leave has left on the Great Migration north. His walk through the abandoned city has filled him with horror – he has seen the shattered remains of once-tall buildings, windows of buried houses peering out of sand dunes, an emaciated corpse leaning against the wall, holding a bundle in its arms that could be a child. He was supposed to join the great exodus – why is he here? The heat is terrible: 37 °C but made fatal by the humidity. Above 35 °C, too much humidity makes it impossible for the body to cool by sweating. There is no getting around the laws of thermodynamics. Death is less than five hours away. He lies on his side, weak with exhaustion, and he sees a lizard on the window sill of the house in front of him. How is it something is still alive here? Oh Dilli, that has existed for 5,000 years to end like this!

'I looked up and saw the flyover, the arches of roadways, against the sky ending in mid-air,' he told Mahua. 'Around me were the relics of our era – the Age of Kuber – abandoned cars, toppled statues of prime ministers. Everything was destroyed, everything abandoned. I knew I was going to die there. I kept looking at the lizard. Magnificent creature, it had a crest going down its back. I thought maybe it was a weird, surreal manifestation of the jiggle matrix. But I desperately wanted it to be real – the only other thing in that devastation that was alive.'

'What happened then?' Mahua said, her eyes round with wonder. They had been talking for two hours straight in the conference reception room, oblivious to the conversations around them, the clinking of wine glasses and the waiters carrying tiny samosas on trays. For both of them this first meeting felt like coming home.

'Well, my friend Vincent happened to come to the lab because he had forgotten his notes for a presentation the next day. Saw me twitching in the sim dome. Pulled the plug. I was in hospital for a week.'

'But why? You weren't really experiencing a heat stroke.'

'Ah, but it felt so real that my body sweated out a lot of water. I was cold, I was dehydrated, going into some kind of shock. Learned my lesson. We've just integrated the entire system with safety nets so thick not even an ant could fall through them. But it takes too much energy to run. So I'm not sure anyone's actually going to invest in it.'

'What's your motivation for the VR immersion? Why not stick to the usual data visualizations?'

Raghu's eyes lit up. 'That's a much longer conversation. Shall we flee this farce and go find a restaurant? I'm hungry.' In the restaurant, over biryani and kebabs, he explained. 'See, the trouble with climate modelling, actually, with any kind of complex systems modelling is that the modeller – that's me – is always on the outside, looking in. That's fine if you are trying to figure out future trends for a company or something that's really outside yourself. But climate is not outside us, we are part of the earth's system, we influence and are influenced by climate. I think if we only look at data at a remove, we will miss something.'

Looking at his eager, earnest face, his hands gesticulating, Mahua had the realization that here, at last, was somebody she could really talk to.

Raghu was as social and friendly as Mahua was quiet and reserved, and he liked frequent, uncomplicated, honest sex with willing partners without strings on either side. His partners always talked well of him, often with nostalgic smiles. But he never treated Mahua with anything other than a friendly regard. As she got close to him, she assumed that she was outside his range of choices, just as she had been for Vikas. Once, they stayed up all night on the steps of the university library, sharing their life histories, and she told him about Vikas. 'I know now that I don't want to marry,' she said. 'My work is my life. But it was the way he assumed that I was not – I could not – be a serious contender for a relationship. Ever since, if somebody gets too close to me, I want to tear his throat out.'

Raghu didn't laugh. 'You've been hurt,' he said gently. 'Give it time. Not everyone is like Vikas.'

Later, she realized that he was attracted to her, but knowing her history, he did not want to push her in any way. He was waiting for her to make the first move. When she first went to him, filled with a great deal of trepidation and terror, it was not easy. For her, it would never come easy to surrender her last refuge, her body, to another person. Raghu's gentleness, the way he looked at her as an equal, a fellow human being with desires and vulnerabilities, slowly took the edge off her rage and confusion, but it didn't feel right. It was always too much of an effort for her to be comfortable with the body's desires. It was easier, in those days, to swear off such intimate relationships. So, they parted as lovers, but their friendship deepened.

Raghu would delight her grandmother by coming home and cooking for them. He learned songs from the old lady in her native tongue, and they would laugh and sing in the kitchen. Mahua's grandmother had been a traditional healer in her village, and he would bring illustrated botanical tomes to her and ask her about this plant or that one. He would break dates with lovers to be with them. Not since Kalpana di had lived with them had the household felt so joyful.

Raghu's restless mind stimulated Mahua's own. He brought her whatever excited him at the moment – research papers, science fiction novels and tomes on radical urban design. Modern industrial civilization had been battling nature for nearly three centuries now, he said, and look at the result – the unravelling of the very systems that provided us with oxygen, fresh air, water, and a liveable temperature range. How could you call such a system a success? The hubris of the Age of Kuber, as he termed the madness of the mid-twenty-first century, lay in the assumption of humans being outside of nature. 'Yet we breathe, sweat, shit, fuck. What a delusion! Mainstream economics – the greatest of scams!' And he would raise a glass of beer, or a cup of tea, in mock salutation.

Outside the citadels of power, uprisings and disturbances were sweeping the countryside. In Bihar and Jharkhand, a network of Santhali women's cooperatives had stopped in its tracks a major project that involved replacing forests with photosynthesis-enhancing artificial trees. In Odisha and Andhra Pradesh, transport workers had declared the largest strike in history when the first robot train made its inaugural run. In Karnataka, fields of experimental crops managed by Ultracorp were set on fire by thousands of farmers.

By this time Mahua thought of herself as a progressive urbanite, a scientist and technologist entirely at home in Delhi. She had garnered some respect for her ideas. Her straight, swift-paced, challenging walk, which she had developed as a defence against the classmates who had teased her in school, could part crowds and silence lecture halls as she strode in. When Raghu talked about the increasing importance of traditional ecological knowledge, she agreed, read the papers on the subject, but felt unable to own her origins. Her grandmother had never forced her to do so, and nor had Mahua ever taken advantage of the reservation system. Even being a woman had become parenthetical to her existence. She was an engineer, full stop.

'For heaven's sake, woman, you're human!'

'Shut up, Raghu, please! Can we go back to looking at the energy distribution simulations –'

Mahua was obsessed with the problem of scale. To move civilization away from self-destruction required massive changes – one small, experimental zero-carbon *basti* was not going to make one whit of difference in a world facing biosphere failure on a global scale. At the same time, extreme weather was driving local conflicts – mass migrations were already beginning from areas that were now uninhabitable due to extreme temperature and rising sea levels.

One evening, Mahua and Raghu met at their usual café, at the corner of Aurobindo Marg and Ring Road. Mahua had an idea that she wanted to share – working non-stop for days, she had missed the news about the elections. She and Raghu had not met for some weeks – sometimes, he would disappear into the heart of the city, not replying to texts or calls. His friends had become used to this. But today, he was here, full of news about the election results. She didn't want to hear about corporation battles. The glass window of the café looked out on Ring Road; there was the muted roar of traffic, the neon trails of cars and other vehicles flashing by. Skyscrapers glittered with lit windows and advertisements, and Ultracorp's lightning bolt icon flashed from a hundred walls and signboards with headache-inducing persistence. On the footpath outside the café, a throng of haggard people returning from work walked stoop-shouldered in the unrelenting evening heat. A group of day labourers, their headcloths stained with sweat, looked enviously into the unreachable cool comfort of the air-conditioned café as they passed.

A long, low sound like a foghorn announced the victory parade, and everyone in the café stopped talking to look. On the main road appeared a flotilla of long, sleek buses, moving slowly. From the video screens along the sides of the vehicles, the prime minister smiled at the public with folded hands. Atop each bus was the ubiquitous global symbol of Gaiacorp, the planet rendered in blue and green, with the word *Gaia* branded in white, glowing letters across it. Gaiacorp had just won the bidding war to run the Indian government – they already ran the New States of America and the Arctic Union. They had roundly defeated the incumbents, Ultracorp, in this election. Victory music blared from the buses as they went past, making the café's glass wall shake. A cartoon of the Gaia icon trouncing a lightning bolt – the symbol of Ultracorp – flashed on the sides of buildings as the triumphant procession went past. All at once, the Ultracorp icons that had decorated the walls of skyscrapers and apartment complexes went dark, and in their place glowed hundreds of little earths. *Gaia wins, India wins! Bringing you prosperity and comfort beyond your wildest dreams.* Enormous waves of blue light swept the canyons between the roadways. Blue was the official colour of Gaiacorp.

It was a spectacle of such magnitude and power that Raghu and Mahua couldn't speak for a few minutes. They sat sipping their drinks, staring into the night, while the café buzzed with excited conversations.

'Who are we?' Raghu said after a while, in a depressed monotone. 'We are nothing. Nothing at all in front of these bastards.'

It occurred to Mahua that the problem of isolated resistance to their political overlords was maybe, and maybe not, connected with her idea about cities and scale.

'Listen,' she said. 'You know that disused road near the hostel? There's a large tree growing there – I think it's diseased or something because it keeps dropping leaves, small leaves. Yesterday, the wind was blowing, and I noticed how some of the leaves were caught in little cracks in the road. I went to take a look. The leaves must have been there for a while, because bits of soil had collected in them, and little weeds had come up. The road was filled with these little tufts of leaves with soil and weeds growing out of them like a bunch of islands in a sea.'

'And your point is?'

'Well, there were places along the side of the road that had already become overrun with weeds by the same process. And some of the islands were connected to other islands through cracks. So it occurred to me – well, the road is so much stronger than a leaf. But when a leaf settles in a crack, it starts a process. Soil accumulates, plants start to grow, and you know what plant roots can do.'

'Split rock,' Raghu said slowly. 'Split the road.'

'Yes. Eventually, if there's no interference, the road will be completely broken up and overwhelmed by vegetation. It's like how biofilms develop or crystals.'

'So small things –'

'If they are the *right* small things, but also if they have the right kind of connectivity –'

'– can topple a monster!' Raghu raised his glass into the air and finished his drink in a gulp. 'But we already know this – just look at history, look at how the mega-corporations insinuated themselves into national governments in the first place – the biggest global coup d'etat in human history, all through the application of network theory and hired muscle –'

'But what I'm saying is more than that! I think, maybe, that the city isn't the right idea for what we're trying to do. You know? All your pestering me about re-thinking the city? So I did. Why would we want to live in the city as it is now – when people don't have time for anything but work? There's constant stress, people don't know each other, don't care either, where democracy is a sham? What kind of way is that to live? A megapolis is beyond the scale of human social adaptation. So, instead, we could have smaller *bastis* like Ashapur, maybe a thousand of them in a cluster, but connected through the Sensornet as well as a physical network of roads and green corridors –'

'Wait. Let's explore your metaphor a bit more, Mahu – the leaves at the sides of the road – positive social change always comes from the margins, but islets of resistance in the mainstream are also important –'

'Can we think about future cities instead of politics just for a minute?'

'Everything is political, Mahu, you know that!'

It was not clear to them at the moment in the café how this vision would grow and change with time and experience, but that was when it first took root in their minds. Networked *bastis*, connected by green corridors, each settlement embedded with sensors, farm towers replacing conventional agriculture. Such settlements would spring up in different parts of the country and the world. Former agricultural lands would return to the wilderness, or to subsistence farming, repairing the damage done to the biosphere's life-maintaining systems.

'What I want to know,' Mahua said, returning to the present, 'is whether an eco-*basti* like I'm planning, Ashapur, can produce its own microclimate. And how many such microclimates, if networked right, can shift the climate on a larger scale? Like my leaves taking over a road? Or a bacterial biofilm forming?'

But when Ashapur had finally started becoming reality, when its buildings and green areas started producing data, Raghu left. He had helped Mahua design and embed sensors in the walls and windows, trees and byways. He had worked on the teams for the suntowers, the most efficient solar energy system ever built. One could walk the *basti* with a Shell unit and a data visor, and information from a thousand sensors would flow into their receivers. They could read energy use, temperature, humidity, carbon flows, the lot. But something had been bothering Raghu. He got moody and sullen, and Mahua realized she had to let him follow his demons. He would come back when he was ready.

Then, when Ashapur was about halfway done, she got a chance to spend six months in Mumbai on a city-sensorizing project.

In the café veranda, there was litter blowing in the wind. People were leaving with paper cups in hand, bags on shoulders. In another hour, the emergency sirens would be blaring the arrival of the great storm. Mahua had just finished talking to her grandmother in Delhi, reassuring her that she would go to a shelter soon. 'Yes, Nani, I will be all right, don't worry.' The current predictions indicated that the cyclone would make landfall about 100 kilometres north of the city, although it was well known that storms could change course near land very quickly.

On an impulse, she unhooked her Shell and removed her visor, stopping the data streams that fed into her mind every spare moment. She sat breathing, feeling naked without the sensor gear, letting the sounds and sensations of the world waft through her, the old-fashioned way. It had been years since she had played the old game of deliberately letting go with each breath, a sense of her limited self in order to sport with clouds, waves and other beings. How strange it felt!

There was the wind, lifting dust and the folds of yesterday's newspaper, and she could see the dust motes forming shapes, like myriad tiny arms turning sheets of newspaper over and over for some invisible reader. With each unfolding, the papers sighed and whispered. The wind said, 'I'm just a breath at this moment, but in a few minutes, I will be a supercyclone.'

There was a tree near her table, leaning a little over her like a dancer caught in a slantwise twirl. The drought had taken most of its leaves, and now its bare branches rattled in the wind. Looking up, she saw the last leaf detach itself from a branch and float unhurriedly down, this way and that, landing to the left of her teacup. It seemed to glow against the dark metal table, trembling for a moment in the breeze. The tip had frayed into a fine lace of veins and branches, but the rest was intact, its very centre still green. It waited, like a gift unopened.

She remembered the leaves of another tree accumulating in the cracks of an old roadway, some years ago in Delhi. Her horoscope in the morning paper, *that* paper rolling around in the wind had said she would receive a gift from a stranger. She smiled. 'Thanks,' she said to the tree, standing up, pocketing the leaf.

She walked to the water-taxi stand, a covered ledge that had once been a first-floor veranda. The water slapped against the building with a hard, choppy rhythm. The wind was now whipping up in great gusts, and the clouds were low and dark, although it was the middle of the afternoon. Nervously, she looked around, the canal was empty; she must have missed the last of the water taxis. Just then, a small barge came into sight. There were shapes huddled on it, and a single figure was pushing a pole with long, unhurried strokes.

'*Arre!*' she called. She was surprised to find that the bargeman was a thin boy in a pair of worn shorts, his half-naked body as dark as hers. The others in the barge were children and a couple of old women who sat hunched against the wind gusts in old shawls.

That was when she first met Mohsin. At the moment, he was only another street urchin, with a shock of straight hair and a gap-toothed, wide grin. The metro had been shut down, its entrances sealed against the expected flood. After he dropped her off at the first share-a-ride on dry land, she had asked his name. She waved, never thinking she would see the kid again.

The cyclone, in defiance of meteorological predictions, made landfall that evening in the heart of the city. The winds howled all night, and there were loud crashing sounds as though a party of destructive giants had been let loose. The rain came down hard. Never had the city seen a storm such as this. The lights went out, and throughout the night the storm unleashed its power.

In the afternoon of the next day, the winds died down. Mahua stepped from her small rented room into a changed world.

The city was ravaged. There was shattered glass underfoot and broken windows in the intact buildings. The storm surges were so high that the entire lower part of the city, all the new highways and office blocks and high-rises, were under several feet of water. The sewers had backed up, and overflowing rivers carried raw sewage and tons of trash into the streets. The cyclone had not spared the rich – the opulent minarets of Billionaires' Row lay toppled, concrete blocks like felled giants, tangled with tree branches, silk curtains, and the bodies of hundreds of staff. The rich had escaped in helicopters. The city leaders returned with their mafia, cracking down on the looters and the desperate, using whatever means at hand to protect their property, but the rest of the city lay abandoned.

In the midst of the devastation, Mahua found herself volunteering with a rescue group that was an off-shoot of a local cooperative called Hilo Mumbai. They were not like other groups she had come across, a motley mix of autorickshaw drivers, some laid-off young actors, retired school teachers, street cleaners and students. How had they come together? Through a poetry workshop for Mumbai's underprivileged, one of the school teachers explained. An elderly autorickshaw driver Hemant had started it in Dharavi years ago, and it was still running with off-shoots all over the city.

Along with Hilo Mumbai, Mahua searched through the rubble for survivors, helped transport the injured to local clinics and dispensed essential supplies when they could get them. The stench of rotting corpses, the cholera outbreaks in the lower parts of the city, made daily life nearly impossible. But the members of Hilo Mumbai worked and laughed and wept together, yelled at and comforted each other – and kept working.

Something shifted in Mahua then. She had thought that getting educated and rising into the ranks of the urban middle class was the only way to bring change to the world. But here were people who didn't have half her education or means, and look at them! She remembered something Raghu had said a few years ago – that change, positive social change, came from the margins. Maybe sometimes that was true. She needed to talk to him, but he was still out of touch, wandering the country.

Months later, back in Delhi, she found the leaf from the tree near the café between the pages of a notebook. It had almost completely worn down to a fine and delicate web. The rest of the leaf matter was a brown powder that had stained the pages. She picked it up by the stem and held it against the light. *A web – the parts connected to make the whole.* Then she put it back and closed the book.

She thought of the great storm, the towers of the rich toppled by the cyclone. Poetry in the midst of the grimness of rescue work. *Maybe I'll go back there some day.*

In the meantime, there was Ashapur. It grew slowly. A marriage of ancient and modern, the buildings rounded, thick-walled, made from mud, straw and rice husk, the inner roads for people and bicycles, the outer ones for buses that connected them to the greater city. Here, there was room for groves of jamun and neem trees, for gardens on the building walls and roofs. Each domicile held families related by blood and by choice, up to 50 people under one roof, cooking together in large common kitchens.

The Sensornet connected building to building, and wearing a Shell unit or data visor allowed a person to eavesdrop on the data flow: the carbon capture rates of green corridors, fluctuations in the biodiversity index, the conversations between buildings and the energy grid. The city government had donated the space because the site was a refuse dump at the edge of a dying Yamuna, and the deal was that the *basti* would displace the slum that had grown on the dump. Mahua kept her promise by inviting the slum dwellers to be the first residents of Ashapur. They were refugees from the coastal areas of Bangladesh, West Bengal and Odisha, escaping violence and privation, as well as the rising seas and salinization of arable land. They brought to the project their survival skills, their traditions and cultures, their ingenuity and desire to learn. Now they had become the *basti*'s first residents.

When she and her grandmother had almost given up hope of seeing Raghu again – he had been traveling the country for several years now, with hardly a message or call to break the silence – he appeared on their doorstep as abruptly as he had left. Over a vast lunch, he told them about living with rebel groups, tailing corporate mafias, living with tribals in the still-surviving forests, joining a maverick scientist's efforts to free a river trapped under a town. He looked abashed when Mahua's grandmother scolded him for his long silence.

'Nani-ji, I'm going to do better from now on. I'll ask your forgiveness first, then commit the crime!'

'What mischief are you planning now, you reckless boy?'

'I'm going on an even greater journey, Nani-ji! Across the world – to Brazil!'

He took Mahua out for a drink and explained. 'Mahua, you've done fantastic work here in Ashapur. But in my travels, I kept thinking – there is one gap we haven't jumped, between the Sensornet and the web of life itself. Then, an idea came to me in a Gond village in Madhya Pradesh. I want to sensorize an entire forest. Not just sensors in trees, measuring carbon capture, but sensors measuring a hundred things in a whole forest. The biggest remaining forest on earth is the best place to start. That's why I'm going to the Amazon.'

She stared at him, stunned. He grinned at her. 'The thing is, Gaia theorists – I mean the old idea of earth as an organism, not fucking Gaiacorp – Gaia theorists have long maintained that the earth is like a superorganism. That the fungal network through which trees in a forest communicate – which you talked about sensorizing in Ashapur last week – might result in an emergent large-scale intelligence, a thinking forest, that we can't yet recognize because we can't conceptualize it. So, sitting in that Gond village, I got the idea that sensorizing a forest is only the first step. Maybe if the sensors are networked right, we can get the forest to become *aware* of the Sensornet, to communicate with it, and therefore with us!'

His eyes shone. 'Imagine, Mahua, the forests of the Sahyadris, the Terai, the Amazon, they're all in trouble because of climate change. Droughts and species extinction. The web of life is collapsing. If we could only communicate with a forest! If it could tell us what was happening in time for us to save it –'

'But we can already figure that out from the sensor data, Raghu! And we still haven't solved the problem of scaling up the *bastis*, and I think that's more important at the moment –'

That was the last she had seen of him. There had been a few letters from Rio de Janeiro and Manaus, but they had got more and more infrequent until she stopped expecting them. After that, silence. More than 40 years of it.

In that time, she had seen most of the old megapolises die through the combined machinations of extreme weather and human greed. She had seen hundreds of Ashapurs rise on the ruins, each adapted to its local ecology, yet linked together via the large-scale Sensornet. She had wanted to tell Raghu that despite a decade of killer heatwaves in Delhi, the *basti* clusters might just have shifted the regional climate in the right direction. *Maybe we averted that future you saw in the simulator.* There was so much she had wanted to share with him! The subcontinent had gone through a long period of chaos and even now, there were mass starvations, violent conflicts, in towns and provinces ruled by brutal mafias where life was precarious. But everywhere else, she could see the fruits of a million mutinies, experiments in alternative ways of living and being, the work and sweat and tears that had resulted in the Great Turning.

She was grateful she had lived to see the change. That she had been a part of it, a catalyst, should have been a source of satisfaction to her now in her old age. But for a few years she had become disenchanted with her work. Not that it hadn't been important, but she was dissatisfied, impatient with her own thoughts and ideas. She would look at her fine, dark hands, see the lines on her face, feel the ache in her knees and she would be filled with wonder. The muscles of her heart, her limbs and sinews, had served her without many complaints through the long arc of her life. Now, with these aches and tremors, lines and wrinkles, her body was telling her something. A reminder of mortality, yes, but something else. For some time now, she had stopped wearing her Shell or her data visor, wanting to listen without intermediaries to the subtle speeches of her physical self.

And now a journalist was coming to interview her with 'some information' about her old friend, Raghu.

Upon arriving, the journalist, a thin, earnest man called Rafael Silva, handed her a carved wooden box, one that she immediately recognized as a gift she had given Raghu before his trip to Brazil. It was meant to hold odds and ends and, in fact, it contained a couple of broken Shells, a small wooden peg, an abstract wooden carving, several sensor cells and optical wires, and a sheet of paper filled with Raghu's handwriting. Wrapped in a leaf, secured with twine, was a five-centimetre long lock of grey hair with a few black strands.

Mr Silva had been covering a gathering of Amazonian tribal leaders near the city of Manaus, he said. The recent droughts in the Amazon and changing water and weather patterns had caused the tribes to come together to share knowledge. He had struck up a conversation with an elder of the local Dessana tribe. Upon learning that Mr Silva was a well-travelled journalist, the elder had produced the box. It had been handed to him by a member of a remote tribe in the Amazon's interior over a year ago, who told them of a stranger and foreigner living with them for several years. The stranger had died from a gunshot wound inflicted during a raid by a gold mining company about two years before that. Thirteen people from the tribe had also been killed. Dying, the stranger's last wish had been that the box be delivered to a city so that somebody could send it to his people in a far country.

The name scrawled on the box was Mahua's, and the address was her old one in Ashapur. The box had taken two years to travel from the interior of the rainforest to the city. Mr Silva had been so intrigued that he had added India to his itinerary of a trip to South East Asia. He wanted to deliver the box in person.

'I am so grateful,' Mahua said when Mr Silva had finished. She wiped her tears. 'Thank you for coming all this way.'

'My pleasure,' Rafael Silva said. After that, she was glad to answer his questions about her life and work, and her association with Raghu. The household gave him a meal, a place to stay the night and then he left the next morning.

All of the next day, Mahua read and re-read the writing on the sheet of paper, held the broken Shell, the lock of his hair in its package of leaf and twine. She thought of the leaf falling from some great Amazonian tree, of the hands that would have picked it up. She caressed the leaf, which was dark green and waxy.

Dear Mahu,

I have forgotten how to communicate in this language, so forgive me.

I came to the Amazon with our technology because I wanted to know the language of the leaves and the animals. I wanted to talk to the forest itself. But after a few years, I realized that the sensors only answer the questions you already know to ask. How do you know what other questions are there? I have lived in the forest with my guides and companions, and through them I have learned that there is a language before language that the earth speaks.

The Amazon once had great settlements along the river, civilizations that never forgot their relationship to the whole, and so they existed for millennia without collapsing – until the Europeans came. No trace was left of them after their destruction except for a few shards of pottery because everything they made was from the forest, and the ruins were absorbed into it. How did they know how to live like this, without modern technology? To learn the answer, I had to learn what the forest had to tell me, merely as human, as an earthling. I came intending to save it, but it saved me instead. Now, I repay my debt by giving myself back to the Amazon. But I was raised by the air and water and soil of my first home, and so some part of me should return there. Will you take this lock of hair, burn or bury it in a forest somewhere near you? Forgive me for not being there for you these many years.

I hope Nani-ji lived a long life. There has never been a day I have not thought of you. I am at peace now.

Raghu

It would have taken him enormous effort to write this missive. From the shapes of the letters, she knew that his fingers had trembled. There was a faint rust-coloured stain in one corner of the page. In the evening she told the family she lived with, 'Call Ikram. I want to go out tomorrow.'

The sense of waiting for something that had come upon her some time ago was turning into a feeling of impending arrival.

Ikram's boat edges away from the river toward the sea. He is a lanky youth with a serious mien, Mohsin's grandson. She sits in the middle of the boat under the canopy, Raghu's box on her knees. The day is suffused with a silver light, the sun is behind the clouds. There will be no rain today, but perhaps the monsoon will build up again tomorrow. The steep, wind-battered slopes of the Mumbai Archipelago are covered with the faintest purple blush. The *karvi* flowers are starting to bloom, obeying their eight-year cycle.

Mahua feels as though Raghu is with her, in this boat. She is showing him the drowned city, the towers like slender pencils over a smudge of old, squat, shorter buildings. It is hot and humid. *Look, the sea lanes are busy with the boats of the fisherfolk and water taxis bringing people and goods from the southern coast.* Ahead and to their right, a skyscraper is slowly tilting into the water. Wagers have been made on when the whole structure will succumb to the sea, but the sea keeps its secrets.

The hills of the five islands of Mumbai rise to her left. As they turn into a channel, hugging the shore, she sees the shrine of Baba Khizr on the rooftop of an old building, only a metre above the water's surface. It is surrounded by boatloads of people seeking his blessings. From here she can see all the way up the slope to where Billionaire's Row had once been. The trees, vines and wild animals have taken over the concrete rubble and, at the very top, there stands a shrine to Samudra Devi, the goddess of the ocean.

This is the age of the small gods, she tells Raghu. *Local deities, long-forgotten pirs. Even Ram is the Ram of the vanvaas.*

Domiciles covered with vines of vegetables and flowers cluster on the hills of the islands. At the water's edge, boats and rafts rock against their moorings. As the boat glides through the watery thoroughfares, they are greeted with waves and shouts, delayed every few metres by conversation because she hasn't been out here in a long time, and everyone knows her and Ikram.

The Baba Khizr shrine, she tells Raghu, holding the carved box in her lap, *marks where Mohsin once saw a vision. An old man walking on water, standing on a fish that bore him through the channels of the city toward the open sea.* Mohsin had heard stories of Baba Khizr from his father, a refugee from the mouth of the Indus River in Pakistan. There are similar stories from as far as Bihar and Arabia, about a pir who was the guardian of the waters, whose feet, when they touched the ground, made flowers bloom.

The boat is moored, and Ikram has helped her off it and up the slope. They are climbing steadily, although every few minutes she needs to stop for breath. She remembers, from a book a long time ago, that the Amazon rainforest used to produce nearly 20 per cent of the world's atmospheric oxygen. At least half came from ocean plankton, and the rest from green plants on land. She doesn't know what the numbers are now, in a climate-changed world. But it is still true that every breath she breathes, she owes to the Amazon, to the ocean, to the trees on the slope above her. 'I'm feeling grateful today,' she tells Ikram, who smiles. At long last they are at the forest's edge. The air is cooler here, and a breeze stirs the leaves. She hears, distantly, the trickle of water, and the bell-like call of a koel from deep within the trees. A muddy path runs into the forest.

Ikram is distracted by a jamun tree, heavy with fruit.

'Go on,' she says. 'Get us some jamuns. I will be all right. I will be at the clearing, where the path forks. Come and find me later.'

'You have your wristpad?' he asks.

'I didn't bring anything,' she says. 'Don't worry, I know this place.'

How strange that the river of her life, which has run sometimes parallel, sometimes away from Raghu's, has been flowing toward the same destination as his. She is walking through the forest, to the confluence, the meeting place. There is a clearing that she remembers from a trip a year or two ago, that he would like.

She walks slowly. In the clearing, a pale sunlight filters through the clouds, illuminating the *karvi* flowers. She looks at her dark brown arm holding the box, feels the heat of the day on her skin.

There is a language before language that the earth speaks, Raghu had said.

Yes, she tells him, *and you can only learn it through the body.*

An animal in a forest, that's what she is at this moment, susceptible to danger and death, but her senses are coming alive to everything. The pattern of light and shadow, the humming of an insect, the cooling of a wood dove, the distant call of a troop of monkeys. Everything about her, from her dark skin to her facial features, have been shaped by her people's particular adaptation to their environment: the slant of the sunlight, the temperature of the air. She feels the crushing weight of the centuries of abuse and exploitation. It is there in the DNA of her cells, in the stories of her grandmother, in the loss of her mother at an early age, in Kalpana di's suicide. The pain stabs her with such intensity that she thinks she might faint. She leans against the trunk of a tree and holds Raghu's box to her chest.

Mahua opens Raghu's box and takes out the folded leaf. Setting the box on a branch, she unrolls the twine, opens the leaf and strokes, once, the lock of hair. Then she ties up the bundle again, and looks for a place where the earth is soft from the last rain. With a stick from the underbrush, she digs a small hole where she places the little package. She covers it up again with earth.

Go free, she says to Raghu, and to Kalpana di. She straightens slowly. Her back aches, her legs ache. All this climbing, she'd better get used to it again. Maybe it's time this old woman learned some new lessons. She cannot own the victories of her grandmother's people – the newly formed Santhal province with its ideal of reverence for the web of life, its model of communities governing themselves through consensus – she cannot celebrate such things without owning the pain of struggle and sacrifice that are inscribed in her very own body, her people's history. And it is thus that she is able to see at last, as her people always have seen, the earth itself: as body, as mother.

At the edge of the clearing, the leaves of the trees murmur in the wind. She feels herself enlarging beyond her own awareness. She is a drop of water trembling on a leaf, she is sunlight on the branch. She doesn't know the names of the trees or the birds, except for a few, but that can come later. For that moment, she is as unselfconsciously free as a soaring bird.

Ikram is calling to her. Mahua clears her throat, takes a long breath. 'I'm coming,' she calls back.

What a privilege to exist in a universe so dynamic, so complex, that one still has something to learn at the ripe old age of 73. She will sit at the edge of the forest with Ikram and look at the sea. They will eat jamuns, stain their lips and hands with purple juice, and she will tell him about that other great forest, the Amazon, half a world away. She will tell him about Raghu.

LIST OF CONTRIBUTORS

Adrish Bardhan (1932–2019) was a writer and translator of science fiction, fantasy and suspense stories for both children and adults, and a champion of the science fiction movement in Bengal. His best known creation is the character of Professor Nut Boltu Chakra. He founded and edited two seminal science fiction magazines in Bengali, *Ashchorjo* (*Astounding*) and *Fantastic*, besides co-founding, with Satyajit Ray, the Science Fiction Cine Club in Calcutta. He also edited several science fiction anthologies.

Anil Menon's most recent work, *Half of What I Say* was shortlisted for the Hindu Literary Prize in 2016. His debut novel, *The Beast with Nine Billion Feet*, was shortlisted for the Crossword Prize in 2009 and the Carl Baxter Society's Parallax Award in 2010. He co-edited *Breaking the Bow*, an international anthology of short fiction inspired by the Ramayana, with Vandana Singh, His short fiction has appeared in a variety of anthologies and magazines including *Interzone, Interfictions, Lady Churchill's Rosebud Wristlet, Jaggery Lit Review* and *Strange Horizons*. His stories have been included in several international 'Best of...' collections, taught in universities and translated into more than a dozen languages, including Hebrew, Igbo and Romanian. In 2016, he co-founded The Dum Pukht Writers' Workshop, a residential workshop held annually in Pondicherry, India. His forthcoming works include a collection of speculative short fiction titled *The Inconceivable Idea of the Sun: Stories* and a novel.

Arjun Rajendran is the author of the poetry collections *Snake Wine, The Cosmonaut in Hergé's Rocket* and *Your Baby Is Starving*. His work has appeared in numerous publications, including the *Indian Express, Strange Horizons, Star*Line, Mithila Review, Berfrois, AntiSerious, SOFTBLOW* and *Eclectica Magazine Best Poetry: V1 Celebrating 20 Years Online*. He is also the poetry editor of *The Bombay Literary Magazine* and was the Charles Wallace Fellow in Creative Writing for 2018 at the University of Stirling in Scotland.

Arunava Sinha translates classic, modern and contemporary Bengali fiction, non-fiction and poetry from India and Bangladesh into English.

Asif Aslam Farrukhi (1959–2020) was a public health physician by training. In his lifetime he published seven collections of short fiction, two collections of critical essays, as well as several translations of prose and poetry by modern and classical writers from the Indian subcontinent. His last publications included a collection of new critical essays on Saadat Hasan Manto; *Look at the City from Here*, an anthology of writings about Karachi; and a study of Intizar Husain, *Chiragh-e-Shab-e-Afsana: Intizar Husain ka Jehan-e-Fun*. He was the editor of *Duniyazad*, a literary journal of new writing and contemporary issues in Urdu, and a founding member of the Karachi and Islamabad literature. He was the director of the Arzu Centre for Regional Languages and Humanities at the Habib University and visiting faculty member at the Aga Khan University both in Karachi.

C.M. Naim is professor emeritus at the Department of South Asian Languages and Civilizations, University of Chicago, and has published translations of works from the Persian, Hindi and Urdu languages.

Chandrashekhar Sastry (1932–2020) was a widely travelled engineer-scientist based in Bengaluru. His first book, *The Non-Resident Indian: From Being to Non-being*, published in 1991, was a pioneering work that dealt with a contemporary subject in an unorthodox manner. His second book, *The Tanjore Painting*, deals with the cultural imports that the diaspora carry to their newfound homelands. His latest collection of short stories, *Long and Short Tales*, was published in 2016.

Giti Chandra is currently Research Specialist with the Gender Equality Studies and Training Programme (under the auspices of UNESCO) in Reykjavik, teaches at the University of Iceland, and has been Associate Professor, Department of English, at Stephen's College, Delhi. She is the author of The Book of Guardians Trilogy: *The Fang of Summoning, The Bones of Stars and The Eye of the Archer*. Her (mostly sci-fi) short stories and (mostly sentimental) poetry have been published in various publications. Sadly, nobody cares about her first non-fiction book, a groundbreaking academic work on violence, although a later publication, *The Routledge Handbook of the Politics of the #MeToo Movement*, has been getting attention. Giti writes poetry in April, paints on Tuesdays, has a Ph.D from Rutgers University, and feels that people would do well to learn that a cello is not an oversized violin. She lives in Reykjavik with a husband, two kids, a dog, and a cat.

Hari Shankar Parsai (1924–85) was arguably the most admired and influential satirist in Hindi in the twentieth century. Born in Jabalpur (MP), he spent almost all his life as a freelance writer in that city. A prolific writer, he preferred writing fiction and essays, and in close to 40 volumes of essays, stories and novellas, he produced a uniquely incisive critique of the follies and hypocrisies that plague Indian polity and society. The story translated here was originally published in a Hindi journal in 1968.

Kaiser Haq is professor of English at the University of Liberal Arts, Bangladesh. A recipient of the Bangla Academy Prize for Translation and the 2017 Sherwin W. Howard Award for Poetry, his writings include eight collections of poetry, the most recent of which are *Published in the Streets of Dhaka: Collected Poems* and *Pariah and Other Poems*; five volumes of translations; two poetry anthologies as editor; and a retold version of the Manasa legends, *The Triumph of the Snake Goddess*.

Keki N. Daruwalla writes poetry, short fiction, plays and novels in English. He spent his career in the Indian Police Service and retired as chairman, Joint Intelligence Committee (JIC) in the Cabinet Secretariat. He was awarded the Sahitya Akademi Award for his poetry collection, *The Keeper of the Dead* in 1984, which he returned in 2015 as a protest against intolerance in India. He has also been a recipient of the Commonwealth Poetry Prize (Asia) in 1987 and the Padma Shri in 2014. His recent works include *Collected Poems (1970-2005)*, *Map Maker* and *Fire Altar: Poems on the Persians and Greeks*, and *Ancestral Affairs*, a novel. His novel *For Pepper and Christ* was shortlisted for the Commonwealth Writers' Prize for South Asia and Europe in 2010. His latest volume of poetry is *Naishapur and Babylon: Poems (2005–2017)*.

Manjula Padmanabhan is an author, playwright and cartoonist. Her play *Harvest* won the 1997 Onassis Award for Theatre. Her weekly comic strip *Sukiyaki* appears in *The Hindu BusinessLine*. Her two most recent novels, *Escape* and *The Island of Lost Girls*, are set in a brutal future world. She divides her time between the US and New Delhi.

Maya Joshi is associate professor of English at Lady Shri Ram College, University of Delhi, and her current research interests revolve around Indian intellectual history. Among her publications are a critical edition of Mary Shelley's *Frankenstein* and a co-edited volume on Buddhist philosophy. She is currently a Fulbright post-doctoral visiting scholar at the University of Pennsylvania and is working on a biography of Rahul Sankrityayan.

Mimi Mondal is a writer and editor. She was a Nebula Award finalist in 2020 for her novelette *His Footsteps, through Darkness and Light*, and a Hugo, British Fantasy and William J. Atheling Awards finalist in 2018 for her co-edited anthology *Luminescent Threads: Connections to Octavia E. Butler*, which also received the Locus Award. She also occasionally writes a column called 'Extraordinary Alien' for *Hindustan Times*, in which she talks about politics, culture, technology and futurism, mostly centering on India. Mimi grew up in Kolkata and currently lives in New York.

Mohammad Salman is a development communications professional and speculative fiction writer from Lucknow, India. His work has appeared in *Kitaab* and other anthologies. He is working on his first comic for the upcoming Indian quarterly magazine *Comixense*. Salman counts Terry Pratchett and Isaac Asimov among his inspirations and dreams of creating a legendarium of his own one day. He has a bachelor's degree in English Literature from the University of Delhi and hold a master's in mass communication from Jamia Millia Islamia, New Delhi. He shares his home with his wife Anam and son Anwar, though it is in truth the dominion of their cat, Alif.

Muhammed Zafar Iqbal (born in 1952) is a Bangladeshi writer of science fiction and children's literature. A trained physicist, he is a college professor. Iqbal, who has been at the vanguard of science fiction writing in Bangladesh, is also a political activist and rationalist who survived an attempt on his life on his university campus in Sylhet, Bangladesh, on 3 March 2018.

Nur Nasreen Ibrahim is a journalist and writer. Born and raised in Pakistan, she is currently based in New York City. She was a finalist for the inaugural Salam Award for Imaginative Fiction, an award instituted for science fiction, fantasy and speculative writing in Pakistan in honour of one of the country's pioneers of scientific research. Her fiction and non-fiction writings have been included in anthologies and collections published by Catapult, Platypus Press, The Aleph Review, Salmagundi Magazine, Harper Perennial, and more.

Payal Dhar writes fiction, mostly for young adults, and has published several books, including *Satin, Slightly Burnt* and *Hit for a Six*. She has also co-edited a unique Indo-Australian anthology of feminist speculative fiction for young adults called *Eat the Sky, Drink the Ocean*. For almost two decades, Payal has been a freelance editor of academic non-fiction and fiction, and a writer on technology, games, sport, books, writing and travel.

Premendra Mitra (1930–88) was one of the most versatile of the post-Tagore generation of Bengali writers. He wrote novels, short stories, poetry, science fiction and film scripts, and also directed films. Alongside his serious fiction – his novels and short stories – he wrote acclaimed works of science fiction and the legendary Ghanada series of stories, which defy genre classification but can be described as historical romps.

Priya Sarukkai Chabria is an award-winning translator, poet and writer. Her books include speculative fiction, cross-genre non-fiction, two collections of poetry, novels, translations of eighth-century Tamil mystic Andal's songs, besides two anthologies of poetry as editor. Her work has been included in numerous Indian and international anthologies, and she has presented her work worldwide. At present she is translating the mystic songs of Karaikal Ammaiyar and Manikkavacakar from classical Tamil. Priya is Founding Editor of the literary journal *Poetry at Sangam*. For more information about her work, see www.priyawriting.com.

Rahul Sankrityayan (1893–1963) was born Kedarnath Pandey in Azamgarh, in present-day Uttar Pradesh, into a family of modest means. In an extraordinary life of largely autodidactic explorations, this polymathic public intellectual acquired proficiency in 30 languages and published over 150 works in Hindi, Bhojpuri, Sanskrit, Tibetan and very negligibly in English. Leaving home as a youth in search of learning, moving from Vaishnava affiliations to the Arya Samaj to Buddhist monasticism in Sri Lanka, he finally arrived at Dialectical Materialism in the 1930s. His philosophical quest co-existed with involvement in the anti-imperial struggle, from the 1920s to the 1940s, as a member of the Congress Party, of the peasant movement in Bihar and, finally, as a member of the Communist Party of India, with Bihar as his primary focus. While he travelled extensively as student, pilgrim and political activist, among his most remarkable journeys are four epic expeditions to Tibet in the 1930s in pursuit of lost Buddhist philosophical texts, travels across remote Himalayan regions resulting in detailed travelogues, and journeys to the Soviet Union where he taught Buddhist Logic. Works in his genre-defying oeuvre are *Volga se Ganga*, a work of historical fiction that reaches across continents and epochs to trace 8000 years of human evolution; *Madhya Asia ka Itihas*, a pioneering Sahitya Akademi Award-winning history of Central Asia; *Darshan Digdarshan*, a survey of world philosophy; and *Ghumakkar Shastra*, a mock-serious treatise for travellers, besides biographies, essays on politics and culture, travelogues, novels, plays, dictionaries and scholarly editions of Buddhist texts.

Rimi B. Chatterjee is an author, artist and teacher. She has published three novels – one science fiction novel, *Signal Red* (2005), and two historical fictions – and a graphic story in the *Longform Anthology*. Her fantasy novel *Ashqabad: City of Stories* is forthcoming in 2019 and she is currently working on *Antisense*, a novel set in the same universe as the short story in this anthology.

Rukmini Bhaya Nair is professor of Linguistics and English at the Indian Institute of Technology, Delhi. An award-winning poet, she received her PhD from the University of Cambridge and has taught at universities from Singapore to Stanford. Awarded an honorary doctorate by Antwerp University for her contributions to narrative theory, she has authored nine books, three volumes of poetry and over a hundred articles. Her first novel, *Mad Girl's Love Song*, was longlisted for the DSC Prize in 2015.

Sami Ahmad Khan writes, researches, teaches, edits and translates science fiction. Sami holds a Ph.D in science fiction from Jawaharlal Nehru University, New Delhi, and is the recipient of a Fulbright grant to the University of Iowa, USA. His future-war debut *Red Jihad* won two awards and his second novel about an invasion of India's capital – *Aliens in Delhi* – garnered excellent reviews. He currently discusses life and literature at GGS Indraprastha University, Delhi, where he also supervises Ph.D research on speculative fiction. Sami's latest work is *Star Warriors of the Modern Raj: Materiality, Mythology and Technology of Indian Science Fiction*, a monograph on India's Anglophonic science fiction writing post-2000.

S.B. Divya is a lover of science, math, fiction, and the Oxford comma. She holds degrees in Computational Neuroscience and Signal Processing and worked for twenty years as an electrical engineer before becoming an author.She is the Hugo and Nebula award-nominated author of *Runtime*, Machinehood, and the short story collection *Contingency Plans for the Apocalypse and Other Situations*. Divya is the co-editor of the Hugo award-nominated *Escape Pod* with Mur Lafferty. Her fiction has been published at *Uncanny, Apex, Tor.com*, and other magazines. Find her on Twitter as @divyastweets or at HYPERLINK "http://www.eff-words.com/"www.eff-words.com.

Shovon Chowdhury liked to refer to himself as 'a slightly disturbed Delhi-based novelist'. His first novel, *The Competent Authority*, was a finalist for *The Hindu*, Crossword, Shakti Bhatt and Tata Lit Live awards, a circumstance he described as 'a massive failure in quality control'. His 2015 novel, *Murder with Bengali Characteristics*, was set in a near-future Calcutta under Chinese rule, a dystopian prospect guaranteed to horrify both the Bengalis and the Chinese. His short story, 'The Man Who Turned into Gandhi', appeared in the first volume of *The Gollancz Book of South Asian Science Fiction*. He was exploring the possibility of writing a novel based on Mahatma Gandhi's life, a project that he felt was rich with comic possibilities and a lifetime of FIRs. Shovon, who died on 26 February 2021, treated all of his writer's bios as a one-man literary protest against pomposity.

Somendra Singh Kharola is a graduate student studying evolutionary biology at the Indian Institute of Science Education and Research, Pune. His poems and articles have appeared, or are forthcoming, in several journals, some of which include *The Hindu, The Four Quarters Magazine, The Missing Slate* and *Strange Horizons*. Some of his most recently published poems were longlisted for the Toto Funds the Arts award in 2018.

Sumita Sharma teaches English literature at Shyam Lal College, University of Delhi. She is currently pursuing doctoral research on science fiction poetry at the Indian Institute of Technology, Delhi. She believes the climate change apocalypse is happening right now and tries to live a simpler, zero-waste life. Her contribution to this volume is her first publication.

Clark Prasad, the alter ego of Suraj Prasad, may be called a mixed citizen of earth, Alpha Quadrant. The son of army parents, he was born in Lagos, Nigeria, in the year *Rocky, All the President's Men* and *The Omen* were made. He has lived most of his life in New Delhi and been educated in Lagos, Delhi, Mangalore and Kozhikode. A pharmacist with a management degree from the Indian Institute of Management, Kozhikode, he works for an analytics and consulting firm. His first book, *Baramulla Bomber*, was published in 2012.

Syed Saeed Naqvi is an author and translator. He has three collections of short stories to his name: *Namabar, Doosra Rukh* and *Tuk Tuk Deedam*. He has also written two novels, *Girdab* and *Baarish Say Pehlay*. All of these works have been written in Urdu, and he has translated extensively from Urdu to English. *In Search of Butterflies*, a translation of contemporary Urdu short stories was published in 2017. His most recent translation from English to Urdu is of Siddhartha Mukherjee's *The Gene: An Intimate History*. He is a doctor by profession, and lives and works in New York

Tarun K. Saint is an independent scholar and writer born in Kenya. He has lived in India since 1972. His research interests include the literature of the Partition of India and science fiction. He is the author of *Witnessing Partition: Memory, History, Fiction* (2010), which was based on his doctoral dissertation. He has edited *Bruised Memories: Communal Violence and the Writer* (2002) and co-edited *Translating Partition: Essays, Stories, Criticism* (2001) with Ravi Kant. His most recent co-edited volume is *Looking Back: The 1947 Partition of India, 70 Years On* (2017), a collaboration with Rakhshanda Jalil and Debjani Sengupta.

Vandana Singh was born and brought up in Delhi, and currently teaches and writes in the Boston area. Her science fiction stories have been published in numerous publications, including several 'year's best' volumes, and she has published two collections to critical acclaim: *The Woman Who Thought She Was a Planet and Other Stories* and, most recently, *Ambiguity Machines and Other Stories*. She is also the author of two children's books about an eccentric character called Younguncle. In her academic life, she is a former particle physicist currently researching climate science at the intersection of pedagogy and social change. Her contribution to this volume, 'Reunion', is dedicated to Ashish Kothari of Kalpavriksh for his indefatigable commitment to environmental social justice, and to the memory of the late Ursula K. Le Guin, extraordinary writer and human, for her radically inspiring visions.

COPYRIGHT ACKNOWLEDGEMENTS

'*Atonker Groho*' by Adrish Bardhan, tr. Arunava Sinha as 'Planet of Terror'. Translated with permission of Patra Bharati Group of Publications.

'*Inspector Matadeen Chand Par*' by Harishankar Parsai, first published in *Parsai Rachnawali* Vol. 2, New Delhi: Rajkamal Prakashan, 1985, tr. C.M. Naim as 'Inspector Matadeen on the Moon'. Translated with permission of the author and Rajkamal Prakashan.

'*Samandar ki Chori*' by Asif Aslam Farrukhi, tr. Syed Saeed Naqvi as 'Stealing the Sea', *In Search of Butterflies*, ed. Saeed Naqvi, Karachi: OUP, 2017, 65–86. Reproduced with permission of Oxford University Press Pakistan © Oxford University Press.

'The Sea Sings at Night' by Mimi Mondal, *The WisCon Chronicles, Vol.9: Intersection and Alliances*, ed. Mary Anne Mohanrai, Seattle: Aqueduct Press, 2015. © Monidipa Mondal. Reproduced with permission of the author.

Excerpts from *Baisvin Sadi* by Rahul Sankrityayan, tr. Maya Joshi as 'The Twenty-Second Century'. Translated with permission of Jeta Sankrityayan.

'Shit Flower', *Brave New Now*, ed. Liam Young, Lisbon Architecture Triennale, 2014. © Anil Menon. Reproduced with permission of the author.

'*Juddho Keno Thamlo*' by Premendra Mitra, tr. Arunava Sinha as 'Why the World Ended'. Translated with permission of Mrinmoy Mitra.

'*Shopno*' by Muhammed Zafar Iqbal, tr. Arunava Sinha as 'The Dream'. Translated with permission of the author.

'Looking Up' by S.B. Divya, *Where the Stars Rise: Asian Science Fiction and Fantasy*, eds. Lucas K. Law and Derwin Mak, Calgary: Laksa Media Group Inc., 2017, 73–89. © S.B. Divya. Reproduced with permission of the author.

ACKNOWLEDGEMENTS

This anthology is dedicated to my parents, for their constant support and encouragement.

~

An SF anthology of this scope and range could not have been brought together without many conversations, helpful comments and interventions. I would like to especially thank Manjula Padmanabhan for her keen interest, unflagging sense of humour and dedicated involvement; without her careful editorial suggestions, this collection would not be the same (especially my own story). Her foreword and endpaper drawings have brought in a further dimension of depth from a seasoned practitioner's point of view, in her characteristically whimsical and witty style. Exchanges with Anil Menon and Sami Ahmad Khan provided vital early impetus and direction, while Alok Bhalla was always a source of critical encouragement as he read the introduction in draft form. Madhavan Palat's incisive remarks helped identify flaws in the argument at an early stage, while Anwar Ahmer's and Geeta Patel's critical responses were invaluable in sharpening the focus of ideas presented. Shaswati Mazumdar, Vijaya Venkataraman and Sachita Kaushal came through with insightful suggestions, references and critical materials and helped amplify the range of concerns here, emanating from their work and discussions about the genre of SF at the Department of Germanic and Romance Studies, University of Delhi. Sumita Sharma was unstinting in her assistance in finding poets who write in the speculative vein. Anil Nauriya's and Giti Chandra's support and guidance have played a crucial role at key moments. It was a pleasure to converse at length with SF scholar Bodhisattva Chattopadhyay after the event on art and science fiction at Khoj Studios.

Poulomi Chatterjee and Thomas Abraham have been involved in the shaping of this volume at every stage, contributing tirelessly with their enthusiasm and considerable knowledge of the genre. Their thoughtful suggestions and comments have helped make this a better book. Thanks to the entire editorial team at Hachette India, in particular to Niyati Dhuldhoya, Sini Nair and Ansila Thomas, for enabling the work on the editing, permissions and proofs to be completed without hitches. The designer, Bhavi Mehta, deserves a special mention for creating the cover image, which captures the strangeness and uncanny feeling underpinning many of the stories.

As ever, a note of appreciation for family members who have put up with my SF preoccupations ever since I was gifted a copy of Robert Heinlein's *Red Planet* at the age of ten; thank you, Debbie Cohen, for kick-starting an imaginative journey of discovery of outer and eventually all manner of spaces, metaphysical and cultural too. Furthermore, a shout-out to the many students who attended the SF classes I taught over the years, for helping me sustain a critical outlook towards the genre, and ex-colleagues and friends for being there.

Finally, special thanks for the efforts of the writers and translators who have contributed to this volume, many of whom are good friends, as well as those whom I have got to know better during this journey. The time taken to compose and translate the stories and poems included here has certainly borne fruit; in their final form, these works do give a sense of the diversity of South Asian SF. Any gaps and errors, of course, remain my responsibility.

Tarun K. Saint

ABOUT GOLLANCZ

Gollancz is the oldest SF publishing imprint in the world. Since being founded in 1927 Gollancz has continued to publish a focused selection of bestselling and award-winning authors. The front-list includes **Ben Aaronovitch**, **Joe Abercrombie**, **Charlaine Harris**, **Joanne Harris**, **Joe Hill**, **Alastair Reynolds**, **Patrick Rothfuss**, **Nalini Singh** and **Brandon Sanderson**.

As one of the largest Science Fiction and Fantasy imprints in the UK it is no surprise we have one of the most extensive backlists in the world. Find high-quality SF on Gateway written by such authors as **Philip K. Dick**, **Ursula Le Guin**, **Connie Willis**, **Sir Arthur C. Clarke**, **Pat Cadigan**, **Michael Moorcock** and **George R.R. Martin**.

We also have a strand of publishing in translation, which includes French, Polish and Russian authors. Gollancz is home to more award-winning authors than any other imprint, with names including **Aliette de Bodard**, **M. John Harrison**, **Paul McAuley**, **Sarah Pinborough**, **Pierre Pevel**, **Justina Robson** and many more.

The SF Gateway

More than 3,000 classic, rare and previously out-of-print SF novels at your fingertips.

www.sfgateway.com

The Gollancz Blog

Bringing you news from our worlds to yours. Stories, interviews, articles and exclusive extracts just for you!

www.gollancz.co.uk

GOLLANCZ
LONDON

SF MASTERWORKS
ALASTAIR REYNOLDS
Revelation Space

SF MASTERWORKS
ARKADY & BORIS STRUGATSKY
The Doomed City

ARTHUR C. CLARKE
Childhood's End
SF MASTERWORKS

SF MASTERWORKS
DOUGLAS ADAMS
The Restaurant at the End of the Universe

SF MASTERWORKS
FRANK HERBERT
Dune

SF MASTERWORKS
H.G. WELLS
The Time Machine

SF MASTERWORKS
ISAAC ASIMOV
The Gods Themselves

SF MASTERWORKS
JOHN WYNDHAM
The Day of the Triffids

SF MASTERWORKS
KURT VONNEGUT
Cat's Cradle

PHILIP K. DICK
Do Androids Dream of Electric Sheep?
SF MASTERWORKS

SF MASTERWORKS
RICHARD MATHESON
I Am Legend

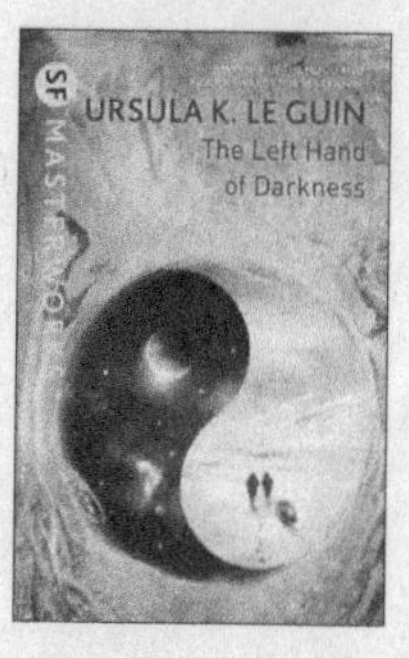
SF
URSULA K. LE GUIN
The Left Hand of Darkness

SF MASTERWORKS
JAMES TIPTREE, JR
Her Smoke
Rose Up Forever

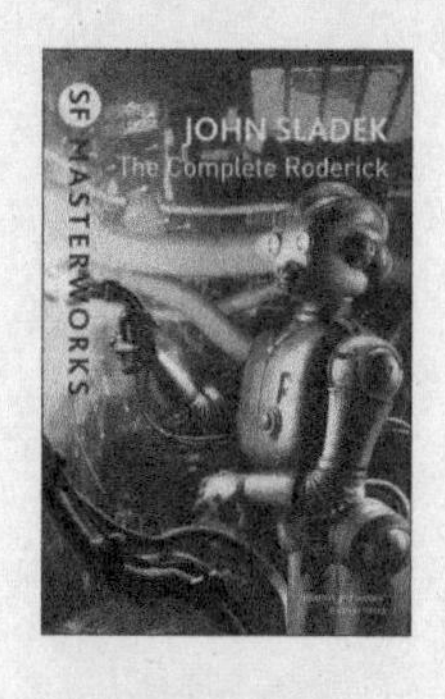
SF MASTERWORKS
JOHN SLADEK
The Complete Roderick

SF MASTERWORKS
GREG BEAR
Blood Music

SF MASTERWORKS
ALFRED BESTER
The Demolished Man

SF MASTERWORKS
THEODORE
STURGEON
More Than Human

ROBERT
SILVERBERG
The Book of Skulls

SF MASTERWORKS
GREGORY BENFORD
Timescape

SF MASTERWORKS
FREDERIK POHL
Man Plus

SF MASTERWORKS
JACK FINNEY
The Body Snatchers

JACK VANCE
Emphyrio

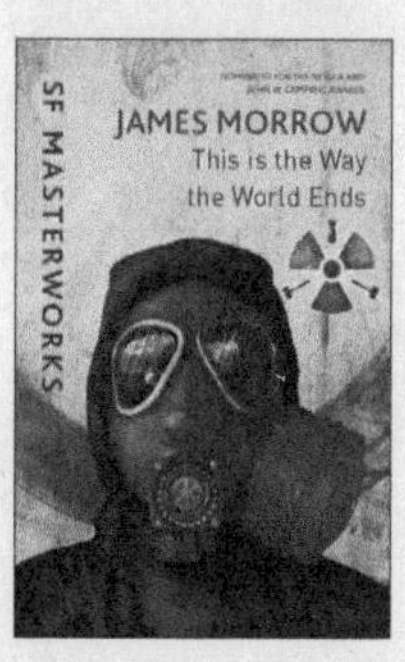
SF MASTERWORKS
JAMES MORROW
This is the Way
the World Ends

SF MASTERWORKS
RACHEL POLLACK
Unquenchable Fire

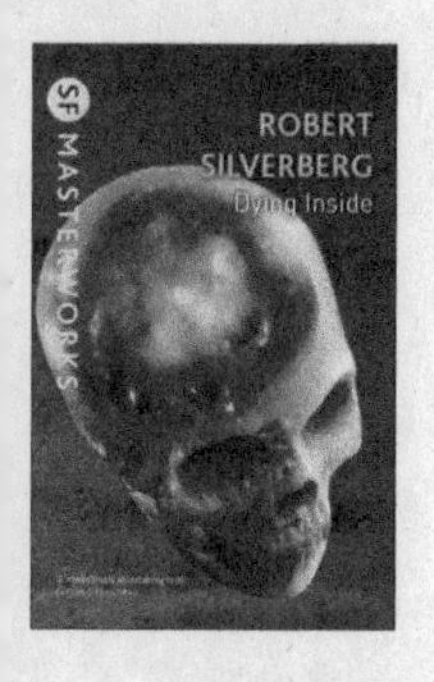
SF MASTERWORKS
ROBERT
SILVERBERG
Dying Inside

SF MASTERWORKS
GEOFF RYMAN
The Child Garden

SF MASTERWORKS
MICHAEL BISHOP
No Enemy But Time

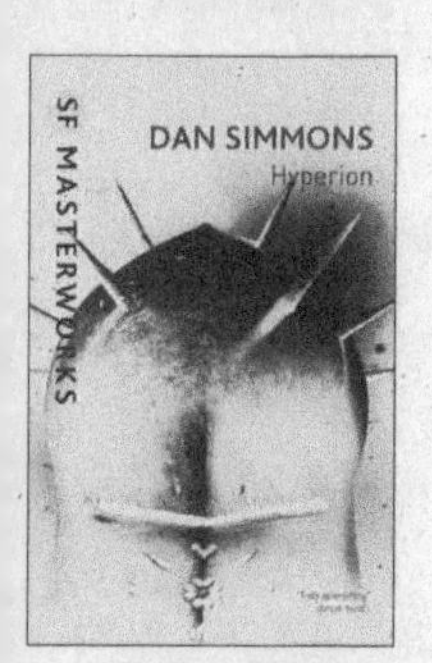
SF MASTERWORKS
DAN SIMMONS
Hyperion

SF MASTERWORKS
LUCIUS SHEPARD
Life During Wartime

SF MASTERWORKS
GEORGE R.R.
MARTIN
Dying of the Light

SF MASTERWORKS
PAUL McAULEY
Fairyland

SF MASTERWORKS
WILLIAM GIBSON
Neuromancer

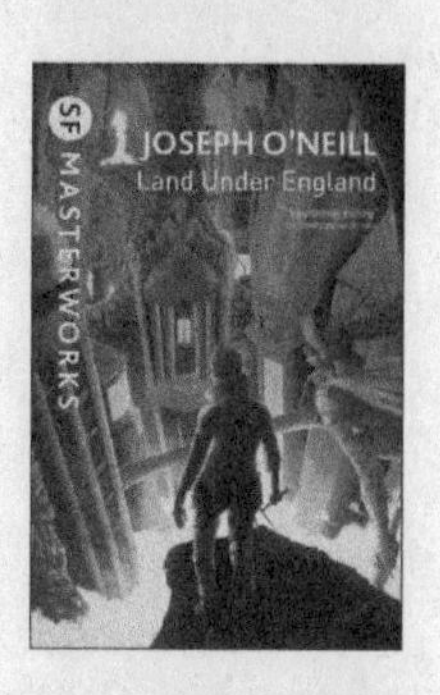
SF MASTERWORKS
JOSEPH O'NEILL
Land Under England

SF MASTERWORKS
WARD MOORE
Bring the Jubilee

SF MASTERWORKS
GEORGE R.
STEWART
Earth Abides

SF MASTERWORKS
DANIEL KEYES
Flowers For Algernon